PLAYGROUNDS &
BATTLEGROUNDS
FOUR NOVELLAS

Also by Robert Scott Leyse

Novels

Tease and Dare: Angie and Ella's Summer of Delirium
Attraction and Repulsion
Self-Murder

Collections

Adoration and Affliction: Novellas and Short Stories

Novellas from the above collection are
available separately as eBooks:

The Urban Primeval
Penelope Prim

PLAYGROUNDS & BATTLEGROUNDS
FOUR NOVELLAS

Robert Scott Leyse

ShatterColors Press
New York, New York

Photography + cover design: Robert Scott Leyse
Photo of RSL: Jason Weber

The four novellas are released individually as eBooks.

ISBN 978-0-9821710-8-0

Library of Congress Control Number: 2025906109

First Edition

Eternal gratitude to the teachers who
seriously made a difference.

Mrs. O'Malley (1st Grade)
Miss Bishop (4th Grade)
Paula Rhine, later Paula Elkin (6th Grade)
Mrs. Digiambattista (11th Grade)
Mrs. Labonte (12th Grade)
Bert Van der Lee (12th Grade)

(University was a joke.
I was self-educated at university.)

Contents

Nighttime Euphoria and the Field of Reeds, or One Can Get Away with What One Dares

"Do not waste a moment of life, not ever, for any reason. Do not allow an employer to badger you at the expense of your happiness, because a new job can always be had at a more sympathetic firm. Failure to live for the moment every day will only yield much self-reproach and regret when death comes knocking. I am pleased that I have lived, and then some, and avoided such self-reproach. I will bid life adieu in peace when the moment arrives and greet the beyond with a clear and strong conscience. It is everyone's responsibility to refuse to endure unconscionable exploitation."
—F. Turlington, JSD, four days after being diagnosed with terminal cancer at 94 years.

Also, from an email sent to his daughter while under hospice care in her home, his wish being that she always have it: *"I am pleased that no one imagines I am 94, for which I thank my love of play and never caring if I was thought of as weird for loving play, because those who stoop to judging others for activities that do not harm others are, to put it bluntly, vermin. Surrender to play and melt care away. It is not always easy to master that skill but the mere act of striving to do so is the first step on the path to contentment and indicates you are already winning. There are people in ill health who are upset that they bought into the lie of working themselves to the bone without a reward apart from more money than they needed and you need to steer clear of that outcome. Place happiness first."*

Chapter One

Although the following narrative strongly advocates circumvention of gainful employment's restrictions, getting away with as much as possible while reimbursed, I'm a law-abiding citizen and proud of it—for nearly two decades a fully documented homeowner, employed first by a corporate law firm and presently by a pharmaceutical advertising agency, both with multiple branches worldwide. My record's spotless—according to official documentation I'm a model American, who'd never dream of hoodwinking my employer at every opportunity. I'm climbing the corporate ladder, all right—aping the part of unquestioningly obedient minion, careful to never remotely hint at harboring subversive sentiments, the better to maximize goof-off time. I take pride in how brazenly I lie to upper management, declare I feel privileged to be part of "the team," during the annual review—the trick's to play the angles without enabling anyone to measure them—the more I'm paid to amuse myself, treat myself to off-the-books recreation, without administration suspecting the more fulfilled I feel. Over 50% of scheduled time's downtime and my sole goal's to obtain more.

I'll cut to the chase: it's minutes before midnight on a worknight, Tuesday about to be Wednesday, in late July in Manhattan and I'm under my building's awning at 1st Avenue and 85th Street with Akila. Akila's Egyptian, we met on San Juan's Condado beach in the rock-sheltered pool at El Presby during incoming tide on her last full day of vacation seventeen days ago. She was running her hands up and down her thighs and midriff, stroking her shoulders and neck—lifting her chin and circling her head, swishing her hair—while on her knees in the rippling shallows near the emerald crescent of eelgrass, intermittingly easing herself backwards onto her elbows on the fine-grained sand, splashing with her feet. I was standing close-by, admiring her from the corner of my eye (not wishing to intrude, turn her self-conscious, via direct staring) as multicolored reef fish, their sides flashing in the clear water, ticklingly nipped me from ankles to knees for reasons unknown. Akila was a perfect picture of enrapturement with the sea's elemental majesty, delightedly watching the waves shatter upon hitting the rocks. As a stronger set of waves smashed into the rocks in rapid succession, spraying titillating mist, she greeted the mist with outspread arms, a sky-wide smile, lilting laughter, more swishing of hair—a woman after my heart indeed.

Suddenly I'm aware Akila's aware I'm admiring her—although seeking to veil my gaze, limit admiration to peripheral vision, I've betrayed myself: attractional tension's tough to conceal, as nature's obviously intended. She rises to her feet, raises sunglasses to hairline, turns to face me with the kindest of smiles—sweet as her eyes are, there's more than a trace of insistence in them, the tone of her stance, positioning of shoulders, thrust of her chest—she's expecting me to face her in turn and I can neither hide nor wish to—subsurface communication, mutual transparency in the electric realms of the nerves, where desire clearly announces itself, often happens miraculously fast. The soft litheness of Akila's body—trusting unselfishness of her body—is already whipping buoyant excitement through my blood—I'm turning to her as if a disembodied spirit's slipped under my skin, appropriated my will. And at the moment I turn to her, I swear, a gust whips her hair across her eyes, flings her sunglasses into the water—I'm alongside her in seconds, assisting her in retrieving them—as the pool's minimally agitated for the most part, the tide only beginning to circle wavelets around the rocks, spray mist over them, her sunglasses readily stand out against the sand—soon I'm handing them to her and she's thanking me—I'm saying something along the lines of, "Happy to help, I almost lost mine a couple days ago—I always assumed they'd float until a wave tore them off my face and they started sinking—I was lucky to grab them before they were gone—they're prescription progressives, would've been a pain to replace—I'm glad you haven't lost yours." An exchange of names and playful banter follows—I'm relishing Akila's immaculate contours, energy and intelligence, the while—she's likewise looking me up and down favorably—flushing with encouragement, happy light: what a gift! Our conversation doesn't flag for an instant, flows as freely as the waves beyond the rocks—there's no trace of wondering-what-to-say-next—emotion's attaching itself to words, sweeping us along, and I've seldom felt as elated. Akila's wild and unafraid to be so.

Akila and I lifted fun to incandescent heights, first thrilling to the tide's advance, increasing churn of the pool, smash of waves on the rocks—quickly comfortable enough to willfully be silly—indulge in splash-wars, games of tag, gleefully shouting—thereafter feasting on fish tacos at La Cueva del Mar, dancing ourselves euphoric on La Placita's dance floors spilling onto the sidewalk under the stars, frolicking in La Ventana al Mar Park's fountain-jets at dawn's approach; and the following day—technically the same day, after a couple hours sleep at best—wandering among tree ferns and flamboyants in my "private forest" (A rainforest made accessible by RV enthusiasts, of all people, who create paths without overdoing it, and I've never seen anyone else there—I've a knack for happening upon unfrequented spectacular places.) ten minutes south of Guaynabo; then we're in Condado again and I'm showing Akila how to catch waves with a boogieboard—she's soon riding the board in the up dog yoga posture, skillfully steering—wondering why she's never done it before; then we're in the rock-sheltered pool where we met, splashing and laughing and yelling, until she needs to catch her flight, when I drive her to the airport, where we're kissing outside the departure terminal up to the last second, sunset blazing, and she tells me she'll be in New York once her schedule allows. So here we are: she arrived from Cairo mid-afternoon—obtained the key to my place from the doorman, caught up on sleep while I was at work—we ordered out for dinner, ate amidst much exchange of additional personal details, thirsting for more—she became curious concerning my terrace, its greenery partially visible through the slats of the shades—I informed her it was a sunrise surprise, entry temporarily forbidden, which led to more spirited teasing, featuring a pillow fight—late night arrived in a flash.

Akila and I are intent upon having the time of our lives tonight, building upon Puerto Rico, and I couldn't be more unconcerned that I'm expected at work at noon—am eager to stay up until dawn and beyond with my darling, confident I'll be buoyed by adrenaline at the office, regardless of how sleep-deprived. I've carved out a cushy niche for myself in the advertising world—a set of specialized online database duties, readily executed robot-fashion, that permit me to be lost in distant thoughts, indulge in unlimited daydreaming, even be outright dazed, the while. My duties are as essential to the completion of projects (I add information in the final stage of production, am often the person who clicks through the sequence that submits them to clients.) as they're mindless, enable me to be a thoroughgoing slacker while receiving accolades for assignments well done—if I didn't have my job I'd doubt it could exist. God bless compartmentalized service industries that bill clients outrageous rates: all one need do is master an essential fraction of the whole, the more specialized and baffling to others the better (If my job's Googled less than a dozen results appear, none instructional.), to be home free—my duties impress management almost as much as they amuse me. Service industries are tailor-made for the ambitious, hungry for promotion, and slackers alike, and I'm proud to count myself among the latter. If promotion were forced on me I'd flip employers—added income's insufficient compensation for added responsibility, intrusion upon attention and freedom. My aim's to minimize employment-imposed mental and emotional clutter, multiply opportunities to pursue worthwhile experiences while being paid. When contrasted with the thousands of generations of pre-civilization human activity the notion of reporting to an office, being on the clock, is as nonsensical as parasitical. Life's far too brief to allow oneself to fall for manufactured morale—circumvention of manipulation's essential.

Enough about my job: allow me to describe Akila. She does right by the ancient Egyptian depictions of women—straight pitch black hair cut slightly above mid-back, unblemished bronze complexion—slender, flawlessly feline of line, unflappably posture-perfect—eyes serene, an endless sea in her gaze. I swear I've seen her in the Egyptian wing of the Metropolitan Museum, along with the other Bastet, Isis, Tefnut, Ra, and Anubis worshipping beauties. Perchance it's my fancy at play, idealistic illusion, but it's as if Akila's disposition pre-dates Christian guilt, has brought pagan affirmation-of-life radiance to the present, her visage untroubled by modern civilization's agitation. But I'm not deluded when I declare Akila's absolutely fearless, game for all manner of jubilant recreation, the more atypical the better, as she more than demonstrated in Puerto Rico. I'll add she's from an affluent family with an estate on the Mediterranean shore—this detail emerged when she declared she adores strolling her family's private beach with nothing on, getting wet and rolling in the sand. Akila couldn't be prouder to be Egyptian.

"Can barely believe I'll be playing with the mirror image of an ancient Egyptian mural woman in my town—the otherworldly's smiling upon me, wilder than any dream," I say, running my eyes from Akila's feet, snug in black leather sandals, to her forehead, passing a hand through her hair.

"Can barely believe I'm in your town with a man who brings out the wildest in me, leading by example," she coos, taking my earlobes between forefingers and thumbs, gently rubbing. "Fun in Puerto Rico's brought me here, and now..."

"And now I'm spinning back through the millennia to when Cleo's Needle was erected," I cut in. "Your white linen dress and black eyeliner and gold scarab ring and spangled anklets and henna-dusted feet, and if you were to turn sideways, strike the ancient murals profile..."

"Way too easy, surfer man—I'll never want to be let off easy," she laughs, wrapping herself around one of the awning's brass support-poles, shimmying to the top, executing an aerial split. Before I can pull the front of her dress down, keep her decent, she shoves it down while grasping the pole with one hand. "Ta-da!" she announces, blowing me a kiss. Instants later she's dismounted from the pole—before me with hands on my shoulders, bouncing up and down on her toes.

"Jesus!" I cry, hugging her. "It's outside imagining I'd get to know an ancient-Egyptian-mural woman in the flesh, and who pole dances to boot. Amazingly athletic pole dancing, that I wouldn't have a prayer of doing!"

"Oh, that's just because I've climbed ropes since a wee little girl, excellent exercise, and I'm flesh, all right, and don't think I'm ancient!" she responds, frowning charmingly—seizing my behind with both hands, squeezing and kneading—undulating her stomach against me. "Huh?"

"Oh, you're off the charts fresh as the dawn, darling, and no mural will ever grab ahold of me, whip through me like liquid fire, transport me to..."

"But of course I enjoy mimicking the murals," she interrupts giggling; then, after she's indicated she wishes to be released and I've done so and she's backed away a bit, turned sideways. "I adore doing mural profiles in the mirror, like so, seeing how close I can come to the originals—compared to my birthright fashion magazines are a shoddy derivative joke, I'll always honor my ancestry. I'm a daughter of the desert by the sea—Puerto Rico was a lush variation, especially the rainforest you took me to, cascades of scarlet flowers in the flamboyants, fresh-fallen petals carpeting the ground, and the piercing soaring songs, miraculously from tiny invisible treefrogs, but nothing compares to home, the vast desert. Not much equals rolling naked down the dunes fronting our beach, pretending I was raised by leopards—screaming myself hoarse, getting messed up and sandy—then leaping into the Mediterranean, swimming until tired *and* fired up."

"You pretend you were raised by leopards? I'm lost in awe!" I declare, swishing her hair. "In fact, I'm positive you *were* raised by leopards—your feline fearlessness, slinkiness, poise is proof. You have courage to burn and know how to live, always welcoming fun—we've been there."

"We've been there *hugely*, Perry—you dream up the most breathtaking cheerful things for us to do, challenge me in the best way," Akila smiles, framing my face with her fingers, tapping my temples. "And speaking of courage, you're an insane surfer, heading straight for those spiky rocks on barreling waves, slipping off the board in the nick of time, turning sideways to escape being grabbed by the waves and thrust forwards, slammed against the rocks. You scared me with that at first, made me cringe, but then I saw it's routine for you—reading the waves, extending your ride on them, pumping your board up and down, exiting instants before serious danger—diving under the waves, swimming sea-wards as your board's tossed around on the surface. You playfully slapped the water soon as you were safely past the breaks, laughing like a toddler in a kiddie pool."

"Sweetheart," I say, tapping Akila's temples in turn, "I was showing off because you were watching—first time I've been that confident in the face of those rocks, your gaze lifted surfing to wilder heights, increased my skill, and the wave-slapping was gratuitous theater. And you took to boogieboarding effortlessly—timed the waves like a pro, leapt into their sweet spot at the perfect moment, rode the sweep ashore—your elation in the froth was priceless." I'm thrusting my right leg between Akila's legs, wrapping it about her left—she's nibbling my left ear.

"Whoa!" she exclaims, pitching leftwards, grasping my shoulders to steady herself. "Slight loss of balance! Ha!"

"Sorry, Akila—no excuse for clumsiness, completely my fault!" I'm unwrapping my leg, seizing her waist, holding her upright.

"Nonsense, Perry—toss me off balance anytime, since I know you'll always make sure I'm safe. *(She squeezes my shoulders more insistently, glances at my hands on her waist.)* Been a spoiled brat my whole life, mostly thinking relationships a joke, but that only frustrated and isolated me. You've opened my eyes—spared me."

"Akila, it's *you* who've spared me from..."

"Not finished, honey!" she breaks in, two-handedly reaching up my untucked shirt—lightly squeezing-teasing my nipples, pressing her belly to mine. "Otherworldly what you showed me in Puerto Rico, nonstop feast of unsuspected places—dancing to salsa bands in the streets, getting tipsy on the beer in the gold cans, buying quenepas from the vendor with the candlelit dancing dolls and metal music in the highway underpass where the multicolored tropical imagery murals were—getting sticky with quenepa juice, streaming from fingers to elbows, rinsing off the stickiness in the decorative pool at the condo building when the guard wasn't looking, the pool's white rocks glowing in underwater floodlights (That sequence alone's as if torn from a dream!)—kissing like crazy later under the ancient gnarled tree smothered in vines in the square with the unreal ghostly amber light where wild chickens were, roosters crowing—playing in the fountain, on pitch black granite, by the beach at sunup, yanking the plastic barrier to the walkway aside—you were kicking it and yelling and I was laughing so hard my tummy ached; then we're on the walkway fronting the sea—waves slamming into the monster rocks, spraying us steady as rain—you climbing over the railing, finding the big snails on the rocks at waterline that were as iridescent, when you flipped them upside down, as pearls—our time in Puerto Rico was as whirlwind as impossible to forget—a normalcy annihilating hallucinogenic blur."

"Puerto Rico's perpetually hallucinogenic but you sped it up, flipped it into an extra vivid waking dream, same as you're doing on this street where I've lived since 1999. My block's never been so electric, as if the expansiveness of the sky's being yanked to earth—the distance between here and York Avenue is deliciously indistinct, falling away. Sweetheart, you're making me fall doubly in love with my neighborhood and my town and we'll blur time together again for sure. I'm on vacation without traveling, because of you—we overcome boundaries together and every day you're here will be a trip to an otherworldly place."

"Perry, I want to live boundaryless and dynamically enough to be worthy of the Field of Reeds, transition from earthly life to the after-life—death's a door on bliss that needs to be blessed by my Gods and they'll judge me according to how uninhibited I've been, whether I've valued abandon over constraint, avoided poisonous halfway emotions, and being with you makes it easy. I've never crossed the earth for anyone or imagined I'd do so but I've done the right thing—the way you look at me and appreciate me, touch and kiss me, laugh with me!"

"Akila, I couldn't be more honored you've crossed the earth to be with me, will do all in my power to make it a valued experience for you—an incandescent experience for you," I say, massaging her shoul-ders. She's flexing her shoulders, rolling them up and back and down, her arms wrapped about my back—the gathering wind's tousling her hair and dress. "But forgive me—what's the Field of Reeds? I'm sure I should know but don't—what a stirring image."

"It's ancient Egypt's heaven," she replies, playfully shaking her hair. "Endless sunlit fields of reeds rustling in breeze, one of our representations of eternity—the same reeds that still flourish on the Nile's banks, remind us of our ancestry. As with Christianity's Heaven, the Field of Reeds must be striven for and earned but there's a lovely twist: the Field of Reeds isn't some separate-from-earthly-life state of being one's never experienced but everlasting continuation of earthly life, assuming one's lived earthly life vividly, gone all out in one's pursuit of vitality and joy. The idea's to live in such a way that one wishes one's life to last in perpetuity—the Field of Reeds mirrors how well one's lived. Is that motivation to embrace every moment, relish every breath—fling oneself into adventure and fun—or what? Death's not something to be feared, it's merely relocation, passage from earthly life to another place, and how happily one lives determines what place that is, whether one continues to enjoy life or is exiled to the nonexistence zone—nonexistence is Egyptian hell. Not having lived in a manner worthy of perpetuity, ceasing to exist, is the terrible end we seek to avoid at all costs. I do my utmost to live each blessing of a day as if it's my last—each day's a fresh opportunity to add to the bliss I'll experience in the Field of Reeds, if I'm so blessed—each day must be greeted with humility, gratitude, urgency, delight. I'm constantly asking, 'Would I like what I'm experiencing today—feeling today—to last forever?'"

"Akila," I say, kissing her forehead, "surely you're a priestess sent by Fate to place me on the right life-affirming path, in answer to subconscious prayers. What better yardstick by which to measure each day than by living in such a way one wishes it to last forever? Your religion's just plain sensible, no pointlessly distracting pomp attached. 'Is today absorbing and intense enough? Am I cheerful and mystified enough? Is this a day I'd like to reexperience forever?' Asking oneself those questions couldn't be more life-affirming, since affirmative responses to them are *essential*. Non-Egyptian though I be, I'm living for the Field of Reeds going forward—pictures of rustling sunlit reeds are already rushing into my head, I'm positive they'll be sweetening my dreams when I'm asleep."

"A priestess?" she laughs, freeing a foot from its sandal, slipping her toes up one of my pantlegs, tickling. "I'm no more priestess than I'm a mural sprung to life, only an often completely silly girl who wishes to do the blessing of life proud—having a human body's miraculous. And I'm certainly not out to convert anyone, I keep my beliefs to myself and family. Accuse me of living in a long-gone age, devoted to a technically dead religion, shrouded in the mists of my ancestry, but that religion promotes well-being better than any other religion I know of. Illusion or not—does it matter when the gist of it's being healthy and happy, living in illumination of sensation and force of feeling? And you don't need to be Egyptian to live like that—living well's open to all, salvational to all."

"But you *are* a priestess, Akila darling—a svelte angelface priestess, impossible not to grab!" I laugh, seizing her by the waist, yanking her close again. Her eyes, silver-inflected grey, rival the light of sun-glistened waves.

"Weeee!" she cries, ceasing to tickle with her toes. "Let me find my sandal!" She taps my breastbone, by way of indicating she wishes to step back—after I've released her and she's re-sandaled her foot she seizes my hands, guides them to her behind, steps close again. "Grab me and savor me, sweetie, your hands on me are sugar and smiles!" I'm grasping her silk-soft globes, squirming musculature, with gusto—she's leaping into my embrace, wrapping her thighs about my waist, as I lift her, we nonstop kissing. At first we're in the illumination streaming from my building's lobby, her visage an effulgent dream—thereafter on our feet in the shadows at the wrought iron grate guarding the brownstone a few doors east.

"Whoa! How'd we get over here?" I inquire a few minutes later, gesturing towards the glow of my building's awning. "Did I carry you or did we float on the air? I hardly know! Tonight's already veering towards the hallucinated place."

"Life goes to the escalated place when we're together—the air's an electric kiss on every centimeter of me, altered states come easy."; then, widening her eyes and passing a hand in front of them, gesturing at the cat sculptures framing the brownstone's door behind the grate, "Am I dreaming? I'm thousands of kilometers from home and those are Egyptian tomb cats, as emotionally and psychologically imprinted on me as glimmering desert sands! Do you like cats, Perry?"

"I unreservedly adore cats, Akila, and recognize these as well, reproductions from the Metropolitan Museum, available in the gift shop—think I need to finally get one for the terrace. The world's in love with the matchless lines, as graceful and sensual as austere, always wildly otherworldly, of ancient Egyptian art—every succeeding civilization that's seen it has fallen under its spell—oft imitated, never equaled. And in my humble opinion cats are one of creation's finest achievements—so svelte and fluffy, affectionate and fun-loving, and they're still matchless hunters, one foot in the wilds, instincts unblunted—amazing creatures. I think cats are faking domestication, in order to be sheltered and fed, while remaining faithful to the wilds—they're aristocrats at the top of the food chain and know it and flaunt it, sleep well over half the day, entitled to leisure."

"But of course I knew you adore cats! Guess what? Another feature of the Field of Reeds is one's reunited with one's pets. Is that icing on the cake or what? I worship all my cats, present and past—have two now, Pluma and Swish—Pluma's a calico with an extra fluffy feathery tail, Swish is a Persian with long swishing fur—I couldn't live without my cats, their affection and playfulness. Simply watching them find the high places in the house and pose like these sculptures brings joy to my heart."

"Wild! The Field of Reeds includes everything of value! I'd love to spend eternity with our cat Omar, one of the most amazing beings ever born. Omar was as close to me as anyone's ever been—he knew me from the first grade until after college, as well as anyone ever will. I often awaken in the dead of night thinking of Omar and missing him, mourn his absence every day. A magnificent grey tiger—mesmerizing of presence, indomitable of spirit. He'd gaze into my eyes, very intent, and inform me he loved me—we played nonstop, shared countless adventures, accompanied each other deep into the woods. Omar knew when I was depressed and would rub against me and cheer me, purr, playfully paw. Nor did he hesitate to inform me when I was behaving foolishly, as grade schoolers and middle schoolers are wont to do—the look in his eyes, tone of his meows and body-language, cut to the core.

Omar had a hand in raising me, showed me how to be decent, helped me negotiate adolescent awkwardness, is one of my most influential friends—I'm supremely privileged and blessed to have known him. Your ancestors were right to deify cats."

"Yes, imagine eternity in the Field of Reeds with the wise and mischievous cats who've brightened your life! And now I'm starting to sound like a missionary! Sorry! But you're also a missionary, Perry, sent by Fate for *my* benefit," she adds, tapping the top of my head. "I'll never forget our last Puerto Rico dance on the sandbar at sunset, making the most of the little amount of time left before my flight—blood-red-striated sky, golden-crimson ocean waves, quickening my blood along with your touch. And the bratty crab that appeared from out of nowhere, pinched my ankle, drew blood, and how you caught it, tore it apart, extracted the meat, and we had crab sushi. I can't imagine anyone else doing that, telling me about the Paleo way of life—pre-agricultural diet and fitness as best we're able to manage in the present—you're a *very* beneficial life-changer for me."

"Thanks for that, Akila, but I'm not out to convert anyone either—all things Paleo are kept to myself unless I'm inspired to tell a special someone because we've feasted on raw crab, alive a minute ago, when we'll soon have to part ways—the time-constraint intensified those moments—sunset-fire writhing on the waves, and you were vein-electrifyingly radiant—unforgettable glimpse of beatitude."

"Perry, that'll be one of my favorite epiphanies, glimpses of beatitude, forever! I've been nearly Paleo without knowing but it's useful to know it, have that affirmation—now I understand why I've been revolted by pizza and pastries, all processed food. My family casts nets into the Mediterranean for fish, as our ancestors did, and we make reed and lotus root and wild onion salads, as our ancestors did, and add lotus blossoms to wine, as our ancestors did, and brew beer from mashed reeds, cloudy with nutrients, as our ancestors did, and dozens of date palms are on our property, bountiful yearlong, and the desert heat's nonstop slipping under my skin, inflaming my veins and imagination, carrying me back to when the Pharaohs reined—their tomb-murals mirror the austerity of the desert, sharp lines and light. I *love* bright hot light—it's my heritage and I can't help but love it—I've always hungered to escape modernity too."

"Lucky you! Wish I had access to such bounty, self-caught fish and self-gathered salad ingredients and fruit, lift Paleo to higher levels—Paleo for me's smart shopping. You escape modernity much better than me."

"But you *do* have access, Perry! Meaning that you're coming to *my* home—refusal's unacceptable. Will you please come to Egypt? I'll show you..."

"Oh, I'll come to Egypt, with all my heart and soul, Akila, and thank you," I break in. "I'm already losing my mind with anticipation, tingling at the thought of it." We've returned to my building's awning—are embracing again.

"You're very welcome," she half-whispers, her voice sultry, sweet, electric—her intonation's assuredly stroking my spine. "We'll roll naked down the dunes night and day, howl at the sun and stars and moon—my family will treat you like royalty. I may have never known of Paleo living, in the official sense, until meeting you but have always been a savage, as uncivilized as possible—I like to dance and scream in the ocean winds on our beach, writhe on my back at shoreline after dark, waves sloshing me, build roaring bonfires, pretend I'm alive thousands of years ago—oh, yes! And you're making me want to completely kiss off caution and dare *anything* and so's your town—there's amazing energy here."

"Speaking of energy, Akila *(I lead her a few yards west to 1st Avenue, wave an arm north towards distant lightning-flickers, thunder.)*, I turn doubly alive when a storm's swooping in—it's reassuring and uplifting when Mother Nature puts puny civilization in its place. Nothing's more Paleo than a storm—being face to face with the untamed elemental, whisked free of calculation and artificiality. The Storm Gods are blessing our night."

"They sure are, Perry—the storm's swooping in so fast and is so vast and can't be caged, just beautiful—thunder's music for me." We're trading cheek-kisses while admiring the advancing clouds, increasingly frequent lightning.

Chapter Two

"Time to take off, my dear," I say as my phone dings, announcing arrival of the SUV I've reserved. Upon confirming its license plate matches the one listed on my phone, I'm opening the SUV's door and Akila's gliding within.

"Smush time!" she giggles, climbing onto my lap once I'm beside her and have shut the door—she's gripping me with her thighs, knees pressed to the seatback on each side of me—grasping the back of my neck, bouncing up and down; then, when the cab stops at the red light a block west, at 85th Street and 2nd Avenue, "So what's the plan, sweetie? I'm up for anything, in case you don't already know! I know we're off to stimulating places, even if we don't budge from this spot."

"You on my lap equals Nirvana and we wouldn't need to go else-where, but we'll be traveling anyway—hang on a moment, honey (*I smilingly tap her forehead.*), be right back." Leaning forward as Akila's hair dusts my face, I inform the driver the destination I entered on the ridesharing app isn't final—after arriving at Dyckman Street and Broadway (in Inwood, Manhattan's northernmost neighborhood) via Henry Hudson Parkway I'd like for him to flip around and return down-town, further instructions to follow; then, addressing Akila, "Forget my homefield advantage—New York's not a place on a map tonight, it's an experience. Tell me how you want to feel and I'll do my best to deliver with the right adventure—our destination's emotional, all else mere backdrop."

"Love it, Perry!" she responds, leaning back to full on gaze at me, delight leaping in her eyes. "As in love with my homeland as I am life's journey isn't a matter of geography but of how we live—anything aside from quality of feeling's insignificant window-dressing, shallow show and tell, and you're bringing that to me."; then, caressing my forehead, "Are you sure you're not Egyptian?"

"One hundred percent Norwegian, Akila—no pyramids or Sphinx-es, roaring metropolises like Memphis or Luxor, in our history," I say, sliding my hands up the sides of her midriff, thrilling to the tightening grip of her thighs. "But we Norwegian's have had our moments—I'm proud of my Viking heritage, maritime technology ahead of its time, destroying the competition—the first Europeans in North America, with settlements to prove it. Columbus is a joke—Leif Erikson beat him by five hundred years. Although I must say the notion of 'discovering' a so-called New World, already inhabited by advanced societies coast to coast, is ludicrous—even Tierra del Fuego was populated by 8,000 BC."

"Longships!" Akila shouts, smacking the car's roof with both palms. "All the world knows about Longships knifing through the sea, spreading conquest and trade and exploration, an archetypal imprint on collective consciousness if there ever was one—something our ancestries have in common. Our ancient civilizations continue to haunt and fascinate and inspire, no one can get enough of us! An Egyptian and a Norwegian! How can incredible chemistry not happen? The fiords' cliffs and Nile's floodplain—tropical desert and arctic forests, permafrost and blazing sun! I think our chemistry's going to constantly carry us to magic places."

"That's as indisputable as the law of gravity, and I'm counting on it," I smile, kissing her forehead, "especially since, Norwegian though I be, I'm also Californian through-and-through, born and raised on the coast. Norwegian ancestry of which I couldn't be prouder, and a child of the California Republic, of which I'm equally proud—the sea's in my blood."

"More luscious alignment, Perry—we're both children of sun and sea. I was born within earshot of the Mediterranean, delivered by a midwife on our estate." She's tongue-flicking the left side of my neck.

"Jesus, sweetheart! I was born within earshot of the Pacific in San Francisco, ocean sounds and breezes and scents greeted me—I've confirmed this—when I was carried from the hospital. I live for the waves, in every sense of the word—especially for the waves of your ocean-motion hair, as I'll never tire of proving." I swish her hair over my face.

"Ummmm," she intones, we immersed in kissing.

"How'd we get here so fast?" I ask once our lips part, gesturing at Henry Hudson Parkway. "The time it took to travel from my neighborhood to here seems like the same as springing off a diving board into a pool! Am I on hallucinogens? Absolutely! You're a hallucinogen, darling—your kisses speed minutes into seconds, escalate sensation—the wind whooshing over us through the windows is as vivid on my skin as churning surf."

"Never been called a hallucinogen before—best compliment ever, I'm sure only a Californian could come up with it! Are Californians tripping all the time?"

"Of course—tripping's a California religion. But tripping often happens without substance-assistance, as when I'm climbing my hometown's sea cliffs north of the Cliff House at Land's End, and it's only about a fifteen minute cab ride, if traffic's light, from downtown. I'm able to go from Chinatown's Dragon Gate to rugged seascape, kiss off civilization's pseudo security, in a flash—suddenly I'm gauging reliability of footholds and handgrips, my life depending on sound judgment as the Pacific thunders into jagged rocks below, saltwater-mist rising on updrafts—the swift alteration of circumstances, contrast between being safe on a sidewalk and clinging to cliff crevices, is off the charts hallucinogenic. I once started sliding while on hands and knees on loose gravel on the slope above the cliffs proper—flung myself to the ground, spread my legs wide and flattened myself, dug my nails and the toes of my shoes into the dirt under the gravel deep as I could—sunny cloudless sky was spinning above, waves hissing below—I *had* to become one with the ground—I would've died if I didn't! And barely over an hour previously I was polishing off a bowl of French onion soup at Café de la Presse, across the street from Dragon Gate—I was flashbacking to the soup, comfort of the café, being on solid ground, experiencing my-life-could-end-soon sensations—priceless! I was bleeding under most of my nails afterwards, that's how forcefully I dug them into the dirt—interestingly there was no pain, only numbness."

"Is it necessary to recklessly place yourself in peril?" Akila inquires, freezing in every limb, her expression dead serious. "Kissing off civilization's one thing, I'm all in favor, but don't let civilization bore or badger you into risking your life—nothing's 'priceless' about that. I doubt pre-civilization humans gratuitously sought out danger—I think doing so's a disease of civilization, misguided sensationalism, and if you die because if it civilization wins. Sorry, Sir, but you're not doing that on my watch!"

"Point taken," I respond, gripping her hands and holding her gaze. "Pre-civilization humans were in constant danger—at the mercy of hungry predators, including saber-toothed cats, for Christ's sake (Isn't *that* wild?), so it's unlikely they deliberately sought out danger. Although another way of looking at it could be that chasing after danger in the present is a means of remaining in touch with ancient emotions, our evolutionary development—resurrecting what we once felt every day so as to remain vitalized, strong. Civilization endeavors to emasculate us via systematic deprivation of vivid experiences, intensity in general—sampling of life-or-death extremity partially liberates us from civilization's nefarious agenda."

"Cute, Perry—you're adept at flipping logic. But if you do something as rash as climbing those cliffs, needlessly endanger life and limb, while we're... Well, I don't know what I'll do—I'm asking you not to, even if being mommyish is presumptuous of me and not my usual approach. I'm sure you know I want you to otherwise be unfettered. But no chance am I going to slide on gravel above a cliff and shrug it off like it's nothing if I manage to avoid dying! That's stupid! Sorry to go there—I just..." Trailing off, she gazes at me questioningly.

"Please don't apologize for extremely sane advice, Akila—I'm done with gratuitous pursuit of serious danger, cliff-climbing and the like, and appreciate your sincerity. I obviously needed a bright bold unfettered woman, whose judgment I trust, to set me straight. You're priestess *and* guardian angel."

"Perry, you're making me insanely happy!" she exclaims, her muscles relaxed and soft—all tension gone as if it was never there. She's tugging the top of her hem from where it's pinned under her knees on each side of me, dropping it onto her thighs—once done guides my hands inside her dress, her smile as stirring as sun on surf. As I run my hands up her thighs she seizes my shoulders, abruptly twists off of me to the right—pulls me from the seat's back, laughingly pushes, shouts, "My prisoner!"—in seconds I'm on my back with my head half off the seat's edge, Akila lying atop me. It's not a situation in which uncorking a bottle of Champagne, even if it's only a demi, is advisable but I do so anyway, after extracting it from the bag on the floor behind Akila's line of sight, lifting it over her head, my biceps mildly pressed against her ears. (To explain the bag: Akila inquired about its contents when I grabbed it as we exited my place—I told her it was a surprise. Soon as we stepped outside I set it on the windowsill of my building's lobby, safe under the doorman's watchful eye—I retrieved it when our ride arrived. Because I'd padded the bag with newspaper, she was unable to discern its contents.)

"Weeeee! Juicy sparkle-shower, fizzy rain—you deliciously deliver on surprises, golly gee!" Akila shouts as foam bursts from the bottle, sloshes us. "Super scrumptious nectar!" She's lapping Champagne from my cheeks.

"Christ! I thought only cheap counterfeit Champagne burst out of the bottle like this—a prankster must've shook it up!" I say, hastening to hold the bottle above the floor instead of us, it still overflowing. "Sorry for soaking you—your hair and dress. No excuse for failing to anticipate chance of..."

"Don't be berating yourself, Perry!" she cuts in laughing, still licking Champagne from my cheeks. "It's not only royally fine but beneficial if my dress gets messed, and your Champagne's too silk-smooth yummy to be cheap! If I was worried about messed dresses I would've missed out on windfalls of fun—I'll never understand favoring replaceable material things over fulfilling abandon. Hordes of girls run from fun in horror if fun involves getting their clothes rumpled, and that's misplaced priority verging on lunacy. I'm glad a prankster shook up the bottle, wouldn't be surprised if the prankster's *you*! And, hey, Mommy Nature's pitching in—luscious rain, let it pour!" She's referring to the rain whipping through the east-facing window, we having entered the storm.

"Speaking of luscious," I say, licking her face in turn, "there's an electric candy tone to your skin, I can *taste* your happiness! Am I with Nefertiti reincarnated? Long neck, high cheekbones, serene gaze, beauty that's as if stolen from wildest dreams—the very sort of detached sophistication that lives for flipping in the opposite direction—flinging reserve aside, running with revelry."

"So sweet, sweetie—Nefertiti's my highest queen! But I need to call you out on that bit about me being detached, since it's the opposite of me. Sure, I know how to appear unapproachable, send pestering guys packing with stern looks and posture without speaking a word—big deal, it's an act. The real me wants to be effervescent and dizzy, even ditzy—run around on our beach only wearing jewelry, kicking the sand—I love the feel of sand shoving up between my toes. I worship the locust swarms that blot out the sun—they really *do* blacken the sky, enough to alter the weather. I live for admittance to the Field of Reeds and detachment doesn't get me there."; then, writhing against me so insistently it's as if she's seeking to submerge herself in my skin, "Do you really think I'm detached?"

"Don't think I said you're detached, Akila! I meant you're able to appear so, as you've said—I'm well aware you fearlessly live for dev-il-may-care fun, seen it firsthand. Detachment's often a yardstick for how wild someone can become—it's the illusion of contradiction, because both require energy—no women get wilder than those who're adept at mimicking iciness, I'm truly blessed to... Uh, oh! Ouch! Ha! *(Here I jerk a hand to one of Akila's shoulders, grasp for upward pull—I feel I'm involuntarily wincing, projecting undue alarm.)* OK, OK! Don't worry, dollface, all's well—smarts a bit but I'm flexible enough to handle surprises like this, thanks to yoga." What's happened is we've slipped off the seat onto the floor—my back's bent over the axle-hump with some of Akila's weight on me.

"Oh, no!" Akila cries, springing off me, eyes distressed. She's on her knees on the seat in seconds—grasping my forearms, gently pulling me off the floor, her strength greater than her slender frame would suggest. "Perry, are you sure you're...?"

Her question's interrupted by the driver, understandably displeased by the spillage of Champagne—informing us he might need to call it a night because his car needs to be spotless to obtain top ratings, keep his job. Would we spill Champagne in our car, carry on as if it's a grand occurrence? Do we understand his car's his living, not a party place, club or bed? The backs of the front seats are high, he feels clients are entitled to privacy, but it's wrong for us to take advantage and make a mess, he's shocked at what we've done. And he wanted to oblige with the open windows, never mind the AC's on, but he doesn't need rain soaking the back of his car—this is stated as the windows zoom up. Thanks to Akila's assistance I'm soon seated alongside her, catching the driver's eye in the rearview mirror, suggesting we go to a gas station with carwash facilities, assuring him I'll clean his car, reimburse him for lost time with cash off the books. "I've been a New York cab driver on the night shift," I say, "before ridesharing existed and the garages were the only option—I know making a living in the streets is tough and time's money. Sorry for spilling Champagne, I know better, and will fix this—as an ex-driver who's been through the lunacy I won't be able to feel right until I make things right. Again, apologies—please head to a gas station."

Within fifteen minutes we're at a gas station somewhere in Inwood, a neighborhood I know next to nothing about, and I'm spraying the SUV's backseat and floor with a thin jet of water in a carwash enclave, angling the hose such that most of the water flies out the opposite side's open door. Then Akila's vacuuming as I wipe with paper towels—once there's no evidence of Champagne spillage, all spotless and dry, I instruct the driver to pull it to a pump so I can top off the tank. The gas station's overhang is bright white, scintillant with fluorescent light—rain's hammering the pavement outside its edges, shattering and whirling into undulating sheets of ghostly light-bending mist. "As far as I can tell we could just as well be in Singapore or Sidney or Helsinki," I say, Akila massaging my shoulders as I fill the tank. "I'm transported to places I've never been while gassing up a car—the buildings and that patch of trees over there smothered in shifting haze, outlines blurring and swapping places with the sky, suggesting infinity like a Turner painting—being with you lifts mundane things into the extraordinary."

"My skin dissolves and expands when I'm with you, Perry—the rain is silver waterfalls and it's as if I'm adrift in its vapor, suspended between the ground and roiling clouds. We're at a gas station, of all places, and it's transcendental because I'm with you, as I know everywhere else will be when we're together—you don't restrict me in any way. How can I put it? It's like there are no boundaries under your skin, no barriers in your nerves—halfway feelings are poison to you and there's room for me to expand, wildly flow, without judgment."

"Spot on description of your effect on me, Akila," I say, swatting the gas tank cover shut and returning the pump to its slot, turning to her. "I think we'd gaze upon beatitude, lift each other clear of our skins, even if stranded in an endless empty parking lot, bleak asphalt in every direction. Not that we'll end up in one, because… OK, I may have misled you about ignoring homefield advantage—after we were flying up the highway it occurred to me where we might want to spend the night and we'll go there, up to you if we stay—there are many options."

"Yay!" she cries, clapping. "I was hoping you'd match our emotional destination with a homefield advantage destination and can't wait to see your choice, it's a given I'll love it. I know nothing about your town, aside from loving its energy—all compass points are the same direction for me here—intensity's my direction and I know you'll take us there."

Then we're on Henry Hudson Parkway, returning downtown far slower than when leaving it, the storm limiting visibility to a few yards—the gusts are strong enough to periodically vibrate the SUV as rain pounds its roof. Akila's on my lap and we're kissing uninterruptedly, but pleasure's not the only reason she's on my lap: I'm seated on a triple-folded cardboard box, obtained from the gas station, to protect the seat from getting sticky again, since our clothes are still partially wet with Champagne. As for the Champagne, it appears Akila and I were too enamored of each other, plus distracted by the mess of the spillage and tumble off the seat and driver's annoyance, to take a sip aside from what we lapped from each other's cheeks—the bottle's seemingly vanished into thin air, I don't recall tossing it. Not that failing to drain the bottle matters: Akila's more intoxicating than anything that'll ever be brewed. Then we're at the southwest corner of 5th Avenue and 79th Street and I'm handing the driver $80 above the fare, saying, "I know your time's money." Then he and I are showing our phones to each other, exchanging five-star ratings—shaking hands, wishing each other well. Mindful of safeguarding our phones against the rain Akila and I wrap them in two plastic bags the driver provides and bury them in her handbag before exiting the cab.

Chapter Three

"Hail beautiful experience-expanding storms!" I shout, lifting fists to the sky, catching raindrops with my tongue. "Civilization will never tame Mother Nature, drag her to its level, and this isn't any middling storm."; then gesturing at Central Park's Cedar Hill, guiding Akila towards it, "Storm-born sensations, as our pre-civilization ancestors experienced, here we come! Are we favored or what? We get to frolic in primeval forces on your first New York night."

"Insanely favored!" Akila cries, jumping up and down and tugging my wrist, eager to scamper ahead. "Storms send negativity and stagnation packing, wash us clear of debilitating mental clutter, false worries—miraculous primeval medicine."

"The real miracle's you're here fresh from Egypt, sweetheart!" I yell to be heard above a sustained thunder-rumble. "You're an exotic import, shimmering light and rejuvenation, shot in my blood!" Akila's already as rain-drenched, her white linen dress semi-transparent, leaving little of her stunning symmetry to the imagination, as if she's leapt into the sea.

"And you're an exotic destination, darling!" she shouts back. "All due respect to my Gods, they didn't anticipate airlines—opportunity to hook up with my male reflection, miraculous emotional double, thousands of miles away! I'm amazed out of my skin I'm in energy-factory New York, where I never thought I'd be—face to face with you under lofty storm-tossed trees!"

"Right, we need to clear out before boughs break and brain us!" I continue to yell, yanking Akila forward fast as we can dash as a renewed flurry of gusts hisses through, alarmingly threshes, the cathedral of foliage above—seconds later we're clear of the trees, below Cedar Hill's unobstructed sky—within minutes repeatedly sliding feet first down the lawn, both of us seated on plastic bags grabbed from a nearby trash can. Rain's falling so furiously the lawn's a water-slide—a couple times we attain such velocity we flop onto our bellies, dig elbows and knees into the lawn, to avoid hydroplaning onto the asphalt path at Cedar Hill's base and the irony isn't lost on Akila. Alluding to my hometown adventure, she laughs, "So now we're doing what I told you not to! Not that there's a nasty sea cliff here, we're only threatened by scrapes and bruises, I don't want to minimize your courage—we get to hug the earth like you did without death looming."

"Guess you approve of my sea cliff escapades after all—nice of you to call it courage, instead of rash idiocy," I tease, we side by side on our stomachs on the lawn. "And Land's End, where the sea cliffs are, is as uplifting a place as any on earth, overlooking the Pacific—the evergreens are so wind-sculpted they *look* like wind. The wind's unceasing, waves endlessly roiling into mist— there'll never be a more beautiful place to plunge to one's death. And I was born nearby, a bit inland from Baker Beach slightly north—dying there would close my circle."

"No!" she yells, poke-prodding me onto my back, straddling me and slapping a shoulder, gazing earnestly into my eyes. "You *never* have my permission to endanger your life! Stupid me for mentioning those cliffs—your insane anecdote about sliding on gravel above a fatal fall froze my bones, robbed me of breath! Do you understand? Luxor has gorgeous bronze-gold cliffs, Hatshepsut's temple's at their base. Will I be monkeying around on them because they're beautiful, imagining it would be glorious to plunge to my death? No! Although I realize you're being facetious this time, I'm still very negative on the sentiment."

"Rest assured, Akila, cliff-climbing's no longer in the picture," I say, running my fingers up her neck to her cheeks, softly caressing. "Your word's law because your word favors life—insane of me to court danger like a dolt and it's over. The touch of you alone's grounding me, demonstrating I was naive and loony to do that."

"And your desire's law, Perry—please look at and touch me like this, surge under my skin, all you want and all *I* want!"; then, after twice jerking her head forwards, bringing her hands to her hair, "Silly me! I wanted to swish you but my hair's too soaked to budge—might as well be glued to my scalp."

"You're a deliciously drenched angel," I say, grasping her shoulders and pulling her onto me, rolling us until I'm on top—rising slightly on elbows and knees, licking her lips. "And would you believe there are people who'd like to rob us of this fun? It's insane but we're breaking the law, even though we're harming no one and couldn't be more respectful of the park. The city administration, spouting self-serving manipulative blather concerning our welfare—shamelessly weaponizing exaggerated danger—has imposed a Central Park curfew. Do I have a clue what the official Central Park hours are, aside from aware we're violating them? Why bother? It's a con, the powers-that-be cynically assuming people will fall for tawdry politically motivated scare-tactics, be misled into believing policing of playtime's a good thing. And is anyone patrolling the park at this hour in the rain? Nope! And what's the penalty? A fine at most, usually only a warning and instructions to depart, so I think we'll risk it! And curfew didn't exist in the '90s, which just goes to show how arbitrary it is. As for the much-ballyhooed danger, it's unlikely we'll cross paths with hostiles at this hour in this storm—I've been here during storms postmidnight before, strolling randomly with friends, covering miles of ground, and have never so much as seen anyone else. In fact, it's a riddle I like to pose: how does one wander for a few hours in Manhattan without running into anyone? All one needs do is hit the park after midnight in a storm—crazy, but New Yorkers tend to act as if rain's lethal—anyone out to rob or assault others would reasonably assume the park's poor hunting grounds during a storm."

"So the city's really out to rob people of incandescence in the park after dark, criminalize being lovingly alive?" Akila responds frowning. "But of course being lovingly alive makes it essential to ignore ridiculous politically motivated rules—nature trumps society's prejudicial shenanigans. It's the city that's committing a crime, since it wants to prevent us from playing in this magnificent storm. I adore that you're utterly indifferent to stupid rules, no trace of fakery, Perry! Too many guys make a show of being bold and unfettered, blab and posture, with no follow-through—wilt when the opportunity to prove it materializes, make pathetically feeble excuses, fail miserably to save face. How can anyone act like that when there's only one life to make the most of, all judgmental stuff a lie? Why the fear?"

"And you're fearless to your fingertips, Akila! Society's undeclared agenda, shadow-war, is to swindle us into putting up with being stomped into the dirt at every turn—new laws are implemented every day and we're expected to mindlessly accept them, *never* wonder why something legal a week ago's now a violation. Screw political grand-standing rubbish!"

"Death to political rubbish forever!" she gleefully shouts, indicating, via tapping my shoulder and glancing towards the ground alongside us, she wishes to be released; then, once I've complied and she's squirmed a couple feet away—still on her back, snow-angeling her arms and legs, "What an out-of-my-senses date this is, tempestuous sky descending to caress and kiss me, rain and wind roaming over me like hundreds of hands—you sure know how to show a girl a good time!"

"And you sure know how to show a boy a good time and make me feel like a boy," I respond, rising to my knees, sliding my fingers through her soaked hair. "Here I am in the park past midnight on a worknight, kissing off what I'm supposed to take seriously as if it's a mirage. Because of you the idea of being shackled to a schedule, employed by the agency, is preposterous—tonight's as unbounded as this storm, obligation's nonexistent. Why would tomorrow afternoon concern me when I'm with enchanting you in unleashed nature? Tomorrow's been erased!"; then, upon rising to my feet and pulling Akila to hers—yelling with upraised arms, "Storm Gods! We thank you for nature's transformative might that liberates us from the sham of civilization, debilitating arti-ficial reality! We thank you for an experience unchanged since humans first walked the earth, privilege of honoring our Paleolithic heritage! Storm Gods! We thank you for the lightning's blinding light, thunder's deafening roar, alongside which the status quo's a flimsy fabrication, and humbly beseech you to look favorably upon us! Civilization's misdirec-tion and contagion and you're our cure and salvation!"

Moments later we're howling like wolves, barking like dogs, meow-ing like cats—soon dropping to hands and knees, running races on all fours, still howling and joyous in knowing it's safe to do so, as there won't be any "making fools of ourselves" judgment (such judgment be-ing something only fools, incomprehensibly hostile towards life, indulge in)—our appreciation of one another, mutual trust, is increasing by leaps and bounds. Inside of five minutes there's a lightning-flash near enough for us to hear the electricity's sizzle, an almost instantaneous thunder-boom vibrating the ground. "Owee!" Akila exclaims, flinging herself onto me. "Serious wake-up call, shock waves cutting to my bones—scary but also a gift! We can yell our lungs out, we're just pip-squeaks! Thanks infinitely for bringing me here in the storm, Perry—no other man's done this—they think I'm unstable when I want to run naked in the dunes, either get scared and make themselves scarce forever or think they can tame me, make me—ha ha!—*sensible*!"; then, after backing away a bit, seizing my hands, "Sweetie!" That lone word, brimming with affection, is all that's needed to convey her wish.

In seconds I've brought her to a wide low-slung tree about three yards shy of Cedar Hill's crest on its northern side and we're crawling under its lower branches, they battered earthwards by the storm—the tree's neither bulky nor tall enough for storm-stressed branches to pose a threat: should a branch break it would be arrested in its fall by the tangled mass of those below it, and none exceed three inches in diameter. "What a friendly sheltering tree," Akila observes. "It's like we're in a tent, far less wind here and no one will be able see through these velvety leaves—ummmm!" She's risen to her knees, rubbing the leaves against her cheeks.

"This tree's an old friend, has cheered me with its scarlet floppy-petaled blossoms every April for nearly thirty years, and I still don't know what species it is—would be easy to find out but at this point I like keeping it mysterious. I stretch out here *(I gesture at the ground.)* in all seasons, spring's blossoms and summer's green and autumn's gold—even in winter when the branches are bare, since I picture them laden with blossoms and leaves. This tree *(I kiss a leaf.)* helped me stay sane, grounded and calmed me, when I was awaiting the co-op board's verdict, go-ahead to buy my place, and had no fixed address, was either holed up at the Chelsea Y or crashing with friends about town—my future was hanging in the balance, acceptance into the co-op wasn't guaranteed. And now this tree's outstripping all expectation because I'm under it with you."

"Oh, I'm all in for outstripping—or stripping—Perry," she smiles, lifting her soaked dress above her waist, swaying side to side slowly, undulating at her shoulders. "And there's a special tree in my life too, palm that's cheered me with the sleek splay of its fronds, rustling in sea breeze, since before I can recall—I'm sure the frond-patterns of palms and the music the wind makes on them were imprinted on me at infancy, indelibly tied in with security and felicity, when my mother nursed me outside underneath them, especially on our palm-bordered brick path. My palm's on the highest dune, where there's a to-die-for ocean view—I stretch out under it at all hours, sunlight or moonlight or starlight beaming through its fronds. I'm old friends with a tree too, *love* my palm—more sweet alignment between us! Our alignment's multiplying and, as far I can tell, there's no end in sight." She casts her eyes towards the ground, sweetness brimming.

"Alignment every moment, my storm-infatuated darling," I say, heeding her glanced request and easing her onto her back, lowering myself onto her. "And speaking of ocean views *(I gesture through the tree's flailing foliage at Cedar Hill, illuminated by one of Central Park's lamps.)*, the lawn's churning surf, whitecaps to the horizon. Remember del Indio? We're on boogieboards again—waiting to catch wild waves."

"Will never forget del Indio," she replies, squirming against me so emphatically it's as if her bloodstream's surging into mine. "The thrill of catching waves on a boogieboard for the first time, flying at the beach in swirling foam! The lawn's waves for sure—I see waves all over the place all the time too, in the swish of palm fronds and wind-sculpted patterns in dunes and in the dips and rolls of locust swarms and flocks of birds, and in fields of rippling reeds, shifting desert sands."; then, her voice acquiring a mellifluous forthrightness that's assuredly delving into my very soul, "I think I was lonely before we met and didn't know."

"Akila, this is a miracle, thank you for telling me. I've also been feeling I was lonely before meeting you and won't hide that I was less clear about it to myself than you are to yourself, plus afraid to say it even if I were clear about it—just like that you say it, translate my feelings into words. You're proof fate can flip on a dime, seconds alter our lives forever for the better, as when our eyes first met and I *knew* I wouldn't rest easy until introducing myself to you—that it absolutely *had* to happen or I'd be feeling isolated and abandoned, as good as flung into a dungeon, cursing myself. I recall those moments as clearly as if they've just occurred—high waves hit the rocks and misted me, as windblown mist is doing now."

"Wow! Same as what I felt, honey—now you're translating *my* feelings into words," she says, seizing my wrists and squeezing, sending sparkles up my arms—joyously twisting her head side to side. "At first eye-touch I *had* to get to know you also, as if I'd sink into a black pit if I didn't, be forever knifed by regret. The sky expanded, became something like twice as vast, when those same waves splashed me, and your eyes were *so* reassuring—scanned and pierced and aroused me, lingered on every inch of me while somehow still looking straight into mine, lusciously encouragingly. I *knew* you'd be coming over to me, giving us a chance. But how could I know I'd be in New York so fast, playing in a storm with you?"

"It's almost as if, from the second we spotted each other, emotion was kicked into motion and nature took its course—brought you here from your side of the world. Simply by being here, dollface, you're altering my home for the better beyond wildest hoping of what's possible—all's a revitalizing waking dream."

"And hopefully, Perry, you'll be transforming *my* home into the wildest of waking dreams soon—the reeds, dunes, and Mediterranean want to show you a good time! When can you come to Egypt? Let's take care of that."

"Akila, the thought of visiting's tingles me silly all over—I have seven days of vacation left, not counting Thanksgiving's four-day weekend and the between Christmas and New Year's break. What time's best for you? I'll book the flight tomorrow. And it's tough to resist coming straightaway but think we should wait at least a month, space it out, since once I use my days that'll be it until the holidays. A golden rule of slacking's *never* attract the attention of distant administration people, invite censure that's easily backed up by hard evidence, as in by exceeding allotted vacation days. By all means bend rules but *always* ensure there's enough wiggle-room to keep doing so, avoid suspicion of intent—I'll never get enough of playing the part of compliant corporate puppet, then sneaking off to sunbathe on rooftops, attend sound bath classes, meet friends at The Boathouse, or... Ha! I've fine-tuned the art of duping my employer, had an insane amount of unauthorized fun on company time, and it would be extremely stupid to jeopardize it."

"Love it," she coos, licking my neck. "Corporate stuff's alien to me, I've even been vaguely intimidated by it at times, and here you're awarding yourself windfalls of fun on your employer's dime, giving the lie to things many take seriously, and... Well, that's downright revelatory, and definitely shouldn't be jeopardized! How's early September for your visit?"

"Perfect," I respond, kissing her forehead. "Labor Day's a bonus vacation day, free and clear of allotted days, so this is how it plays out: I use four vacation days for Labor Day week, three more for the next week, then... Well, it would be a shame not to spend a third weekend with you due to being a paltry two vacation days short, so I'm inclined to violate what I just said, dream up an excuse that enables me to get away with taking extra vacation days for the first time—I don't care about pay being docked, completely fair. Flights are cancelled often enough to lend credibility and it's far-off Egypt, this my golden opportunity. What's also in my favor is I've never taken a sick day. Not sure what excuse to use, but..."

"Trust in Egypt for a foolproof excuse!" she interjects giggling. "Say a locust swarm's stalled traffic because it's impossible to see more than two meters ahead, darkness blotting out daylight. Use a video I took, stripped of the date taken, to prove we're stranded on a desert high-way—the din of locusts surrounding the car's guaranteed to amaze the administration people. The swarm swooped in and engulfed the car of a sudden, smothered all in whirring wings, it's me and two girlfriends but we're not in the video, saying anything—we had to stay in the car, going outside's out of the question. Imagine every centimeter of air crammed with desert locusts, six to eight centimeters long each, and they're scraping your skin with tiny claws, bodies and wings battering your face—add wind to their flight-velocity and they hit you hard as hail. If you're outside they're landing on you, clinging, chewing—hungry for everything, hyper-amped up, as if possessed. And smushed locusts on the road are slick as ice, add that to limited visibility—no chance to get to Cairo's airport on time. Hit them with *that* excuse for missing a flight and you'll have wiggle-room to burn, no one will dream of doubting."

"Whoa! It's not only a foolproof excuse, management will be totally floored, I couldn't have dreamed it up in a thousand years—I'd pay to see the aghast faces, dropping jaws!" I laugh, licking her lips. "Perfect example of 'so far out it must be true'—I'll be hitting them with a plague-of-Biblical-proportions experience! I'll book the second Wednesday as my return date, then my return's regrettably and distressingly—ha ha!—postponed due to desert locust interference! I'll send a screenshot of the receipt to management with your video, complain about the change-of-flight penalty that doesn't take locust disruption into consideration."

"Wonderful," she smiles—tightening the grip of her thighs wrapped around me slightly below my waist, vibrating them. "Knowing our Egypt adventure's in the works is pure honeysuckle sweetness, and our New York adventure's barely started and already surpassing imagination, a tough act to follow! But I'll say this: you'll walk among the real rustling fields of reeds on the Nile's bank and taste of them too—succulent salads unchanged for thousands of years. I'll show you the dawn of recorded civilization—show you a civilization that lasted longer than any other—show you the invention of architectural wonders, rooted in feats of engineering used to this day—show you our otherworldly dunes and beach, verdant oases amidst stark desert sands—we'll feast on fresh-netted fish, baked in bonfire embers on the beach, and skewered barbequed locusts and lotus."

"And could I in wildest dreams have anticipated an adorable sophisticated woman, who lifts breathtaking-as-the-dawn to mind-altering heights, would inform me we'll feast on skewered barbequed locusts and lotus? You're a hallucinogen like no other, angel! No night will be more flush with vitality and joy than tonight and those that follow—we won't be lonely anymore on *any* level, consciously or subconsciously!" I'm massaging her shoulders, kissing her forehead again.

"We've entered our safe harbor, Perry—actually been in it since Puerto Rico! I'm blood-flooded by your texts alone, keeping me soaring and in wonderment. And our time-erasing phone calls, hours flying insanely fast—your voice strums my heartstrings, seems to *land* on me! Tonight's as joyful as my childhood universe, limitations inconceivable—I'm a little girl again, thank you!" Moments later, without saying a word and as if with one will, we're seated upright and undressing, assisting one another as needed, our drenched clothes clinging—we can't stop touching each other, kissing and laughing. When I finish pulling her dress over her head, Akila helpfully wriggling, she gathers it into a ball and throws it at the tree's trunk, whereupon it makes a *Splat!* sound and she's clapping, yells, "Direct hit!" Soon we're repeatedly throwing our wet clothes at the tree's trunk and retrieving them, triumphantly yelling when the *Splat!* sound's achieved.

"Civilization wants to fool us into thinking it's tough to get away with much and you're smacking that deception down, darling," I say, embracing Akila from behind. "I'll be forcing myself to return to the office at noon and, instead of tossing a damp towel on fun, it's spice in tonight's sauce—it's invigorating to not care tonight's a worknight! Contrast is the name of the game and you're lifting contrast to bacchanalian heights—I've no doubt you'll inundate me with warm lingering emotionally surfable waves of excitement, thoroughly protect me, turn the office into a joke once I'm in it again. Dare and thou shalt receive! Daring to have fun in the face of opposing forces, supposed responsibility, is downright godly, and..."

"I thank my Gods you know fun's godly, Perry!" Akila breaks in, falling backwards onto my lap, scampering her fingers up my chest, blithely gazing. "Too many guys are serious in the fake way, won't allow fun to happen, adhere to oppressive guidelines concerning intimacy, I've never figured out why. If they're uncomfortable with having fun how can I be comfortable with them? Being with you's as expansive as sun-shimmered horizons, and I'm thankful!"

"I've unfortunately also encountered anti-fun lunacy—will never understand the judgmental killjoy approach," I say, framing her temples with my fingers. "How can fun be the enemy? I've heard variations of, 'We can't do this, it's not what a relationship should be, we need to be mindful of the future,' while having a good time with a woman—had the good time abruptly halted, endured tiresome lectures. What was the crime? Casting care aside was the crime, which is plain insane. Mindful of the future? Ha! I'm very mindful of the future and anti-fun people need to be ditched! But why dwell upon those suffering from the death-in-life mentality? Akila, you're high surf and I want to catch *all* your waves!"

"Please catch your fill of me, ride me until I'm spent, sweetie—I want to break on your shore until I'm too deliciously dazed to know I'm thousands of miles from home!" She rises from my lap to her knees, faces me—seizes my shoulders, gently but firmly shoves me onto my back, flings herself onto me. The lines of her litheness are intermittingly illuminated, compellingly ablaze, depending on whether lightning's flashing bright enough to penetrate the tree's foliage.

Spoken words are largely done away with. Communication's primarily via caresses, gestures, stretches, glances—the tone of our breathing, gasps and sighs, ebb and flow of muscular tension, nerve-vibrations—press of our lips, tongue-undulation, while kissing. It's breath-stealingly beautiful that the rise and fall of Akila's chest, tautness of her thighs, positioning of her shoulders, or tap-tap of her fingers anywhere on me seizes ahold of and dizzies me inside out, pulls me deeper into her depths, as if entrusting me with many of her carefully guarded secrets—wellsprings of sensitivity, vigor, fearlessness. I'm willing to bet we're the only people in town making love in Central Park or in any other park in this storm, an achievement of which I'm inordinately proud. At one point Akila's raised on her knees, gazing upon me as tenderly as I'm sure I'll ever be gazed upon: I can see, and feel, delight sparkle up her spine as she arches her back, twists her hands among the leaves, one of the park's lamps close enough to flow ghostly illumination through the foliage, and what pops into my thoughts is that they're hands, despite being soft and delicate, that are swift enough to seize an asp by its tail before it's able to strike, whip it dead against a palm's trunk. Because Akila's also very fit and athletic and eager for challenge—hungry for commonplace-eclipsing experiences, opportunities to surpass and amaze herself.

Chapter Four

It's not until sunrise gold's glistening on Cedar Hill's storm-flattened lawn, Akila and I on our backs, remnants of rain sporadically dripping from the foliage above, that I'm aware of speaking in complete sentences again. "Wild! The night's whipped by as if it occurred in a couple hours, storm clouds gone as if they were never there—what a kaleidoscope of possibility this new morning is!"

"Sweetie, I couldn't be more elevated by a new morning, swimming out of my skin, and I've seen sunrise swathe the Sphinx in vermillion waves, dissolve horizons bleeding into desert sands. Field of Reeds or Paradise or Elysian Fields or Valhalla, whatever people choose to call boundless joy: I'd say we're tasting of such joy at this very moment—I've never been more overflowing."

"We're there, all right, Akila—I've never been more tingled electric simply by breathing, every moment an expansive gift, as wild as..."; then, cutting myself off, reluctantly switching topics, on account of perceiving unwelcome movement in the corner of my eye, "Bloody hell! A guy's on the path already, good thing we can't be seen from there—people need to be nearly on top of us, bless our tree's wall of leaves. Sunrise suggests immortality, rejuvenation in a new day's freshness and promise, but also means privacy's out the window—we're mortal after all, at the mercy of civilization's censure, pointless prejudice. Apparently the park's officially open again, early risers, possible spies, swarming in—we should get dressed." I'm gesturing at our clothes, heaped near the tree's trunk.

"Wise suggestion, even if I'm—ha ha!—wanting more of the freedom in daylight we had to do the things we did in your private forest, unmolested by worry of anyone intruding," Akila smiles, rising to her knees, the man on the path having vanished from view—only to drop to her stomach, a woman with a yapping Yorkie having appeared. "OK! So we definitely need to dress once the coast's clear, avoid risk of observation by unkind killjoys inclined to pigeonhole us as being maturity-challenged-mud-caked scamps! *(She runs a finger up one of her arms, gathers mud, grinning ear to ear.)* I've been muddy to the roots of my hair on the Nile's banks, where they're lush with our reeds, but never dreamed I'd be muddy in Manhattan—thank you, I appreciate it—I feel right at home."

"Never thought a woman, and especially one who's the embodiment of sophistication, class, delicacy, and grace, would thank me for getting her muddy! But shame on me anyway—ridiculous that it never dawned on me there's hardly any grass under here due to lack of direct sunlight, mostly bare ground waiting to turn to mud in rain. My flimsy excuse is I never had a pressing reason to notice, since I've never brought a cutie here, didn't know I'd do so in a storm."

"So I'm the first girl you've brought here? I couldn't be more tickled sweet! I can't wait to show you transcendence where *I* live—we'll play on the Nile's banks in blazing sun, have mud-fights, swim the mud off, then have more mud-fights—behave as if unleashed in prehistory, before splinteredness of mind was possible—no ability to be judgmental. We'll build bonfires on the beach, I'll get you tipsy on ancient-recipe beer, lotus blossoms in the mix—we'll dance and yell under the stars, mirror the writhing patterns of flames on the sand. You know my birthplace on the Mediterranean and Cairo condo are your homes as much as mine, right? I can't wait to experience my homeland through your eyes."

"And I can't wait to arrive in your legendary homeland, where I could've never imagined I'd be—infinite thanks, Akila, for inviting me," I respond. "I'll kiss the Sphinx's paws at vermillion sunrise, roll onto my back and howl, even if dozens of tourists are around—please hold me to that. Vacation in Puerto Rico leads to this incandescent night which leads to the land of your Gods, your glorious heritage—life's humbling me with its beauty, as are you. I don't believe how blessed I am."

"I'm insanely blessed, Perry—meeting a man who treats me to an all-night Central Park storm's a dream I never knew I had come true—you're expanding aspiration's boundaries, and that's incredible. And we both value seeking to escape civilization's stultification, behave as if doesn't exist—our alignment's my favorite miracle."; then, tensing with alarm—cupping my ear, whispering—as a half dozen noisy gesticulating tourists burst onto Cedar Hill's path from below, snapping pictures, phones glinting in the sunrise, "Getting *way* too crowded!"

"Getting to be a zoo," I whisper in turn, crawling about a yard on elbows to grab our clothes—soon we're flipping onto our backs, arranging our clothes atop us, mimicking being dressed, they clinging on account of being soaked. "We'll dress for real when the coast's clear," I continue. "Movement might be detected through our tree's leaves, abundant as they are, if anyone seriously stared over here—they probably wouldn't know it's people but... Well, who knows what these tourists will do?—where they'll wander, what they'll photograph and film?"

"Social media shenanigans could get us! And I'm amused by that but also not, if that makes any sense. Maybe I should say social media's revoltingly, and unjustifiably, invasive at the same time it can be titillating—the latter because it makes hovering on the edge of a threat possible in ways nonexistent when I was born, requires greater creativity in getting away with frowned-upon, or outright taboo, amusements. Assuming we get away with being birthday-suited outside in Manhattan at daybreak—aren't filmed, broadcasted—we'll be tickled pink about it forever, right? But it's disgraceful that we could be plastered all over the Internet by tabloid-imitating losers with no decency—I can't imagine willfully violating the privacy of randomly encountered people who aren't harming anyone."

"Yeah, we'll be laughing ourselves dizzy if we get away with it, likely but not guaranteed—social media's threats of exposure send elation sky-high when exposure's avoided, since it's tougher to do nowadays—welcome to the ultra-modern-people-victimizing-to-tal-strangers-for-clicks world. Crazy how hordes have been brainwashed into believing it's commendable to behave like sniveling grade schoolers, tattletale at every opportunity—informing on others has become a worldwide contest. Two decades ago I wouldn't have cared if tourists caught us in our birthday suits—social media's done its best to destroy devil-may-care and promote paranoia, enable an unofficial worldwide police state, law enforcement routinely examining the posts. Tourists could randomly stroll over here, part our tree's branches for no particular reason, feel they've struck gold at the discovery of us—promptly film us, stream us live with condemnatory narration—invite their followers to watch and for it snowball around the world, people as far off as New Zealand and Iceland categorizing us as irresponsible, chastising us in the comment fields—something neither Orwell nor Huxley nor any other enlightened author warning of oppressive technology-enabled futures foretold. But I refuse to be suckered into getting negative, just want to grab and lick you as if it's thousands of years ago!" I slide sideways, press against her—sling a leg over hers, caress her from midriff to neck—the sight of her heaving chest alone's a flood of joy.

"Yummy," she coos, reaching to grasp my shoulder, writhing against me; then, after planting a row of kisses up the side of my neck, "Not going to shortchange our fun by worrying about social media either—have a technology-splintered head, be preyed upon like that—society fosters self-disunity, schizoid mental states, how sick! Nah-nah-nah, civilization and stupid rules, the incomprehensible war on fun! *(She briefly thumbs her nose at the air.)* I think we're going to get away with being naked under our tree after our luscious night, and get away with a lot more the more we're together! Oh, yeah, I'm gloating! And tingling too!"

"Only having one life we're sure of should be motivation for everyone to seek elevating experiences instead of indulging in tawdry busybody meddlesomeness, but curiously isn't. Wielding a camera at the expense of others is snitching, pure and simple, and snitches have traditionally been rightly despised. We're not afflicted with the snitching sickness—we live for euphoria and being carefree and indifferent to judgmental trash and I thank my lucky stars for that, and for you."

"We absolutely do, sweetheart, and that's our heaven—channeling storm-energy tonight, loving you while rolling in mud under a roiling Manhattan sky, is fire stolen from the Gods—your home's a magical otherworld for me, gloriously permissive and primitive."; then, inclining her head towards the tourists, who've gathered to chat in a semi-circle at the top of the path, not above fifteen yards away, and are turning away, "Oh! Looks like they're leaving—we can dress."

After the tourists head west across the East Drive we don't squander an instant or gesture—the fact our clothes are sopping wet and tough to manipulate adds to urgency. Once Akila's dress is on and I'm pulling its hemline down, smoothing the rumples, she rising high enough on her knees for her head to touch our tree's leaves, I'm saying, "Your dress is too transparent in the wrong place, the mud's not strategically splattered—waterlogged white linen's not an effective veil."

"No, it isn't!" she giggles; then, tapping her chest, "Mud's only veiling me upstairs—downstairs will get me stared at in a way I'd rather not be and is surely a public exposure violation but it's easily fixed." She's gathering a handful of mud.

"No need to add mud—I'll wrap my shirt around your waist."

"But it's a t-shirt—the sleeves are too short and won't wrap around me, can't be tied together. It'll fall off the moment I move."

"I'll fasten my belt around you, slip my shirt up between it and your waist in front. You'll be covered more appropriately than with mud—if it's only mud you could come off as being overly wanton and careless, like you're indifferent or unaware and it's only by accident that you're covered up."

"But you'll be shirtless! And what does it matter if more mud's on my dress?—it's already trashed, I'll be tossing it—nothing will get the stains out. And who cares if being covered up by mud appears to be accidental, or wanton, so long as I'm covered? No reason for you to be shirtless."

"And being shirtless isn't a public exposure violation for me, so end of discussion," I respond, removing my t-shirt and twirling it. "And, anyway, what sort of man allows a darling to smear mud on her dress, even if it's already muddy? Now, if you please." I gesture for her to discard the mud.

"OK, and yes, Sir," she salutes smiling, wiping the mud in her other hand onto the tree's trunk. "What sort of girl refuses a chivalrous gentleman's thoughtful gesture? May the Gods smite me if I ever do."

Akila's massaging my shoulders as I remove my belt and fasten it about her waist, pull my t-shirt up under it in front and fold it over, drape it down. "There, now you're veiled—won't be violating public exposure laws, are right and proper and legal," I announce upon completion. "It's safe to leave our tree."

"Thank you, sweetie, for making me legal in an unfamiliar land," she giggles, running her hands up and down my arms. "I'm very willing to be stared at, just not for the wrong reasons. I think we're going to be stared at like crazy, for the right reasons—mud on us, our disorder of presentation, like we've been stranded in a remote oasis for days—subsisting on lizards and insects, drinking spring water, licking dew off leaves, using mud as sunblock and to forestall dehydration. And our elation in the face of tribulation, refusal to be smacked down—I'm looking forward to being disheveled in public with you, attracting stares."

"And thank you, darling, for flipping geography on its head, encouraging me to dare more closer to home. I've been a happy resident of the Upper East since April, 1999, my favorite NYC neighborhood by far, and have never been shirtless and muddy in the streets, liberated as if on vacation worlds away. The difference is I'm with an Egyptian princess, who does the ancient murals proud, brings pagan serenity and sweep of emotion and aspiration and light to the 21st century. You said my home's a magical otherworld for you? Well, because of you it's also one for me—you've turned my backyard into an exotic place and I can't wait to parade on the sidewalks with you, carefree as if in Puerto Rico's rainforests. I'm a kid with a new toy, transported by courage at home I previously lacked."

"You lacking courage?" she cries incredulously, waving a hand in dismissal. "Rubbish! I've told you about the guys who think I'm weird for rolling down the dunes and yelling—you couldn't judge a girl for worshipping abandon if your life depended on it, only prod her to carry it further, and have courage to burn, enough said!"; then, after licking my neck and cheeks, rolling her tongue about her lips, lightly poking my ribs, "But I *do* agree with the new toy thing, since I never thought I'd be courageous enough to be a messy muddy girl in mighty Manhattan—your courage expands my safety zone, I'm feeling very protected."

"Yeah! New toys and expanded safety zones here we come!" I shout as we drop to hands and knees, crawl below the ground-kissing ends of our tree's lower branches—in a flash we're standing on Cedar Hill's lawn.

"Didn't realize we're *this* muddy, direct sunlight's spelling it out—a true badge of honor," Akila laughs, looking me up and down and lifting her legs perpendicular to her waist in turn, examining them as well as her chest and arms; then, upon crouching, running her fingers through the lawn, "I'm completely, and proudly, a girly-girl, fond of out dressing and showing up other girls—being stylish, polished, fluffy—but likewise live for being thrashed around by Mommy Nature, unleashed and primitive. I've traipsed about my town fresh from rolling in the dunes after a swim, covered in sand—hair mangled, make-up mussed, looking ratty—I rip up my mesh cover-ups for added effect, walk erratically to appear lost and glazed. It's fun getting people who've known me all my life, seen me being the belle of the ball—ultra fastidious, not a lock of hair out of place—to do the disbelieving gape-mouthed thing. Some have communicated concern to my parents, wondered whether I'm wholly right in my mind—very endearing indeed, more motivation to put on the act. Modern life's way overrated—overmuch pampering, protection from the elemental, leads to inertia, enervation, depression, undermines the immune system, invites illness—nature can't be cheated by cheap tricks. Ha! That's me paraphrasing you, Perry! You're a super positive influence, have added to my vocabulary and aspirations, ability to communicate what I value."

"I'm in awe of how much we value in common, Akila, out and out floored, and of course you've added to my vocabulary and aspirations as well—the Field of Reeds has taken my imagination by storm. It's straight out of fiction, an author inventing a man and woman who're hungering for a lost, less artifice-informed, past; and they find each other while on vacation far from their homes and effortlessly mirror each other's ideals and inclinations, both aware the powers-that-be are seeking to swindle us into falling for artificial versions of life, digital pseudo-experience figuring prominently in the plan—both avoiding such flimflam as best they can. I'll say it again, darling—your night-black hair and illuminated visage and light-kissed gaze and ethereal grace are ancient Egyptian beauty miraculously reborn, thriving and alive, in the here and now. And the Met's behind those trees *(I gesture towards the Metropolitan Museum's roof, glints of its glass piercing the foliage.)*, where I've thrilled to Egyptian beauty too many times to count. And Cleopatra's Needle's just over there. *(I gesture further to the left.)* Thirty-five hundred years old and just about the most uplifting work of art in town, line-perfect quadrilateral obelisk stabbing the sky—so symmetrical, erect—flawless posture, like yours. I think our night won't be complete until we visit Cleo, pay our respects to your heritage—Egypt's a beckoning light."

"Cleo's over there? Wow!" she cries, jumping up and down and clapping. "If you hadn't read my mind (you're amazingly good at it) I would've suggested visiting Cleo myself, even if not today, since I had no idea she was so close—I don't know much about your town but have always known Cleo's in it. I've been at the other three obelisks—in Paris and London as a little girl, Luxor every year. Now I get to complete the set—never thought of visiting all four as a pilgrimage, mainly because I never thought I'd be in New York, but now realize it is. And that I'll be greeting Cleo on this incandescent morning after all-night frolic surpasses wildest fantasy! And Luxor's obelisk and temples, by the way, are on my list for your visit—we'll take the balloon ride, you'll see the desert's expanses sweep into the sky, unite horizons—a visual depiction of infinity if there ever was one."; then, upon skipping a few yards ahead, turning to face me, extending her hands, "Please show me the way, Perry—Cleo might be close but I'm still a stranger in a strange land, where south's the same as north." Seconds later we're scampering down Cedar Hill hand in hand—angling left, heading north, per my lead.

Chapter Five

"Obelisk irradiant in sunrise—stabbing the golden sky and seeming to stream it to our feet, flagstones ablaze," I say as we circle Cleopatra's Needle hand in hand. "It's always as if I'm seeing Cleo for the first time, she's as fresh as if sculpted yesterday—far younger in spirit than the present sorry excuses for architecture, dated within decades. Ancient Egypt knew how to intensify experience within civilization's limitations, invest living with multidimensionality, dynamic cat and jackal and ibis Gods: if civilization needs to exist (I'll always feel it's a psyche-splintering affliction) Egyptians were the best example of how to go about it. Akila, you're breathtaking beyond measure and the sun streaming over you delights in your beauty almost as much as I do—you couldn't be more of an antidote to falsity, unaffectedly unbridled, nonstop overwhelming me—it's still nighttime, our adventures shimmering me in blood and bones."

"Perry, you can't help but will me towards the best versions of myself, shimmering in blood and bones indeed, and I love that you're calling it night when we're in dawn's resplendent light, you couldn't be more right—I'm still speeding with night-feelings, as if safely swathed in the permissiveness of darkness. When night-feelings follow me into daylight my energy overdrives—my energy's shooting up Cleo's hieroglyphs to her tippity-top, tilting me dizzy! Are my feet on the ground? Maybe I'm afloat on shafts of light! Help me defy gravity!" She's indicating via downward rub of her fingers, one of our dance-signals, that she wishes to be dipped.

"Looks like we could be upstaging Cleo," I whisper, aware the dozen or so tourists in the vicinity are watching as I bend Akila backwards deep enough for her body's arc to suggest yoga's wheel-posture, she wrapping a leg about mine above my knees, smiling a glimpse-of-heaven smile. "Holding you while resisting the urge to lower you onto the flagstones, grab and lick you all over—this state of energetic suspension, desire deliciously needling—and with Cleo alongside us, has to be one of the most bracing waking dreams I'll ever have—tilted dizzy's spot-on." I hold Akila in her dip until we're trembling, muscles tightening, then hold her longer—it's as if I'm falling into her eyes as awareness of the tourists blurs.

"Whew!" Akila sigh-exclaims, two-handedly fanning her face as I pull her upright awhile later, we shaking off muscular tension. "Wild heaven to be this turned loose, messy and muddy and primitive in morning's light, charged with up-all-night energy, and we're not in any Sahara oasis or Puerto Rican forest but in Manhattan and Cleo's here! We need a picture, for me to keep always—let's ask them, they look like nice people." Moments later she's approaching three German women, inquiring if one would be kind enough to photograph us—employing flawless tact and manners, utterly opposite of our disarrayed appearance.

The women, exhibiting no surprise, as if mud-spattered lovers are only to be expected in New York, cheerfully oblige. Soon one of them's aiming Akila's phone, counting off one-two-three as Akila and I nestle cheeks in front of Cleopatra's Needle, arms wrapped around each other. Then the woman announces, "I think you should want more photo—maybe you do to get in dance standing. You doing dance stand when we come here and you dance good." Her English isn't perfect but we readily comprehend, particularly as she clarifies with gesticulations—seconds later I'm twirling and dipping Akila as the woman snaps multiple pictures. "There, you look to see if photo good," the woman says, returning Akila's phone. Upon examination of the pictures—over two dozen—we inform the woman they exceed expectation, thank her profusely, then photograph her with her friends, encouraging them to be by turns serious and silly. When the women depart a few minutes later, myself having recommended they visit Belvedere Castle and The Ramble and The Lake and Bethesda Fountain and provided directions, the five of us exchange blown kisses.

"Look how aglow we are, on happy energy fire," Akila says, once we've finished admiring Cleopatra's Needle and reached the Metropolitan Museum's northern wall, smothered in an ivy and Virginia creeper mix, where we're perusing the pictures. "I don't need photos to affirm I'm out-of-my-skin elated but they don't hurt and I'll always treasure these. Our photographer and her friends were priceless—found it charming we're muddy, no judgment, just smiling. Give tourists their due—they're often a breath of fresh air, I've seen it at home. They're away from home, free of servitude to obligation, maintenance of appearances—out for fun, less likely to care what others are up to. I'd say fear of public opinion's mostly a local affliction: people want to escape it and travel helps that happen."

"Couldn't agree more," I say, backing Akila into the vines—she's winding her arms through breeze-fluttered leaves ablaze in the sun as her chest arrestingly rises and falls, curvature ripples, under the cling of her dress. "Travel's freedom from constraint—I do things in distant locales I wouldn't dare do here, or at least not until this morning. This is just about the most kissing-off-of-care vacation I've taken and it's blocks from my home, which makes it all the more hallucinogenic—I've traveled further than Australia without catching a flight. Is my job a figment of my imagination? It's just plain *weird* that I'll be setting foot in an office in a few hours—performing repetitive tasks, pretending to take nonsense seriously."

"But are you really going to work, honey?" she asks, rubbing a cheek against my chest, gazing up at me with sky-wide eyes, seizing my hands, squeezing. "I know you're tough but I'd dread winding up in an office on no sleep after our night—having to stifle elation, focus on duty. It seems like a harrowing experience to me! Why not call in sick?—since you're the healthiest man I've ever known, it's virtually guaranteed no one will suspect you're faking. I think people will be thinking something like, 'It must be serious if Perry's calling in sick.'"

"Akila, I appreciate that you're looking out for me but, to echo your sentiment, cavorting in a storm all night on a worknight with fetching you's a dream *I* never knew I had come true, an absolute kicker to the marrow of my bones, and I want to continue riding elation's wave at work. I've never flowed into work fresh from an out-of-bounds night of frolic on no sleep and am blessed to have the opportunity—reporting to work's been transformed into something of high adventure, and I relish new challenges. Not everyone can have the night I've had and turn up at a place that's won a prestigious 'Mid-Sized Agency of the Year' award, where corporate protocol's law and assignments must be executed to the letter, and get away with it and I need to be someone who can. After being in the storming elements with you on mud I thought was grass under our dancing-in-gusts tree how can I pass on the chance to hum with tonight's energy while handling whatever assignments come my way?—thrill to the contrast, laugh all the way to the emotional bank? It'll be fun! It's my love of fun that'll carry me—frivolity's strength! But what do you do for a living, Akila? We haven't covered that, have been too out of our heads. I don't peg you for being idle rich, as I'm guessing you could be if so inclined."; then, checking myself, "Please don't take amiss the...

"Impossible to take anything you say amiss, Perry," she breaks in, lifting her head from my chest and facing me. "I know you'll always be one hundred percent for me, as I am for you—the sound of your voice alone's silky soothing. Yes, I *am* protected by family prestige and money, I won't hide it, but have been raised to fend for myself, thank God. I train people to ace standardized tests—LSAT, MCAT, SAT, ACT, all of them. I've always been a test robot and love helping people get into the schools of their dreams and am also fully independent, no third party agencies taking a cut, as they did when I started out, before I made a name for myself. Word of mouth's a beautiful thing—my students and their parents, who're footing the bill, promote on my behalf, and teachers and guidance counselors do so as well. Sometimes I teach at my students' homes, other times online—I've had students in Shanghai, Reykjavik, and Surabaya, Indonesia. My students book my classes on my website—I'm able to block time I want off, as I've done for this trip. And it's slower now, a between test-cycles lull, or I wouldn't be here yet—not because of lost income but because I'd sooner die than leave my students hanging when they need me. The next frenzy, when I work eight to twelve hours a day every day for almost a month, starts later."

"Many thanks for squeezing in this visit and my early September one," I smile, kissing her forehead. "You've bested me with *your* job, eliminated offices altogether. I may have an optimum slacking job, with none at work suspecting it's such and making trouble, but I'm still tied to an office—obliged to forestall inquisitiveness by tossing off a doctored personality, appearing strait-laced and afraid of fun—a game I could do without."

"I'd say the game's kept you razor sharp, Perry—I envy you the opportunity to lead a double life, use the distance between your office persona and the primal man you *really* are to nurture emotional fluidity, open up new psychic space, experience transcendence in a tedious place—it's crystal clear why you want to go to work today. And a confession, dearest—my suggestion to call in sick was partly motivated by selfishness, since I'd *love* to cuddle all day! Sorry for..."

"*Really*, angel? You're apologizing for wanting to cuddle, when I'll never be nearer to heaven while mortal than when in your arms? Please continue to be selfish in that manner, since I am too!" I interrupt laughing, pulling her against me, she wrapping her arms around me. "But let's head home—I actually *do* need to think about getting ready for work, where I'll be thinking about you constantly, hungering to cuddle—it'll be the most rhapsodic *and* agonizing interval I've spent at work. Where does euphoric anticipation end and knifing impatience begin? I'll be getting very acquainted with *that* borderline today, oscillating back and forth!"

"I'll be engulfed in sweet torment all day too, going crazy dizzy just outright totally loony, waiting lasting forever!" she beams, springing from the ivy and seizing my hand. "Please be my guide and steer me home, Perry, since I've no idea where home is, am as good as in a not-on-any-map place, and that's an absolute kicker for me—one of amazingly many." Within five minutes we've scampered down the incline of lawn to the walkway, crossed 5th Avenue, advanced a block north, are strolling east on 86th Street's south side, with the sun before us— reflecting off, seeming to ignite, rows of windows to our left and right.

Chapter Six

"Sweetie, were you really a cab driver or did you dream that up to settle down the driver when the Champagne spilled?" Akila inquires, gesturing at a cab. "Dreamed up or not, it worked." We're paused on Park Avenue's traffic island, waiting for the pedestrian signal to change to "Walk."

"One hundred percent true," I respond. "Back in my East Village days, upon arriving in New York from Paris seemingly a century ago, I signed on for the night shift at a garage in Long Island City, as exploitative as every other garage—with a parasitical puppet union running the show, demanding monthly dues for zilch in return, due to kickbacks to ownership—and in hindsight I wouldn't have wanted it any other way. Because also in hindsight I consider cab driving to be atonement for a sheltered upbringing, even if I accidently fell into it, since it was the first job I got wind of that didn't require commitment to a schedule—I only drove when I needed money. But I *was* thirsting to taste of the raw uncensored streets—there *was* an urge to knock the, shall we say, spoiledness out of my system, go contrary to the common perception of me, including my perception of myself—I'd like to think I wasn't romantic about it. And I *did* experience what it is to live hand-to-mouth with no economic leeway, financial security or benefits—there *were* days when I arrived at the garage hungry, with only the two dollars I needed for the per-shift lease permit, another union scam. I'd be praying my first few fares didn't require change for larger bills because I had no change, and once I hauled in enough cash would head to the nearest place with healthy food. Never mind mom and dad would've happily bailed me out—I blotted that option out, felt it was only decent to keep them in the dark, tell them I was supporting myself with freelance editing (Which turned out to be prophetic: following a chance conversation, I submitted a fictional resume to temp agencies, bluffed my way into getting signed, wound up on legal and medical editing jobs, have breezily earned a decent living ever since.), as they would've been as shocked as worried sick. The backed-up-against-the-wall sensation as a driver, being at the mercy of the volatile streets, was priceless, even if I was far from thinking so at the time—I remind myself of it always, will cling to it always, draw strength from it always. I learned far more about life in the streets than I did in school, acquired greater gratitude for my time on earth—survival leads to joy. I'd say driving a cab in New York City on the night shift and emerging stronger—happier, wiser, more centered and self-assured—is the street-equivalent of graduating summa cum laude from MIT."

"You sure know how to surprise a girl!" she smiles, playfully poking my ribs. "Not to naysay the profession, but you don't look anything remotely like a cab driver, I would've betted you made it up! You *so* look and act like—whoa!—this man's leisure class—your aristocratic aplomb, down to finest details of posture and diction, can't be faked. Actually, you look and carry yourself like you grew up surrounded by priceless art! And like a goody-good also, so innocent-faced! Hahaha!"; then, frowning at herself, becoming stock-still, "I'm not making fun, Perry—I adore that you look goody-good, convincingly play the part, and admire you all the more for your street education, opposite of your upbringing. You love the sweep of life and are doing right by it, are truly one of the happy few." We're still on the traffic island, having ignored changings of the traffic light.

"As are you, Akila—only the happiest of women would unreservedly fling herself into our Central Park adventure, not for an instant wonder if it's weird or inappropriate or whatever other anti-life terminology unhappy people employ and, also, the goody-good observation's a compliment—I'm delighted I look too goody-good for people to suspect what I've done in my past—things I did as a cab driver that I've never told a soul, including fellow drivers at dawn gatherings (when the tales ran thick and fast, our nights unfailingly eventful), and never will, statute of limitations or not. An older driver once said, 'We get every psycho in town in our cab and it rubs off and we turn into psychos too and do things we never thought we'd do.' And I got there, all right! Forget stashing guns, crowbars, knives, machetes under the front seat, as some drivers did—I felt handheld weapons would get me into far more trouble than they'd get me out of, there's the issue of incriminating evidence, plus I'm not exactly a hulking weightlifter who'd triumph in physical confrontation. The cab was my weapon: when faced with guys who leapt out of their vehicles to threaten me would jerk it, a Crown Victoria, straight at them, stopping just short, and they'd elect to retreat, often with an 'I didn't think of that, this guy's insane!' look on their faces. Perhaps such self-defense could be considered justifiable by some but I reached the point where I'd chase people onto the sidewalk with the car because of a bad tip, or throw bottles at the windshields of cars that cut me off—it became normal to indulge in such lunacy—that's how far I was yanked into the alternate world, where law and order's mythology. The streets get white hot—hordes are out to scam drivers, including the filthy rich. I began to want to kill for disrespectful tones of voice, glances that may or may not have been patronizing—was often swept into inability to distinguish emotion from fact. Another older driver once said to a group of us, 'Had an arrogant deadbeat last night and he got his. If a guy doesn't want to pay the fare, fine, but he'd better *run*. Don't insult me by walking in front of my cab after not paying and give me *that* look. I rammed the son of a bitch, broke both of his legs.' All of us were shouting approval, pumping fists. Yeah, I went there, all right! Three days later was in the same situation—a fare picked up at FIT, exiting at Junior's on Flatbush without paying, deliberately walking in front of my cab, giving me *that* smug I-dare-you-to-come-out-here-and-try-to-get-your-money look, derisively jerking his head away—at first I bump him with the bumper, enough that he's scrambling to stay on his feet, arms flailing, barely avoiding a fall—he turns to face me again, is about to yell, then sees I'm glaring at him, realizes it's intentional, runs like blazes towards Flatbush's opposite side—I flip a U-turn, and... Well, suffice to say I quit driving that morning, fearful of what further insanity might grip me—fled to an indulgent aunt's hospitality on Lake Michigan's shore, didn't return to New York for over a year. I won't deny I'm pleased to have turned psycho for a spell, verified I'm capable of going to unsuspected dark places, scaring myself to death, but don't want to go there again. Be *extremely* nice to cab drivers, especially those who drive at night when people are more unhinged, some apparently feeling dutybound to make trouble. It's a given drivers have been flung into dozens of highly stressful normalcy-redefining situations, whereby it becomes too easy to lose sight of what constitutes criminal activity, begin to believe one's survival depends on indulging in it—the unexpected breeds lawlessness. I'm proud to have been a night driver for four and a half years, instead of dabbling in it for a token month, for novelty's sake, as some trust fund kids did—it was vaguely fashionable at the time."

"Thank you for sharing, Perry," Akila half-whispers, massaging the back of my neck. "I'm going to be *so* sweet to you, don't want your past troubling you—we'll keep each other's phantoms at bay." She's winding an upraised leg about me at my hips—her mud-spattered hemline, having dried enough to allow it, is sliding down, the bronze of her thigh bright in the sun—a bed of multicolored chrysanthemums, customary for Park Avenue traffic islands this time of year, is to my right.

"You're electric honey in my veins, Akila," I respond, wrapping an arm around her back. "Forget the cab driving stuff, it's not troubling me. I'm sheltered again and at peace with it, no more rashness-bordering-on-lunacy—the days of flipping into psycho and scaring myself are long gone, another life. I'm a happy go lucky sun worshipping surfer and slacker—God bless the sun! And bless these flowers, and bless your miracle-of-creation legs, I'll never get enough of dollface you!" I'm gripping her upraised thigh, yanking it against me, with my other hand.

"Ooooo!" she coos, licking my lips—lightly circling her nails about my upper back, tickle-hinting at scratching, her chest and belly pulsing against mine—her breath-rhythm's as stirring as incoming tide. "You help yourself to all you want, sweetie—use me up anytime, anyplace, anyhow. I'm your on-demand girl, game for anything—no questions, no judgment, no rules." She's tilting her head towards the flowerbed: in a spin of sight, my eyes relishing the leaping silver of hers then dipping into the chrysanthemum-colors, I'm guiding her onto her knees in the flowers, easing her onto her back—kissing her as flower petals brush my cheeks—my fingers dancing in her hair, sun rippling gold over her rapt visage...

We're out of the flowerbed, on our feet, in under a minute—I'm saying, "*That's* one way to escape Internet publicity—in and out of the flowers too fast for anyone to decide to access their cameras. Hand-held technology's subservient to human response-time, thank God—a few seconds is just the amount of leeway we need to get away with tasting of frolic in a Park Avenue flowerbed on a sunny morning. Who, us? We weren't in the chrysanthemums moments ago—anyone who says different's deluded—nothing's provable without photos! Hahaha!"

"An out-of-my-senses taste of frolic in a New York City flowerbed on a busy morning in the wide open!" Akila declares. "Every instant so intensified it seemed to distort time, suggested infinity—on my back in the flowers, tingling silly, then on my feet again lickety-split with no mis-behavior-in-public consequences! I'm sure I'll never be more oblivious of my surroundings, celebratorily or foolishly or entrancedly or otherwise, even if only for a flash! And speaking of a flash I was flashbacking to the Puerto Rico rainforest, when we were under flamboyants with all the time in the world, scarlet petals raining down upon us, carpeting the ground. Perry, I couldn't in a thousand lifetimes have imagined I'd be in your streets looking like when playing on the Nile's banks, slopped with mud!"

"And I couldn't in a thousand lifetimes have imagined I'd be bare-chested and slopped with mud in the streets blocks from my home with an exotic sophisticated-to-her-fingertips beauty who delights in getting muddy and parading it," I say as the "Walk" sign appears and we continue east on 86th Street.

"Rest assured we'll be muddy and primitive and nearer to naked than we are here in my town too, where just about everyone knows me and can squeal about it to my mother," Akila giggles, rubbing against me. "Although I'll own up and say my mother will adore that I'm being an attention-magnet, upholding family tradition—she was extremely daring and mischievous as a youngster. My grandmother, no wallflower either, once told me there were times when she thought my mother might be certifiable. My mother will adore you, Perry."

"I look forward to meeting your mother, Akila. As for me looking like this on my home turf, no one can squeal about it to my mother because she's in California, and also wouldn't care, is amused by her offspring's antics, even if she'd never admit it. But it would be extra special if a coworker were to see me now (some live nearby, it's possible) and tattle at work. Of course such attention flies in the face of my under-the-radar approach but I'd enjoy the new game. How could I not be proud to be seen all messed up with off the charts gorgeous you and for coworkers to be speculating, especially as I've always been—ha ha!—stone-faced stoic? The more bafflement flung my way at work the more I'd be laughing—anyone with half a soul will wish they're having half as much fun as I'm having and judgmental killjoys don't count. I'd *pay* to be seen by a blabbermouth coworker."

"Judging by some of the double-takes, halting stares, we're getting a random busybody could be eager to tattle by filming us, spilling us all over the Internet. Looking like this in Manhattan's streets on a bustling morning could easily be considered Internet entertainment—we're almost asking for it. A stranger might turn your office into gossip-city for you for free—no need to pay."

"Ha! So here I'm momentarily forgetting invasion-of-privacy postings are something only no-life losers desperate for attention lower themselves to do—not only admitting I wouldn't mind if we were posted looking like this but would enjoy it. My dear, this is our story if a no-life pest posts us and it's publicized enough for us to find out: we're a respectable image-conscious couple and are accidentally disheveled, through no fault of our own. We went for a dawn walk in the park and were on The Lake's shore, admiring the view, then slipped on rain-soaked ground, fell into the lake, got muddy while climbing out. I used my shirt to make you as decent as possible downstairs—we're doing our best to be presentable with the means available to us while hastening home. Could happen to anyone."

"Clever boy, now we're covered: if we're posted we can be hurt and outraged in the comments field—ask how anyone can be unfeeling and cruel enough to publicize our slip and fall misfortune, unconscionably exploit a couple's bad luck. Because of course we're distressed and dis-combobulated at being bedraggled in public—if we were pleased about it we'd be an irresponsible thrill-addicted couple, heaven forbid! We couldn't possibly be thanking our lucky stars for gifting us with this fantasy-exceeding experience on a shimmering summer morning."

"Right, how could we possibly relish being in this deplorable state? I'm bare-chested and muddy in my neighborhood so of course am mor-tified! Our mishap happened in Central Park and we regrettably need to run the gauntlet of looking a mess from 5th Avenue to 1st Avenue, and during rush hour to boot, since hailing a cab in our muddied state's out of the question. And someone's filmed us to acquire social media traffic? I'd ascend to the soapbox, all right! 'You're beyond loser,' I'd write, 'so starved for attention you feel it's acceptable to persecute a respectable couple for slipping on mud. You have no pride and no honor and if you think honor's an antiquated notion it only shows how soulless you are.' And, hey, maybe we ought to pretend to be ashamed of what's befallen us—hang our heads, blankly stare at the pavement?"; then, after Akila attempts to do so, "Not convincing, sweetheart—your expression's only superficially glum—you're clearly amused below the surface—there's a glow about you that gives the game away."

"Well, yes, you've caught me, even if I'm hardly trying to hide it," she giggles, flinging herself onto me. "Anything can be spun, doll! So what if we're filmed happily embracing while a mess? We counter by saying we were putting a brave face on a nasty situation for sanity's sake, challenge people to think that's a bad thing—stress it's important for couples to support one another. I'll ascend to the soapbox as well—say I'm a woman who's found a good man, ask why a stranger's harassing us, intent on humiliating us, simply because we slipped on mud, point out such negativity's typical of unhappy creeps, jealous of the cheerfulness of others. Positivity always—a sunshine smile on unkind twists of fate always—couples united in countering adversity always."

"Instead of allowing misadventure to beat us down, bury us in self-blame and shame, we're rising above it with hugs and kisses, uncaring who observes—judgmental creeps can drop dead!"; then, after we've scampered laughing all the way to 2nd Avenue, pausing a couple times to kiss, "Is it stupid to not care if we're filmed? What's *extremely* stupid is worrying about what's stupid, hesitating to have a good time. If we're posted I think another comment should be, 'We have the relationship you *wish* you had—eat your heart out, loser. We couldn't be paid to trod on others, we're far too happy. Wake up, imbecile—life's brief.'"

Then we've crossed Second Avenue, are strolling past the Q Train elevator's high glass rectangle, gleaming in the sun, and Akila's waving her phone aloft. "Perry, are you OK with more documentation—selfies to go with Lena's photos?" she inquires. (Lena's the woman who photographed us at Cleopatra's Needle.) "Why not be total showoffs, revel in our messiness? We're in an embarrassing accidental situation, putting a brave face on it, turning it into a game, as people in healthy supportive relationships do—fun's to be had in unexpected ways."

"Totally in favor of being total showoffs—count me dead if I ever run from fun," I smile, swatting her behind.

"Oooooweee!" she cries, jumping and twisting, such that several heads whip in our direction. "Uh, oh!" she continues quietly, signaling for us to stop and face one another, "Shame on me, looks like some people may have gotten the stupid idea you're bothering me! But easily fixed." She's framing my face with her hands—licks my lips.

"Yeah, lightning swift impressions in the electric streets—emotions race, energy surges, and it's too easy to misread reality, jump to mistaken conclusions. The big guy in the Yankees shirt by the convenience store was about to save you from perceived aggression, took a number of resolute steps towards us, eyes flashing nastily. Now he's smiling, wishing he was me."

"I want him dying to be you, eating his heart out," she grins; then, raising her voice, "Whatever you want to do to me, sweetie, is my pining heart's deepest desire! *(She wraps her arms around me, repeatedly kisses my cheeks.)* My world's wildest bliss when you're in it and unbearable torture when you're not, I'm your obedient girl!" Instants later we're snapping selfies while nestling cheeks, or embracing and kissing, or gazing into each other's eyes, all the while heading east, taking a few steps between pictures. We make a video near 1st Avenue, in front of the supermarket's high wide windows—set Akila's handbag on the sidewalk, use it to angle the phone at us—are jumping up and down, saluting and blowing kisses at the sun—towards the end of the video I say, "Glorious life-sustaining orb, we're madly in love with you!" after which we bow towards the camera, hands joined.

"Well, here's some fun defiance, where I couldn't have imagined I'd dare indulge in it—Manhattan's concrete and angles in the background, New Yorkers deigning to look surprised and stare at us," Akila giggles, hip-bumping me as we scroll through the pictures while continuing home. "Then again, calling it 'defiance' downgrades us—we're healthily oblivious, just don't care—have worry-free faces, you're so cute! Maybe we should post some of these photos? I'm very proud of them! We could totally go in a making-the-best-of-a-bad-situation direction—fib about falling in The Lake, add commentary such as, 'At first we were apprehensive about leaving Central Park in our muddy condition, scared of inviting ridicule. It's our trust in one another that rescued us—we resolved to turn our mishap into a fun adventure, since we couldn't otherwise change it—couldn't stay in the park forever, make the mud on us disappear. So we took these photos to celebrate overcoming fear, carrying one another along, having each other's back.'"

"Will be proud to post them, even if I never thought I'd be tinkering with social media in that manner—can't imagine better photos and commentary to debut with, and the gawking that's in the background of some's a bonus," I say, we having crossed 1st Avenue a block north of my residence; then, sweeping an arm south, "I call this the 1st Avenue Grand Canyon, high-rises framing the avenue, and today the high-rises, usually sharp of outline, are soft-edged, blurry—the air's bouncy, dancing—ocean wave motion's swirling the light. It's the up-all-night-alteration-of-perception effect, intensified because I'm with you. Are we on a sunny beach?"

"Looks like a beach to me: the sidewalk is a white sand shoreline, the asphalt is dark water lapping against it. And speaking of beaches, my favorite beach is twenty minutes from ours and also on my list for your visit. It's crescent shape slingshots one's gaze along a rocky promontory straight at the horizon—incoming waves are shoved up, roiled and accelerated, by twin mini-islands near shore—gain over a meter in height between the islands, turn deep azure, surge at the beach over a sand bottom. We'll roll around among the iridescent seashells, scarlet and pale blue and even silver, that are washed ashore there and nowhere else I know of."

"Roiling azure waves and iridescent seashells? Wonderful pictures you've placed in my head—I'll be out of my senses in Egypt every day."; then, aware of the barking Maltese in a window above my building's entrance, gesturing there as we cross 85th Street, "Pastry's announcing us—one of the sweetest dogs ever born—leaps onto your lap, bounces and squirms and licks your hands like crazy—I call her Energy Dog, nonstop charged up, eager to socialize and play."

"She's well-named—fluffy confectionary frosting fur flying all over—adorable! Hi, precious!" Akila blows Pastry a kiss.

Then we're entering the lobby and I'm bumping fists with Luis the doorman, asking, "So does it look like we've had a stratospheric night or what? How many people have been in Central Park in a storm all night before going to work?" "Whoa!" he responds grinning. "Never heard that one before—you guys look *great*! I mean because you're so relaxed, good for you." "Yeah, I get it—we've had fun but need a shower, no argument there." "You've clearly had a good time—everyone needs to forget about things now and then." "No argument there either—thank you and catch you later, time to clean up." Akila and I advance to the elevators and when one arrives a man I've probably exchanged less than a hundred words with emerges, bursts out laughing, says, "Always thought you might be crazy—congratulations!" Waving farewell, he's gone before I can respond.

"Positive responses from the first two people met in my building, one basically a stranger—I'd call that a good omen," I observe once Akila and I are ascending in the elevator. "We should post our photos—it appears there would be plenty of approval. As for naysayers, who cares? We can push back with, 'If you were happy you wouldn't be criticizing our happiness and that's *your* problem, not ours.'"

"A meddling pest once told my dad I was inappropriately dressed—suggested I was overindulged and spoiled, might benefit from discipline; and, yes, I *was* technically topless in the afternoon in the town square, but wet sand was covering me more thoroughly than my half-cup bikini tops do, which are deemed acceptable. My dad's reaction was to buy me an Aston Martin, inform me when criticism's motivated by envy we're obligated to laugh about it and reward ourselves, and that only losers, desperate for a personality, spread slander. 'I know you're not snotty,' he said, 'and nothing will ever go to your head. You're as down-to-earth and hardworking as anyone I've ever known—your mother's mirror image inside and out, no father could be prouder of his daughter.'"

"Your dad's an absolute stud, Akila—you've been raised to tell meddling pests to drop dead. We're posting our photos and it's a given some meddling pests will judge us unkindly, act as if their opinions count, but we'll just laugh."

Then we're inside my apartment—undressing each other, depositing our muddy clothes in a shopping bag, showering. Afterwards I fix a breakfast of fried eggs, lox, and avocado slices, which we devour as if we haven't eaten for days.

Chapter Seven

"Welcome to my jungle, Akila," I say, drawing the blinds and opening the door to my east-facing terrace after breakfast, leading her outside. "Sorry for—ha ha!—forbidding you to see it yesterday, I wanted your first time to be in the morning, was hoping it would be sun drenched, kind of the weather to cooperate—hopefully it's not anti-climactic." I'm sweeping a hand through the lemon-yellow flowers, similar to sunflowers but lacking their dark center, swaying on yard-long stalks along the length of the terrace railing's ledge, they crowding the flowerboxes.

"Wow! A jungle for sure, oasis on the edge of the sky, it couldn't be more fabulous—overflowing with flowers and entangled vines in evergreens, even wildlife—bumblebees and butterflies." She's gesturing at the variegated butterfly, orange and red and black, on one of the lemon-yellow flowers.

"That's a Painted Lady—its range circumnavigates the northern hemisphere, probably as far south as Egypt—there's a chance you've seen them at home. I've seen them all over the US and in France and Belgium."

"As a matter of fact I *have* seen them at home, including on the flowers on our deck—crazy! It didn't occur to me it could be the same kind of butterfly—our homes have a butterfly in common, what a fun connection. I *love* that you know the butterfly's name and where it's found."

"There's more where that came from—I've seen emerald-on-black Spicebush Swallowtails and yellow-on-black Tiger Swallowtails and red-on-black Red Admirals and Angel Wings and Blues, as blue as their name, and Monarchs and Coppers up here—fluttering gems. A Praying Mantis was once awaiting prey in the Morning Glories on the trellis. One afternoon a Nessus Sphinx moth, hovering like a hummingbird, laid eggs on the Virginia Creeper, this vine on the wall—it's the only plant the caterpillars would eat, I watched them grow until they pupated underground. And, hey, it's nuts that I know a few things about insects, right? Chalk it up to wanting to get acquainted with my outdoor neighbors, residents of my private ecosystem. But I haven't a clue what kind of flowers these are. *(I gesture at the lemon-yellow flowers.)* They were in a seed assortment of northeastern wildflowers I planted over a decade ago, I stupidly tossed the packet before reading the list of species it contained—can't believe I did that."

"But it's wonderful that you know so much about insects, Perry—I'm dating a naturalist! You can reel off butterfly names and your terrace is a 'private ecosystem.' It makes me wonder more about you and I love to wonder, as much as I love to roll naked in the dunes, yowl like cats in heat—I'd say your terrace jungle's your version of my dunes."

"Well, I can't exactly get naked and yowl out here but you're right—doesn't matter that I'm surrounded by countless windows, the potentially prying eyes behind them, this is my freedom-place and I come here in board shorts at all hours in all weather, summer heat and winter ice alike—I do yoga in the rain, whether warm or frigid, and in falling snow. If people think I'm loony because of in beach attire during blizzards they're welcome to it, but no one's ever bothered me. The trick's to keep my eyes to myself, *never* look at any windows, lest I be suspected of not minding my own business—it's an important unspoken rule. No technical privacy but, strangely enough, I feel very private, ignored and free, out here—my home's one of my ideas of Paradise and I thank my lucky stars every day."

"Darling, I sensed that unspoken rule the second I stepped out here, the windows and not knowing who's behind them instructing me how to behave. We're thoroughly exposed, your terrace couldn't be more of a stage, but we'll be left alone so long as we don't glance around intrusively—delightfully counterintuitive freedom in an unexpected place. And among butterflies, flowers, evergreens—I'm in touch with nature on your terrace and this isn't a country village, you've brought nature to you in New York City—nurtured a mini-forest." She's facing me, softly circling the edges of her nails about the sides of my neck.

"Akila," I say, stroking her cheeks, "you're a flesh and blood magic spell—sprightliness on no sleep when we're together's as easy as if I've awakened after sleeping half a day. And your crimson and gold summer dress *(I gently push her away, look her up and down at arm's length, clasping her hands.)*, almost as silk-soft as your skin and cut to your every bewitching curve, is icing on the cake—your immaculate lines are screamingly vivid under the fabric and I never want to sleep again. Not that I need special dresses to appreciate you—at the slightest glimpse of you, whatever you're wearing or not, my blood will surge."

"Perry, the scrumptiousness of you eye-raping me under my dress is keeping me as charged awake, thrillingly energetic, as I'll ever be—you're enclosing me as completely as ocean waves, stroking me all over and inside out, without laying a finger on me." She's escaped my hold, scooted backwards—is fluttering her hem, lifting it and letting it fall—dipping to her heels, rising—running a hand up and down a leg, giggling—shortly extending an arm towards me, bidding me approach.

Then I'm within a foot of her, wordlessly pressing spread-fingered palms to the air between us, breastbone-high, in lieu of grabbing her—tightening every sinew of my body, freezing. Akila immediately understands, is hovering her palms fractions of an inch from mine while likewise motionless, silent. I'm sensing the surge of her blood and sparkle of her nerves as surely as if embracing her, can almost feel her skin against mine, and am aware, via the tone of her tension, the same's true of her with respect to me. We're caressing one another inside and out with our electrical fields—avoidance of speech and physical contact is opening up deeper avenues of intimacy. Every couple aspires to such subsurface communication—spontaneous transparency and intuition, unity in their depths—and Akila and I are already here. I close my eyes, continue to align with her nerve-emanations—it's as if we're seizing a portion of space together, intensifying it. Awhile later she's whispering, "Ummmm," extending her arms aloft, twirling her hands, swaying—I can feel, still with eyes shut (admittedly assisted by interruptions of sunlight's warmth on my face, shadows of her movements, rustling of her dress), the motion of her arms and hands and hips. A minute or two later we're rubbing foreheads, quivering our legs against each other's, drawing deeper breaths—soon grabbing each other, me easing Akila to her knees while dropping to mine. I'm saying, "Up all night with a beauty in the storm-tossed park and the office is looming—I should actually already be on my way—and I'm feeling as emotionally chiffon-smooth as I'm sure I ever will, indifferent to schedules and employment, soaring on energy seemingly undying. It's like we're in the rock-sheltered shallows where we met."

"I'm positive I'll never feel more chiffon-smooth, Perry," she responds, turning about and scrunching her back against my chest—soon we're seated on the terrace tiles—she's stretching her legs across my extended legs, lightly bouncing them while grasping my hands. "I could hover between earth and sky on your terrace with you until I forget my name and where I was born and who my Gods are!"

"Akila, we can easily increase the hovering sensations, if you'll be kind enough to release my legs," I say, tapping her knees; then, once she's lifted her legs from mine and folded them against her chest and I'm on my feet, pulling her to hers. "Grab my shoulders and close your eyes and trust me."

"Trust always, Perry, and I love wondering what you're going to do with me, she smiles, doing as instructed; then, as I bend her backwards over the terrace-railing—perfectly safe, since it's as high as her mid-back—with an arm around her waist, leg wound about hers, "I'm sure I know where I am, sweetie, but am your ever-compliant girl and my eyes stay shut until you OK me to open them."

"So open them, dearest, and rest assured I have secure grip of you."

"Wooooo, baby! Manhattan topsy-turvy in blazing sun—down's up, the sky's a blinding whirl falling on me—and there isn't a scared bone in my body, I know you have firm grip of me, feel extra safe, and that's a huge part of feeling free!" She's back-bending further over the railing while thrusting her belly at mine, extending her arms earthwards, tickling one of my ankles with fluttering toes.

"Akila, I've been coming out here for almost twenty years and have seldom felt so free, your trust's a drug, lifts me—I'm loving my terrace jungle all the more through your eyes. Would you believe some people won't come out here because it's fifteen floors high?—never mind the garden and sweep of skyline, and that it's a terrace built on brick and concrete instead of a flimsy dime-a-dozen balcony with only air under it. You haven't flinched for an instant, no surprise there."; then, combing her hair with my free hand, "I could pet you forever, fearless feline."

"How can anyone run from the dreamiest of skylines among flowers on a terrace that's as structurally safe as indoors?" she inquires, bending a handful of the lemon-yellow flowers towards me without breaking their stems, brushing my cheeks. "Seeming to ascend and descend at once while firmly wedged between you and the railing, held fast, is another undreamed of experience come true—you don't stop at showing a girl a good time, you make her feel otherworldly."

"And you transport a boy to phantasmagorical places, Akila—flower petals swishing me, and your svelteness sparkling electricity under my skin, and the office is *still* looming! Going to work's never seemed so absurd! Why does restriction exist? What imbecile invented restriction?"

"But are you *still* going to work?—you said you ought to be on your way but haven't budged. And, yes, you also said you'd like to flow into the office elevated with our escapade—fly on adrenaline there, relish the difference between coworkers perception of you and the reality—and I understand that aspiration. Being left alone's against my interests but I don't want to keep..."

"Don't want keep me from heading to a beige office, its appearance as bland as the tasks I perform?" I cut in smiling, pulling her upright away from the railing. "Ordinarily I'd ask you to forbid me to go but, yes, I *do* want the office-on-zilch-sleep adventure—this is the best opportunity I'll have, mainly because I'll be flying on adrenaline *you* inspire."; then, upon checking my watch, "Ha! Always easy to lose track of time in the sun, it's no accident I've only been late for work on sun-drenched days. And, Akila, you're more beneficently distracting than the sun and I'll be setting a new tardiness record today—thank you! But, yes, I ought to finally get going—please assume control, kick me out the door."

"As if I could control you, Perry, or want to! But since you're requesting and I'm your ever-compliant girl, let's see what I can do," she giggles, tugging me towards the terrace door; then, whirling about to face me once we're indoors, "Thank you for saying I'm as distracting as the sun, maximum compliment—the sun's our birthright and in our blood, dazzles us always, keeps us fit and feisty, sharp and cheerful and bold. We're not immortal but intensified emotion can foster the illusion we are and who cares if it's illusion?—being electric to our bones is an end in itself. Delusion's relative to whether it's healthy, right? Idiots call Don Quixote delusional and he's a shining example of how happy mortals can be."

"Believe I said you're *more* distracting than the sun, angelface—I've never seen a more time-beguiling smile. And I love that you know Don Quixote, it's one of the three books I've reread the most. The Don knew how to cast the world in a more enthralling light and ramp up his emotions to match it, make every day magical—nothing delusional about that, perception's relative to what it inspires us to feel. No trace of delusion in you, Akila—no one's more level-headed, firmly grounded. Oh, and that's nice—*very* nice!" We're in the entryway near the front door, she's brought me here while skipping backwards, me having grabbed my phone from the dining table—is pressing my back to the wall, slipping her hands up under my shirt, caressing my chest while tickle-nibbling an ear, breathing deeply. "I told you to get me out of here but maybe that was the wrong..."

"Shame on bad disobedient me—I'm not trying to tease, sweetie!" she breaks in, springing away with brow charmingly knitted in self-reproach. "Couldn't resist prolonging, even if only for instants, our outside-of-imagining night."; then, upon standing straight and squaring her shoulders, saluting, "You told me to get you out of here so that's what I'll do, although I'd vastly rather you stayed!" She turns to the door, grasps its knob.

"But you've made it impossible for me to go!" I laugh, pulling her from the door; then, upon lifting her hair aside, kissing the back of her neck, "I'll always be spellbound by the swish of your hair, abounding with a kaleidoscope of fragrances I'll never pin down, and the miracle of your skin—your hairline's one of my favorite playgrounds."

"And your touch racing down my spine and radiating every which way—making me softer and tremblier and cuddlier than I already am, extra heated somewhere—I know you know where," she whispers, shivering. "You do me proud, Perry, and I'd say pretty please take me again—that I'll be itchy nuts if you don't—but don't think we want to settle for halfway measures, be limited by time-constraints. I'd want you to linger over me, foreplay me dizzy, like under our tree when we had all night. I'll never comprehend the quickie thing—quickies only increase craving, dissatisfaction stabbing. We can wait, even though it'll be rough, right? Waiting for you to return after you go will be knives in my nerves." She's reaching behind her shoulders, stroking the back of my neck, squirming.

"You said you weren't trying to tease?" I ask, sliding my hands up the back of her legs under her dress, squeezing. "You can't help but tease, darling, simply by being here, and I think we ought to surrender to teasing, and anyway it's impossible for me to resist. Once I leave we'll be apart for torturous hours."

"Yay!" she cries, about facing and smushing her chest to mine, kissing me up and down my cheeks. I'm pulling her to the floor, reclining onto my back, and she's straddling me, squeezing my midriff with quivering thighs—bending low, nibbling my neck gently, her hair swooshing my face. Sunlight's streaming onto us through the windows of the eastern wall, the said wall being at least 80% glass—I'm reaching behind my head, by turns raking my nails on and smacking the door, saying, "Dollface, I thought I was on my way to corporate tedium but I'm in the sun's gold with you instead—thanks for flipping my timeline upside-down."

"Sweetie, no one flips my timeline upside-down as well as you! Seems like weeks since I was last in Egypt, when it's under two days—no vacation's blurred and blissed me this fast." She flings herself lengthwise onto me, licking my face anew—sunlight's glancing off one of her shoulders, whirling into my eyes...

Awhile afterwards I'm consulting my watch again, saying, "Akila, I may want to kick myself for saying this but please *do* kick me out the door! There'll never be a better chance to be in emotional Elysium while surrounded by agency nonsense, blissful in the face of bleakness—you've vastly increased the contrast and I need to milk it. Like, whatever will I do at work with all the energy you've pumped into my blood, pictures you've placed in my head? I'll be insanely adrenalized."

"Oh, I'll be insanely adrenalized too," she smiles, rolling off me and scooting to the door and sitting with her back to it, bouncing her extended legs up and down. "Your effect on me's like stepping into fierce wind after a cool night's immersion in the Mediterranean, wet and wind-chilled, then a bonfire's heat hits me and I'm roasting! You're my bonfire and I'm *very* heated—waiting for you to return and seize me will be a wild rollercoaster ride. But let's get you out the door, I'm neglecting my duty." She's placing her palms on the floor, about to rise.

"Requesting delay of said duty, Akila," I laugh, motioning for her to stay put. "You've so deliciously distracted me I've overlooked the obvious. Meaning I'm already seventeen minutes late and even if I fly out the door without changing first, as I need to do *(I shake my rumpled shirttail),* will be at least an hour late—looks like I need a good excuse for the first time and that I shouldn't leave until having one in place, texting in advance. And it's shameful that I've never been an hour late before—you're the most beneficial influence imaginable."

"Excuse manufacture time!" Akila gleefully shouts, raising her arms and twirling her wrists, writhing against the door forcefully enough for its hinges to creak. "What's believable? I'll help!" In a flash she's on her heels, squatting with legs splayed and knees raised, preparing to stand—the top of her hemline's sliding down her thighs as the lower portion's dipping to the floor and sunlight's darting within the gap, illuminating her lusciousness—there's a squirmy amused tone, immensely magnetic, about her.

"Let's postpone excuse manufacture as well, angeldoll," I say, tapping her knees, inducing her to spread her legs wider. "It would be a crime for me to shut us down, not to mention impossible, and I'll get to work when I get there—knowing I'll be using an excuse is a game-changer, I'm sure we'll dream up an excellent one." I'm lowering myself to my stomach to better enjoy the sight of where Akila's thighs conjoin, crawling to her on elbows—she's reaching for my shoulders...

Chapter Eight

"It's fitting that an Egyptian beauty, freshly arrived from golden sun drenched beaches and deserts, has treated me to this golden morning," I say, Akila and I rump-bumping as I grab my work-phone from the entryway's sunken bookcase, we on our feet. "Good fun to intend to fly out the door and then *not* fly out the door, delay work as I've never done before—fun keeps tromping on duty, making a joke of schedules and obligation, distorting time—I'm even late announcing I'll be late. How long are you going to exercise your powers, delay my departure?"

"No more delays, Perry, unless you want more," Akila giggles, springing a couple yards away. "As for my supposed powers... Cute of you to say, but we both know we sway each other equally—it takes two to prioritize fun, delightfully distract each other, distort time—this morning's been *insanely* golden, honeysuckle feelings gushing. Anyway, my new project's helping you get away with being so late, lots of lies can be told, let's see... But get a load of presumptuous me—corporate stuff's alien to me, you know better than me what lies will work."

"What's funny is coworkers have unwittingly informed me what excuses work best—protocol dictates we send lateness notices to the production department email, and we all read them. The most common excuse is public transportation delays, followed by home emergencies, plumbing predominating, nor to forget medical situations, a surprising amount of people going overboard with cringe-worthy specifics, and once a guy announced he got drugged and robbed at a bar and needed to contact credit card companies. OK, so a plumbing emergency's plausible and can't be fact-checked like public transportation issues, and I couldn't be paid to fake a medical situation, come off as unhealthy, so let's go with plumbing emergency." I'm entering my work-phone's code to unlock it.

"We should add photos—hold that email, give me that phone!" Akila cries, advancing and seizing my work-phone, holding it behind her back. "We can clog the bathtub drain with our muddy clothes, fill it up and snap photos, send the nastiest ones to them—no one will see our clothes through the muddied water, know it's faked. What do you think?"

"I think it's unadulterated genius," I answer, kissing her forehead. "Providing photographic evidence is as priceless as your locust-swarm excuse, I couldn't admire this mischievously brilliant side of you more, am absolutely..." I break off because my work-phone trills, announcing a text, which I quickly check, Akila handing the phone back. "Is everything OK? Are you coming in?" I read aloud, adding, "Uh oh! That's my manager, I don't blame her—it's 12:52, for Christ's sake."; then, reciting as I type, "Bad plumbing mess here, can't leave, will update when able—sorry for no notice—no excuse except it's nuts, never happened before, filthy water."; then, showing the text to Akila, "I misspelled words on purpose, ignored punctuation—better communicates confusion."

"A masterpiece," she responds, likewise kissing my forehead, "and the best part is it leaves the door wide open for our photo project—you won't need to leave anytime soon, or at all! As for our project, let's begin!" She scampers to the pantry, grabs the bag containing our muddy clothes and carries it to the bathroom—soon we're tossing the clothes into the bathtub, shoving them against the drain with a broom's handle, turning the water on high. The broom, used for sweeping the terrace, reminds me of the bag of potting soil under one of the terrace's chairs. "More dirt!" I yell, dashing outside, grabbing a half-handful of soil, returning to add it to the tub. "Wouldn't do to have our fun backfire, clog the drain for real," I say, explaining why I don't add more. Meanwhile Akila's stirring with the broom's handle. "Witches cauldron!" she declares, acting the cliché part of witch with snarly face, arched back—curling her fingers in a manner that suggests evil, hissing through clenched teeth. "Jesus!" I'm laughing, "I'm in grade school again, seeing how far I can bend rules! And, hey, we can make it more believable with tools!" Thereafter I'm leading her to the kitchen, where I keep tools in a drawer—we're grabbing screwdrivers, a hammer, pliers, crescent wrenches—soon in the bathroom again, setting them on the bathtub's rim. "And the plunger too!" I say, grabbing the plunger from behind the toilet, throwing it in the tub.

"Looks authentic—I'm proud of our work," Akila smiles. "But is there someone who works for your building who could bring plumbing stuff here, act urgent and bothered, pretend to fix the drain? We could take his picture with the mess, below the neck if he prefers anonymity. No chance will anyone doubt it's an emergency—they'll be feeling sorry for you."

"Absolutely brilliant, darling—thank you! Here I was imagining no one was better at bamboozling my employer than me and you're teaching me new tricks! I've never felt so free in the face of the office—sunny mornings dazzling and delaying me in the past or not I've always cautioned myself against carrying it too far, never been over a half hour late. But today there's zilch to worry about, all bases are covered with your plan—people will definitely be feeling sorry for me."

"Just taking cues from you, sweetie—your predicament's my inspiration, as is our fun—every second together on this amazing morning's a treasure wrested from time. I take it there's someone who'll put on a good act."

"The handyman Ramiz is our man. He's an unflappable Bosnian refugee with a bullet lodged near his spine—attempts at extraction would imperil his life. He's literally lucky to be alive, having survived genocidal hell, including imprisonment and torture, and relishes frivolity as few people do—having come close to losing his life in a terrible manner, he gives thanks for life every day and will enjoy playing our game." We're seated on the couch when I phone Luis the doorman, inform him of our plan, ask if Ramiz is available. "You're crazy and I love it!" Luis exclaims, then states Ramiz is on a minor repair job, after which he puts me on hold, transfers the call to Ramiz. Once Ramiz is on the phone he's saying he'll be honored to oblige, Luis having filled him in—he's never had a like request, can't stop laughing—also says he'll bring Amilcar, another staff member, along for added authenticity—they'll be up in about ten minutes, is that OK? "Absolutely—thanks, as always, for your help," I reply. When I hang up Ramiz is still laughing.

"All set, Akila. Ramiz and another man, Amilcar, as jovial a soul as you'll ever meet, will be up shortly—I *love* my building."

"What's not to love? Your building lifts full-service to an entirely new level, excuse manufacture assistance on demand—first time I've encountered *that* perk." Seconds later she's springing to her feet, heading for the terrace—casting me an over-the-shoulder-come-hither glance, yanking her dress tight against her behind. She's among the lemon-yellow flowers, running a hand through them, once I step outside—murmuring, "Come here, please."; then, once I'm within her arms, "You're just plain fun to be with, Perry—I'm revisiting grade school too, when I'd arrange ribbons and bows and flowers on my bed before school to choose the prettiest ones to wear, and I adore pranking your agency with you."

"Slacking's what I most aspire to at the agency, but pranking's up there too, and if honesty was advisable I'd declare such in the 'goals' section of my annual review! And guess what, sparkle-eyes? Clasping hands like this *(I seize her hands.)* is one of my secret tests of a girl's responsiveness, energy, mettle—whether her hands come alive like yours, stimulatingly quiver and squeeze and caress—a girl's hands should *attack* mine without being clumsy or jellyfish or angular and jarring—effortlessly shimmer my blood, birth hunger for more. But rest assured no hands' test, or any other, was needed with you—all was stunningly clear the second I sighted you, such is your vivacity of presence, liveliness of eye."

"Very pleased and flattered you didn't feel you needed to test me!" she laughs, extracting one of her hands, tapping my forehead. "But the clasping-hands thing's a perfect test—straight to the point, an infallible reading easily administered early on. I won't pretend I've *consciously* administered the test but now realize it's always been one of mine too. Obviously lame jellyfish hand-holding indicates someone needs to be ditched—hand-pulsations need to lift me and yours are electric sweet."

"Could pulse hands with you all day, darling," I say, grasping her free hand again. "This alone's..." It's here that the doorbell rings and I break off—instants later we're indoors and I'm yelling, "Door's open—come in!"

When Ramiz and Amilcar enter Akila and I are advancing to greet them. Following introductions, they clearly impressed by Akila's beauty and intelligence and charm, we lead them to the bathroom. Without instruction, as if they routinely stage sham plumbing emergencies, they pull two automated plumbing snakes out of bags, unwind them in the tub, spread the coiling about—place the motors on the floor, toss the outlet-ends of the electrical cords out the bathroom door. Then they put on goggles, face masks, bright yellow rain jackets. "Action," Ramiz says rather casually once everything's in place, nodding towards my phone. Moments later he and Amilcar are leaning over the tub, yanking at the plumbing snakes—shouting, scowling, stomping, gesticulating—as I snap pictures.

"Good enough?" Ramiz inquires within two minutes, he and Amilcar pulling down their face masks, turning to Akila and I.

"Far above good enough, impossible to doubt this is a nasty emergency—take a look," I laugh. Soon I'm flipping through the pictures, all of us raucously shouting approval, after which we take celebratory selfies—Amilcar manning the phone for most because, at six feet four, he has the greatest reach. Some are of us pointing at the mess in the tub, putting on looks of dismay and horror—others are of us shaking hands and congratulating each other, or standing shoulder to shoulder, arms interlocked, smiling ear to ear. "I think another star of the show ought to be given due credit," Akila says, reaching into the cloudy water, lifting her muddy dress from the drain. "Without my dressy none of this would've happened, let's show her some love!" "Hear, hear!" we're applauding as Amilcar photographs Akila's dress. "Classic white linen dress journeyed from Egypt to give me a foolproof excuse!" I announce, kissing the dress. Our final selfies are of us toasting one another with glassfuls of coconut water in the kitchen, after which I give Ramiz and Amilcar each a bottle of Napa Valley late harvest wine.

"Diversity's stressed at the agency," I observe once Ramiz and Amilcar are at the front door, about to depart, "so it's only fitting a Bosnian, Honduran, Egyptian, and Norwegian have teamed up to prank the agency, create a lateness excuse masterpiece second to none. Thanks again, Ramiz and Amilcar."

"And thank you," Ramiz says, "for a fun break at work. It's gratifying to help fake an emergency for a worthy cause, I'll always be eager to participate—the gift's unnecessary but appreciated."

"My wife and kids will be laughing hard when I tell them about this," Amilcar grins. "I'd *pay* to help fake the emergency, so extra thanks for the wine."

Then we say our goodbyes—shortly thereafter I'm writing an email to my department on my work-phone, Akila observing over my shoulder.

The email is as follows:

"Hello Team,

Apologies for late update, an insane plumbing thing happened, interrupted breakfast and blew my routine apart. There was hissing in the bathroom, dirty water bubbling up in the bathtub, a flood could've happened if the building staff didn't come right away. Will head out when I can, hopefully soon, have had enough of this. The handyman and his assistant are working to stop the gushing sewage water."

To the email I attach three pictures, Ramiz and Amilcar extra frantic in them, muddy water abundantly splashing. "It might be too wordy—more details provide more opportunities to read between the lines, detect lies—but the photos will dispel all doubt," I laugh, clicking *Send*.

"Believe me, Perry, your email works just fine without photos—adding 'gushing sewage water' is perfection, anyone who reads that's going to be thinking, 'Glad it's not me!' But what I especially like is you haven't set a departure time, left it open due to events beyond your control. Now I'm free to keep you here another hour or two, or all day!" She circles around to face me, seizes my shoulders, gleefully repeats, "*All day!*"

"And I'd get away with it free and clear," I say, reaching for her waist. But then I check myself, yank my hands away, slap one with the other. "OK, Akila! If we're in this situation again I will most assuredly the carry the fakery to its logical end, reap its full benefits and stay home with you—say the plumbing problem's come back to bite me, worse than before—but I *need* to go to work today, you know why. If I wait much longer I'll run out of time, since the game depends on the agency being at capacity, having an audience—most people leave at around 5:30, will be gone in... Christ, three and a half hours! I really *do* need to..."

"Say no more," she cuts in. "Trust your fierce disciplinarian!"; then, as I'm retrieving my personal phone from the couch, "No slacking! Hurry, and I mean now, now, now!" She's emphatically clapping as parents do when spurring their offspring to action, albeit with mirthful eyes. Soon we've exited, are racing down the hall, then kissing in the elevator, stepping hand in hand into the lobby.

The moment we're in the lobby Luis the doorman calls out, "Welcome!" with upraised arms; then, as we bump fists, "Did Ramiz and Amilcar do a good job? Will your boss buy it?" "Oh, she'll buy it, all right—Ramiz and Amilcar never botch a job. And this is Akila, from Egypt—faking a plumbing emergency and having Ramiz and Amilcar lend authenticity was her idea." "Honored to meet you, Akila—welcome to New York, anything I can do, just ask," Luis says, bowing. "Thank you, Luis, honored to meet you as well and happy to be here, love your town," Akila responds, curtsying. "So now you see I'm not always a messy muddy scamp." "It was clear you'd had a good time; and Egypt must be a crazy party place, Perry looks very relaxed, you're a good influence." "That she is beyond measure," I agree. "Never thought I'd have a night and day like this on a workday, all wrapped up in a tidy bow with a lateness excuse no one will doubt—I'll totally get away with it. As for the excuse, check it out." *(I show him my phone, flip through pictures.)* "Very good," Luis chuckles. "Looks just like what we call professional plumbers in to fix, bathroom disaster zone." "And it's all smoke and mirrors, here's the bathtub now—pristine clean. *(I tap on a picture further down the list.)* All we did was drain the dirty water, spray soap and turn on the shower. Good fun to snow-blind my employer—thanks again for your help." "And thanks for making my day," Luis says, exchanging thumbs-up with us as we exit.

"So we were last here like this last night," I say, referring to being face to face with Akila under my building's awning, "and, darling, the interval between then and now seems to have whipped by in seconds—it's day instead of night, you're in multicolor instead of white, but elation's unaltered. I'm off to work thirsting to be there, something I never would've dreamed possible, and that's your doing—the office will be a rare and exotic adventure today, doubly so since it'll be happening in a place previously tedious, dispiriting, stifling—I'll be shimmering insanely, losing my mind, with anticipation of grabbing and kissing you again."

"I'll be in opposites while waiting, Perry, itchy agonized while enrapt—be in honeysuckle feelings while stung to my bones! Mainly, I'm not sleeping either—am staying awake all day so I can meet you in the same sleep-deprivation-intensified-senses state—we'll crash heaven's gates."

"Akila, unity in insomnia-accelerated senses is the stuff of wildest dreaming, incomparably uplifting and rare—crash heaven's gates indeed!"; then, after kissing her, "Until this evening, angeldoll! It'll be an agonizing infinity of waiting but you're rapture at the end of the tunnel so time will also fly blurringly fast—contemplation of tonight's fun's already rushing at me like high fast waves."

"Sweetie, I'll be texting like mad, sending cascades of photos—our energy will travel between us!" Akila's hands are framing my cheeks, her visage luminous, as I spin away. The traffic light's in my favor, I cross to 1st Avenue's west side as if weightless, am glancing back—her dark-eyeliner-accentuated eyes, as hungry as kind, vivid as touch, are beaming their sweet silver through daylight's glare, and she's dancing her hemline up and down again—sophisticated frolicsomeness personified, as aristocratic as earthy, and we're blowing kisses, her fingers fluttering at her lips, butterflies in the breeze. Then I've advanced south a block, turned 84th Street's northwest corner, vanished from Akila's view—am on my way to work in earnest, with her beauty ablaze in my mind's eye, tingling me up and down my spine, seemingly lifting me outside fleshly boundaries.

Chapter Nine

My commute's a walk across Central Park, which I enter at 79th Street and 5th Avenue, to Central Park West and 72nd Street, where I catch the B Train to Bryant Park, its southwest exit yards from the office. I could take the most direct route across the park, enter north of the Metropolitan Museum at 84th Street, be on the B train platform at 81st Street in twenty-eight minutes; but, as my excuse is firmly in place, won't trouble to shave off commute-time—I'm already over two hours late, at liberty to dawdle at will. Aside from rousing exercise, rock climbing in The Ramble and on The Lake's west shore often included, crossing the park creates the impression I'm not headed to work—given what I've experienced in the park through the years being in it points to freedom, obligations momentarily fading into the background, half unreal. I cross in all weather, excepting during the rare ice-storm, when weighted branches crash to earth and incautious people sometimes die—otherwise nothing, driving rain or blizzards or subzero temperatures, will turn me back. Crossing the park establishes a more positive tone for my workday—it's easier to remain even-keeled, avoid irritation, laugh at annoyances.

Shortly after entering the park at 79th Street I'm strolling up Cedar Hill, making a beeline for my favorite tree—parting its branches and snapping a picture. "Behold last night's bed!" I announce, texting the picture to Akila. "The fun we had here juxtaposed with going to work's priceless!" "Oh, joy!" she responds. "Why didn't you tell? Could've come with you!" "Because if you were here I'd probably abandon the plan and kiss off the office, don't underestimate yourself! Bye for now, before I change my mind! Turning off phone until at office!" I'm recollecting I told Akila I wanted reporting to work on no sleep to be something of high drama, a scary undertaking, test of fortitude and resilience, and am laughing at myself, thinking, "Nothing like inventing conflict, dreaming up phantom hostility, to get my blood racing!" I stroll south of Turtle Pond past Belvedere Castle through The Ramble over Oak Bridge and along The Lake's western shore to 72nd Street, as entranced as I'll ever be while alone in Central Park.

By 3:20 I'm logged into my computer, ascertaining what assignments are in store, in the dismal low-ceilinged claustrophobic sinkhole center of the agency, where there's no window in sight, not a flicker of non-artificial light—as exposed to everyone's view as if in a vacant parking lot, cubicles having been abolished in keeping with current trend, as in saving money by going open-plan and then informing employees privacy is counterproductive via slick PR-firm-crafted communiques. But the office is powerless to dig under my skin, make me feel hemmed in—I'm safe in emotional upwelling, awash with tingles, courtesy of lovely Akila and last night's storm and our street parading and delay-of-departure games—itching to jubilantly yell. There are inquiries concerning my plumbing emergency and as I rattle off fictional details, indicate I'm grateful my building's staff is knowledgeable and proactive, always eager to help, am as if suspended outside my body, watching myself perform from a distance. It's reassuring and revitalizing, does wonders for morale, that I can spend the night under wind-whipped branches in blinding sheets of rain with an unbridled darling dollface and thereafter report to work, confident performing my duties will be child's play, no one doubting my abilities or discerning I haven't slept for over a day.

Compartmentalization's agency protocol: each item in an advertising campaign, be it as minimal as an envelope or discontinuation notice, is a series of rigorously separated steps from conception to completion, only producers authorized to communicate between departments. Meaning I'm discouraged from contacting other departments without go-betweens—if I don't hear something from my manager I'm not supposed to hear it and couldn't be happier, as such spares me a great deal of interaction, enables me to better elude notice, undetectably goof off. My manager's on the front line, I'm under the radar—in a sense I'm my manager's boss because if I need anything I inform her and she handles it—many aspects of official corporate structure are conducive to slacking. I tend to think earning a living in a 21st century office requires at least as much playacting as a supporting role on Broadway—the majority of my coworkers are persuaded I'm all business, lack a sense of humor, am allergic to fun, and I love it. The distance between what's scintillating in my veins—animation via all-night exertion, my secret activities—and the stoicism I'm faking's an indication of what I'm able to get away with, far more than I could've imagined before scoring this job. My duties require minimal mental exertion in readily mastered databases—I take pride in how mindless they are. My coworkers have far more of this advertising business in their heads than I'd ever want in mine, nor am I required to attend tedious brand team meetings, as they are, and I've no intention of sacrificing freedom on the altar of promotion, for the sake of a higher salary I don't need. As for elevated status, it's institutionalized flattery—corporate marketing—calculated to swindle people into striving for added intrusion on their time and attention. The higher one ascends in the ranks the less one's left to oneself and the more one's owned. My humble position ensures I'll always be able to report to work, and keep my job, after being in the park with a sweetheart all night, dancing with her at Cleopatra's Needle at dawn while mud-splattered—I measure success by how adventurously I live. I'm persuaded existence counts time spent in civilization-imposed bondage against us—I need this job to feed myself but needn't be a corporate pawn, only mimic the role. The difference between believing in corporate culture and exploiting it to one's advantage is as expansive as the sky.

Three assignments are waiting when I arrive and two more follow (one lasts twenty-seven minutes, another lasts fourteen, the others under ten) and I execute them on routine-based autopilot, no great amount of attentiveness required, on their associated databases as recollections of last night spin kaleidoscopic in my mind's eye, tingle my nerves and blood: Akila's rapt countenance, wellspring glances—svelte anatomy in the wind and rain and thunder, joyful body language, elation evident in the slightest twist of her torso or tilt of her head, the tone of her touch—are buoyancy like no other. Ha! My ranting concerning civilization's falsification of experience aside, God bless technology—I *love* technology! Technology not only enables me to rake in good money without overmuch effort—often at home, more on that shortly—it enables Akila to drive me deliciously nuts via texted photos. At first she's in a diaphanous hip-high lavender nightie, indigo-lace-fringed—pursing her lips, putting on a little girl pout; then a sleeveless low-necked mid-thigh-high lemon-yellow one-piece, winking as she bites a lime wedge—two photos, frontal and a profile; then with three or four floral print scarfs wrapped about her throat, spilling down her sides, her breasts snug in scarlet-lace half-cups—everything below her waist left to my recollection; then on the terrace dripping wet in last night's muddy white linen dress, cheeks finger painted with wavy lines of mud, commenting, "Messy again and tribal for you, honey, in honor of last night's storm and our plumbing prank—think I need another shower!" To which I respond with a picture of the office, stating, "Zilch windows and sun, unbroken barren beige—usually it's smothering gloom, downright creepy, but today I'm rapturously excited! Your photos are shots of bliss, princess!"

It's nearly 5:00 PM—I've been awake for over thirty-one hours, highly active for most, and am as exhilarated as I'll ever be. Akila's nonstop whetting my appetite with photos and it's as easy to remain alert and responsive as when surfing head-high waves. And who knows what my darling will be wearing when I return home? Is it superficial to be absorbed in speculations as to what makeup scheme she'll adopt, how she'll fix her hair, accessorize?—whether dustings of henna will be utilized?—to what degree she'll be naked, as for instance nothing on underneath her dress, or in a flimsy nightie or veil instead of a dress, or not bothering to wear anything besides makeup? Only anti-life killjoys, accustomed to being resentful and miserable, could think so. God bless women who know how to deliciously toss one about in one's imagination, blaze in one's blood, lift one out of one's skin.

Additional assignments aren't projected to be handed off for at least a half hour and I could hightail it outside, monitor the work-email via my phone (Should an assignment materialize ahead of schedule I'd immediately return to the office and pounce on it—every accomplished slacker knows conscientiousness is key to getting away with maximum slacking. The irony of slacking's that "Work first, then slack!" is the golden rule.), but I pass on going outside for the same reason I'd never turn out of a wave prematurely, forgo the full sweep of a ride. As I've texted to Akila, "Thanks to you, the office is enchanted and I'm tingling to my bones!"

The benefits of indulging in what's conventionally, and ignorantly, classified as "behavior befitting a child" are incalculable. I'm far older than anyone comes close to guessing and my physical of last February indicates the "blood-pressure of a teenager" (A no-nonsense nurse practitioner's precise words.) and I credit, among other things, eagerness to behave like a child for my enviable medical records—I'm convinced that if one behaves like a child the health and vitality and high spirits of a child follow. So-called mature people, incomprehensibly averse to play, invariably age prematurely—suffer from chronic aches and pains and allergies, are often out of sorts, visit doctors every week—whine about lacking energy, slowing down. It's invigorating to laugh at departmental expectation propaganda, inform myself, "If they only knew I was in the park all night in the storm with a woman who's as fearless and stunning as any ever born, and that's why I was three hours late and the plumbing emergency's fiction, but they'll *never* suspect in a trillion years!" I routinely text friends from about town on company time, gleefully detail my unauthorized activities, documented with pictures—kayaking on the Hudson, attending aerial yoga classes, taking dips in rooftop pools, hopping cabs to the East Village, Chinatown, and Central Park. Assorted phrases from my texts are: "Slacking is my God!," "Promotion's for masochists!," "Screwing around for $!," "Paid to play!," "Money for monkeying around!," "Reimbursement for irresponsibility!," "Salaried slacker!," or simply, "Hahaha!" Let those who'd presume to lecture me concerning "acting my age" be as healthy and active as I am at my age first; otherwise, they're unqualified to do so. What best exemplifies responsibility? Remaining healthy and never taking a sick day, or tallying up multiple sick days due to failing to remain healthy, thereby burdening others? If "acting my age" includes the compromised health, loss of eagerness for adventure, resignation to sluggishness, those my age often succumb to then count me out. I've seen people become unrecognizable (sometimes within months, frightful how fast it can happen) before hitting their mid-thirties—their predominant ingrained expression suddenly one of disappointment and worry—their gaze uncertain, wobbling, as if their will's abandoned them. Well, not for me! I'll continue behaving like a child, thank you! The dirty little secret of those eager to snipe and critique concerning whether others are "acting their age" is they're endeavoring to rationalize their loss of animation, mask envy of those healthier and happier than they are. In my humble opinion the benchmark of responsibility's whether we're doing our utmost to experience joy at every turn—remain spiritually, emotionally, physically healthy. And, sure, there's abundance of ego in these assertions—so what? It's part of indulging in "behavior befitting a child," maintaining the "blood-pressure of a teenager"—it's fun to thumb my nose at debilitated judgmental slobs. Again, let those who'd naysay me surf the waves I surf at my age, or ski the slopes I ski, or take three hot yoga classes in a day, and I might consider listening to them. Any takers? Thought not. And, hey, why not reveal my age instead of concealing it, as I've done since turning twenty-one? Then again, nah! Hail yoga and surfing and skiing and the sun!"

Staying put in the office is proving to be inspirational: I've resolved that going forward it's my *duty* to turn at least one worknight a week into an all-night adventure and my imagination's on overdrive with the options. Such as renting a car and spending the night on a Long Island beach, boogieboarding at dawn, reporting to work reverberant with ocean-motion—never mind I know nothing of Long Island surf, the spots are easily found via surfing apps, and should the Atlantic be flat I'll still have been on the water, perhaps seen sunrise ignite the sky while hugging my board. Or what of renting a boat at Sheepshead Bay, fishing near shore until dawn?—bluefish and stripers, if I'm lucky, flopping at my feet? Or heading upstate, spending the night in a forest campground by a lakeshore or stream? As for hooking up with other women once

Akila's flown home it's impossible and how miraculous *that* is—I've waited a long time for a special woman to blind me to others, and we'll chase delirium together when she's in Egypt. Midnight here's 6:00 AM for Akila and she'll accompany me through the night—I foresee us egging each other on as she tumbles down Mediterranean dunes at 9:00 AM Egypt time while I race around in Central Park at 3:00 AM New York time. She'll be showing me the desert's expanses and oases, Cairo's streets, her family's estate, the Nile's rustling reeds—treating me to shoreline bonfires—while I'm at work. Ha! Despite rapt contemplation of anticipated escapades it's impossible to remain in the office at the approach of 6:00—stinging stir-crazy's an understatement and Akila's the cause, since she's sending photos of how she'll be dressed when I return—is in a silver-polka-dotted emerald summer dress, hem mid-thigh high and low neckline, silver bangles on her wrists, gold scarab barrette in her hair, barefoot—toenails gold, legs swirled with henna. Of course the sight of her lissome figure's shimmering my spine but her hungry affectionate eyes upstage all. After a flurry of photos, shot from multiple angles, she announces, "I'm flaunting me so maybe you'll want me—I'm only a hopeful girl!" "Darling," I text back, "are you kidding? I'll always want you as if it's my last night alive—you're fetching to die for, flogging me out the door!"

So there are the account executives and producers for whom I perform my duties and then there are the upper management bureaucrats, would-be enforcers of outdated pre-digital policy, attempting to oversee from a distance. The former are allies, generous with accolades (Because I spare them wait-time and worry, execute assignments quickly without compromising accuracy.), who couldn't care less where I work from. The latter are enemies, who'd like to treat me as if I'm in grade school despite how efficiently I work, the primary imbecile among them—painfully strained of face, visibly perishing of stress—having announced, "Remote work is unacceptable. Employees need to come to the office. No excuses." Meaning the trick to leaving early's to let the account executives and producers know I'll be home in a flash (it takes a half hour tops), handling what needs to be done, and keep the bureaucrats in the dark. I do so and am on the Q-train platform within five minutes, texting Akila once there, as in, "Dollface, my home's otherworldly in the background of your selfies, aglow with you—your spirit electrifies familiar surroundings—and I can't wait to bask in your glow!" To which she responds, "Starvation for you's taking me by storm, dearest! The floor's rippling—I'm topsy-turvy, need to be balanced—please fly home to me!"

I met Akila in Puerto Rico when her flight home was barely over a day away—we became close enough to thirst to be together again and now she's here, and things that were previously annoying no longer are—it's impossible to feel desolate at the office or anywhere else—I swear I'm reporting to work after all-night escapades every day during her visit, may the Gods disfavor me if I don't. As for tonight, the groundwork's been laid—I'll be subcontracting my work, without my employer being the wiser, to the precocious ninth grader, trained by myself and in whom I have unwavering confidence, who lives with her family down the hall. (She has my agency-issued laptop and will log in as me, plus I've provided her with a Notepad containing phrases good for virtually every contingency—if an unanticipated situation occurs and she's uncomfortable with winging it she'll call and I'll advise. And I'll be paying her what I'm paid—I'd never take a cut.) In the meantime Akila and I will feast on the salmon, steamed vegetables, and fruit salad she's prepared, catch up on sleep until midnight or thereabouts, and thereafter... Well, as I've texted: "My mission's to see to it New York's nonstop incandescence for you, new surprises every day, and for you to want to return ASAP!"

The Field of Reeds are forever and employment at a firm's fly-by-night—a brazen lie existence-wise, unnatural splinteredness-of-the-self—so I know what I'll be valuing and living for. Secular-minded people, casualties of modernity's self-serving manipulation, will insist elation in perpetuity's illusion. Even if so, so what? Nothing's illusory about living to the emotion- and mind-altering utmost, seeking to intensify experience at every turn—our species has aspired to soar free of earthy confines for thousands of generations and I side with time-honored instinct. When I was face to face with Akila on Cedar Hill in the flashing lightning and crashing thunder—grasping her shoulders as she gazed upon me with starshine eyes, then flung herself onto me with a mirthful cry, insistently writhed—I was shimmering to the roots of my nerves, as if suspended outside perceptual restriction. Our united desire dissipated every worry I've ever had as the slope of rain-glistened lawn blurred into, became indistinguishable from, the gust-tossed treetops, tumultuous sky.

I conclude with our seven most up-to-the-minute texts:

Accompanied by a photo of the subway platform, I state, "Filthy, cheerless, claustrophobic but I'm immune! Emotionally I'm in a sun-blasted Puerto Rico rainforest clearing and that's your doing, darling! Soon I'll be grabbing luscious you after craving you for seemingly weeks!"

Accompanied by a photo of sunlight reflected on the windows of buildings opposite my terrace, shot from indoors, Akila responds, "All's rosy and cozy here, easy to be in that clearing with you! I'm glimmering like those windows and that's your doing, Perry! Can't wait to present myself to you! Spill me on my back on your carpet, smush me into the fluff, take your fill of me while filling me!"

"Invitation to Paradise and I love you SO much, Akila! I'm saying it outright and direct instead of obliquely, not worrying anymore if it's too soon! And here it's coming out in a text, I couldn't wait to tell you I LOVE you! I LOVE you, Akila, am going nuts to tell you while holding you!"

"I love you SO much too, Perry! Just LOVE you! Breathing's delirium, I'm one deliciously dizzied girl—thank you, that'll be my favorite text forever, saved forever! Loved one, our song's the sound of the waves where we met, right? Do you think the waves are our song?"

"Absolutely, sweetheart! How blessed can I be? My beloved loves the sea-rhythm as much as I do! You're my kaleidoscope, Akila—my new wilder life, my blood-beat, all! You're the life I've always wanted and never knew I'd get! Train's arriving, the ride to you will be delirium! I LOVE you!"

"Insanely blissful now, flowing over the floor, up the walls—loving you lifts luscious to wildest heights! I LOVE you, Perry! I SO love saying I LOVE you, Perry! Hurry hurry! I'm dying to grab you and be grabbed by you!"

"Saying I LOVE you, Akila, is the measure of my newfound freedom, more than I could've dreamed I'd deserve! Switching off my phone, so I can say all the things I'm dying to say to you while gazing into your eyes! I LOVE you!"

Playgrounds and Battlegrounds

"If you die before you die, you won't die when you die."
—Greek saying

My latest bordering-on-hallucinogenic trip to Puerto Rico, communing with the tropical Atlantic's deathless rhythm via surfing and boogieboarding—Condado beach yards east of El Presby's rocks, more dependable for surfable waves than not, even if it's flat at del Indio two minutes away—and Luquillo's La Pared, head-high waves when none are elsewhere in the northeast, optimum reef and sandbar configuration birthing them—is over. I'm reverberant with ocean-motion, Puerto Rico's blazing sun and beachside yoga and rainforest exploration, while wandering Manhattan's streets at 10:00 PM's approach, relishing the city's hum and energy, dancing light—in post-vacation mode, as if in two places at once. A Latin club's entrance materializes as I turn a corner—Salsa's the most inviting dance music by far, another gift of Puerto Rico, La Placita in Santurce. Gorgeous women, decked out for the dancefloor, are crowding the sidewalk outside the club, animatedly chatting in lilting tones—their joyful fidgetiness, eagerness to dance themselves dizzy, charging the air—and their lively eyes, sultry smiles, radiant complexions, long legs, milk-soft chests, muscles and flexibility, all accentuated by the club's kaleidoscopic neon lights, echoes and beats of Salsa within. I could step through the club's door and find a dance partner, catch waves via dancing, another deathless rhythm. But I refrain—refrain while increasingly stirred, fervor rising—my skin heated, twitchy, tingling—blood-beat throbbing at my temples.

Nine hours ago I was boogieboarding El Presby's breaks in early afternoon light, a hard wind driving them high. I returned on a 3:40 PM flight, arrived home shortly after dark with saltwater-residue on my skin—I like being able to lick my arms, taste of the waves, for hours after arrival—am enamored of contrast, Manhattan's streets juxtaposed with the sea and tropics—Puerto Rico's uncaring calm giving way to wariness, stress, strife. It's healthy to expose oneself to swift shifts of extremes of temperature, take an icy shower after sweltering in a sauna—such fortifies immunity—one should guard against being swindled into placing overmuch faith in civilization-encouraged comfort, calculated to foster laziness of disposition, flagrantly at odds with nature. Taking my cue from such, I believe exposure to swift shifts of emotional extremes is also life-sustaining, bracing and healthy: what applies physically surely applies emotionally—restricting experience to flatness of feeling stifles self-development. Are the streets my playground or battleground? The two are interchangeable, depending on what mood I'm in—where I've recently been, what I've recently done, am doing now or believe I intend to do, or simply on account of random thoughts, accumulated impressions. The streets are a means of becoming mercurial enough to baffle myself—spur desire, daring, disorientation—blur sensation and interpretation of sensation, fling my comfort-zone sideways, flip it upside down, the further from predictability the better. Playgrounds can easily be battlegrounds and vice-versa—again, it's purely a matter of moodiness, emotional interpretation.

So, regardless of the beguiling women outside the Latin club—their aura of antsiness quickening my pulse, punching electricity into my stomach, inducing sensations of topsy-turvy weightlessness, crowding my head with sparkling imagery—I'll be denying myself the delight, redirecting my arousal towards the beckoning shadows of distant streets. It's thrilling to be uncertain what I'm after, not know if I'm authentically feeling a certain way or only imagining I am, be at sea as to what the outcome will be—predetermined aspirations are self-limitation, unfulfillingly one-dimensional, devoid of mystery. I wish to do my best to reap the most from my allotted time on earth, behave as if today's my last. How do I know I'll be alive tomorrow?—that a mugger, after obtaining my wallet, won't slash my throat for kicks?—that an improperly secured air conditioner won't tumble from a window onto my head?—that a cab won't jump the curb, pin me to a wall or mow me down? No one's exempt from wrong place at the wrong time.

I've resided in Manhattan for over three decades and have a knife in my pocket in public for the first time, having previously been fearful of possessing a weapon in the streets; the knife's altering the cast of my nerves, inducing what I'll call emotional vertigo—going so far as to toy with my vision, obscure depth-perception—almost make the treetops seem close enough to touch, sidewalk faraway as the sky—and, far from retreating from these unfamiliar sensations, I'm eager to discover what the consequences are. There's an urge to inundate my veins with paranoia, taste of unexplored amplitude of foreboding, despite myself. Being self-divided can be as enlightening as gazing at the stars above timberline in the Sierras, where they're bright with ancient light, unobscured by artificial light—the distance between one's divided parts suggests the vastness of the universe—unprobeable mysteries pulsate in our blood. I routinely wander the streets at night but have never dared do so with a switchblade rubbing against my thigh with each footfall, placing pictures of violence in my head. Not that I've planned the adventure—I'm not intentionally tempting fate, it's occurring by chance. I happened upon a man offering items for sale on the sidewalk. Am I to blame the knife was among what he arranged on the blanket and it caught the streetlamp light and glimmered, attracted my attention? I seized the knife spontaneously, unsure as to why—at first touch it, although an inanimate object, jolted me in an unaccustomed manner—my unease suggested subversion of normalcy—I was handing the man five dollars before half aware of what I was doing. *Weapons are double-edged—able to discourage conflict but may also attract it!* flashed through my thoughts but, instead of reconsidering my purchase, I was aroused due to suddenly encountering new emotional territory—come what may, I'm resolved to see this accidental impulse through.

I'm a few blocks, and three or four turns, away from the Latin club on a tree-lined cross street—the trees are partially interrupting the streetlamps' amber light, casting fitfully shifting shadows, extensive patches of darkness—many features blurred, obscured. To walk all night in random directions with no clear destination, surrender to being drawn on and on... There's no telling what might occur—what secrets, as enticing as forbidden, one might stumble upon. In the night-streets one's permitted to get a clearer idea of one's psychic and emotional potential—better able to lift oneself apart from society-fabricated boundaries, avoid being hoodwinked into settling for a fraction in place of the whole of possible experience—everyone has the right to ward off exploitation, dilution. So-called civilization seeks to pass off manufactured desires as authentic desires—dupe people into squandering precious time on all too convenient, as in sanitized and unfulfilling, distractions—the night-streets have zero tolerance for one-dimensional flimflam—one must be hyper-vigilant at all times, with 360-degree directional awareness, and doubly so when carrying a knife.

Now I'm southbound on Riverside Drive's Riverside Park side, towering trees swaying to my right, breeze whispering through their leaves—a couple are on a bench ahead, lost in each other's mouth, and I'd be the first to declare few activities are as enjoyable and rewarding as kissing a loved one. And I mean no harm but apparently I've observed them for slightly longer than is polite, unintentionally fostered misapprehension. Because the man's noticed, is turning defensive—glancing up from the woman's happy countenance, whipping his eyes at me. Time to erase my face, appear oblivious of them, continue walking as if they're not there—indicate I'm not dreaming of doing anything but mind my own business. At my back I soon feel the man's glare fade away, cease to follow me. No great amount of drama involved but, all the same, I'm thinking how easy it would be to get in a scuffle over nothing more substantial than mistakenly perceived presumption—a stranger compelled to raise his fist against me due to unfounded disturbances in the jealousy/aggression regions of his brain. And then myself, in turn, obliged to fend him off, lash out with the knife—he thrashing on the sidewalk, suffocating on blood flooding his throat, because of thoughts he thought I was having. Just think about it—a killing traced back to stressful pulsations, momentary overload of synapses, in an accidentally encountered man's brain—pulsations that owe their origin to the degree he's enjoying kissing a cutie—the degree of his enjoyment directly proportional to the likelihood he'll misinterpret a glance, regardless of how cursory, as being invasive and offensive. Just think how ridiculously easy, like misreading a map, it can be to kill or be killed—how frighteningly arbitrary, blind as the lottery, a great deal of murders surely are.

Or perhaps most, if not all, of the misapprehension's been in *my* head? I'm dozens of yards distant from the couple, reviewing what occurred, and realize there's a chance the man wasn't disposed to hostility—he briefly glanced up in an understandable invasion-of-privacy response—whatever annoyance he may have experienced was soon dismissed. It's an indication that the knife's delivering on my intuitive expectations, prodding me into being on edge disproportionately to actual occurrences—making me skittish, suspicious, claustrophobic—claustrophobic even though outside, under the sky—imbruing the air with additional shadows, pressing them against my eyes, not allowing me to feel soothed by the breeze. I'm tingling but there's a cutting edge to it—it's wariness-driven more than elation-driven—I'm losing faith in the accuracy of my judgement, wondering to what extent perceptual distortions, emotional mirages, are manipulating me; and on account of the novelty I like it but am also becoming increasingly alarmed—apprehension's countering the pleasure of curiosity. It's different than surfing in front of jagged shoreline lava rocks—I'm always aware of when I need to turn out of a wave to escape being torn to ribbons, never afraid of failing to do so in time. Will I be able to accurately gauge danger's approach tonight?—able to turn out of the knife's influence in time to escape involvement in life-jeopardizing conflict, perhaps a heinous crime? This situation thrills me as much as it chills me.

I've circled back to Broadway, my stride seemingly rapid as storm-driven swells—the sidewalk's an ocean of motion, rising and falling, shifting and swerving—the knife's whipping me through the streets with surfing's swiftness, cutting across a wave's face before it curls over me, crashes, foams—it's as if I'm racing to stay one step ahead of the knife's emotion- and perception-bending pull—each second's winding tighter with tension. And the people gathered outside this bar, chatting in the light rippling onto the sidewalk from its interior... Are they looking at me in a funny way? Can they discern something's amiss and I'm not wholly myself? I *must* be coming across as disoriented and hesitant because of still adjusting to these new sensations—out of my element, something of a dolt. Are they snickering at me, laughing?—about to verbally abuse? But... Well, now it's me that's laughing at me! These people are nine-to-fivers having a well-earned good time—out to seize a few hours of healthy freewheeling on this Tuesday night before obliged to acquire enough sleep to be alert enough to function at work tomorrow—they don't mean me any harm.

I'm definitely being tugged towards misapprehension bred of escalating excitement and trepidation, under the influence of rationality-disarranging stimuli, if I'm questioning what these peaceable people think of me, assuming they're even noticing me—it would be difficult to find a more persuasive barometer. Just look at them through *my* senses, the way they're flickering in and out of clarity, sliding under and then out from under my skin: now the mocking and hostile people they aren't, now the inoffensive out-for-a-good-time people they are—one moment I'm hopped up and defensive, primed to counter aggression, the next I'm laughing at my exaggerations, sighing with relief. And with each cycle, swing from anxiety and fear to laughter and relief and back again, I further succumb to the knife's influence. Increasingly, the knife's effect is similar to choppy water hitting a wave I'm surfing—catching me off-guard and requiring greater skill, threatening to spill me from the board, spin me under the surface.

But my stride's deserted me—I'm lingering a few yards from the bar, leaning against a building, unsure why... And maybe those people can perceive there's a knife in my pocket, accurately read the giveaways, and... Am I carrying the knife because I want to get in a fight? And is such obvious to others? Frightening thought! Maybe some of them will call my bluff—take me up on my hunger for a fight, slam my head against a wall to teach me a lesson, drive home the fact I've no business playing this unfamiliar game, straying this far outside habitual feelings—am out of my depth. But what a fool I'm making of myself! I stress anew they're decent law-abiding people, safely removed from violent thoughts! Why would they have violent thoughts? They're out on the town, having fun!

How would they know what's transpiring within me?—why would they care? And full disclosure: I *am* one of those people, have a steady job (as I assume they do) and a cushy one at that, am due back at the office at noon tomorrow; and here I am wandering the streets with a knife—scaring myself with this unexpected experiment, sampling of what I've never experienced before. Bottom line: I need to get lost, disappear from their sight. I don't want to think any of these nice people might attack me—don't want to be beguiled into reaching into my pocket for the knife. And I'm by no means eager for a fight—I'm sure of it! But the knife's beginning to do its best to persuade me I am!

Oh, I dash to the end of the block, all right—clasp the corner of the building at block's end as I turn it to maintain velocity during the 90-degree switch of direction without veering towards parked cars—am running as if hell's hounds are nipping at my heels. Paranoia may be starting to dizzy and befuddle and sting me in earnest, swirl the light into glaring haze, amplify traffic's hiss into a wail, but I still—thank God—possess enough presence of mind to spare blameless people its possible consequences, remove myself from their proximity. Palpable in the air, somehow detectable on the building-fronts, is the wound-up stillness of a snake poised to strike—every agitated pattern of shadow, flutter of a leaf in the trees, is the urgency of a spider responding to vibrations in its web—the sky's rushing earthwards as if diving for prey. And the knife seems to be a living thing, have a will of its own—not for an instant is it allowing me to forget it's in my pocket—an insistence of presence, warm and rigid and quivering, is hard against my thigh. When I run my fingers up and down the handle inside of which the blade, like a cat's retractable claw, is concealed I'm subjected to a shock—sparks flare in the blackest pits of my nerves. When I dare to firmly grasp the handle, fondle the button that springs the steel of the blade outward fully erect, I'm terrified by what could transpire—my familiar world, accustomed conception of safety and security, is as insubstantial as mist in the wind.

Will I, God forbid, be forced to use this knife?—exchange speculation and fantasy for action, cross the line between emotional curiosity and traumatic encounter? I swear the knife's exerting a pull suggestive of gravity—my fingers can't stop stroking it, my hand's increasingly twitching with the urge to yank it from my pocket—I can't stop envisioning blood soaking the sidewalk. Such is how the knife's toying with, prodding and tempting, me—nothing's commendable about a killing. Heaven help me if I yank the knife from my pocket and its blade springs free of the handle, flashes silver in the open air, vanishes inside someone's chest—the last thing I want to do is kill, be remorse-flayed until the end of my days. Yet I can't resist being drawn further into the spell the knife's casting, continuing to explore the boundary, toe the tightrope, between lawful and criminal behavior. Is it necessary to kill in order to achieve authentic liberation from society-endorsed paucity of experience? I hope not! Hopefully merely contemplating the possibility of killing—imaginatively projecting myself into the deed, permitting mental pictures of murder to daze me scared without following through—will suffice. I *so* wish to smash through my comfort-zone, sample of the forbidden, but also wish to remain law-abiding, smiled upon by society. Can I have my cake and eat it too?

A man, about six feet four and two hundred fifty pounds, and as if wrestling with demons, deviled by unrest, is rapidly approaching... I'm on another dim cross street, I believe between Broadway and West End—shadows are writhing under the trees, the trees' leaves are hiss-whispering, air's breath-stiflingly dense... Being face to face with a stranger, heavy and fit as a football player and apparently disturbed, while alone in the night-streets isn't conducive to ease of mind, faith in being safe... He doesn't appear to be a civilization-bamboozled zombie, could be one of the unimpressed and unreachable—an authentic savage, immune to mandated manipulation. So can *he* discern I'm tempting fate tonight?—might *he* be inclined to demonstrate I've no business overstepping my allotted boundaries, put me in my place? I'm under the impression separation between my inner and outer selves is illusion—that I'm a window, transparent as glass—that my gathering distress and loss of equilibrium are crystal clear and it's impossible to hide—that I'm being flipped inside out, robbed of secrecy and privacy, by the intentness of his gaze: I'd give anything not to have the knife on me, be under its baleful spell. And the man's looming larger and larger—the distance between us is fast disappearing, we'll soon be sharing the same sidewalk-square—I dare not slow my pace, risk flashing a fatal signal—projecting added disquietude, vulnerability—there's no time to frame a fragment of thought, seek to collect myself—I'm jittery and off-kilter head to toe and he senses it. And my hand's *too* wound up, as if being stung—poised to jerk the knife from my pocket, press the blade-release button, thrust out the steel, slash! I'm seeing blinding white!—the sensation of walking, feel of my feet on solidity, is haze in a dream!—swift silver's cutting through, blurring and curving, the air! And entry, resistance!—it's as if I'm stabbing prime rib, encountering bone!—my arm, its muscles strained, is shoving with all its strength! Then a final push and twist, followed by a backwards yank—squishing sounds accompany extraction of the blade—a wide tall shadow, fraught with convulsive motion, falls from view—a choked yell fades...

I spin leftwards, encounter a building—am pressing my chest and thighs to the masonry, extending my arms across it, spreading my fingers to grip, striving to remain upright on rubbery legs—shaking, hyperventilating. An approaching truck, engine growling, is seemingly inches from my back and it's as if I'm about to tumble backwards off the curb, be struck, dragged across asphalt. Ha! Just the slightest bit more of an edging into my panic, wrapping the cape of paranoia-fueled fire about my nerves, and I may very well have gone to the point of no return—either the man or myself could be wounded, bleeding, dropping to the pavement, or outright dead. Because I didn't attack him and he didn't attack me—the sequence flashed in my imagination, was substitution of thought and feeling for action—frightening approximation of drowning in the dark place. He's strolled on by—both of us are safe—now I realize he had no inkling of my unsettled state.

Which isn't to say I'm not tasting of blood-on-my-hands side effects—I was alarmingly close to killing-mode, haven't been cheated. I'm barely able to stand, hovering on the edge of a swoon—nausea's coming and going, throbbing like a hangover headache—my stomach's rising to the back of my throat, acrid—I, who haven't thrown up for nearly two decades, might be sick. And the lingering heat, as of that rising from pavement after sundown on a sweltering day, in my nerves—writhing blue and violet patterns, shot through with vertiginous depth, are inside my eyes. Is my head tilted up or turned to the left or right as I cling to the building? Am I gazing at the sky or sideways or effectively blind? I don't know! And is perpetration of murder unmistakably stamped upon my countenance, quivering my cheeks?—is a guilt-divulging glaze overspreading my eyes? If my disorientation isn't proof I've flailed before the prospect of taking a life, teetered on the threshold of irreversible transgression, then the sun isn't rising tomorrow.

Murder can indeed be an instance of striking at fancied peril, mistakenly believing self-defense is called for: inoffensive people sometimes die through no fault of their own. The sense of danger and vulnerability, accelerating conviction that if one fails to realize it's a kill or be killed situation and resort to violence first it'll be too late, that compels one to reach for one's weapon. The out-and-out strangeness, unexpected aspect of innocence—as of being engulfed in sensations outside societal restriction, exempt from the law—which accompanies the act. The suspension of belief, ability to distort acceptance of responsibility, afterwards. It's understandable why killers are able to believe themselves blameless—murder can occur due to being involuntarily swept into panic-inflamed frames of mind, torn from better judgment—a hijacking of the will. Civilization declines, or is unable, to take such frames of mind into account—civilization can't begin to explain, much less police, the full range of human emotion—innocence is relative to circumstances. Ha! Do I believe the half of what's contained in these musings? It's immaterial if I do or not—what matters is I've sampled of some of the thoughts and sensations that lead up to and accompany a killing, been brought face to face with them via the stabs in my nerves. As I wouldn't have been able to conceive of indulging in these musings prior to tonight's explorations, my explorations are already paying dividends.

Many of society's prohibitions contain loopholes, cannot be 100% enforced—there are more ways to circumvent the law than society cares to admit, or is able to anticipate—laws are emotionally one-dimensional, whereas emotion knows no boundaries, flows freely as water through cracks in stone. I've tasted of murder's emotions but the law only recognizes the limp body and bloodied blade—one's permitted to indulge in murder-experimentation, thoroughly taste of a kill, so long as one refrains from sticking in the knife, soaking the sidewalk with blood. Here I am: dizzy, nauseous, numb, shaking, shattered, half-blind—my heart at once stunned into stillness and beating loud enough to deafen me to all else—and no one's going to arrest me, suspect what I've felt to the marrow of my bones—society will never have an inkling of the crimes I've come close to committing. Yes, if society could get inside me and measure my nerve-vibrations, confirm they matched tit-for-tat those of someone who committed *actual* murder! But society isn't able to do so.

But I need to cease with thought-absorption, cast musings aside—quiet my nerves and blood and muscles, reunite with perceptual accuracy, put a stop to the impression I'm reeling towards the sidewalk. My scrambled state could project vulnerability, an inability to protect myself, invite aggression—the night-streets insist upon undivided clarity of attention, my life may depend on accurately ascertaining what's happening in the here and now. I hear steps to my right, feel a presence—someone's close. "Fella, I want some words!" a man announces in a strident tone, almost as if I've provoked him—have I unknowingly glanced at him with glittering eyes, unintentionally communicated disapproval? Gripping myself from the inside out with all the will I can muster, commanding myself to not visibly shake, I turn to face him, with only my left shoulder pressed to the building—I still need the latter for support, am hoping such eludes his notice. Apparently he hasn't showered lately, he's as ill-smelling as his hair's matted with grease—I'm anticipating a request for financial assistance—a down-on-my-luck-can-you-help-me-out act, appeal to pity or attempt at intimidation—I'll hand him a couple dollars to be rid of him, am not fit to be around anyone—he could be in danger—I've no idea what my overexcited imagination, altered perceptions, will compel me to do. But the man's not nearly as predictable as I'd like—doesn't want money, won't be easily brushed off. "What do you think about the bad politics?" he asks. "I think they're no good!" There's a disquieting aspect to his eyes—they're too intent and inquisitive, fastened onto me, while also lost in the distance.

"Sorry, I don't know about politics—I know I should but I don't," I respond, evenly spacing my words in a measured tone—the extent of the man's imbalance, alienation from rationality, is becoming more obvious and alarming by the second and I'm seeking to defuse possible acrimony, dispense calm—hopefully my professed ignorance of politics will discourage additional discourse.

Instead of abandoning the conversation and leaving for elsewhere the man frowns, stamps a foot, raises his voice, "It's not right what they're doing—there's bad exploitation! The powers think they're right but they're bad and want to steal everything—rich people are bad!" He's staring at me unkindly, as if I'm one of the "rich people." I've the unpleasant impression nothing I say, including feigning sympathy, will settle him—that the more I speak the more unsettled he'll become. Evidently I'm someone for him to project inner conflict onto, expend frustration upon, simply because he randomly stumbled upon me—if I wasn't his reference point, cast in the role of mirror of what bothers him, someone else would be. He's sweating profusely, jittery in his stance, cheeks twitching—periodically whips his eyes about, as if scanning for enemies, only to fasten them on me again.

It's impossible to know what's passing for logic in a street crazy's head, what will incite or mollify him, bring a smile or scowl to his face, and such is the source of my fascination—partially unwilling fascination—as I stay put instead of making tracks. I've stepped apart from the building, no longer needing support, able to stand steady without wobbling—I feel perception's been reunited with response-time. I'm examining the man's face for signs of imminent hostility—one of my hands is hovering near the bulge of the knife, prepared to dart inside my pocket and grab it. If there's an abrupt step in my direction—if there's an assertive gesture, fist headed my way—I'm confident I'll be quick enough to protect myself. I'm thinking I'm fortunate to possess a means of self-defense at the same time mounting panic's informing me it's preposterous I'm in this situation—rapid-fire flashes of my doorman building co-op, safe as a residence could be, whirl through my head: what's motivated me to court this amount of peril? In addition to living in a secure building I work in the corporate world in a non-stressful capacity, thereby being sheltered on all fronts. But being over-sheltered's the source of my unrest, right? How's one to reinvent oneself and mature via challenge in situations where challenge is absent? Then again, is it necessary to go so far as to jeopardize my *physical* well-being in the streets? Is the office so stiflingly predictable I need to compensate by dealing with this unbalanced individual? But forget the office, it's a mirage—security's fiction. Chance life-menacing encounters, courtesy of the impartially capricious streets, can materialize at any moment, regardless if one's indulging in experimentation. Meaning I might need to slash and cut, expose this man's blood to the air to spare my life, before he has time to hold me responsible for his distress, attack and incapacitate me. If he's entangling me in his frustration, projecting hostility onto me when I mean him no harm, about to become violent... Well, all unjustifiably hostile creeps deserve to be stopped in their tracks, right? And—God!—vein-jolting chills are seizing me—I can hardly believe these thoughts are mine! Are they?

"I think you're...you're maybe a rich boss—bossing workers, stealing everything!" bursts from the man's throat; then, while yanking at his shirttail with one hand, his other arm twitching, "Exploitation bad, the bad politics are beating me! Government bad, market...stock market, bosses there, no good—cuttlefish, sea creatures, starfish, tentacle, squid...bad creatures squirm on the ground, look out!" He jerks his glance at the sidewalk for an instant, briefly recoils, half-steps back, then turns immobile, albeit while tremulous head to toe—is clinging to me with his eyes again, breathing heavily, as if gathering himself. Is he about to spring on me?

"I'm no boss," I hear myself say, raising a hand to ward him off, no longer caring to conceal annoyance. "I like being left alone and that's not boss behavior—bosses are in everyone's face, can't mind their own business. And what's that to you? I mind my own business, leave people alone." Is an altercation a given? My non-raised hand's in my pocket, clutching the knife—a finger's confirming location of the blade-release button—I'm ready to leap sideways, acquire firm footing, let fly into the middle of his belly. What happens instead? The man, wonderment widening his eyes and his features softening, takes a slow, one would say respectful, step forward, gently places a hand at the back of my head, and—amazingly—I allow him to do so. His manner, curiously enough, is that of a doctor listening with a stethoscope—apparently he's taking some sort of reading on me—interpreting nerve-pulsations, determining if I vibrate at an acceptable frequency, or can be trusted not to be a boss, or... Who knows?

I understand it's because I've spoken testily, neither minced tone nor words, that the man's placed his hand on me and it's a highly intrusive gesture indeed but I'm unable to detect a trace of accompanying hostility—there's a naive quality about the gesture, as if it's his manner of responding to the rare occasions when people react to him forthrightly, regardless if negatively—he's doubtless accustomed to being greeted with silence, ignored and avoided. I'm not only amazed but strangely pleased I'm tolerating his hand on me—there's next to no impression of being caught off-guard, even if by all rights there should be. Which isn't to imply I'm not wondering if I'm in danger—I'm seeking to mimic unconcern, banish tension from my muscles, halt all nerve-emanations, erase my presence—an instinctual reaction at such close quarters, which will hopefully incline him to remain calm. It's the state I went to when a mother bear and three cubs came into our campground after midnight in the Sierras, scavenging for food. Fellow campers had warned us of the chance and my friend's English Setter, fearless Zuke, announced their arrival, barking from my friend's tent a couple yards away. I was instantly on my belly in my sleeping bag, raised on forearms, feeling myself drift into the distance while remaining hyper-alert—there was no fear, I was seeking to be invisible—for no trace of electricity to radiate from my body, attract the bears' attention—the mother bear was seated a few feet from my tent, her voluminous shadow cast against its nylon by the moonlight—the cubs were scampering every which way, making squealy sounds, conducting the search. Upon determining no food was available, we having stashed it in the bear-proof lockers and disposed of all trash in the bear-proof bins, with nothing in our tents that could attract via scent, the bears departed and I resumed sleeping as if they were never there. I'm using the nerve-memory of that interval to assist with projecting collectedness, appearing tranquil. After about half a minute the man lowers his hand to the small of my back—is cocking his head, furrowing his brow, while applying the same gentle pressure.

Suddenly I feel there's too much crowding-of-space emphasis, suggesting a threat, in the man's stance—that the softened aspect's vanished from his expression, his gaze unnervingly probing again. Of course I've been on edge the while—now it's occurring to me I'm unable to conceal it—that endeavoring to erase myself is futile and something of my essence, whatever he's been taking a reading on, will irritate him, nudge him towards malice. Are my eyes uncertain of focus, lost in wobbly silver light?—are my pupils dilated in a telltale manner, advertising agitation? Each time the man scans my face, as he does too often, panic flares under my skin—certainly my cheeks are quivering, betraying uneasiness, inviting an assault!

"You're all right, friend," the man unexpectedly says, withdrawing his hand and nodding, backing away a couple steps. "You've been there—you *know*." Upon falling silent he stares at me fixedly.

Been where and know what? flashes through my thoughts as my nerves turn to electric ice—as I twitch, shiver, tense tight. *Why is he trifling with me? If I'm "all right" why isn't he leaving me be?—why are his eyes stabbing at me? I know why! He wants to unhinge me! What have I done to him? I don't know him, was minding my own business! What is it about me that's invited undue familiarity, made him feel it's acceptable to touch me?*

Instants later I'm convinced the man's well aware I have a knife—that my nerves are emitting telltale vibrations, aligning with a weapon's presence. Below the gloss of appearances is a separate world—the air we breathe's in actuality crisscrossed with the invisible strands of nerve-webs and I'm being bound fast in those webs, because of the knife. If the knife wasn't on my person I wouldn't be unduly self-conscious—fretting about muscular tension, questioning the cast of my gaze, fearful of behaving in a manner that invites misgiving, possible violence. The nerve-webs, more sensitive than an insomniac's frayed senses, are measuring and transmitting my disquietude—any attempt to counter transparency in the subsurface realms, conceal my unease, ward off suspicion, is futile—there's no privacy, gut-level or otherwise, for me. I'm not even sure what to do with my hands or arms, how to position my shoulders—the simple act of occupying space is suddenly problematic—some postures might breed belligerence.

The way the man's intently examining my facial expressions while shamming comradeship and sympathy's surefire evidence that he's relishing my uncertainty—he's counting on me to continue second-guessing the circumstances, fail to act. Why doesn't he have the decency to end the farce?—stop dissembling, show his hand, attack? The creep clearly believes he's duping me with an I-identify-with-you act, his "You've been there!" charade! Does he really believe he can toy with me without me being wise to the game? Does he get his kicks spouting rehearsed nonsense to random strangers, aping looniness, sowing fear? He's mistaken if he thinks I'm going to tolerate being a source of cynical amusement, tricked into dropping my guard, for much longer—I ought to slash a red X into his face, slosh the sidewalk with his blood! Slashing him would be sensible self-preservation—it's not smart to persist in placing myself in peril! But, no! Not yet! I need to make more of an effort to cling to the safe world—the rationality-framed world—the non-slipping-towards-disorder world! I'm unexpectedly imagining I'm in a 4-seater high in the sky, as during my first and only flying lesson at sixteen when my father was interested as to whether I was interested, would've gladly financed pilot certification; and I declined at the time, on the grounds there was nothing up there. I'm feeling I'd decide in favor of flying given another chance, so as to do the things that can't be done in cars or boats—fly upside down, sharply bank turns, climb in a curl, flip perception of the horizon on its head. It's interesting how tonight's adventure is inspiring me to flashback to vivid experiences. Occasionally while surfing or skiing it occurs to me I'm exceeding my ability, precariously close to incurring serious injury—frightful moments, yet incomparably vivid—euphoria surges as dread knifes through it, reins me in. I believe that if one isn't periodically compelled to ask oneself, "Are you completely *insane*?" one isn't living as intensely as one should. I'm clearly addicted to gut-punching experiences. Why else carry a knife tonight?

But given current circumstances, it could be life-threatening to permit flashbacks to clutter my attention, erode reaction-time—the man's in front of me, still impudently staring! And if he knows I have a knife and isn't making tracks doesn't it prove he's packing a weapon as well? Do I have an instant to spare before he reaches for a knife—or a gun—and gets the drop on me and I'm the one gagging on blood? God! The thumping of my heart, stings in my chest! My nerves are flaring embers, spine's a stake at which I'm being burned! No! No! No! I'm extracting the knife from my pocket in earnest instead of in imagination—the erect blade kissing the air, glinting silver-white! I'm jumping sideways to make it tougher for the man to hit *his* target, taking aim! Am I able to strike before he strikes me? Is he wounded, incapacitated, unable to strike back? Am I safe? The end of the block, convergence of buildings, whirls leftwards, abruptly halts—the trees and building fronts are wavery, slithering—the stars, indifferent diamond hard stars, are on the ground—all city noise, evidence of light, fades...

What I'm next conscious of is that a man's crouching close enough to brush me with his knee, obstruct my view of all but his shoulders and chest—tapping my forehead, offering a drink from a flask—cognac's flowing over and tingling my tongue. What's transpired? I'm halfway into fetal position on my right side on the sidewalk—apparently I blacked out, dropped to the pavement, and how long I've been here's anyone's guess. There's neither pain nor numbness, but there's abundance of stupefaction—my vision alternately blurred and approaching clarity as I forcefully inhale and exhale, test my limbs and torso, ready myself to rise. Is it safe to attempt? And who's offering aid?—cautioning against moving, stating he'll summon help? It's the man I was close to cutting! Thankfully I swooned before I could harm him—what a nefarious mind-poisoner a knife is! My hand's in my pocket, all but glued to the knife's handle, trapped between the weight of my body and the pavement! I jerk my hand from my pocket as if my pocket's red hot, never mind the asphalt scraping my knuckles, biting my skin—I don't want the knife sparkling against my hand, shooting evil energy into my veins, overriding sanity, thirsting for blood!

Turns out I'm able to stand as easily as if I've sat on the sidewalk instead of tumbling onto it, with negligible smarting in my right hip, readily shaken off, for which I credit yoga's reinforcement of strength and flexibility. Not that all's rosy—the air's overheated, stifling, heavy. Uppermost in my mind's the need to make myself scarce—I don't want to be in conflict with this man or anyone else—don't want to be at the mercy of groundless suspicion, fabricated danger, anymore—hemmed in, turned claustrophobic and desperate. I was frightfully close to blindly lashing out due to the knife and there can't be a relapse. What excuse will allow me to get lost without causing offense? Hey, didn't I promise Claire I'd pop over tonight? Right! I inform the man I've neglected my girlfriend—that if I'm not in her arms within the hour she might phone the wife out of spite. "Being caught between two women's as heavenly as hellish," I say. "I can't give either up—my main mission in life's getting away with having both, striking the balance—it's never easy but I'm never bored. You understand, right? I'm way too late already and if I don't go to her will be in *big* trouble! Thank you, Sir, from the bottom of my heart *(Here I cross my arms across my chest, then shake his hand.)*, for bringing me back to the living—some people would've left me on the sidewalk, walked away. You're a saint!"

The man appears to accept my excuse (I neither have a wife nor steady girlfriend.), cracking a smile—albeit while shuffling a foot, his brow vaguely furrowed. Again, there's much that's off about him—it's scarily easy to see how his inner-disarray-bearing paved the way for the knife to whip me towards fancied danger. In any case, I'm quickly gone.

Once safely away I'm marveling at how I allowed the man to draw me into his befuddled world, infect me with uncertainty and apprehension—wondering why I didn't bolt the second he approached, as most people would. Why listen to the ramblings of an individual of dubious mental stability, trouble to respond, go so far as tolerate him touching me? But of course the knife's responsible! The knife's taking advantage of my thirst for the novel—seizing upon opportunities to shove accurate perceptions aside, alter emotion, yank me into the strike-first-or-be-struck mentality—and I need to put a stop to it before an actual altercation occurs.

As I continue walking as rapidly as possible without breaking into a run, as running's likely to attract unwanted attention, the blocks flick-er-flash in and out of view as if intermittingly lightning-illuminated in driving rain. Before long I'm on a deserted cross street—gradually aware I'm in a particularly posh area. If I didn't know I'm on the Upper West Side I'd think I was on the Upper East, with which I'm more familiar, between Park and Madison or Madison and Fifth—it's as quiet as a NYC street will ever be. The quietude combined with soothing breeze and sight and scent of flowerbeds at the bases of the trees lining the street, rhythmic sway of the trees against the sky, suggestive of the ocean's ebb and flow in a sheltered bay, is enabling me to more effectively distance myself from the knife's vein-invading electricity, thrust its infernal prodding aside—I need to ditch the knife before it grips me anew, fuels another paranoia-attack, deceives me into doing God only knows what. The storm drain at the curb here's truly heaven-sent... What relief—my nerves instantly lifted from the fire, as if massaged—is the sound of the knife tumbling through the grating, landing outside my reach. I'm done with scaring myself, getting in over my head, with night-street experimentation, indulging in perilous extracurricular emotions! Time to sit on this brownstone's landing, where trees aren't obstructing the cloudless sky—gaze at the vastness between the building tops, seek to soar free of tension and worry, gather and ground myself.

But my thoughts are declining to cooperate, flipping in directions I wish they'd avoid—I'm contemplating my multifaceted personality and aspects of it are scaring me to death. A knife's in my pocket? Then I'd best be wary of the portions of my personality that're only too willing to be dazzled and seduced by it! And I ought to be chiding myself in no uncertain terms for having carried a knife, allowed it to scramble perspective, bring me under its sway, vowing never to repeat the experiment, but—would you believe?—there's pride, a sense of accomplishment, in the mix. (So perhaps I ought to amend the above, admit I don't entirely mind where my thoughts are flipping.) Not many gainfully employed individuals, fully on the grid and documented, get to experience what I've experienced. By noon I'll be dutifully dealing with pharmaceutical material approval process, linking claims to supportive documentation in digital submission platforms—safe and secure on all fronts according to society, with comprehensive health coverage. Tonight I've wandered the streets with a knife in my pocket, been swept into frames of mind where murder can seem essential for continued survival: I can't help but congratulate myself on having lived in opposite worlds within a brief space of time, facilitated sharp contrast—overcome civilization's behavioral boundaries. Overmuch safety's enervating—shocking experiences forestall emotional stagnation—stepping outside of society's dictates, however temporarily, is healing and healthy, gives one an advantage over those who never have. Knowing I've infiltrated an advertising agency, hoodwinked my employer with a compliant minion act, then about-faced to flirt with murder in Manhattan's streets is priceless—it's *beautiful* to be fired up, hyper-alert and -cautious, transported to an intensity-altered world where complacency's impossible.

Did I rid myself of the knife prematurely, before it could wholly transport me to the intensity-altered world? The streets aren't white hot, shot through and through with the urge to undergo personality-metamorphosing experiences, anymore. The air's absent of depth and shadow, no longer bending and blurring the light—no more invigorating pursuit of danger, facing off with the unknown. All's dead and hollow and ordinary, equivalent of a concert hall after a performance, the audience gone—same as when ocean waves are flat, no surfing possible. Without the urgency the knife instilled... But do I *really* want to chide myself for ditching the knife? No!

And I actually packed a knife, permitted it to jumble perception and judgment?—inundate my veins with paranoia, tempt me towards killing? Absolutely insane! I'm shaking to my bones now—two-handedly gripping the landing's edge, staring hard at the concrete steps, seeking to steady myself. I suppose I could classify my agitation as moodiness—declare it's temporary deprivation of positive impressions concerning tonight's adventure, an attack of negativity that'll soon pass—but such would be avoidance of owning up to having idiotically surrendered to life-endangering rashness. Does contemplation of death magnify appreciation of life? Perhaps, but it's the height of stupidity to *risk* death. It's essential to flush the knife's residual stimulation from my senses, never dream of flinging myself into another night like tonight. Priding myself on leading a double-life—duping society—is ill-advised, since there's always a chance the dark side of double-living could get the better of me, swallow the light.

So how arrest the side effects—persistent anxiety, stabbing nerves—of indulgence in ill-advised activities?—reacquire rationality-informed bearings, balance?—persuade myself I'm sane, fit to report to work later today? The surefire means of restoring stability I'm aware of is that nothing's more healing than the embrace of a gorgeous darling of a fit flexible woman, and many were buzzing about the Latin club—women who live for delirium via dancing *never* come up short. I've been privileged to know the type—their unapologetic hunger, fearlessness and feistiness, delight in their bodies, willingness to do many things many other women won't is nothing short of magical. Thank God for force-of-nature women—I admire them without reservation, will never be able to praise them enough. And I'm not counting my chickens, mind you, but... Then again, I'm sure I'll find a sympathetic dollface on the dance floor, because I *need* to. Women aren't given nearly enough credit for keeping us men out of trouble—freeing us from pointless disquiet and aggression, restoring contentment with being calm, enabling us to simply be happy with life.

I'm not as distant from the Latin club and its spirited beauties as I believed. Upon shaking my head and widening my eyes—chasing off my absorbed-in-musings state, examining my surroundings straight-on—I realize I'm within six blocks. That I was under the impression I'd strayed far further downtown, despite knowing Manhattan through and through, is added indication of the knife's distortional influence, ability to create false situations. Soon I'm back on Broadway, heading north, and can discern the club's welcoming facade, neon rainbow-colors. Then I'm admiring the svelte profiles, energy and exhilaration, of the women taking a break from dancing, socializing outside—their mellifluous voices alone are immensely uplifting. Then I'm within the club's entryway, paying a reduced rate, postmidnight Tuesday discount, and receiving my hand-stamp (a scorpion, tail and pinchers raised in readiness to strike), receiving a deft pat-down (unable to not smile at the thought of the discarded knife), stepping through the second door (specifically, steel gate)—surrounded by multicolored flashing lights, propulsive salsa-rhythm—alongside the dance floor in seconds, looking for any cutie eager to join hands and be twirled.

"Hi there," I hear in a crisp friendly voice, a tap at my shoulder turning me in the voice's direction. "You were at home in the fabric—guys usually don't take to it that well." I don't recognize her at first glance but her comment nudges recollection—in aerial yoga class her hair was tied tight to her head and she was in a yoga bodysuit plus semi-hidden by the fabric hammock much of the time—now her hair's falling free in abundant waves, over halfway to her waist, and she's in a crimson and emerald and gold floral print summer dress. She was highly animated in aerial, wringing as much as she could from each posture, exceeding the instructor's guidance—routinely lifting herself high in the fabric, extending herself parallel to the floor head to toe, or spinning while dangling upside down, executing back-flip dismounts with flawless landings—making exceedingly difficult maneuvers, requiring strength and precision and verve, look easy.

"Thanks for that," I respond, aware my eyes widen in surprised delighted recognition—a detail she notes and smiles at. "I love aerial—it's a wild new yoga world for me, suspended above the floor, learning to manipulate the fabric, almost like learning to swim—half-defying gravity, a lot of fun. My humble aim's to have fun and get a good workout without making a fool of myself—that was my third aerial class and there will be more." Suffice to say an exchange follows during which I ask questions pertaining to aerial yoga—how to deal with the fabric when it's bunched into something of an inch-wide rope, digging into the bottom of one's foot, during single-leg standing postures, and the like. On the surface we're discussing the particulars of mastering aerial—in the subsurface realms we're sizing each other up, exchanging magnetism, aligning in our blood and nerves, confirming we'd like to continue getting acquainted.

Her name's Solimar—she's told me so in a sultry dip of her voice accompanied by the sweetest of smiles, brightening of her visage. God, she's gorgeous! Just take a look at her: cascades of curling pitch black hair, silver-flecked gray eyes piercing and intelligent and kind—sweat-glistened back and arms and shoulders and chest, her dress being sleeveless and backless, with a deep V neck. She's been dancing nonstop and wants more.

Our timing's effortlessly in sync on the dance floor—Solimar's intuitively quick, stunningly so. We're reading each other's joined hands, finger-twitches, palm-pressure—the tilts of our heads, expressiveness of glance—as if we've been dance partners dozens of times. I always do my best to avoid cornering women, presuming consummation's a given—they should be allowed to be sweet and giving, treat me to dance floor delirium, without fear of being held to promises they haven't made. I'd sooner die than be a tactless dolt, pressuring women is as tacky as dishonorable—as wild as they want to be and I'd like to think I give them space to be wild. If they're inclined to have a good time in bed they'll signal such and if I fail to read the signals shame on me. I'm grasping Solimar's waist, undulating like wind-kissed waves, and she's matching my steps, eyes beaming delight—when I dip her I slide a finger down the center of her face forehead to chin, or slide a hand from the nape of her neck down her back, relishing the responsiveness of her muscles while encouraging her to lift her breasts towards me, which she readily does. Solimar's signals—laughing eyes, fervent grasping and caressing of me—frequent hair-flicks, pride and joy in advertising her attributes, flexing and stretching—appear to be pointing in the direction I'd like but, again, it would be imprudent to presume.

But when I lead Solimar from the dance floor after I've no idea how many time-eclipsing songs, we sweat-drenched... What a breathtakingly forthright invitation is the tossing about of her hair as she thrusts out her chest, stretches taut, sighs deeply, eyes leaping. She seizes my arm, inclines her head towards the corridor leading to the stairs ascending to the second floor, yanks me towards it—blessed be, she's dispelled all doubt.

Soon I'm gently pressing Solimar to the corridor's wall, kissing her as she wraps a leg about mine. So electric's the rippling of her belly—wrap of her arms, massage of her fingers, spill of her hair about my shoulders and neck—I'm being swept into impressions of boundlessness as when surfing high fast waves, seemingly suspended between sea and sky. Before I have time to care what others might think—we being in full view of people ascending and descending the stairs—I'm kneeling at Solimar's knees, thrusting my hands and head up inside her dress, seizing the globes of her behind—inhaling deeply, savoring her scent, rubbing my cheeks against her thighs. Solimar's widening her stance, grasping my shoulders through the silk of her dress, bending forwards, her mouth near one of my ears—trembling, whispering, "Goodness gracious, Steve! You *are* girl-starved and I'm going to feed your appetite as much as you're feeding mine!"

Just as I'm about to pull Solimar's diaphanous panties slightly aside, tongue flick her source-of-life place, she's urgently tapping the back of my head, saying, "So sorry, Steve—we need to stop," while stiffening, yanking her hands from my shoulders, standing straight. Upon emerging from under her dress, smoothing its hem southwards, I follow the direction of her gaze, wordless exchange with someone else, and perceive one of the club's employees, physically imposing, is indicating via gesticulations we're violating the rules. It's clear he means business and is to be promptly obeyed but he's also not troubling to conceal amusement—the look in his eyes roughly translates as, "Good for you, lucky son of a bitch!"

Then I hear, "Get a room, you weirdos!" in a slurred snarling tone from a soused-to-the-gills-half-slumping-to-the-floor individual, his cheeks swollen and varicose-veined, and my spine turns razor-edged. I'm flashbacking to the knife-amplified streets, thinking how careful people need to be in their dealings with those they know nothing about—thinking if I still had the knife he could wind up suffocating on his blood. But, no! I don't want to be recollecting the knife, yanked into violence bred of tonight's experimentation—be impelled to slam his head against the wall, pull him to the floor, kick him unconscious. Every so-called man who's yelled "Get a room!" in a nasty tone's an emotionally impoverished loser who wishes he was enjoying the company of a wild willing beauty and never will—I can't imagine mouthing such tackiness, rife with frustration and envy, in a trillion years, I'd feel I deserved to be kicked dead if I did. The club's employee, bless him, turns to the slob, says, "Sir, your outburst is uncalled for—either hold your liquor and or you will be asked to leave, harassment of guests is not tolerated," while stepping between the latter and myself. Solimar, alert to my aggressive tension (We're already so attuned I can feel, via electrical pulsations, her nerve-stream ascertaining the disturbance in mine, sympathetically surging to place me at ease.), hugs me close and caresses my ears, whispers, "Steve, he's a drunk and doesn't matter—let it go." So soothing's her affectionate intonation and touch. I'm vaguely aware the slob's stumbled away but no longer care if he's dead or alive.

Within ten minutes Solimar and I are exiting the club arm in arm—the club's a blur of motion, indistinct as choppy surf in dappled moonlight, as we near the exit—we'll soon be safe from prying eyes, unrestricted by rules. But I need to describe Solimar in greater detail. She's Puerto Rican, Guánica born and raised. Guánica's west of Ponce on the southern coast and known for its pristine beaches and tropical dry forest, the latter a UN Biosphere Reserve, and she's the embodiment of the beauty and wildness of the terrain surrounding her town. (Including clouds of bright white butterflies, and how could I know I'd be hooking up with a Guánica native in New York, informing her I spent three days in her otherworldly birthplace eleven months ago?) I've alluded to the wonder of Solimar's hair—I've never seen a more pulse-quickening abundance of black-as-a-moonless-night curls, falling nearly to her waist, lavender highlights framing her radiant bronze visage—with a high forehead, elevated cheekbones, unblemished chiffon-smooth complexion. Her predominant expression's placidity of the energetic, unity of opposing impulses, variety that hints at a stormy past, as if her balanced disposition's hard fought for and won—she'll never be undermined, infected with frustration, by mean-spirited creeps. Solimar's svelte and graceful and fluffy and elegant, feminine to her fingertips, and also happens to be solid muscle, able to lift herself in aerial yoga's fabric, solely utilizing her arms, and kiss the ceiling, then bring the twin streamers together with her knees and spin and flip upside down, joyous the while. She's a size six, five feet seven or so, and fond of fiddling with her hair—changing it from free-fall to ponytail to lifted high, her fingers deftly adding or subtracting ribbons, barrettes, and pins, either plucked from or returned to her shoulder clutch—swishing her hair during transitions. Perhaps it's my, readily admitted, admiration of a fine head of hair at play but

I'm persuaded women who enjoy altering their hair are more playful, vivacious, and daring than those who don't and, in any case, Solimar's playful, vivacious, and daring to the tips of her tapered fingers. She's also penciled in a beauty mark slightly to the northwest of her lips—reserved women are rarely inclined to do such—wild how the addition of a dot indicates pronounced tendencies towards adventurousness. Solimar's glance unites kindness, sensuality, boldness, intelligence—I couldn't be more honored she's favored me.

Solimar and I are hailing a cab on Broadway while embracing, each of us raising an arm—yellow's soon alongside us and we're climbing within. I barely manage to voice our destination—my address—before I'm spilled on my back on the seat, Solimar atop me, gigglingly licking my face. I was wandering about with a knife earlier? What knife? Solimar's inundating me with euphoria and I'm unable to be troubled by having indulged in rash experimentation—my doings of earlier seem like something that took place in someone else's life, nothing I'd dream of doing myself. From the moment she tapped my shoulder Solimar's been dispensing sweetness and light, enabling me to slip free of the extent to which I scared myself, vanquish the dread. Ha! To think I was wondering if my dabbling-in-murder-emotions game would haunt me for years, or that I'd be tempted to repeat it! *Now* I know for a fact, thanks to Solimar, I won't be playing knife-in-the-streets games again—recklessly gambling with well-being, sanity, life. Solimar's glance and touch rejuvenate as when the sun scatters morning fog.

As stronger gusts are whipping through the open windows, I'm aware the cab's accelerating across a Central Park transverse. Solimar's still atop me and we're kissing, legs intertwined—we're embracing so emphatically it's almost as if I'm submerged in her skin to her bones. The phrase "Stars, sea, eternity, blessed be," pops into my thoughts and I couldn't be more grateful for being alive than if surfing head-high waves in tingling rain.

Idleness and Unrest

"Civilization is an enslavement vehicle, calculated to dull the senses. Civilization invented boredom."
—Barnave

Chapter One

It's a sunny mid-July Tuesday in Manhattan, the thermometer's nearing ninety, the specific location's Tudor City Greens opposite the United Nations, where many employees of midtown firms are passing their lunch break, relishing verdant respite from the city's clutter and clamor, hues of grey and beige. Hilaria Hath, a slender fit woman of above-average height, mid-back length vaguely wavy red hair, animated almond eyes, comeliness that frequently attracts lingering glances on Manhattan's sidewalks—a former yoga instructor, who easily passes for over a decade junior of her thirty-three years—is seated on a bench in the shade of one of the towering trees not toppled by Superstorm Sandy. She's a surgeon's wife, married for two years and three months—the marriage is childless, her husband's too preoccupied at the hospital to desire children. He's often too preoccupied to pay little more than cursory attention to her—habitually climbs into bed with the sole intention of sleeping, disinclined to become intimate. Hilaria didn't marry to be treated like a showpiece instead of a person, the security and status of being a physician's wife means nothing to her. So she's become intimate with Alexander Alexis, even if she was never consciously casting about for extramarital relief.

Alex is twenty-seven years old—over six feet, under one hundred fifty pounds, with broad-shoulders, high forehead and elevated cheek bones, full lips, sandy hair cut close enough for the mole on his head's left side to be discerned. He's easily excited, often restive, but also given to solitariness, not overly talkative—his dark brown eyes tend to either be piercing or abstracted, rarely midway between the two—sometimes he appears to stare too intently, other times to not trouble to pay attention. He works for a pharmaceutical advertising agency and his official title is "Regulatory Operations Coordinator," a position new to the industry that your humble narrator, never having previously heard of it, is at a loss to describe. All that matters from Alex's perspective is that his employer services clients with extensive budgets and billing's the key to being a valued employee, regardless of how much work he does. He delights in announcing (but only to people outside the industry, lest word filter back to his employer) that his area of expertise is a silly gimmick, which affords him an abundance of "goof-off time," "adventure opportunities," "reimbursed fun"—something he never thought would be possible with a five-days-a-week job. Suffice to say Hilaria's awaiting Alex, he having texted her thus: "Perfect that you're free, honeydoll! Easy to ditch the office today, there's nearly zilch to do! TC in forty min! Dying to grab and kiss you!"

Alex is thrilled at having become involved with Hilaria. She's the stunning audacious married woman, thirsting for attention and excitement her husband declines to provide—the former yoga instructor, eager for physical expression, who has a two-year stint with a renowned dance company, as well as glowing reviews in Vogue and Cosmopolitan, on her resume—the beauty with more time at her disposal than she wants or knows what to do with, who realizes life is brief and doesn't wish to be shortchanged. So she's cheating on her husband to avoid being cheated by life. Alex would love to broadcast their relationship to the skies but, given Hilaria's marital status, such would be ill-advised—he hasn't told a soul.

"Hey you," Hilaria calls out at Alex's approach, beaming elation while flicking her hair behind her shoulders, springing to her feet, extending her arms.

"Been far too long, Hilaria, the delay torture," he smiles, stepping into her embrace. While kissing her he's alternately caressing her neck and shoulders, seizing and squeezing her waist, circling a hand about her back, tracing his fingers over her cheeks, smoothing her dress downwards against her thighs.

"Intervals between meetings are a seemingly unending walk across blazing coals, but every meeting's salvation, my multi-handed-man," she mirthfully responds once their lips part, fervently rubbing against him. "Your text was a super plus moment, sweet of your agency to turn you loose when the coast's clear for me. But I'm still not sure what you do—you've never told much, always waving it off." She's clasping his right hand as he strokes the nape of her neck with his left.

"Waving it off because it's boring—would rather appreciate your luscious locks," he laughs, fluffing her hair and splashing it over his face, inhaling deeply.

"Yet you often mention your job—boast about what you get away with on the agency's dime, rooftop swimming and floatation therapy, aerial yoga and tanning time, Central Park and Chinatown excursions, research at the Public Library, shopping at Macy's. So I'd like to *finally* know why you're able to get away with all that, be with me today."; then, upon gathering her hair, flattening it against the top of her head, "Yeah, extortion! Either tell, or my hair's off-limits!"

"But, sweetest, your plan's flawed—all I need do is touch your tickle-spots and you'll liberate your locks straightaway and I'll be playing with them all I wish, your extortion's doomed to failure. Our time together's tough to come by, infinitely precious, so I'm not wasting time, spoiling things, by describing what I do for a living. Who cares how I flimflam the agency, so long as I do? Results speak for themselves." He's wiggling his fingers, reaching for her midriff.

"Jesus, Alex!" Hilaria giggle-cries, releasing her hair—swatting his hands, leaping back, executing a 360-degree spin. "Our fun's my lifeline and sanity, especially since I come here from a sterile world of pretense for appearances' sake—you don't need to touch me to tickle me!"; then, stepping close again, flinging her hair at him, "I adore that you adore my hair, but what's the issue with describing what you do? It's not like we're going to suddenly get stilted and cerebral beyond recall, lose the ability to be carefree brats."

"Impossible for me to refuse you anything, Hilaria, when your hair's waterfalling down my cheeks, delighting and disarming me!" he laughs, embracing her anew, inhaling deeply, one hand grasping her waist as the other slips up her dress in front. "My job's digital database stuff, officially designated as 'Material Approval Process Tagging and Linking,' unofficially a slacker's dream come true, ticket to goofing off galore. It's not needed for most projects, but in some circumstances is very much needed; and the real kicker's that no one else, including my boss, is sure what I do—I'm entrusted to do my job when need be and take care to deliver, as botching an assignment would jeopardize the extent to which I'm under the radar, as ignored and free to play around as anyone in corporate bondage will be, vastly exceeding what I imagined possible. I do zilch more than half the time and chances are few would care if they knew, although I'd never take such for granted. Bottom line is there's no one else to do my job and I spare people in other departments, including those at the top, a great deal of stress. There's a lot of money, as well as the agency's reputation, at stake."

"No one else to do your job? That's loony!"

"Loony and surreal and 100% in my favor—I'm low on the totem pole but disproportionally have clout—many higher-ups are scared of me, since I can make or break a submission, but always meet client expectations—I can hint at quitting, subtly blackmail, worry people—no one tangles with me. I don't really have a boss since my boss, having next to no idea of my job's particulars, is unable to oversee my work, needs to accept it on faith, plus—a special bonus—when I'm on vacation the ill-trained freelancers reliably screw up the jobs and I'm sorely missed. My profession's new to the industry, few have heard of it, Googling provides no info (I've confirmed). My fill-ins seldom know enough to fly solo, and the official guidebooks are—another bonus—more confusing than instructive. But do you really want to hear this stuff? I don't want to be the guy who bores his girlfriend to death blathering about his job—my job's a joke and I'm thankful for that."

"Sweetie," she smiles, hugging him tighter, "need I point out I had to threaten a hair-strike to get you to tell more about your job? Not that I'd be able to follow through, please be assured of that! But since I've—ha ha!—wrangled you into addressing the topic, what are client expectations? Call me a sheltered girl, no exposure to corporate doings. I'm interested, because you're dealing with it."

"Touches upon more of what I could've never believed possible, had I not accidently stumbled upon it. I'm in a humble support position, don't participate in pitches or campaign development or attend meetings, and what the entire agency knows is that if I don't do my job accurately the client will fail the job, regardless of how otherwise perfect; and then senior people can kiss their bonuses goodbye, and the agency can say hello to a three-grand-per-failure penalty, plus threats of account cancellation. I'm often the last in line when major jobs are submitted to clients, click on the final submission button, since jobs are electronically submitted via the databases in which I work—there are no checks and balances in place for me, which is amazing. Other departments review each other's work but no one reviews mine because, again, no one has more than a vague idea of what I do and no inclination to learn. My instructions are generally along the lines of, 'Please work your magic and submit the job and inform us when done.'"

"OK, Alex, I understand it's fun to claim to be the most irresponsible person at the agency, but I'm not buying it. You succeed when called upon and there's no one else to do what you do, so I'd say the agency's lucky to have you."

"Again, Honey, succeeding when called upon's solely in the interest of adding to playtime on company time, being left alone when not on assignment, indulging in more unauthorized extracurricular activities," he responds, two-handedly grasping her waist. "Think I want the agency to win new business? No! The only thing I get out of new business is more work and less playtime and I'm delighted when clients (too rarely!) take their business elsewhere, even if I'd sooner die than be the reason why. Only performance matters, my attitude's immaterial."

"Performance is everything for sure," she coos, grasping his shoulders and winding a leg about both of his, leaning backwards—soon flat-out dropping towards the ground as he holds her, an arm wrapped about her back. She's gazing up at him, circling her tongue about her lips. "Remember?"

"No chance of forgetting the miracle of being with you for almost a day," he smiles, pulling her upright and twirling her twice, then dipping her again.

"We *so* need to hit a Latin club again soon as the coast is clear!" she says, eyes brightening, grasping the nape of his neck. "The radiance of that night's haunting me, even stalking me—twinges of yearning, as sweet as tormenting, ambushing me anytime of day. Sinking melting into you on the dance floor, wanting you with all my heart to make me too wiped out to recall my name, worry about anything—our energy was undying! And our hand-communication, touch-telepathy—words became clumsy vague things, our gestures and glances so vivid new worlds were born—our night into day of dancing's invading my dreams, nothing devils as deliciously as bygone bliss—fragile bliss." Tugging downwards on her dress at her waist to lower her neckline, reveal the lacy tops of her brassiere-cups, she thrusts her chest closer to him. "Sorry for teasing, sweetie—simply can't resist wanting more of how you look at me, light of your gaze sweeping through my veins."

"It's not teasing, it's a preview of fun to come. It's only teasing if you keep me hanging, and you never do."

"May I be flogged senseless if I ever keep you hanging, Alex! And not just because such would be absolutely disgraceful behavior but because whatever you want of me serves me fully, ever your humble servant," she smiles, lifting a leg nearly to his waist, winding it about him. "Love this gorgeous day."

"Hilaria, we both know you'll never be my servant, may I be flogged senseless first!" he laughs, one of his hands seeing to it her hemline doesn't slide in the wrong direction, reveal an immodest amount of upraised leg. "You challenge me always and I value that beyond measure, I live to be flung in new directions by you. Of course we'll hit a Latin club again—for an amazing night I united with the fantasy of having you to myself constantly, as if obstruction's a mirage."

"Alex, I was losing my mind imagining the joy of being together constantly, as if no marriage was shackling me—our night of dancing was a sun-shimmered sea."

(It's here we'll mention that our couple are referring to their adventure seven weeks ago on a Thursday, when Hilaria's husband was at a seminar in Salt Lake City, and they were free to be together all night—the only instance of such. After dinner at The Boathouse they danced until dawn at a Latin club, then were at Alex's residence until late morning, not sleeping a wink, when Hilaria returned home and he arrived at work twenty minutes late, his shift being noon to eight. Hilaria snatched enough sleep to appear adequately rested upon greeting her husband in the evening, nothing about her manner striking him as questionable. "Not that he would've noticed a change but a girl can't be too careful, complacency's our enemy," she'd observed via text. Alex was so inspirited, drugged on adrenaline, the office had never been easier to endure.)

"Speaking of sun-shimmered, love your dress," Alex says, raising Hilaria to her feet as she unwinds her leg. "Bronze silk playing silver waterfall games with the light, sensuously floppy pleats swishing over your legs like waves, in rhythm with your movements, hemline's black lace trim dancing; and above your waist your dress hugs you as tight as I wish I could, so snug with your curves it appears inseparable."; then, upon sliding a hand through the pleats, lightly fluttering them, "And your dress feels even better than it looks—the way the silk sends static crackles through my fingers almost makes me believe it's alive. I'm jealous of your dress, wish I could grab as much of you at once as it does—it must feel like you're being felt up by dozens of electric hands when you move."

"Happy you appreciate my dress, Alex, but need to dispel your misapprehensions," she responds, wagging a finger in mock strict-teacher manner. "First of all, you hug me more blood-stirringly than fabric ever will—your touch is alive and my dress is inanimate. Second, men like to imagine we women are stimulating ourselves all day long in our dresses, scrunching our legs together under cover of floppy fabric in sheer stockings and tingling to high heaven, but that's false—we're no more stimulating ourselves in our dresses than you are in your pants. Surreptitious leg-rubbing is male-invented mythology."

"Sounds like an admission, Hilaria, especially since I didn't mention anything about rubbing legs together and you're the one who brought it up," Alex laughs. "You've vividly, lovingly even, described under-your-dress stimulation, and have especially given yourself away with the word 'scrunching,' as well as the phrases 'tingling to high heaven,' 'stimulating ourselves all day in our dresses' and 'surreptitious leg-rubbing'—highly revealing imagery, I'm getting excited. Maybe I ought to try wearing a dress, see if I can go to that self-stimulation place."

"Oh, be quiet you," Hilaria says, playfully swatting one of his shoulders before reseating herself on the bench—briefly lifting her arms skywards, gazing into the sunlit foliage above, stretching—delightedly swishing her hair.

Within seconds Alex is alongside her. "Are you scrunching now?" he teases, referring to her crossed legs, tapping her topmost knee.

"Scrunching against you, silly," she replies, cuddling close, nuzzling cheeks. "And the glint in your eye's speaking volumes, a dead giveaway, adorable—you're itching to tell about another exploit and I'm itching to hear."

"Just so!" he says, wrapping his left arm around her shoulders, squeezing. "Can't hide anything from you and don't want to! There was a prank."

"Yay!" she cries, seizing one of his knees. "I'm extra super curious now, you don't designate just any exploit a prank, only special ones—the nuts ones."

"Last Wednesday," he chuckles. "Finally I can relax, since the prank's done and I'm turned loose from the tension leading up to it. Advance preparation was enlivening but also oppressive, since I was firmly committed to execution and there was no escape. Like, once the prank was conceived it possessed me and I *had* to deliver, regardless of risk and stress. I blame the sterility of the office, it makes me restive, vexed, defiant—sometimes too eager to see what I can get away with, how far

I can go before a worst-case scenario swats me down. Under ordinary circumstances, by which I mean real-life instead of office-life, I don't need to dream up kicks to keep boredom at bay."

"But I thought you have it easy—slacking galore and you're often free to be with me, I never would've thought corporate jobs could be routinely circumvented. The corporate stereotype's rigid supervision, which clearly has nothing to do with you." She lifts his right hand to her lips.

"I *do* have it easy, am blessed, grateful," he says, Hilaria softly nibbling his fingers, mock biting with lips instead of teeth. "The best accomplishment I could list on my resume (and obviously won't) is I've scored a getting-away-with-an-insane-amount-of-recreation position at a top-tier firm—mindless with no one suspecting it's mindless. But slacking or not, I *still* have to report to work and put on an obedient stooge act. As long as I'm *in* the office I have more leisure time than I know what to do with and few opportunities to put it to worthwhile use—fidgetiness accumulates, there's no immediate outlet—I'm constantly gazing out the window, imagining I'm at liberty to do as I please when I'm not. Surfing the Internet's emotionally hollow, sorry substitution for action—I want to be active for real, worthwhile challenge jumpstarting my pulse, and pranking enables that to happen. And ditching the office to be with you, Hilaria, will always be the pinnacle of pranking—you're my ultimate prank-enabler, thanks for keeping me sane."

"And thank *you*, Alex, for turning me loose from restive idleness, sensations of being slammed against a wall, at *my* office, AKA my so-called home. And never thought I'd be called a 'prank-enabler'—priceless." Slinging her right leg across his lap, she thrusts herself against him, licks his neck.

"Yeah! Strategically-placed-tote time."

"You bet," Hilaria giggles, slipping her left forearm through the straps of her tote bag, placing it on Alex's knees, blocking observation. They're deep-dish kissing by the time he's reaching inside her dress, up her leg that's slung over his lap. One reason Hilaria's never worn a dress that's skintight below her waist or less than knee-length is because such is unacceptable in her husband's world. The primary reason is Alex routinely reaches up her dress in public and flowing folds enable greater freedom of movement and better prevent detection, no outlining of caress-motion. He's stroking her thigh where her stocking ends and skin begins, relishing the contrast, while spilling her hair over his head with his left hand.

Chapter Two

"Whaaa...what's, uhh, gohun on? Somethun I nuh like...it blasphu-hous...bad sinfuhl behavyuh, God nuh like, hawk in sky muhbuh dive duhn huh, tear off face," a man—unwashed, disheveled, shabbily dressed, holding an empty pint of gin—announces, scowling at our couple from about four yards away.

Our couple instantly disentangle, sit bolt upright and apart, assume on-guard-mode, Alex confronting the drunk with eyes and body language, ready to leap to his feet, land blows if necessary. The drunk's wobbling, erratically wringing his hands, looking towards but not entirely at our couple, eyes bleary, glazed. "But we're in love—surely you understand," Alex states loudly in a firm measured tone, well aware his words are wasted on the drunk—he's speaking for the benefit of those who've whipped their heads in the situation's direction, wants it clear he's calm and composed, would sooner die than allow the drunk to harm Hilaria.

"Nuh unerstan nuhthun, wuhld evil, swallowah buh the devuhl Sat an... Holuh Bibluh says nuh do sinfau behavyuh, whaa yuh dohun...nuh relighun nuh more, only bad devuhl stuff..." Trailing off, the drunk staggers away.

"Well, we're on stage now because of a loony drunk, go figure," Alex observes, kissing Hilaria's forehead. "People are wondering why this doofus, even if plastered blind, went off on us and I'm liking it—he's done it for free, I would've paid for the attention. Hahaha! What man wouldn't be elated sky-high to be gawked at while with just about the most ravishing woman ever born? *(He kisses Hilaria's neck.)* I'm thinking splits are called for but it's your show."

"Optimum time for splits-time, " she smiles, rising to her feet and facing him, tapping his knees with hers—seconds later she's doing the splits on his lap, legs extended to each side of him atop the bench, they in its center; then, while smoothing her hemline down each of her legs, adopting a mock instructional tone, "Firstly, our usual rule applies: so long as I'm decently covered, adhere to basic guidelines of decorum, we'll be able to get away with more. Second, it's doubtful an audience member wants to be associated with the drunk, placed in his company by aping his behavior, so it's less likely we'll be told we're out of line. Finally, we need to show we're at ease, because if we sit here looking too scared to do much because a drunk yelled at us another loser might be emboldened to be unkind—cowards wait for opportunities to latch onto mob mentality, go for a ride."

"Love the way you think, my dear, and the way your body mirrors your thoughts," he says, placing his hands high on her thighs, thumbs brushing her waist. "How long are we staying this way? You're in charge."

"Why not let smooching decide? Smooching's wiser than I'll ever be—desire's in charge, not me," she laughs, leaning in to kiss him while continuing to hold her hemline at both knees.

"In smooching we trust—hallelujah," he responds, kissing her while wrapping his arms around her back.

"OK, time's up, honey," Hilaria says about three minutes later, scooting backwards off Alex's lap—is swiftly seated alongside him, chin on his shoulder. "And, yes, splits-time's been cut short but that's your fault, because I need to know why you called Wednesday's prank risky. Never heard you call a work-thing risky."

"Your athleticism's otherworldly," he smiles, running a hand through her hair. "A slide off my lap, then a leap from nearly a split and a twirl and your tongue's on my neck—insanely easy for you. Flexibility and grace that's as if seen in…"

"Sweet, Alex," she cuts in, clasping his hand, "but please address the riskiness issue. You've never called our assignations risky and I'd like it to stay that way. Why jeopardize a job that enables our fun and pays you handsomely for it?"

"Pays handsomely for fun!" he gleefully echoes. "But the agency's still out to force me to put on approved personas, parrot sanitized vocabulary, censor myself—rob me of my existence-given right to live as vividly as possible. So the hell with it! I'm going to thumb my nose at the status quo, resist being herded into society's self-serving corral—going to combat one-dimensionality, add depth to experience, play pranks! And sometimes pranks are more than a means of fending off boredom, quickening the blood—sometimes they're justified retribution."

"Alex, sweetie," she says with mock impatience, swatting his wrist, "could you please stop whetting my appetite with mentions of risk and dastardly deeds done, only to tangent into the evils of society herding us into corrals. I'm all too familiar with being corralled and the emotion-police, I'm a wife who's expected to make husband look good by attending socials and hosting dinner parties, nonstop calendar-clutter—must grit my teeth while faking I'm the luckiest woman alive, privileged to have the husband I have, never mind he emotionally casts me to the curb. Social ornament's *my* job description—my marriage is a *job*—and the fawning I'm subjected to makes me nauseous, I liken it to choking on sawdust. And, unlike you, I can't play pranks on my job. Wait, strike that—*you're* my life-saving prank, Alex—the measure of my sanity."; then, upon slinging her right leg across his lap, slipping her left arm through her tote's handles and placing it on his knees again, winding her right arm about his shoulders, "OK! We're back to how we were before the drunk's interruption, so please tell your adventure."

"And I'll love telling it, but first... And I swear I'm not delaying on purpose, doing a tease thing, it's just that I should check in. *(He extracts his work-phone from his pocket, consults the email.)* Zilch, as expected, but I know better than to assume—sometimes people, no matter how many advance queries I send, spring surprises. The downside of people not having a clear idea of what I do is they don't always realize I'm needed until the last moment, plus underestimate the size of assignments, think a three-hour job will take one—there's no such thing as safe."

"Appreciate that you're covering the bases, Alex, careful not to place our meetings in peril—without our meetings I'd be as good as drained of my blood, thank God you're adept at gaming the system." Hilaria's alluding to the fact that, except when her husband attended the seminar in Salt Lake City, it's only reliably safe for her to rendezvous during regular business hours and she needs to be uptown come evening. While generally working late, her husband's capable of springing surprises of his own, as in short-notice requests that she attend the aforementioned socials and dinner parties, or host affairs at their residence, some having occurred as early as 7:30 PM.

"It's technology that enables us to meet—credit where credit's due," Alex laughs, tapping the satchel, containing his laptop, at his right.

"It's your manipulation of technology that enables us to meet—I'm tickled to death by your exploitation of remote capabilities," Hilaria responds, bouncing her leg that's on his lap, kissing his cheek and massaging his neck. "And now please *finally* tell me about Wednesday's exploit. What justified retribution?"

"OK. One of the senior people is only senior because he has a client in his pocket—a highly lucrative account. As always, follow the money. Money's why this schmuck's given the velvet carpet treatment, showered with laughably exaggerated accolades in official emails—never mind he has zilch social skills, including refusal to practice elementary hygiene. He's in his mid-forties, neither bathes regularly nor wears washed clothes, often smells like a dead animal. His hair's clotted with dandruff and greasy, matted to his scalp—his nails are over a quarter inch long, twisted and cracked and blackened—he's constantly digging at rashes on his neck. He's rude and arrogant to all but the two men who run the place (One decent and sane, the other a grasping goo-goo eyed dolt who has no business running anything and ought to be terminated by the parent company.) and lives with his mommy. The creep's influence with the client is due to family connections: maybe his mommy plays bridge with the CEO's wife, or his cousin's married to a board member's daughter, or his aunt owns the buildings where the client rents offices, or his daddy co-owns a marina or country club with a major shareholder, or it's simple trading of favors among the filthy rich. But enough speculation: what's pertinent is the creep's revolting behavior. About six weeks ago, as I was exiting the office and holding the door for an intern, a sweet-dispositioned schoolgirl, the lout was in the elevator well and brusquely entered—crowded the girl, outright blocked her way, caused her to recoil in alarm, and sneezed in her face—instead of apologizing, he darted her a nasty look. Then, aware I'd witnessed the sequence, he derisively glared over his shoulder at me—shamelessly gloated, confident of being above recrimination, out of my reach. At that instant I knew I'd be smacking him down, even if I had no idea how—what also flashed into my head was it would be advisable to bide my time before doing so. He knows the majority despise him—appears to enjoy it, clearly doesn't care—but I still felt I ought to wait at least a month before administering discipline so he wouldn't have a reason to suspect me above anyone else."

"Cute how you kept that to yourself for weeks, didn't drop a hint," she smiles. "Clearly sticking to your talk versus action principles."

"Not sure if they're principles, sometimes I think superstition's in the mix," he laughs, "but I feel blabbing about doing something in advance of doing it, especially if it involves gathering courage, lessens the likelihood of following through, as if words are able to displace action, wrest it from one's will. Plus boasting in advance is vainglorious assumption of success—a done deed's boast-worthy, a planned deed doesn't exist. And it's also about staying focused on what needs to be done, not getting sidetracked—thoughts of slamming the creep were increasingly preoccupying my attention."

"Oh, I've seen plenty of cowards talk big and never get past the words—the words are their limit, it's cringe-worthy how emasculated they are. It's admirable that you kept your mouth shut while planning your prank, just so long as you spill every last thing now! I'm especially curious about the stressful things—I find it tough to believe you were overly stressed." She's stroking the back of his neck.

"But how am I to place myself back in the stress, accurately convey trepidation, when your presence *(He slips his hand up her thigh under her dress.)* is eliminating all conception of fear? And if I manage to overcome your effect on me, focus enough to tell the tale, won't you feel slighted? Shouldn't I stay spellbound?"

"Oh, right!" she cries. "As if I want you to be a fumbling schoolboy who gets too befuddled by women to add two plus two. I live for making you feel good—am your willing toy, no questions asked—but you're not one to lose your bearings, thank God. We women want our men to adore us but want them to do it from a position of strength with clear heads, otherwise it's worthless. It's easy to bamboozle weaklings, but that's no better than snatching a baby's candy."

"OK, then, candy-snatcher," he laughs, widening his eyes and shaking his head. "Let's see if I can avoid getting too befuddled by you—regain my orientation, concentrate on narration."

"Oh, shush! Why was the prank stressful?"

"The stressful part's that I recalled a college prank, whereby one lines a cereal box with a plastic bag to prevent leakage, then fills the box with a nasty concoction, with the aim of... Wait, sorry—I'm jumping too far ahead, will start over: when the lout sneezed in the intern's face and made her fearful, nearly brought her to tears, plus haughtily glared at me, it was tantamount to an unforeseen, demanding and dangerous, mission being assigned to me from out of the blue with no option of refusal. I absolutely had to punish the creep, regardless of the chance of sabotaging income and career—being in good-standing with my employer was suddenly a precarious situation. It was as if a separate personality—a lurking-in-the-background-shadow-personality—hijacked my will: while realizing I had no choice but to strike and pleased with myself on that account I was also alarmed—wondering if the risk was worth it while knowing I'd take the risk. I waited over a month before commencing preparations, the certainty I'd do the deed causing me to be doubly cautious. I went so far as to wear blatantly conservative attire, including the occasional tie, although I detest the strangled feel of them—almost no one at work wears ties. And, sure, conservative attire was overkill, but who cares? The more conservative I dressed the more invigoratingly fixated on smacking the creep down I became. I, so to speak, overhauled the chore of reporting to work, intensified the atmosphere: when one knows one will be indulging in job-jeopardizing behavior the job acquires depths of emotional participation it previously lacked—goodbye predictability, hello blood-quickening, even if occasionally unnerving, uncertainty—the offshoot was it almost became *adventurous* to report to work."

"Yeah, dressing blatantly conservative was *extreme* overkill, you already look like a choirboy!" Hilaria laughs. "Your little boy haircuts alone *(She taps the top of his head.)* make you look insanely innocent, and you know how to put on *that* face—your 'What? Who, me?' surprised little boy face. Your little boy face deflects suspicion when we're playing in secret *(She vibrates her leg in response to his touch, his hand still inside her dress.)*, you fearlessly go further than anyone'll ever suspect—I positively *adore* my choirboy."

"First time you've called me a choirboy, I like it a lot! Turns out I've always gone in for the choirboy look, even if I never thought of calling it that—choirboy's the optimum public image for me."

"The first time? Could've sworn I've called you choirboy before—strange if I haven't aloud, since in my thoughts it's one of my terms of endearment for you. Unless you're monkeying."

"Absolutely *not* monkeying—choirboy's priceless and I would've said so had I heard it before," Alex responds, kissing her cheek. "Choirboy encapsulates the fun of projecting false images to get away with more, is going to be another of my slacking rallying cries—I love how it's so obvious and I never thought of it, thanks for bringing it to my attention. 'Don't judge a book by its cover,' they say. Cute sentiment, but most people judge a book by its cover anyway. Forget getting creative with my hair, dying it red or purple or green—forget mohawks or shoulder-length hair, my head shaved on one side—forget tattered jeans, studded leather wristbands, skull-and-crossbones belt buckles, arms smothered in tattoos. Those are the guys who were frisked by the cops in the Metro when I lived in Paris, never mind if they were model citizens who'd never dream of being in a country illegally for over two years, as I'm pleased to have been. And to think that as a child I'd get upset when adults thought I was a goody-good, until an older and much wiser girl pointed out it was a good thing. I'll be forever grateful to Julie for setting me straight—I started taking advantage of the situation straightaway, became doubly daring in the mischief department—being thought of as a goody-good became a badge of honor, I was honing my craft. Did anyone besides my closest friends know I worshipped at the altar of pyromania?—built robust fires faster than anyone else, concocted

Molotovs that reliably spread long-lasting flames? (So many incandescent memories!) And as far as appearances go, you're picture perfect Upper East Side respectable—your black-lace-trimmed dress mildly suggests kinky, especially as it's body-hugging from waist up, but its fanned-out pleats and below-your-knees hem offset that, as does your minimal amount of make-up, cream stockings, flat-heeled shoes, immaculately manicured nails with clear polish—all as elegant as restrained.   You *so* look like just-dropped-a-grand-at-Bergdorf's-and-reside-in-a-Park-Avenue-penthouse-and-will-be-dining-at-The-Pierre-tonight-and-forget-about-hitting-on-me-because-I'm-faithful-to-my-husband-through-and-through. Or maybe it's the drop-dead-gorgeous-but-aloof-and-unobtainable-bookish-librarian look, minus the glasses."

"Well, it's a wonder we've hooked up if *that's* how you think I come across," she grins, swatting his shoulder. "Then again, I appreciate the informative feedback: I'm not always sure I'm any good at playing at female choirboy, being the—ha ha!—standoffish librarian character, bloodless ice maiden. In husband's world resentful people are looking for the tiniest reason to make trouble, pour on gossip—faking aloofness, dressing conservatively, is survival."

"Right, plain women get apoplectic at the mere thought of beautiful women—nothing awakens tawdry envy faster."

"Can assure you the microscope I'm under in husband's world, hostility lurking under the polished surface, has nothing to do with my appearance—it's collective resentment of income and supposed prestige. Women and men are equally willing to think the worst of a surgeon's wife and my best friend in husband's world, who turned sixty-seven in May and is one of the wisest people I know, an authentically regal woman, mother of three, is scrutinized as much as me—we buoy each other by laughing about our situation, have met for tea at least twice a week since about a month after my marriage, thank God. But the endless charade, pretending not to be who I am, concealing myself..." Here she briefly trails off, allowing her eyes to speak her affection; then, whispering, "You're my salvation, dearest, and I don't need anyone suspecting that without you I'd be in a desolate place."; then, ceasing to whisper, "Alright, enough of that! Please finish your exploit—I want to hear *everything*."

"OK, first there's the agency's layout—you've peered into its north side from the hotel but I'll add on. It's the current fashion in office-design: zilch privacy, people seated barely over a yard apart, advertised as 'cutting edge' and 'enlightened' when it's regression to how offices were before cubicles introduced a modicum of sanity. Supposedly open-plan facilitates equality, inclusion, and communication, but the true motive's cost-cutting—cubes are more expensive to install and maintain and more people can be sardined into smaller spaces. And, no surprise, some people are 'more equal than others.' The senior people, including the creep, have private offices—the token concession to equality consists of the glass walls of their offices, it's their way of saying, 'Hey, we're in the open too!' when they're not. Of course administration makes flowery announcements concerning equality and reverses direction when it comes to those who oversee the agency or bring in the most cash. So the sneezing-in-the-face-of-sweet-interns-and-still-living-with-mommy schmuck has his own office—it's centrally located, near the right angle of the agency's L-shape, such that its windows face south.

"There are ceiling-mounted cameras throughout the agency, exemplifying technology's nasty side, but there are blind spots—quite a few. I had no idea the information would be useful when I was in the facilities office a few months back and happened to notice where some of the cameras point, and where they don't. I refreshed my memory by dropping in to chat with the man—an ex-cop, always jovial and helpful—who *really* runs the agency, in a behind-the-scenes sense. He has far more influence than the senior people would care to admit. I had an ulterior motive when discussing the Yankees' chances of securing the division but don't feel bad because he detests the hygiene-averse creep as much as I do. But I digress: what's important is I committed the relevant camera blind spots to memory.

"Was it necessary to hang fire for over a month before having at the creep? Doubtful, but why take chances? Although a textbook case of a mediocre moron getting by entirely due to nepotism, the creep could still be capable of narrowing the field of candidates following execution of the prank, recollection of our encounter possibly influencing his deductions. Instead of glancing away when he glared at me, as he surely expected, I felt myself flare inside and glared back—I wanted it seen his family connections meant nothing to me."

"I've no doubt you memorably conveyed your opinion," Hilaria smiles, reaching up under Alex's shirt while kissing his cheek. "My choirboy's eyes can flare and warn very vividly, make meddlesome drunks stop dead in their tracks!"

"I was thinking maybe too memorably and didn't care if my imagination was multiplying the danger—I was all for caution intensifying the office-atmosphere, didn't want it to abate. Although I'll admit it occasionally occurs to me I could simply relax and let the incident slide, walk away—if I forgot the cough in cutie pie's face, forgot the glare the lout flung at me, I'd be free of the tension and fever, return to being safe. And here's where I tell you part of my motivation to see the prank through was so I could tell you about it. I was often thinking, 'Hilaria will love it!' You were my guiding light—added incentive to do it right, not get caught."

"Well, that's just..." she trails off, clasping his left hand—the one not inside her dress—to her heart. "Honey, I'm honored to have been in your thoughts that way but hope you'll never use me as motivation to get overly reckless, for the sake of a tale to tell—the part about me being an incentive to not get caught is what I like best." She's requesting he resume his narrative with her eyes.

"But of course," he smiles, softly kneading at her heart and thigh alike—thrilling to her quivering. "The designated day for action—last Wednesday—arrives and I bring a cereal box, flattened and hidden inside a newspaper, to work. The box is lined with three plastic bags, each placed within the other, duct-taped to its top. The top of the box, reinforced by the tape, is as flexible as tough to tear. The bottom drawer of my desk is conveniently deeper, at sixteen inches, than the cereal box is high and that's where I toss the newspaper, after which I extract and unflatten and open the box, pin it upright against a side of the drawer with books. That done, I fill the box with my recipe's ingredients at intervals in the late afternoon. The ingredients are orange juice and honey (brought in the previous week), and blood and entrails from a butcher on 9th Avenue (obtained during lunch-break, disguised in an Italian restaurant take-out bag). At the last moment I'll add a bottle of glue, so the mixture better adheres to whatever it lands on.

"So far nothing special—anyone can fill a plastic-lined cereal box with foulness, fresh enough to not smell, at work. Here's the dicey part: last Wednesday was chosen because no accounts were active enough to compel people to stay past their shifts—a nearly vacant office is essential if I'm to carry out my mission, but also places me in a vulnerable situation. As my shift's noon to eight, I've reason to be in the office past regular business hours but the fact remains I'll be among the few recorded by the cameras at that time, if anyone cares to consult archives. Not that calling off the prank's an option: the lout absolutely *must* be punished, my peace of mind's at stake—I won't be able to respect myself if I fail to follow through. And, if it comes to that, I'm almost certain no one would rat me out—my target's as close to being universally despised as anyone could be: people who seldom agree about anything are united in their dislike of him. It's similar to the locker incident in high school, a fond memory: a bully was picking on me, it's not important what he did. What I did was squirt lighter fluid through the slots of his locker and set the contents on fire. Then I dropped hints to gossipy people, who promptly broadcasted them—I was the prime suspect but there was no proof, and the bully had few friends. Among the hints I dropped was, 'Maybe the locker's the first fire and his house is next—a spool of unoxidized magnesium ribbon would do the trick real nice. If I was the firebug, which of course I'm not, I might consider it—he shouldn't be pushing people around, assuming they won't push back.' Apparently the bully got the message—he never bothered me again."

"Poor bully!" Hilaria laughs. "He didn't know the choirboy look's a put-on."

"It's the downside of the choirboy look. The typical bully's a loser driven to dominate others to compensate for being a loser, doomed to live a boring uneventful life of utter frustration, and sometimes one will get the idea it's safe to screw around with me because I'm well-mannered and clean cut. I've had to waste time troubling to acknowledge a bully's existence and retaliate, have better things to do. I don't seek conflict, am peace-loving at heart."

"Alex, sweetie, you certainly bring peace to me! I'm never as free from caring what others think as when we're together and want to get carried away with that now but hear children approaching."; then, upon looking over her left shoulder, "Alert! Nannies setting up shop—we need to stop." She's referring to the group of nannies who've congregated about eight yards away and are spreading blankets on the ground, lifting children from strollers onto the blankets—scattering stuffed animals and toys. It's true our couple's stimulating activities—Alex's hand up Hilaria's dress, Hilaria's hand up Alex's shirt—are undetectable to others, but our couple have a strict never-play-when-children-are-present policy.

"Absolutely," Alex says, withdrawing his hand from her thigh, she removing her leg from his lap and tote bag from his knees—seconds later they're on their feet. "A good place to go's behind those flowering shrubs," he continues, tilting his head towards a row of bushes. "They're far enough away and the bonus is bees are crazy about their flowers—nannies won't be letting kids anywhere near bees."

"A living flowering fence, with guardian bees—beautiful," Hilaria smiles, they strolling towards the bushes. "Can already see bees mobbing the flowers, never seen this many in Manhattan, it's almost like there's a hive—those flowers must be overflowing with nectar."

"Honeydoll, you're the flower with the nectar I live for and there's a vacant bench so let's grab it," he says, seizing her wrist and quickening their pace.

Chapter Three

Our couple are on the new bench, closer to the southern border of Tudor City Greens, separated from the children by the high row of bushes and over thirty yards—in the sun instead of shade, the wide stump of one of Superstorm Sandy's victims a couple yards behind them. "OK, sweetie," Hilaria says, slinging her leg across Alex's lap again, "I'm dying to hear every minutest detail of your exploit and to help that happen am zipping my lips—hopefully no more distractions." Joining her thumb to forefinger, she slides them across her lips.

"With pleasure," Alex responds, kissing her cheek. "Although the prank's technically over and done, it won't be wholly out of my system until I tell you about it. So last Wednesday was a slow day, few people in the office past six. I was anxious in Bryant Park, seeking to calm myself with yoga on the lawn, between around 6:15 and 7:45. At the approach of eight I'm back in the office, half-hoping a situation outside my control, such as anyone lingering near the creep's office, will force me to postpone revenge while also eager to be done with it. Are there butterflies in my stomach? Ha! There's grinding heat and dread in my stomach, a swarm of bees! This isn't high school shenanigans, as with the bully—I'm an adult and this is my living, it's a tightknit industry and I could be blacklisted via word of mouth. But at the same time that I'm uneasy I'm slipping into *magical* autopilot mode, where blind courage is shoving self-preservation considerations aside, sweeping sparkling exhilaration up my spine. I do indeed owe the creep a backhanded thank you, because he's jolted me from boredom at work into fulfilling action—I'm imperiling my job without being able to stop myself.

"The moment for action arrives and I empty the bottle of glue into the mix in the cereal box, place the latter in a shopping bag—the bag's packed with wadded newspaper to ensure the box remains upright. Then I'm advancing to the center of the agency, where my target's office is located. My hyper-alertness, sense of being surrounded by danger—the fact I'm engaged in a project that could alter my life for the worse... Well, it's flat out *beautiful*! The agency as good as changes into a primeval forest, rife with mystery and threat—its features, desks and the pathways between them, are startlingly clear and close while also blurry and distant—the walls are hemming me in at the same time they're flying into the distance; and don't ask me to explain how contrary perceptions are happening simultaneously, although I'll opine it's on account of heightened caution. Who knows who might appear at the wrong moment, catch me in the act? Chance could easily swing against me! The carpet all but silences footfalls, it'll be tough to hear anyone's approach, so I'm listening as intently as if there's a tiger loose—my eyes are peeled every which way, I keep turning to check if anyone's at my back—I'd like to think I'll be able to pick up electric pulsations of presence, as when it's not necessary to see with eyes to realize someone's near, but it's not a foolproof ability. All seems to be happening in slow-motion, although I'm moving swiftly.

"As mentally rehearsed innumerable times I cut to the left and approach the creep's office while up against the wall, thereby avoiding most of the sweep (as noted in the facilities room) of the camera covering the area, which doesn't include the higher surfaces of the walls: only my legs, from mid-thigh down, will be recorded. I'm also wearing red sneakers, swapped for my customary shoes under my desk minutes ago, to further avert suspicion should camera archives be consulted—it's the first time I've worn red sneakers in my life. And I've padded my jeans, shoved newspaper up inside them from below, to appear less slender—as for jeans, they're ubiquitous at the agency. When close to the creep's office I pause, as there's a camera directly above me that monitors the area which includes the front of his office: as long as I'm pressed to the wall I'm outside its range. I blind the camera with a cotton ball held in place by a thin strip of tape (Cotton so adhesive residue isn't smudging the lens afterwards, providing an unwelcome clue in event of an investigation.), then dart to his *locked* door. Once there I extract the cereal box from the bag, press the long sides at its top together, and slip the flattened top under the door until it's protruding a few inches inside his office. After glancing about and listening one last time, ascertaining the coast's as clear as it'll ever be, I jump on the box and propel its contents into his office—the glass walls allow me to discern the extent of the splash, which discolors a sizeable area of the carpet, soaks the front of his desk, flies onto its top—highly gratifying. But I don't linger to gloat, instantly pick up the spent box and return it to the shopping bag, am quickly under the camera again, removing the cotton. The interval between taping the cotton over the camera and removing it isn't above twenty-five seconds, I know this because I timed myself when rehearsing with an empty cereal box at home, executing the identical tasks at an identical distance. After retracing my steps along the wall I duck behind a yard-wide support pillar, then make a beeline for the corridor, about three yards distant, that leads to the rear exit.

"Once in the stairwell I swap the red sneakers for my other shoes, also in the shopping bag, and remove the padding from my jeans—as the stairwell's a common area of the building, landlord property, it's free of my employer's cameras. I pause a couple times while descending the stairs—set the bag down, punch at the air while hyperventilating to dissipate tension, steady my nerves. When I exit the stairwell I'm about four yards from the building's rear security desk and, as customary, bid the guards goodnight. I stop at the kiosk, situated midway between the guards and the building's exit, and purchase a pack of batteries to reinforce appearance of unconcern. Unexpectedly, I'm as if adrift in a gentle eddy of calm—similar to soaking in a hot tub after skiing all day—as I stroll towards the bustle of outside, visible through the glass doors at hallway's end.

"Once on the sidewalk I'm reflecting upon what I've done as if it's happened in a dream from which I've been jolted awake, feeling like an animal must feel when released into wilderness after prolonged confinement in a cage. What relief in knowing the deed, anticipated—seemingly united with my heartbeat—for weeks, is behind me! Manhattan's bustle and noise are fading and I'm gazing up at the open spaces between the building tops, offering myself to the dimensionless sky—awareness that earthly concerns are less than a mirage when contrasted with the vastness of the universe is welling within me. It's not that I've never experienced the sensation of falling upwards into the sky and laughed at earthly restrictions, I do so frequently, but in this instance I have a livelihood-imperiling act to set it in relief, doubly electrify me. It's as if I'm already a different person than the one who befouled the dolt's office—a seeming infinity of moments separates me from taping the cotton to the camera and jumping on the cereal box. Unable to endure enclosed spaces—the subway or a cab—I head for Central Park, where I climb rock outcroppings, run around in the Ramble, splash in The Lake's shallows, lie on my back on the lawn laughing. Upon arriving home I fall onto my bed, twist and shout and laugh louder. I sleep for nearly half a day."

"Goodness gracious!" Hilaria exclaims, stroking Alex's temples, gazing lovingly into his eyes. "Honey, I understand why you felt you needed to swat the creep down, settle that score, but aren't sure I ought to approve, even if I couldn't be prouder. And researching camera directions, blinding one with cotton?—wearing red sneakers, padding your pants, to throw off anyone checking video archives? I'm dating a *spy*! Would love to have seen the creep's face when he saw the mess in the morning, was trying to figure out how it got there through a locked door! Then again, given what's at stake if you're caught I shouldn't be thinking such things, going there... Ha! As you can see, Alex, I'm somewhat divided in my opinion of your exploit—admiration's tangling with worry."

"Hilaria, I'll never pretend it was a wise thing to do," he responds, stroking her temples in turn. "I appreciate that you're introducing a note of caution into the equation, being sincere and sensible as always—you're mirroring my opinion. Obviously I shouldn't be gambling with my living because a pathetic still-living-with-mommy loser misbehaved—if I'm caught he wins and I come up empty big time. I might joke about the slacking I get away with, but I've worked hard at honing my act so I can get away with it. On paper my job's not a cushy job, it comes off as technical and demanding, like one will be pestered nonstop, but I've turned it into a cushy job for me."

"Well, *duh*!" she laughs, placing her tote in the strategic location on his knees again, jiggling her leg that's on his lap. "You've wrangled a slacking job out of a job that sounds scary and I understand your urge to take more chances, and love that you do since it means we have our time together, but please be careful not to lose sight of..."

"Well aware overconfidence is poison," he breaks in, reaching his hand up her thigh inside her dress (As a reminder, the move's safe from observation when her tote, a foot and a half high and equally as wide, is on his knees.), "and always seek to guard against it, but... Jesus, a sensation of unbounded freedom, I kid you not, flooded me after I was done with the prank—perceptions so vivid it was as if I'd stepped outside my personality's boundaries, was glimpsing a fresh self, emotional shedding of skin. But of course whether I've a right, in the end, to rejoice in that freedom depends on whether I get away with the prank—the jury's still out. And, yes, it's an amusing mystery for the creep to solve: his office door was locked, I'm sure he and facilities have the only keys, but a foul liquid was sprayed all over anyway. He'll be twisting in the wind and tormented, serves him right."

"OK, so the creep's too mentally impoverished to figure it out on his own but what if he has help? You say the jury's still out and that worries me. Any blanket-email reprimands from administration, anonymity-guaranteed invites to provide information, threats of doubling down on strictness? I'm thinking of high school here but have a feeling corporate methods of fishing for rats aren't much different."

"Spot on, darling—there are many high school parallels. Once we had to gather for a lecture about billing because a handful of imbeciles weren't doing it with regularity, routinely missing end-of-quarter deadlines. Reminded me of high school assemblies when the whole school had to listen to tedious rubbish simply because one kid did something, such as filch blasting caps from a construction site located in the district. Like, it didn't even happen on school property."

"Woo hoo!" she gleefully cries, grasping the nape of his neck. "Was my choirboy responsible for that high school assembly?"

"Sorry, I can't claim the glory of swiping the blasting caps, that belongs to Sal, I'll forever be in awe of the deed! Anyway, there's been no mention of my wee bit of mischief, which I daresay's a good sign. Once a bottle of wine vanished from someone's desk and there was communication from HR straight off, disbelief and outrage in the tone; and another time the head guy was incensed because someone turned a garbage can upside down and used it as a seat in a conference room—he included two photos in his email."

"So those offences were pounced on but there's been no mention of yours, even though it's more egregious! Good sign!"

"So far so good but what most keeps me guessing, could do me in, is that after I removed the cotton ball from the camera and backtracked along the wall my senses half abandoned me—I wasn't listening or looking around anymore—only seeing straight ahead, single-mindedly intent on vanishing down the stairwell. It was only a few seconds but maybe chance was against me and someone saw."

"So what's in your favor is the creep's so disliked it's unlikely anyone will gratuitously tattle, and what's against you is a witness could also be a suspect, since few people were there. A witness might mention spotting you if self-preservation's in the picture."

"And I wouldn't blame them one bit, don't want anyone accused in my place. But another reason for squealing on me is some people are directly benefiting from the account connected to the creep, apart from the agency as a whole—doesn't matter how much they detest him on a personal level so long as they're raking in bonus cash. If one of them saw me I might wind up being ratted out."

"All the same, Alex, I'd say the odds are against a rat at this point—rats usually can't wait to pounce, glory in their pseudo version of power. I'm unfortunately familiar with the type."

"Usually, but no guarantee—I'm not congratulating myself on being free and clear just yet, and that's OK by me since feeling like I might be hunted down, wondering if my days at the agency are numbered, isn't wholly bad—the office hasn't reverted to being boring and that's a gift. And, hey, if I'm found out and fired I'll head straight for Bethesda Fountain, watch the water shoot up, spread into spray and swirl earthwards, the mist sparkling—will gaze across The Lake's rippling water, reflect upon the mutability of life, offer thanks for the unemployment benefits—six months of semi-paid *vacation*."

"But what about blacklisting? It's dreadful that they..."

"Sorry, Hilaria—didn't mean to exaggerate the blacklisting thing," he breaks in. "In the end, blacklisting's more of a rumor and bluff calculated to keep people in line than a real situation, I wouldn't be surprised if HR departments dreamed it up. It *is* a tightknit industry and word of mouth's rampant, but agencies can be willing to overlook indiscretions committed elsewhere—competition for proven talent's fierce, money's to be made, and everyone knows I execute assignments quickly and clients never kick back my work."; then, catching the mildly alarmed look in her eye, "Hilaria, don't worry! I'm not trying to act like it doesn't matter if I'm caught! I'm pleased to have pranked the creep, flipped the bird at his nepotism-enabled parasitism, but a repeat would be as stupid as prodding a rattlesnake nest, or allowing black widow spiders to crawl across my hand."

"Thank goodness," she responds, bouncing her leg up and down on his lap again. "I don't want you being too rash for your own good, going off on a prank-craze because it's intoxicating to feel like an animal freed from a cage. Choirboy dissimulation only goes so far."

"Well aware of it, angeldoll," he smiles, stroking her with greater emphasis under her dress. "But speaking of being too rash for one's own good, here we are in broad daylight, only shielded from view on this side *(He glances towards the row of bushes.)*, and you're a married woman. Your spouse might be occupied but who's to say someone who knows who you are doesn't happen by and see you with me and snap a picture and post it to social media—public opinion's newest battering ram? Manhattan's population-dense but its popular places are small area-wise, I run into neighbors and coworkers all the time. Maybe we ought to be more mindful of *your* safety, head to the hotel. If a coworker sees us I'll likely be the talk of the office and my goody-good act will be shot to hell—I'll cease to be as under the radar, won't be able to get away with as much—but it's hardly world shattering, I'll adapt. My situation's a joke compared to the risk you're running."

"I beg to differ, Alex," she responds, slipping a hand up under his shirt again, stroking his midriff and chest. "Being together in public like a regular couple, simply sitting or strolling around, is too much of a sanity-sustaining treat to pass up. I know you're proud to be with me—your manner screams it—and I'm proud to be with you, I'm not going to worry if anyone who knows me happens by and that's that! A nightly ritual of sorts is I pray to escape being found out by husband and I'm starting to wonder why, since being found out might be for the best. If there's a divorce, then... Well, maybe that's precisely what I need! I'm not helpless, I made a good living before, can do so again. Experienced yoga and fitness instructors are in demand—my pedigree, if I say so myself, places me in a rarified zone. No divorce will get me blacklisted, probably the contrary—not only is my situation less precarious than you think, it might be less so than yours."

"Granted, I'm the one in corporate bondage but apart from the office I'm free, don't need to fake emotional attachment—the acting I do's nothing compared to yours. But you're mentioning..."

"Yes, I might be closer to taking the plunge than you think," Hilaria breaks in whispering, her lips at his ear. "Quality of life, time spent in bliss, is infinitely more precious than the empty ego-massage of status—the need to lord it over others via society-conferred entitlement, with no foundation in nature, is mental disease. Life wouldn't be worth living if I stopped seeing you, Alex, so what's the logical course of action? Why tread water in a dead marriage?"

"Darling, this is amazing news—the closer you are to taking the plunge the better," Alex says, withdrawing his hand from under her dress, framing her face with his palms. "A monumental life-change and I couldn't be more ready for you to move in with me—say the word and it's open sesame, my home belongs to you. I want to fall into the heavenly healing light of your eyes every day."

"So close yet maddeningly far! I'm dead set psychologically but practical implementation's a brick wall; for one thing, there's the daunting legality."; then, perceiving he's about to respond, placing a finger on his lips, "Sweetie, please let me continue—I want to say this. There's the cliché about adultery making some marriages possible but I don't want to live a lie. It's become *essential* to recall our time together when we're apart—you're my cure-all for suffocation. You've given me more time to give my marriage a fair chance, see if it'll work—without you it might've been over months ago. Maybe I'm lazy—it's too easy to succumb to inertia when someone simply ignores you. But a husband ought to know a wife needs attention, and maybe I... OK, enough! I'm not going to wonder if I'm good or bad, or bewail my lot when hordes of women would kill to be in my place. Alex, please assure me everything's kosher at work and you won't be shown the door."

"Hilaria, I don't feel I'm deluded when I say if it wasn't for the inescapable circumstance of being one of the very few people at the office afterhours on Wednesday I'd be just about the least likely candidate in the drenching of the dolt's office. I'm a thoroughgoing bore, right? A database geek averse to fun! At any rate, I do my best to reinforce the perception—avoid agency-sponsored outings, act staid and restrained at all times, frown if anyone talks about hitting bars after work—I don't even want to be caught smiling. I measure my freedom by the amount of misperception with which my coworkers view me, which is a *huge* amount—I've worked hard to create my phantom personality and am proud of it, as it pays incandescent dividends, such as..." Trailing off, he kisses her.

"So, Alex," Hilaria smiles once their lips part, "have I told you lately how much your ability to emotionally be in two places at once—or, to phrase it another way: doubleness and duplicity—stirs me? How little your workmates know! Emotionally speaking, you're running wild in untrammeled wilderness, laughing at civilization, and they've no idea, which is just so positively *cute*!"

"And you're an untamed tigress in a Bergdorf dress—quintessential uptown decorum and sophistication, manners and grace far superior to finishing school cookie-cutter versions, while being as unapologetically lustful for action as any bar wench. But, sorry! What I *really* mean is most bar wenches would blush at the thought of getting as wild as you love to do, and that's *my* Paradise!"

"Are you sure you're not projecting fantasy—indulging in selective perception, only seeing what you want to see?" she teases, swatting his shoulder. "I blush all the time and it's not always an act. My dirty little secret, which I'm proud of, is I'm a lady at heart, knock-down-drag-out dance competitions in the past or not, and rivalry at the studios. We dancers lock arms and look for all the world like we're best friends forever in the group shots and sometimes want to swat our neighbor to the floor. But that's contradictory, isn't it? Hahaha!"

"Yup, you've owned up to being a tigress despite yourself, involuntary admissions reinforce the truth—the bit about swatting a rival's especially revealing, love it! *(Here he lifts her hair high, spills it over his face.)* And who's the darling who fearlessly pushes frolic-in-public boundaries, doesn't hesitate to do the splits on my lap even though it once riled up an authentic loony, yelling about 'visual assault' and 'temptation horror' and something about Sodom?"

"Sorry for the let-down, sweetness *(She playfully squeezes his arm.)*, but I'd sooner die than swat a fellow dancer for real. It was an in-joke on one of our tours, we exchanging love-tap slaps, acting like bratty schoolgirls on purpose, rallying around the game—surefire release of tension, lifting of spirits, before hitting the stage. As for the splits, I've done them since preschool gymnastics, no big deal—conditioning from an early age renders them easy-peasy. And you keep us safe in public, always on your toes. If a drunk or loony or other unkind person pesters us, so what? You handle it and protect us, I never need to feel like I'm fearless. I'm a spoiled sheltered kitten, no tiger—meow, meow!" She's nibbling his ear.

"We agree you're a feline and that's enough," he laughs, reaching up her thigh under her dress again, toying with the top of her stocking—lifting it, letting go.

"Ooooo, baby! Ticklish tiny stocking thwacks!" she giggles, pitching against him, gripping his lap tighter with her leg. "And thank you, as always, for policing my hemline, pulling it down when it rides up—I do *so* wish to remain socially acceptable, to all appearances a proper lady, while you're feeling me up."

"Speaking of policing, I'm overdue for a check-in," Alex says, consulting his work-phone with his left hand, his right hand continuing to have a good time on her thigh; then, upon perusing the email, "Bloody hell! An assignment from out of nowhere, zilch advance notice—it's eight minutes old, a bunch of people are cc'd—someone's asking for an ETA, I don't blame them! I'm an idiot!" He withdraws his hand from under her dress, reaches for his laptop bag.

"I know the drill, ever your good soldier—hup two!" she responds, saluting and removing her tote from his knees and leg from his lap, resettling herself with knees pressed together, smoothing the rumples in her dress. "Are we in danger?"

"No, but considering what I get away with on the agency's dime it's advisable to maintain my reputation for executing assignments quickly, plus—here's *my* dirty little secret—I have a nasty work-ethic streak in me. Truth be told, I cringe at the thought of letting coworkers down, since they're mostly very nice people who mind their own business and leave me alone—no one questions my time spent outside the office during working hours, as they well could, and I'm grateful. No one even texted about this assignment and I wish they would more often—I've told them to not hesitate. I hate that this team will be waiting eight minutes longer than they should have to for me to finish." He's logged into his laptop.

"And I'm *super* grateful no one questions your time spent outside the office, am all for nice people getting their work done—we all win. I supposed the corporate world was oppressive, employees remorselessly monitored and shoved around, and it turns out some of it's friendly. Going to watch you work your magic *(She tilts a hand towards the laptop.)*, if that's OK! I want to see what it is you do that gets people to leave you alone, gives us windfalls of playtime."

"Sure thing," he responds, accessing the required database. Then he drags the PDF he needs for reference from the agency's server onto his desktop and copies it. Instants later he's clicking about on pages in the database, opening comment-fields, cutting and pasting information from his copy of the PDF into the fields—cutting's a best practice means of keeping track of what needs to be done, neither omitting nor unnecessarily duplicating pertinent information.

"My goodness, you're fast—this is *fun*!" Hilaria declares, leaning in closer, her hair spilling down his chest. "Swarms of windows appearing and disappearing, digital ballet, and while snuggling! Said it before and I'll say it again: never knew the corporate world was anywhere near to being open sesame to a good time."

"Well, it's fun when you're with me," he smiles, briefly sliding a hand from her waist to her knee. Inside of fifteen minutes he's done, notifies those concerned as follows: "The linking's finished, item's been submitted for QC to Dina," and claps the laptop shut. "So that's what I do, darling—the *only* thing I do, there are no other responsibilities—a gimmick and scam if there ever was one, and I know I'm very fortunate to be benefitting from it. I'll bill the client an hour and a half for this and if no other work comes in will grab more billing codes off today's hot sheets—lists that conveniently facilitate padding of billing, even if it's the opposite of their stated intent. Management, and the finance department, surreptitiously approves—I'd be scrutinized if I failed to be one hundred percent billable."

"The choirboy look might be a smokescreen but you also deliver on what people expect from choirboys. I couldn't explain what you did if my life depended on it but you're clearly an expert, the agency's lucky to have you. The assignment was done fast and certainly perfectly, so where's the harm if we're hooking up on company time, especially since you're always one hundred percent billable?"

"Hilaria, I could teach you how to do this stuff in half an hour—it's the ultimate slacking enabler, looks intimidating but is thoroughly mindless. It's nuts how coworkers are mystified by my job when I could've done most of it in the fourth grade, the only real requirement's ability to focus on details—big deal, the details are mostly idiotic repetition. The real kicker is people dread when I go on vacation—I thank the freelancers who botch jobs and annoy clients when I'm gone and make me look good, help keep the scam going—I ought to gift those freelancers with gift cards."; then, kissing her cheek, "OK, enough! The best part of my gimmick of a job is it allows us to hook up during your safe window."

"Without which, as I can't say enough, I would've likely fled my marriage by now," she responds, returning his kiss. "We can talk about pranks and duplicity, me putting one over on husband and the society people, but who cares? The drama of leading a double-life—being a decorous social-asset on the one hand, an adulteress (Don't you just *love* that word?) on the other—means nothing to me. It's the positivity that counts—our time together enables me to thrive."

"You're my Godsend, Hilaria," Alex says quietly, thrilling to the sweetness-brimming intentness of her gaze. "You energize me, make me bolder and brighter, outright irradiate existence. You're off the charts amazing and who would've thought...?" He trails off, betraying mild uncertainty.

"Thought what?" she inquires tenderly. "Please tell me."

"Hilaria, sometimes I feel you're out of my league, being so crazy gorgeous and fit and perpetually cheerful, not to mention well-off, and with your dancer and modelling history and multitude of ex-students who adore you, are fans of you, and wish you were still teaching, as is clear on your secret pseudonymous Facebook, that your husband's unaware of. You could have any man alive."

"Sweetie, surely you're kidding—the out of your league thing's insane," she whispers, placing a finger over his lips. "Sometimes I wonder why you're bothering with a disillusioned older married woman when you could be cavorting with surfer- and ski-girls—sports you're a maniac at and I've never attempted. As for being well-off, that's husband's property, not mine—nothing in his place belongs to me except my wardrobe and laptop, a handful of keepsakes. And of course I get oodles of envious looks from other women when I'm with you. Earlier there was the blond schoolgirl in the lemon yellow dress, probably an aerobics addict (as an instructor, I can spot them), salivating at the sight of you playing with my hair, and then sort of abstractedly flicking her hair like she couldn't help it—an auto-response, attempt to attract your attention. I'm sure you noticed."

"You're the woman of my wildest dreams, Hilaria, so why would I notice? And right back at you: that filthy rich guy over there *(He inclines his head towards a mid-fortyish man seated on a bench a few yards away, on the opposite side of the main walkway.)* feels it's a sorry shame you're with a guy who can't afford to helicopter you to the Hamptons, can't stop bringing his eyes back to you after looking away—he wants to shake you off, since we're together, but can't manage to do it and he isn't looking at other women, is only spellbound by you. As for women giving you envious looks it's because they'd kill to be as radiant as you, has nothing to do with me—at most, they're only incidentally aware of me."

"That's nonsense and you know it, Alex," she says, lightly swatting his shoulder. "Soon as we're together a contest starts between me and other women—some are out to draw your eyes from me to them, often quite blatantly, and I know you're too perceptive not to...."

"Doesn't matter—they don't exist to me, I don't care," he cuts in, clasping her hand. "You're my end-all-and-be-all ideal miraculous woman and that's that!"

"And you're my gift from the Gods, prayers at last answered! As for that pompous dolt over there who'd like to *buy* me, take me to his penthouse or whatever... Pah! I've already been bought and once is too much! Who knows how long I'm staying married? I'm scattered and wan and jittery from inattention and the esteemed surgeon has no idea—I'm searching the Internet for herbal sedatives in the dead of night and he has no idea—I'm crying in the bathroom and he has no idea—I'm screaming in my bloodstream to my bones and he has no idea. What I mean is that was my life *before* we met and you rescued me! Now I get life-sustaining assignations with you, hotel heaven, but maybe I ought to nix the marriage and be an instructor again—I was happy every hour then. And, hey, come to think of it I'm an *unwilling* slacker! I'd much rather teach than put on a surgeon's privileged wife act and so what if a meddler in husband's world sees us and snaps a picture and posts it? Yes, let a meddler come—let his *mother* come—and see me *now*!" she outright-shouts, kissing him for all she's worth.

"Take her home!" is shortly heard from a few yards away. A half dozen Yankees fans, wearing Jeter and Mo and Bernie numbers and pumped for today's game, are passing by. The man who's yelled isn't chiding—there's admiration in his tone. From the corner of his eye, as he continues kissing Hilaria, Alex perceives the men are smiling with approval while continuing on their merry way. "A good omen, I'd say—signal from on high," he laughs, interrupting their kissing. "I think we ought to heed the advice, our room's waiting."

"That wise man read my mind," Hilaria smiles, springing to her feet and slinging her tote over her shoulder. "But of course home's all too fleeting in my case—our hotel rooms are my true home, the other one's... Well, forget negativity—let's go!" Seizing Alex's wrist, she pulls him from the bench.

Chapter Four

"Our town turns otherworldly when I'm with you, angeldoll," Alex observes as they approach Grand Central Station on 42nd Street's north side, arms about each other's waists as they lean into one another, playfully sway side to side in their stride. "The Park Avenue Viaduct *(He gestures towards Pershing Square.)* is a fairytale bridge, exotic and ancient and strange—sunlight swirly blurry in the curlicue latticework, spinning the air alive—suggestive of lapping waves, ocean spray, dawn mist. Darling, I firmly believe love's a psychedelic happening—emotional hallucinogens. Senses accelerate, scenery twists and brightens and blurs, blood shimmers and surges, time warps—minutes flick by quick as seconds."

"Time definitely deliciously warps in love-elation—seems like seconds since you arrived at the Greens, wondrous whirl of buoyancy! Past and future go *Poof!* when I'm with you, sweetie—there's only a vibrant *now*. Civilization invented measurement of time, the better to enslave and prey upon and exploit us."

"What's more insane than sectioning off the day, stipulating what's to be done when? Civilization's our fall from grace, expulsion from Paradise."

"Yes! Always important to bring that up, since we enable each other to overcome and laugh about it!" Hilaria smiles, rubbing against him. "And hallucinogens? That too! Of course seeing you's perception- and mind-expanding, a trip to an alternate sensory-intense world—love's the only drug I love."

"I'm feeling *silvery*—seemingly floating over the sidewalk! What do I mean by 'silvery'? Ha! Damned if I know—it just popped into my head. Maybe it's because silver's the sheen of surf in sunlight, sparkle of mist and wave-froth, or reminds me of stepping out of a club around noon to salute the sun after dancing all night—the shivery electricity, thrilling jolt. Do you remember when...?"

"I'll remember our first night into day forever," Hilaria cuts in. "Stepping into daylight after you danced me blurry, shock of the sun... Feeling silvery's perfect terminology, all the energization—bustling daytime people were mirages."

"Speaking of bustling people, I vote for going to a less crowded place, trading 42nd Street for 41st—doing the doorway thing. I'm *lusting* for it, darling!"

"Yay!" Hilaria exclaims, two-handedly seizing Alex's arm—skipping alongside him like a little girl, slinging her hair about, rolling her tongue about her lips—as he steers her towards the crosswalk under the viaduct, between Grand Central's main entrance and Pershing Square Cafe. When the traffic light flips green in their favor our couple cross to 42nd Street's south side and thence to 41st Street, where they turn right, continuing west. Before they've travelled a third of the block Alex tilts his head towards a doorway and Hilaria, giggling, pulls him within, backing up against the white brick wall—lifts herself on tiptoes, stretches to full height, flings her hair behind her shoulders, thrusts out her chest.

"Your sky-wide eyes and waterfalling hair and all-encompassing delectableness, fetchingness to die for, are my world," he smiles, sliding his hands up her legs under her dress in back, she happily wiggling.

"We're in America's loudest town and I'm deaf to all but your voice-candy, Alex! Your voice instills equanimity and courage—constraint's illusion, my sham marriage ceases to be real."; then, after nudging him with a knee, darting him the look he knows well and adores more, "Clear for jump and clench!" Stepping forward to avoid scraping her back on the wall, she seizes his shoulders and jumps—wraps her legs about his waist as he, gripping her behind, lifts her. "And clear for trap and smush!" she continues, framing his face with quivering fingers, licking his lips, kissing him. Instants later he's pressing her to the wall.

Perhaps a split-minute thereafter Alex hears the building's door open, footfalls of someone exiting—sees by the aspect of Hilaria's gaze she's in vigilant cat mode, ascertaining whether the person's apt to turn troublesome. The footfalls vanish and Hilaria's eyes soften: all is well. As an aside, we'll mention our couple's love of doorway adventures has inspired a vocabulary: "Doorway Thing," "Jump and Clench," "Trap and Smush," and "Vigilant Cat Mode," are part of it, as are, "Precariousness Kick," "Hiding-In-Plain-Sight Stimulation," "Sidewalk Subversion," and "Street Oasis," as well as numerous code-phrases and -gestures. "A minimum of one doorway thing per assignation regardless of difficulty, no excuses," is a rule our couple have imposed on themselves, love to obey.

"Oh, yeah!" Alex exclaims once they cease kissing and he's easing Hilaria's feet to the pavement, savoring the downward slide of her body. "Hiding-in-plain-sight stimulation's always as fresh as our first time, stirring as high surf, and sorry for analyzing, but... Hell, it's like I'm a grade school brat on the playground again, racing to hidden places to get away with stuff, and... Ha, in grade school it was stressed adulthood would be a serious challenge and we'd need to behave or suffer dire consequences, fail to be successful, wind up in the gutter, and here we are! We're in plain view on the sidewalk one moment, and the next... I mean, it's wildly against what we've been taught! We duck into a doorway, we're not really out of sight but it's as if we are—a doorway's only an indentation in a building, rarely over a couple yards deep, and numerous people are passing by, but it's a refuge anyway, where we're free to go a great deal further with fun—emotions intensify in the marriage of precariousness and daring. How magical is that?"

"Alex, doorways are our special altar, where we indulge in life-elevating subversion. When thrust back into the putting-on-a-show-despite-a-dead-marriage world, I sustain myself with recollections of our doorway doings—elevation surging back to me, whirling me, during forced idleness, needling unrest, in pseudo home, or while attending dreary obligatory functions. The doorway thing's as uplifting as when the sun shafts through grey clouds, gloom flipping to jubilation, and pointing that out's healthy and supportive, so please no apologies for analysis! Our doorways are hallowed ground, our religion and sacred rites."

"Every moment with you's on hallowed ground," he responds, hugging her anew; then, after she nods towards her chest—pulls her hair forward and spills it down, wraps her arms about his shoulders, to provide cover, "I'm in a Paradise-place with you, sweetheart—no boundaries—no second-guessing—mundane things vanish." He's cupping her breasts with his palms, caressing—nothing apparent to others, they'd need to be near enough to rub shoulders to see. Our couple are practiced in the move, having confirmed indiscernibility from all angles in front of mirrors—they rehearse their doorway maneuvers in hotel rooms.

"Laps of the Gods, Alex, and what's wildest about the doorway thing is it's merely whetting of appetite, even if I'm turning-inside-out-tingling to my toes! And here's another treat for us." Stepping from his embrace and turning her back to him, brushing her hair forward over a shoulder and exposing her neck, she reaches high as she's able up the wall with one hand while yanking her dress tight against her rear with the other. "See panty lines, sweetie? If not, I'll fix! I'll never get enough of your heavenly eye-stab on me, delving *so* deep!"

"Seeing heavenly clear, my dear—moments like these make me infinitely grateful I'm a man! If you could suspect what it's like to be a man admiring your miracle-of-creation body snug in your dress—silk clinging tight as you stretch taut—you might want to switch sexes to experience the euphoria, float outside your skin! You're my wildest playground, as close to Nirvana as I'll ever get."

"And it's moments like these that make me infinitely grateful the Fates flipped the dial in my favor and made me a woman," she giggles, turning to face him again, shaking her hair to behind her shoulders, yanking her dress backwards to outline her legs—raising herself up and down on tiptoes and circling her shoulders backwards, breasts rising and falling. "If you could suspect what it's like to shimmer under the influence of the eye-feel of a man like you, be stared transparent, you might want to become a woman to experience it—assuredly Nirvana when you beam your energy under my skin!"

"But I *do* shimmer under the influence of your eye-feel, turn inside out straight up my spine! And, yes, I know I started the sex-comparison stuff—silly of me considering that we exchange our worlds."

"We sure do, Alex—each rendezvous brings me closer to turning into you! But of course there are individual identities to be maintained, as for instance..."

"As for instance, honeydoll," he cuts in laughing, "since I'm the male I'm expected to be aggressive and bend you to my will, take whatever I please whenever I please, right? And so..."

"So be a big bad man for me, show me stern action, instead of talking about it!" she counter interrupts, playfully rubbing her forehead against his while tapping his breastbone. "*Prove* to me I'm your toy!"

"Ha! We might exchange our worlds but in the end I can't imagine being anyone besides a man," he says, pressing her to the wall again. "I'm never happier than when grabbing yoga-doll tush!"

"Please take whatever you please whenever you please, Alex—it's an open invitation forever, my fervent hope! My names are 'Compliance,' 'Acquiescence,' and 'Surrender'!" Widening her stance and thrusting her pelvis forward, she grasps one of his hands, guides it up and front and center inside her dress.

"I live to comply and what a nice coincidence that our wishes are identical, and that your dress enables success," he smiles, stroking the front of her panties as she pulls the pleats of her dress forward on each side of them, veiling their fun.

"It's essential to adhere to the conservative dress codes of husband's world, and likewise to select dresses that facilitate our frolic—what a nice coincidence that long hemlines and abundant pleats pull the wool over eyes in both worlds. Frolic-facilitating fashion, dressing to dupe, pays delicious dividends and I can't wait to be able to yell, 'Take me!' in our hotel room and for you to follow through! (*She thrusts forward more insistently, licks the side of his neck that's not facing the sidewalk.*) But I *always* say that, don't I? The doorway thing's energy infusion, turning me tingling antsy, and when... (*Here she abruptly switches topic and raises her voice, jerks her eyes at her shoulder.*) Did you get all the dust?"

"Pretty sure I did," Alex responds with like raised voice, withdrawing his hands from under her dress, heeding their alert. (*Did you get all the dust?* means an unfriendly observer's close.) Seconds later Hilaria's stepped forward from the wall and he's vigorously rubbing his hands together a couple feet from her, mimicking getting rid of dust. "Crazy how dust clings, almost as if it has glue in it."

"Clings insanely—dust on me's icky!" Hilaria says, shivering with feigned revulsion; then, upon craning her neck, examining the back of her dress, "Yeah, all gone, thank you! Not even sure how it got there, which is scary!"

"Turn around again, angel—want to make sure every trace of dust is gone," he says. Hilaria presents her back to him.

Our couple are putting on the act because a forty-something couple, obviously tourists, have come to a dead stop on the sidewalk to glare and scowl. Then the woman loudly announces to her companion, "I don't like this city, everyone's rude and acts like animals."; then, peeved that our couple are declining to respond, "You should be ashamed. Hugging like that in public and not paying attention to who might see you doing it is indecent and it wouldn't happen where I'm from."

"No reason to care what mean-spirted suburban creeps think, it's not like they'll ever have half a brain or a clue what decency is," Hilaria says rather casually to Alex; then without speaking another word and steadying her eyes on the woman, she kicks higher than her eyes. Even though Hilaria's over three yards away, the woman flinches and backs away in alarm, at which Hilaria shrugs her shoulders. Then she grasps Alex's arm and our couple exit the doorway laughing.

"Dead silence from the twit now," Alex says as they continue west, the New York Public Library directly ahead. "That kick really shut her up—flawless fluid grace, perfect execution, beautiful to behold."

"Was only exercising, innocently limbering up—I do those kicks all the time in many places, a dancer needs to stay in shape," Hilaria smiles mischievously. "I wouldn't dream of kicking anyone but am pleased she became uneasy."

"Serves her right—poisonous people, who want others to be as miserable and hateful as they are, make *me* uneasy. But what's funny is the only thing the twit noticed was us hugging—she was staring hard at us, out to think the worst, and had no clue what was happening under your dress. That's useful feedback."

"Right! Many thanks, poisonous people, for being test subjects, providing additional evidence frolic-facilitating fashion works like a charm and we should continue fearlessly playing in public! *(She turns about to face east.)* Oh, look—they're not there anymore, guess I..."

"Scared them clean away," he breaks in grinning. "They were originally headed this way but have about-faced and skedaddled because of a harmless kick in the air that wasn't very close to them! Interesting that the other one who scolded us for public affection was the drunk—maybe the three should get together to be miserable together."

"But *we'll* always be blissful together—it's as sure as the laws of gravity," Hilaria smiles, kissing him on the cheek as they turn west again.

Chapter Five

"Tally the hours and I've been paid a tidy sum to add to my tan here," Alex laughs shortly after they step onto Bryant Park's lawn. "I once tracked the time for two weeks and it came to over fifteen hours. I swap my boxers for board shorts in the men's room then put my pants back on and come here and strip to the board shorts, looking like I'm on a beach when the agency's a couple minutes away. In theory I could easily be spotted by coworkers, but don't think I have. Most are so mindful of pursuing promotion they could be afraid to take the leap from office to park—the psychological distance must be huge for them, since the physical distance is so small. Competition for promotion's a scam I won't be falling for—the only person I compete with is myself, always out to get away with more, and you're my muse and accomplice, enabling me to scale greater heights."

"Very honored to help you improve performance in the reimbursed recreation department," Hilaria giggles, stopping to face him—sliding a hand up inside his untucked shirt, squeezing his midriff.

"Yeah, reimbursed recreation! Screw agency-authorized promotion, I promote myself! And you promote me too, honeydoll, every time we meet—the amount of time spent in bliss during my shift exceeds wildest hope." He kisses her forehead.

"We're kids too," Hilaria says, tilting her head towards the merry-go-round at their left, in the shade of the towering trees framing the lawn, where children are laughing and yelling on the rising and falling horses. "Indifferent to authority and opinions—we hardly notice what others think—and I'm *never* that way unless we're together. You carry me back to the Montair Elementary playground, four square and spinning on the bars with a sweater under my knee, parading with pink parasols under live oaks—liberate me from my age and marriage-shackles, the social status sham—I didn't know I had such playfulness left in me until we met."; then, upon thrusting a leg between his legs, seizing his shoulders, yanking him sideways and down, onto the lawn, "Thanks for the awakening!"

"Well, that's a laugh, schoolgirl brat," Alex says, rolling onto his back and sliding his hands up Hilaria's arms as she straddles him, her legs folded and pressed to each side of him, knees at his armpits. "The notion that you didn't know playfulness was in you's the most ridiculous thing I've heard all year, and certainly isn't what leapt out at me when I first laid eyes on you—first impressions are lasting impressions and you're playfulness incarnate. You awakened *me*."

"Bound in chains, trapped between tight walls, before we met, Alex," she responds, leaning in to lick his lips. "Energy wasted, turning on me at every turn, making me fretful—I was backed up on myself, all exits blocked, until you restored my flow. Like the advice, from I don't remember where, that goes something like, 'When you're feeling low sweep an arm across the sky and follow the sweep with your eyes, travel to the expanses and let low spirits go—let everything go.' You're my expanse, Alex, and life's a kick again."

"Well, I might be in slack city at work over half the time but slack city sometimes becomes boredom city, where I begin to wonder if mind-bending joy's mythology—whether I'll be stranded in what I call the zilch zone, where all's nauseatingly predictable, emotionally icy, shallow. So thank you, Hilaria, for turning *me* loose, seeing to it I won't be stranded in the zilch zone! And nice takedown, by the way—first time you've done that here. Bryant Park's always liberating and going forward it'll be more liberating—when I'm here alone I'll be reliving the sun streaming through your curls as your thighs grip me."

"I was never in Bryant Park until we met and now it's one of my special places of liberation. And as a bonus it's at our hotel's doorstep."

"Speaking of our hotel, why split up and enter it separately when you're already on top of me in the wide open, for all to see? It's time for me to stop caring if a coworker spies us entering our hotel togeth-er, broadcasts my secret activities—enough of kowtowing to caution, proudly accompanying you into our hotel's insanely overdue! Although I don't want to place you in peril, overlook..."

"Peril-schmeril," she breaks in, massaging his shoulders. "We absolutely need to enter our hotel hand in hand, like the proud madly in love couple we are—enough of splitting up and then doubling back to secretly meet in our room, as if we're criminals. We're in love—why hide it? We should be *screaming* it! And, as you've pointed out, I'm already straddling you in the wide open! And, hey, dare we do an up-skirt here? Ha! Your answer's in your eyes—no need to speak." And with that she rises to stand near his feet, then slowly strolls forward alongside him, searching inside her tote bag to appear oblivious of the view she's affording, until she's standing close enough to his head for her ankle to be brushed by wisps of his hair. "For your eyes only, sweetie—it's not like I'm lifting my hem to my tummy."

"Well, I'm too absorbed in removing a glop of sticky stuff from my palm to notice there's a view," he says, holding a hand in front of his face, picking at it with the thumb and forefinger of the other, affecting annoyance. "How can anyone know I'm looking past my hands at the glory of you? People are welcome to suspect, they'll never know for sure—all's deniable. So much fun to be flashed here!"

"And so much fun to flash you here, hide intent in plain sight—I'm too absorbed in fiddling in my tote, fretting about failing to find what I'm looking for, to know you're sneaking glances! But an interruption's about to happen—the wind will blow a napkin away and I'll need to chase it down, lest I be a litterbug." She lifts a napkin to the top of her tote and releases it, the breeze whisking it over the lawn, whereupon she springs after it. By the time Alex is on his feet to assist, Hilaria's clutching the napkin—when he reaches her she's mirthfully glancing towards their hotel, saying, "Why did I do the runaway napkin thing? Because I want to flash you where you can do what I know you want to do! Shall we go?"

"Absolutely," he replies as she, seizing his hand, tugs him towards Bryant Park's southwest corner. Upon reaching the sidewalk at the said corner they cross 6th Avenue and proceed to their hotel's entrance on 40th Street, where they arrive within two minutes.

"Glory be," Hilaria says, rump-bumping Alex as they enter the lobby. "On the surface checking in together's a nothing thing—something that ought to be taken for granted, not worth a thought—but it's a universe away from our former meetings. Farewell skulking in the shadows, fretting about being found out, and hello doing right by our love. This new freedom we've awarded ourselves, always for the taking and staring us in the face, insanely overdue... Well, I want to relish the change, linger here and let it wash over us!" She steers Alex towards the chairs along the wall, not to sit but to be out of the way of people entering and exiting.

"Right, the phantoms have been routed—goodbye constricting frame of mind, hello expansive one. Suddenly it's easy to enter our hotel together, do what we've every right to do, and it's taken too long to happen—I've been holding us back. On the one hand I thumb my nose at the agency, laugh about all the stuff I get away with, and on the other I've been afraid to be seen by a coworker with stunning you, and that's plain insane! So what if my corporate milquetoast act's compromised and I'm no longer under the radar as much? I get the work done quick without botching anything and that's all the agency really cares about, God bless the bottom line, so why have I been so afraid? Sorry for..."

"Shush—I'm not listening to you berate yourself, it's ridiculous for you to do that!" Hilaria cuts in, clapping her hands to her ears. "Seems to me you've never worried about being found out on your end—you were watching out for me because I'm married."; then, perceiving he's about to disagree, her hands still covering her ears, "Nay! I was the one worrying too much and holding us back, being the vulnerable married woman! As if having a husband who ignores me's a marriage, shame on me! Alex, you're my heaven-sent salvation and I'm not allowing you to go negative on yourself, *period*!" Uncovering her ears, she seizes and squeezes his hands.

"And don't be going negative on yourself, I'm not having it," he smiles, kissing her forehead, they still gripping hands. "Love's the law that trumps all else, births and nurtures courage in the face of those who'd like to beat us down—we've shed illusory trepidation together. Without you there's no chance I'm free of caring if I'm gossiped about. So what if I am, right? Thanks for the insight!"

"And if a neighbor were to see us having fun, alert husband and force a divorce, then... Well, maybe I'll owe that neighbor a case of champagne! Maybe what I most need's a swift kick in the rear, wake-up call to action."

"And such a matchless rear it is," he laughs, freeing one of his hands and swatting her.

"Ooooo!" she giggles, lifting his other hand over her head.

"Heaven here we come," he says, twirling her twice (lifting one of his hands high as she rolls her tongue about her lips is their double-twirl signal), after which they advance to the reception desk.

Chapter Six

"Hello again, sweet sanctuary," Hilaria says as Alex opens the door and she enters their room. (As always, it's on the fourth floor in the rear of the hotel, windows facing south onto 39th Street.) "Arriving here's the same jumping-out-of-my-skin jubilation that hits me when I step off a plane in the tropics, lushness everywhere and heat rising."

"We've entered an uplifting tropic zone, all right, temperature soaring—always a miracle to have you here away from prying eyes, unlimited frolic a given."

Hilaria's flattened her back to the entryway wall, reaching for Alex's shoulders. Just as he's about to step within her arms she darts away giggling, kicks off her shoes and leaps onto the king-sized bed, shouts, "Ha! Tricked ya! Maybe you ought to get over here pronto and put me in my place for being a brat!" She's bouncing on her knees, bunching her dress at her waist to avoid landing on it.

"Yee-haw!" Alex yells, dashing at her. But he halts midway, squares his hands on his hips, says, "Ma'am, clearly you think I'm an easily manipulated puppet, will be pouncing on you without being able to help it, and... Well, you're absolutely right and I'm glad you are, it's a Godsend to be in thrall to you! But I'm staying over here for a bit anyway, resisting your pull, because the sight of stunning you bouncing is stimulating in itself—call it disembodied feeling-you-up."

"Well, that's just *too* cute!" she frowns. "Will you kindly entertain the notion of treating me to some molestation like a man instead of babbling about disembodied stuff!" She slings a pillow at him.

"Ha! Missed! But you *did* hit the door almost at the top and that's tough to do from that distance—an athletic line drive of a throw, smooth sidearm motion—location's off, but admirable power." Seconds later he's kicking off his shoes and racing at the bed, leaping onto it; then, once he's jumping up and down, frenziedly stomping, a couple feet from her, lifting his palms to the ceiling to avoid striking it with his head, "Surf's up—mattress waves rolling in—whoosh, swoosh!"

"Whoa!" Hilaria shouts, pretending to be tossed off-balance by the rising and falling mattress—tumbling onto her side, writhing exaggeratedly—seconds later she's seizing Alex's shins from behind and tugging, whereupon he falls forward onto hands and knees. "Yay! Another fake-out! I only fell down to take you down! And take this too—I won't miss *this* time!" She starts smacking him with a pillow and soon he's also grabbed a pillow and they're exchanging blows, rolling around—using the bedspread and blankets as shields, or seeking to fling them over each other, wrap each other up in them. At one point Alex tosses a pillow and it glances off Hilaria's shoulder, just misses hitting the desk lamp a couple yards away. "If we were mature adults we'd dial it down," he laughs, "but we're not!"

"Maturity's wasting disease and fun's the cure!" she yells; then, raising her hand in a pause gesture, "Temporary truce—I have a mission." Once Alex nods in accord, settles the pillow he was about to swat her with onto his lap, she takes aim at the desk lamp with another pillow, knocks it to the floor with a direct hit. "Wrecking hotel property's thought of as a guy thing and I take exception to that."

"No guy could've walloped it more decisively, my dear—you're setting higher standards. *(He mimes tipping a cap.)* Looks like we'll be hit up with another damage assessment, hope it's as amusing as last time—I *insist* on taking the blame so I can put on the contrition act at the front desk again, instead of letting it be an impersonal credit card deduction after we're gone. Good sport to fake excessive remorse, apologize profusely for being an irresponsible lout, offer to kick in an extra $40—the desk people were dumbfounded, vehemently rejected the offer. And hotel anarchy's reasonably priced, only got charged fifty-nine dollars! Wonder what the tab will be this...? *(He breaks off, abruptly yanks his hands away from her, smacks his forehead.)* Unbelievable! Stupid overeager me, no excuse for clumsiness, very embarrassing! Sorry!" He's referring to the fact that, in his haste to remove her dress, he's torn it along a line of stitching under her left armpit.

"No such thing as overeager when you're stripping me, sweetie, and you couldn't be clumsy if your life depended on it!" she declares, dismissively glancing at the tear—soon gripping his shoulders and pulling herself tight against him, they facing one another upright on their knees. "I thrive on your hunger, pure tickle-me-inside-out-tingly, and, besides, I was fidgety, squirming—you saw that, right? The wardrobe malfunction's my fault and I'm glad! *(Noting he's about to speak, she places her right hand's fingertips over his mouth.)* Yes, glad! Because now that my dress is torn and won't be worn again just rip it to ribbons while ripping it the rest of the way off me—ultimate freedom's feeling your hunger rising! Oh, baby!"

"OK, now I'm confused, although... Well, clearly you won't be going home in your underwear, there must be backup clothes." He gestures towards her tote in the entryway.

"Yup, and not just any backup—an *identical* dress."

"Identical?"

"Mirror dresses!" she gleefully shouts, licking his lips. "I've not only anticipated the chance of a torn dress I've had shred-my-dress fantasies—thanks for making them happen."; then, upon tapping the area of the tear, "So finish what you've started, sweetie—totally maul it! I'll report home in the duplicate looking like I've been idling in museums and cafes and stores all day, absorbed in tame and lame wasting of time, just like a proper surgeon's wife's supposed to do."

"Priceless that each time we meet I discover unsuspected things about you—you're a multifaceted gem, ever refracting and combining reality in wilder ways. Sophisticated Upper East Side beauty wants her dress destroyed! A highly compelling fantasy—turns out it's also one of mine, even if I'm only finding out now."

"Am flattered you feel I keep you discovering, Alex, especially as you're constantly surprising me," she says, sliding a hand down the left side of his face while lifting her hem to her waist with the other. "I'm in awe of your revenge prank, sheer guts and spy skills."

"Spy skills of your own, Hilaria—a twin dress is genius," he says, smacking his palms onto the globes of her behind. "You've left nothing to chance, all bases covered."

"Ooooo! Hands where they belong—always appreciated!" she giggles, squirming against him. "And husband hasn't noticed I have twins of over a dozen dresses and isn't apt to but if he does my reason's ready, as in I adore them so much I want extras in case of mishap. (Fun irony, that!) Married over two years and he still doesn't know me well enough to know I'd avoid doubles like the plague if I wasn't up to adulterous rejuvenation. I'd say I'm safe."

"Maybe safe from him—not from me!" Alex announces, pulling her to the head of the bed, out of the bedding's way, after which he kicks the bedding off the mattress, flings the last pillows away—only the gleaming silver-white bottom sheet remains. "So our bed's a clean slate, yoga hottie, ripe for molestation of you—forget about safety!" Seizing her by the shoulders, he spins her onto her back.

"Don't want to be safe from you, honey!" she responds, unbuttoning his shirt and kissing his stomach. "Although that's a contradiction, since I feel extra safe, get warm and fuzzy, when you're having at me—call me yoga hottie again!" She's bouncing up and down on her back, circling her tongue about her lips, swats his knees.

"Yoga hottie honeysuckle angeldoll—all for fun and fun for all!" he yells, removing his shirt and pants, tossing them away. Then he positions himself on his knees between her shins and seizes her ankles, spreads her legs wider.

"Yumsters! Staring me transparent so sweetly, and you mean business!" she cries, extending her arms into a T, twisting her head side to side, her smile wide as a starry sky. "Rip and tear, make me bare!"

"There's a challenge here—the lacy trim looks delicate but the stitching attaching it to the primary fabric's extra reinforced, please assist," he smiles, signaling for her to raise her knees by tapping under them, whereupon he yanks at her hemline's trim, tears it off all around, flings it aside, she lowering her legs again. Then he stretches her hemline taut and takes it between his teeth, initiates a tear, pulls in opposite directions. "My oh my! Seeing the bronze of your dress rip up to the white bullseye of your panties, your immaculate legs framing the picture, is just about the most stirring thing I'll ever see! Reality's turning otherworldly, like when the..."

"Eeeee-yow! For shame, evil brat, catching me off guard like that, no fair! My goodness gracious!" Hilaria interrupts shouting, wriggling wildly and laughing as Alex tickles her stomach, her dress now rent up to her neck; then, upon seizing his hands, arresting the tickling, "I'm *so* tempted to take a selfie of us in all our glory, text it to husband—abolish the sham, shred the veil of lies, be a free woman forevermore starting *now*! Maturity's for (to use one of your favorite invective-words) *stooges*—constraint's too often synonymous with victimization."; then, upon releasing his hands, "Finish the job!"

"With all my heart, Ma'am, but the neckline's not giving—stitching's also reinforced, more than with the trim. No chance am I going to tug, risk hurting your neck, so please sit up and lift your arms so I can strip you the smooth way."

"With all my heart, Sir. *(She complies with his request.)* Love how you've ripped my dress up the middle when I could've slid it off all along. New games constantly—our fantasies alter reality."

"Nice trophy!" Alex exclaims upon pulling her dress over her head—he's twirling it aloft, it's winding into a rope. He lets go and it flies to the left, strikes the curtains forcefully enough to cause the rod to creak. "Uh, oh! You're too distracting, I wasn't paying attention—don't want to be knocking drapes down."

"Especially since we need them to spy on your office!"

"Righto," he grins, crawling across the bed to the windows that are about two and a half feet from its left side. Then he's parting the heavy silver-gray primary curtains a few inches, peering through the semitransparent secondary ones. "Looking over at my desk, watching coworkers be busy corporate bees while we're here, never gets old—the contrast is as tingle-me-dizzy as surf rushing in! That's right, people," he continues, raising a fist, "the allergic-to-fun database geek's cavorting with a yoga hottie on company time across the street and you'll never know! And, yes, I say that every time and will *always* say it! Long live rejuvenating frolic on the company's dime—maturity's for browbeaten stooges!"

(We pause to fill in our reader geography-wise: our couple's room is on the north side of 39th Street, directly across from Alex's office on the south side of 39th Street. The distance between the hotel and the office is that of the typical width of a Manhattan cross street and Alex's desk, situated near the office's high wide windows, is readily visible from their room. As a reminder, the hotel's entrance is located on its opposite side on 40th street, thereby enabling Alex to enter and exit the hotel without being seen from his office.)

"Maturity's a myth, abstract fakery, invented by society—means of swindling us into being tame, overly self-critical, and having no fun but *we* won't be falling for it!" Hilaria responds, scampering across the bed to join Alex—soon they're side by side on hands and knees. "I'll always remember our first time here, when we didn't know if these diaphanous inner curtains *(She taps them.)* were any good at keeping us from being seen from your office and you went over there and looked over here and I was holding up fingers to see if you could count them and you couldn't see my hand, or my silhouette. I was dizzy with joy, running around and dancing, when we confirmed there would be *no* invasion of our privacy!"

"Surveying our battlefield, measuring the enemy's strengths and weaknesses, was a kick in itself—it wasn't easy to maintain my unsmiling workplace demeanor, stop myself from laughing, when I was over there seeing if I could see you here. And then the additional investigations at different hours in different weather, since we're—ha ha!—extremely mindful of light-reflectivity physics! Good thing, since when it's overcast or after dark we need to turn our lights off when the main curtains are open so we can't be seen from the office, since there's not enough outside light for the inner curtains to reflect—the city's lights don't cut it."

"I'll always be very respectful of light-reflectivity physics, and nah-nah-nah, ad agency! *(Here she waggles her tongue and thumbs her nose at Alex's office.)* We'll always be able to see you while invisible to you, especially when it's bright out like now and the light's bouncing off the curtains back at you, blinding you to us! Flaunting fun in the face of the enemy's ticklish priceless—when the heavy curtains are open there's the sensation that people ought to be able to see us, some prodding of vulnerability, but we know they can't!"

"Light reflectivity's a beautiful thing, especially the play of light on your svelteness and through your hair," he says, raising himself to his knees and fluffing her hair.

"Weeeee!" she cries, falling sideways and rolling onto her back, raising herself into yoga's bridge posture. "Sweetie, I'm still not completely your birthday suit girl! Maybe you'd like to finish what you started?" She's smiling towards her panties and stockings while reaching behind her back, unfastening her brassiere.

"Seems I no longer care what's across the street!" Alex laughs, slipping her panties and stockings down her legs. "What's an ad agency? What's a job? What's institutionalized claustrophobia, wasted energy? You annihilate all that's unhealthy, honeydoll!" He tosses her panties and stockings onto the nightstand.

"What's an empty obligation, sham marriage, playacting while wilting inside? Everything negative vaporizes when you undress me!"; then, after rolling onto her stomach and rising to her knees, reaching behind Alex to grab his socks, "Hey, boyfriend! How come I'm always the first one stripped? Sexual discrimination!"

"Maybe it's because I want you naked more than you want me naked, adore you more than you adore me! Sexual discrimination? Oh, yeah, and plenty of it—I'll always want you in all your glory ultra-fast lickety-split."

"Well, I adore you *infinitely*, Alex, and you know it and I know you adore me infinitely too so enough nonsense about who adores who more!" she responds, shoving him onto his side. "And enough resisting—your socks are coming off!"

"Dream on, darling!" He yanks his feet out of reach, slides them randomly about too quick for her to get a grip.

"Dream on yourself, sweets!" she counters, flinging herself across his legs, immobilizing them—she soon pulls his socks off. "I win!"

"Wouldn't want it any other way—when you win I win!"

"Will always want lots more winning," she smiles, pulling him up to a seated position, his legs extended in front of him. Then she's on his lap, gripping his waist with her thighs—nibbling an ear, lightly pinching his nipples, tapping between his legs with her other hand, softly stroking, and while bouncing up and down, squirming, at varying speeds—she play-bites his shoulder, licks his neck.

"Have I told you lately how much fun you are, honeybunch?" He's by turns swishing her hair over his face, cupping and caressing her breasts, sliding his hands up and down her legs and midriff and back, grasping her behind, probing her moisture in front, while kissing and lip-nipping and licking wherever he's able to reach, today's favorite spot being the base of her neck, where her collarbones meet.

"It's lifesaving that I can be me with you, Alex. Husband would think me a whore if I dared have this much fun—go dead silent and freeze, indicate I should never go there again. Not that there's any wish to go there with him, desire's long dead. And your intuition's spot-on—you know my body as if it's yours."

"And you teach me new things about my body—expand my range of feeling, open up depths in me I didn't know were there."

"Hey, no fair—*I* wanted to say that about you!" she giggles, falling onto her back such that her head's half off the edge of the mattress, her hair spilling towards the floor—she's extending a leg towards the ceiling as daylight, rippling according to the motion of the diaphanous curtains through which it's passing, slides about her curves. "I've been teasing and tormenting myself all week thinking about the sweet storm, sweetie—bring it on!" She reaches for his shoulders and he eases himself onto her, she promptly wrapping her legs about his waist.

Chapter Seven

Roughly two hours later Alex is seated at Hilaria's left on the bed's edge, they facing his office across the street. As mentioned, they're able to see within his office without being seen via the diaphanous secondary curtains of their room's windows. There's been an interruption: about twenty minutes ago Alex, obliged to address a database-related question, made a point of doing so at greater than necessary length. After obtaining an instructional manual from the agency's server, which would've sufficed, he accessed the database, took several screenshots, and added commentary. Shortly after emailing the information he received the following response: "Alex, you are amazzzing! Thanks as alwaysssss!"

But to resume with the present:

"Supremely lucky this hotel's here," Alex smiles, rubbing his shoulder against Hilaria's. "Like, what are the odds of a hotel being directly across the street from my office? I've freelanced in probably over three dozen places around town, from Water Street to 54th Street and 1st Avenue to 8th Avenue, for law and financial firms back in the day and advertising more recently, without encountering the situation. I swear I noticed this hotel seconds after being shown my desk and what flashed into my head was something like, 'Golden opportunity to frolic with a cutie yards away from the agency in all freedom, no risk of detection, during my shift.' But how could I know I'd be head over heels in love with the woman I brought here? Initially it was a bucket list thing with any woman at all, simply to play a prank and laugh, thumb my nose at corporate oppression, but it's become life-altering necessity, lifted bliss to dizzy heights." He kisses her.

"Ummmmm," Hilaria murmurs once their lips part, standing to face him—thereafter seizing his shoulders, pushing him onto his back—soon brushing his face with her hair, gazing at him with love-glittered eyes, while above him on hands and knees. "Honeypie, whatever would I do without the leniency your job allows you, and your creativity, urge to push boundaries? Since we're limited to husband's working hours, we wouldn't be able to meet nearly as much if you weren't a prankster slacker. Will never tire of telling you how much it excites me that your coworkers have no clue you're brave and sharp enough to arrange play-time yards away, and you waylay suspicion with a choirboy act. I was tickled out of my skin when you first suggested coming here, told me your office was across the street—never thought I had a fetish until you brought me here and my pulse raced up the emotional ladder, thanks for enlightening me."

"Thanks for that, sweetheart, but bravery and sharpness have little to do with it," he says, grasping her thighs in back up high, twisting in rhythm with her hair's motion. "I'm here with you because it's necessary balance, water seeking its own level—it *must* happen, I've no choice and don't want one. And, anyway, you're the married woman who's braver than I'll ever be—risking all to be here."

"We both know I also have no choice and, as for risk, it's a joke—with each meeting I care less about consequences, to the point of perhaps welcoming them," she says, grasping his arms by the biceps, sliding forward and back, her chest massaging his. "And duping your employer while remaining in good standing *is* the very definition of smarts, and your courage is off the charts, case closed! Come to think of it... Maybe what I called a duplicity fetish is basic love of freedom, resistance to restraint. Duplicity's a kick so long as liberation's the pay-off."

"You've driven it home, darling," he responds, clasping her thighs tighter. "Duplicity's a kick but in the end it's a side-effect—freedom's the pot of gold. All the time I have on my hands at work, I like to put it to better use than pointlessly spacing out at a desk, goofing on the Internet and my phone. Slacking's superior to attending tedious meetings for hours a week like most coworkers—courting the favor of upper management, enslaved to the dangled carrot of promotion—but I want to be enthralled and active instead of idle, prodded by unrest. And I'm here with you, my dear—you're absolutely my salvation, I've achieved more on company time than I could've yearned for in wildest dreaming."

"This room's sacred—unhealthy influences don't exist here, frustration's an unreal dream," she half-whispers, circling her fingers upon his forehead. "Being vitalized by desire—sating hunger, scratching itches, becoming serene—was denied me for I can't believe how long. Summer heat's always a welcome shot in my blood and you see to it I do right by it, instead of gnawing at myself, pining away—all that you bring to me, Alex, my goodness, I could swoon for joy! We've travelled emotional light years together already, and..." Trailing off, she scampers away on hands and knees, is soon seated on the edge of the bed again with her feet on the floor, smiling at him over her shoulder. "Snuggles from behind, please!"

"Home luscious home," he says, having advanced to wrap his arms about her belly and press his chest to her back, lift his legs over hers from each side. "Darling, thank you for reaching out and touching me after yoga class, changing my life—our first meeting's sacred, I'll remember every second crystal clear forever. Considering your marital status, that took serious guts."

"Alex, the way you were looking at me in class emboldened me—your eyes sliding up my legs to my eyes, taking their sweet time along the way, while minding their manners, not a bit intrusive—your stare, even while steady, was tempered with discretion and smooth and inviting, no jarring abruptness, tacky leering, and... Well, I was getting tense, tingly! Even when I turned around to demonstrate postures best understood when seen from behind I could feel your eyes on me. In all my experience as an instructor I'd never encountered the like and was liking it more and more—starting to worry if my response to your eyes was becoming obvious to others at the same time that I was, curiously enough, embracing the chance it was. Your eyes were bright with promise."

"I'm always very much aware of being surrounded by gorgeous women in yoga but usually glaze my gaze, veil my glance. I don't think women are out to hook up in class, as there's wellness, fitness, and spirituality in the picture—yoga's a highly beneficial end in itself. The main part of the art of admiring women without alerting them to it is making sure emotion doesn't leap directly at them from my eyes, as by focusing my gaze on the air between them and myself, or slightly to the side of or above them. But I couldn't stop my eyes from bare nakedly relishing you, betraying me—desire hijacked the situation."

"Couldn't stop your eyes big time, Alex! Wonderful how desire grabbed the reins, served us both! At points I was wondering if you cruise yoga classes for action, first come first served, and didn't much care if such was the case—you were focused on me and I was warming to it. I'd never had it on with a student, as a matter of principle—caution was flying out the window."

"Funny you thought I was prowling when yoga's my version of church, where I've always been a choirboy for real. But hooking up happened with us spontaneously—I was turned loose from overmuch thinking because you're so fearless and discerning. I thanked you for your fabulous class afterwards, and the way you grasped my arm while lifting yourself to tiptoes, your eyes brightening, vanquished hesitation—I couldn't help but ask you out, I didn't think I had it in me to do that. Hugging you when you accepted was as otherworldly an experience as I'll ever have—the impossible was reality, shimmering my spine."

"And I didn't think I had it in me to accept, hug you for all I was worth, and when your hands slid to my waist, grasped me, your fingers pulsing... My goodness! I couldn't help but dance to your touch, and glimpsed myself in the mirror behind you, and what flashed into my head was something like, 'What *am* I doing? Is my mind gone?' But I still couldn't stop responding—wow! A fling's what I'd been thirsting for without daring to admit it! And what I mean by 'fling' is my perception of what was happening then, out of the blue with no expectation of anything life-altering and lasting. How could I know I'd struck the motherlode?"

"You were so radiant while teaching—few teachers take their entire class while teaching but you didn't skip one posture, did each perfectly while still present as a teacher, compassionate and caring, with precise direction. 'Wow—she's amazing!' was in my thoughts from the get-go. I found myself fantasizing about being with you without being able to stop myself, but how could I know fantasy would become reality? A force stronger than me was steering me towards joy."

"Crazy how that class was a one-off, me deceiving husband in the sense he doesn't want me working, seems to feel it's best for a wife to be sheltered and idle, never mind how much I love teaching. A surgeon's wife simply isn't supposed to have a job, even if it's passed off as a hobby! But I'm getting sidetracked—sorry! A friend begged me to sub for her, because her boyfriend surprised her with a proposal and engagement getaway and the other instructors were busy, and the class happened to happen at 2:15, well within my safe zone."

"And also happened to happen at the studio two blocks away, where I take classes on the sly—a calculated risk, since it means I'm incommunicado for at least an hour, and it's not every day I feel comfortable with taking a class. Wild and beautiful how so many unrelated circumstances, from our very different worlds, needed to conjoin and how fast we sealed the deal once they did!"

"I was crazy aware of you every second, magnetically drawn," she purrs, sliding her hands down his thighs to his knees, rubbing her right cheek against his left. "You were a row back dead center, inspiring me to—I own up—show off. But what really..."

"Yeah, right!" he cuts in, sliding his hands up her belly to her breasts, she arching her back. "As if you aren't able to flawlessly execute the toughest postures as casually as if you're sipping tea—showing off's irrelevant at your level. Others might try showing off and never come close to what you do effortlessly."

"So maybe you'll let me say what I want to say," she laughs, swatting one of his knees. "What really swept through me, on what I'll call an elemental level instead of only mental understanding, was it would be safe to grab you if you were near me after class and—another confession—it was no accident I wandered near the shelves when you rose to return your mat and blocks. Yeah, and I wasn't above tugging my top down a bit to show some cleavage, seeking to disguise intent by fiddling at my waist, as if needing to adjust my leggings—I'd never done flirtatious stuff as an instructor, was too fixated on you to be surprised."

"I would've come up to you wherever you were, felt suffocated had I not—no expectation of hooking up, I didn't dare assume. I simply wished to thank you for an incandescent class. And then, wow—what a spin into bliss! Infinite thanks, darling, for paving the way and vanquishing doubt, making it easy for me to ask you out. And so we circle around to how you seized my arm, emboldened me. Yes, I noticed your top inching down but couldn't possibly imagine it was deliberate—all was transpiring in a fast blurred dream—in a flash I was out of my mind overjoyed I'd be seeing you again outside of class, amazed at the touch of you."

"My marriage ceased to exist once you were near me—gazing at me so sweetly and intently. 'Yes! Yes! Yes!' burst into my head at first syllable of your voice—a fast blurred dream's right, we ferried each other to freedom. Silly me, I was folding my wedding ring under my palm to hide it while aware it was highly unlikely you'd missed noticing it—rationality was out the window."

"Yeah, I noticed the nasty stones on your ring finger—violet center-piece and constellation of rubies, highly intimidating. But that information flew out of my head when you grabbed my arm—you're the first married woman I've..."

"As you've told before," Hilaria breaks in, "and I'll always treasure that! Always a treat to review how we met—learn new things about our frames of mind at the time, what facilitated hooking up—more evidence the Fates were favoring us. Free will or not? Who cares, so long as the outcome surpasses wildest hope?"

"I'm all for kissing off free will, being Fate's pawn, so long as being with you's the outcome—joy's the supreme God."

"You've led me to the laps of the joy Gods for sure!" She's tapping Alex's knees and he doesn't need to be signaled twice—removes his legs from atop hers, unwinds his arms from about her, whereupon she springs to her feet to face him, shoves him onto his back. At first she makes as if to straddle and pin him, then—giggling—cries, "Faked you out again!" and scampers to the head of the bed, where she walks her hands up the wall, gazes over her shoulder mischievously. "Here's something I haven't told: I'm immune to the nails-on-blackboards thing, and plaster walls like this aren't too different from blackboards—used to have fun making schoolmates cringe." She claws the wall in figure eight motion.

"Ha! We share that immunity, I had loads of fun raking my nails on blackboards, making classmates cover their ears for protection. The *screeeee!* sound's music to my ears, brings back amusing memories."

"What a fun thing to share, Alex—come join the chorus!"

No sooner is Alex at Hilaria's back, reaching up the wall to claw it (as she raises herself higher, quiveringly stretches), than his work-phone trills, announcing a text. "Uh, oh!" he reacts. "That's a sound, considering the source, that *does* make me cringe—office texts aren't sent willy-nilly, usually mean urgency. Sorry—need to check." He scoots to the right, grabs his work-phone from the nightstand.

"I'll never argue with the hand that feeds our fun, it's only right our corporate sponsor's prioritized," she smiles, immediately scampering leftwards, exiting the bed. "Shame on me, and flog me, if I ever hinder assignments getting done."

Chapter Eight

Upon accessing the text, Alex reads it aloud: "'Are you available? We have a Stage 2 for you! Client changed status! It's HOT! Sorry for short notice!' 'No problem—on it!'" he continues reading aloud while replying; then, addressing Hilaria directly, "Annoying interruption or not, I'm glad they texted—always want to pounce on work right away. Part of my standard message in emails to brand teams is, 'Please text if a job is hot, so that I prioritize it.' The option's appreciated and their self-interest serves mine. I use the word 'prioritize' a lot, because it implies I have a crowded schedule—a beautiful thing's that no team's sure what the others need from me and I can play them off against each other." He's soon seated at the desk to the bed's right, the one lacking its lamp, clicking about on his laptop. His laptop's always prepped when they're at the hotel, with his agency's VPN and server accessed, work email open. He frequently checks the email.

"Sweet of them to oblige with a warning system," Hilaria laughs, standing behind him, massaging his shoulders while periodically bending to kiss his forehead, holding her hair away to avoid obscuring his view of the screen. "And what's a Stage 2? Sounds like rocket launches, technical and complex."

"A Stage 2's the opposite of technical and complex, but it's nice that it sounds complex—my job's technical jargon facilitates the scam.

High-sounding words do wonders for baffling people and enabling slacking."

"Yeah, your job title alone sounds intimidating, as if a PHD's required. But what's a Stage 2 anyway? I'm curious about the pharma aspect, for no real reason at all."

"I take great pride in knowing very little about the pharma aspect—I've infiltrated the pharmaceutical advertising industry, am paid white-collar cash to do what doesn't require much more mental exertion than stocking shelves. The greatest challenge is flimflamming management, maintaining mystique."

"OK then, Alex, *prove* to me your job's as mindless as you say—that's what I'm *really* curious about. Just because it's easy for you doesn't mean it's easy."

"Sure, if you'd like to be royally bored! The gist of it's that claims made about drugs in pharmaceutical advertising need to be supported by references, articles in medical journals or published clinical trial outcomes or prescribing information or others, and I digitally link the claims to the references without needing to read the references or advertising copy, have a clue what the drugs are for."

"Whatever 'digitally link' means! Please show me what it *does* mean so I can decide if it's mindless."

"OK, the annotations next to the claims, as in statements about product efficacy, on this piece *(He points at several annotations with the cursor.)* indicate the locations in the references that support the claims. In other situations, for instance in scientific papers, annotations can be drawn-out elaborations, but these don't interpret or explain anything, are only locations in references. In other words, the reference name, then the page, column, paragraph, lines in the paragraph. So I transfer that info to the copy of the advertising piece in the database by creating links, which is nothing but copying and pasting the annotations into a search field, then clicking on the info that appears in the pop-up—a joke."

"But the database is an absolute wilderness of windows, sidebars, menus—you're not selling that it's mindless, sweetie."

"And it's priceless that it looks nasty! People at work sometimes peer in at what I'm doing, then say something like, 'Glad I don't have to do it!' and exit quickly. But it becomes rote in no time—all that's required is robotic attentiveness in a small region of one's head while the remainder of one's head's free to roam elsewhere. I daydream galore while doing this stuff—recall playing with you, all our adventures, or playing in tropical waves, or playing with my parents' sweet beautiful cat, Sasha, during the holidays—all manner of playtime."

"Right—Sasha! Wish I had eyeliner like hers, and love the videos of her wildly scampering about, or adorably purring, gazing at you—no yogi will ever be as pitch perfect in movement like Sasha, amazing flexibility and serene poise."

"Sasha's pure sweetness and light and joy, like you, and I play hundreds of videos in my head, travel all over, while doing this mindless job. My job's so mindless I'll be able to tear through this assignment while you're on my lap *(He gestures for Hilaria to sit on his lap; she's there in seconds, face to face.)*, which is the ultimate proof, since the touch of you's mind-bending distraction bar none."

"But, sweetie, I'm unable to stay still, resist wanting *all* your attention—good luck with the assignment, let the games begin!" she gleefully announces, bouncing up and down and squirming; but she soon stops, leaps from his lap. "Silly short-sighted me! Delaying your job's the last thing I want! Why should I care if it's mindless or not, so long as it gets done?" She's skipped to the bed—quickly facing him while lying on her side, raised on an elbow, palm supporting her chin.

"So here I am blotting stunning you from my peripheral vision, whipping through this child's play of a job!" Alex declares, busy with the mouse he's attached to the laptop. Inside of fifteen minutes he's finished the assignment and joined Hilaria on the bed, saying, "Darling, hungering to be with you was motivation like no other—I've never done a job in Veeva Vault so fast. I may have been avoiding looking at you with my physical eyes but you were ultra-vivid in my mind's eye and emotions, sweeping me forward every second."

"The database is called Veeva Vault? Very appropriate!" She's pulsing her belly against Alex's back, he lying within her posture's curl. "Your job's too funny and I'm glad it's mindless for you, even if I'm sure it isn't for most. I only saw rapid-fire sequences of patterns, windows appearing and disappearing—I understand the function of annotations but zilch about any big picture."

"Actually you fully understand what I do, have totally nailed it," he responds, flipping about to face her—caressing her shoulder, running his fingers through her hair. "My job's a few patterns of mindless repetition done in databases that appear more complicated than they are—no need to bother with big pictures. Many doors are open to me at the agency—aspiration for advancement's encouraged and senior people gladly help others climb the ladder, since assigning responsibility minimizes their responsibility—but I've imposed a need-to-know rule on myself. I need to know two things: one, the skills that allow me to remain in my slacker niche, and, two, how far I can go with slacking before attracting attention. Bless the databases that enable my slacker ride!"; then, upon licking her lips, "This is hands-down the most paradisiacal place I'll ever be in while discussing databases."

"And the database is Veeva Vault," she giggles, shoving at Alex's upright shoulder until he's on his back; then, once she's above him on hands and knees, "Please come inside my vault anytime and often, it's always open for you! Viva vault!"

"Thank you, Hilaria! A boring database is now a synonym for frolic—love the association! Going forward when I log into Veeva Vault your energy and verve will return to me, elevate me sure as a breaking wave's spray! Viva vault, honeydoll! The sun shimmers on ocean waves and you shimmer in my blood.

"As you do in mine, Alex, ever revealing my depths to me, expanding aspiration, bringing on emotional vertigo, where everything limiting goes poof! So why do we need to return to the one-dimensional world? I return to my farce of a marriage, you return to playacting at work, and we get re-infested with forced idleness, stabbing unrest—splintered feelings, disunity, persecution. Goodbye balance and serenity, hello suffocation. What's the point?" Hilaria's flipped onto her back alongside Alex and they're rubbing shoulders and hips and ankles, their heads near the edge of the bed's base.

"No point whatsoever," he says, caressing her chest and stomach as she lifts her legs perpendicular to her hips, opens and closes them.

"We've been born into so-called civilization—cut off from nurturing nature, robbed of our in-the-wilds birthright, inner division forced upon us. Society's out to splinter our psyches, have us hungering for pseudo self-completion via consumerism—sucker us into chasing manufactured illusions of self-fulfillment—and anyone who denies it is either naive, a willing victim, or profiting from it. Fabricated spirituality's central to marketing—false hope sells product like nothing else—escapism isn't necessary in a non-civilization-contaminated world. Escapism itself is a marketing ploy."

"Humpty Dumpty sat on a wall /Humpty Dumpty had a great fall /All the king's horses and all the king's men /Couldn't put Humpty together again!" Hilaria mirthfully shouts, slamming her legs down on the mattress, then raising them again. "Maybe Humpty's a secret warning against society's soul-sapping agenda? The wall stands for civilization, since walls are unnatural divisive structures built by humans; and so by sitting on civilization's wall Humpty falls from grace, is splintered to bits—we don't want to be Dumpty! I think we ignore the hand-me-down fairy tales, instructive allegories, at our peril—it's healthy to open our subconscious to the secret messages, archetypal truths, lurking beneath their surface, including encouragement to revolt. Since society's out to subdue and exploit us, doesn't it follow that fun's subversive by nature?"

"Right, the last thing society wants is for us to have fun—morose people, lacking inner reserves of healing joy, are sitting ducks for manipulation. Those who'd like to turn us into unquestioning stooges are legion and it's our responsibility to elude their debilitating agenda by being as silly as possible as often as possible—it's essential to ignore judgmental losers, the misery they exemplify. I think the ever-popular zombie-genre's an allegory based upon what society wants to do to us—it's our responsibility to rebel against zombiism, defiantly be high-spirited and happy, decline to join the living dead."

"I'd surely be one of the lost living dead if we couldn't meet, Alex! I might cast a wilting glance at my uptown life of decorum—being pampered materialistic-wise, malnourished emotion-wise—but it's all a joke, can't depress me a bit, once we're together: fun easily vanquishes dry cerebral stuff. And, hey, if I'm not mistaken, it's shoulder stand time!" Hilaria's feet hit the mattress and she springs upright into a seated position, after which she tugs Alex upright—they're shortly on their backs in the center of the bed, executing shoulder stands side by side. "You have a fierce shoulder stand, sweetie," she says at one point. "Fully erect expression, firm alignment from a foundation of strength."

"Probably because I've been doing them since grade school, when they were a limber-up exercise in diving practice, and way of seeing how our legs should look when entering the water. Shoulder stands whirl me back to my diving team summers, prepping on the lawn under palms at poolside, California sun blazing."

"Do much jousting in diving practice?" she giggles, sliding a foot down one of his legs, then pushing, spilling him onto his side.

"Illegal move, brat! Advance warning's stipulated per official rules, ambushes are a violation, and so the referee of good sportsmanship awards me a rematch!" He's laughing too hard to manage another shoulder stand at the moment—finally shoves Hilaria over. "So take that, and bear in mind you broke the rules first."

"Disqualification because you weren't in a shoulder stand—the referee awards me a new contest, stipulates it's to be a snuggle-tussle!" Hilaria announces, scooting to sit on the edge of the bed near the windows, presenting her back to him. "The challenge is for me to escape your hold, run to smack the front door, after you grab me, and if you hang onto me for five minutes you win—good luck!"

"An easy win for me—thank you!" he laughs, embracing her from behind. "Although it's not about winning, it's about relishing luscious kissable you!" He brushes her hair aside, kisses the nape of her neck.

"As if I'd dream of escaping—I'm holding tight," she coos, seizing his wrists. "The object of this game's for me to throw the game, I win by losing—your touch is the beginning and end of all that matters to me, an out of my..." Detecting Alex has started—the sudden tone of dissonance in his embrace, wince upon his face she can feel rather than see—Hilaria breaks off, inquires, "What, sweetie?"

"It's the creep I pranked," Alex replies, jerking an arm towards his office. "He's hardly ever on this side of the agency and clearly hasn't learned a lesson from the prank, is being his usual pompous self, bullying the print production woman—nasty expression, disgraceful body language. He's at the table over…"

"Oh, I see the creep—a sickening sight, instant nausea—blah!" Hilaria cuts in, tightening with distaste. "Reeks of negativity and resentment, complete loserness. If you weren't here, honey, I'd feel as if clammy hands were reaching for me, yanking me towards gloom—I'm not looking anymore, don't want to see that *thing*!" Two-handedly gripping Alex's right forearm she twists towards him, seeking his eyes—moments later is on her feet, facing him as they hold hands.

"Shame on me for pointing the creep out, going negative—should've shut up."; then, after kissing her left wrist, noting her broadening smile, "But he's really just a little mommy's boy loser, still living with mommy and sponging courtesy of family connections, can't accomplish anything on his own. Bet his mommy…"

"Of course he's a joke—shame on me for getting dramatic over a twit," Hilaria mirthfully breaks in. "I still think he's creepy, but only because being that pathetic's a version of creepy. Tries to be intimidating, bullies because of fake achievements and mommy protection, I'm delighted you pranked him—poor weensy baby probably whined about it to mommy for days."

"Yup, pranking the creep's immensely gratifying! Forget what I said about the jury still being out: all signs are pointing to me getting away with it, since I'd surely be fired by now if there was incriminating evidence. But all pales beside the supreme delight of being with you, darling. When I'm at my desk again I'll be looking over here and placing myself back in your embrace, annihilating the very idea of negativity. Your eyes shine bright in my mind's eye day and night."

"And your eyes are my third eye, Alex! *(She taps between her eyes.)* Your glance and caresses and energy stay fresh in my skin in between rendezvous, comfort me constantly. Each morning when I align with pranayama, do my sun salutations, you're there as well—I feel you caressing and stimulating me as I commence to stretch, your fingers across my back and up my neck—doesn't matter how long it's been since we last hugged, you're twisting and turning through my blood and nerves, reinforcing my faith in my right to be happy."

"So maybe we ought to twist and turn our way out of New York, kiss unwanted obligations goodbye, find a place where playtime's less policed," Alex suggests, falling onto his back and pulling her along. "We'll be parting ways far sooner than we want to, which is insane, and I'm getting tired of the intervals between rendezvous, each more unbearable and seeming to last longer than the one before."

"All for relocating to an unpoliced Paradise, eliminating the bleak intervals between rendezvous, and being with you constantly," Hilaria smiles, lowering herself onto him. "Where are we going?"

Chapter Nine

It's here that our couple commence playing The Game, whereby they indulge in free-association fantasies, have fun building upon each other's elaborations. They never plan on playing The Game: it simply happens, as naturally as plants flip their leaves towards the sun. Sometimes they're contemplating highly appealing possibilities, other times immersed in thoroughgoing fiction, or summoning unmitigated silliness—they often create characters and put on accents, the French, Southern, and British being favorites—they never know where The Game's going to carry them in its particulars but always know it will bring them closer. As Alex has stated: "The Game's a path to discovery, helps lift our hidden places into the open, I learn as much about myself as I do about you—we're unguarded in The Game, free to enlighten each other unreservedly." And as Hilaria responded, "Freeform role-play leads to transparency the likes of which I never imagined possible—anticipating each other's thoughts and desires, as if we're flowing through each other's bloodstreams, is a gift beyond measure."

"Why not Puerto Rico, where I was for ten entranced days in October? Most of the population's in San Juan and environs, there are uninhabited rainforest mountains near the sea. I've been randomly off the road all over in the east, surrounded by unbridled abundance, primeval lushness, seemingly seen in a dream—trees smothered with vines, bromeliads, and ferns bottom to top—land snails clustered by the dozen on the trees and shrubs, sweeping branches to the ground with their weight—multicolored butterflies flitting among cascades of scarlet and gold blossoms in emerald foliage, collecting in shimmering clouds near puddles, sipping minerals from the mud—lizards, green and grey and even blue, scampering about and stirring the fallen leaves in such profusion it's as if the forest floor's alive—birdsong and coqui-song lilting and echoing nonstop—prawns in the streams. Nor to forget—ha ha!—the banana spiders, over three inches long, with webs over two yards wide and nearly as strong as string. I wave a stick in front while exploring the forest, lest I stumble into one of those webs—I enjoy the primality of having huge spiders around but don't want one crawling over my face. We could pool our resources, buy raw rainforest acreage, live off the land."

"Love how you're describing Puerto Rico as if it's new to me! I attended summer camp on the southern coast, am fluent in Spanish, have been all over in the forests and on the beaches. So, yes, we buy a parcel of rainforest, clear a tiny bit for home and garden, plant fruit trees here and there—avocado, papaya, mango, citrus, plantain, quenepas. Good chance coconut palms will already be there, having spread island-wide from plantations. I'm absolutely receptive to living in our very own rainforest preserve, keeping our footprint to a minimum."

"You went to camp on my favorite island, speak Spanish?"

"Surprise! I spent six summers, late elementary through middle school, west of Ponce. Otherworldly mangrove islands and thickets, emerald in Caribbean aquamarine, interspersed with bright white sand beaches—sun-heated sauna pools in mangrove-sheltered shallows, sea softly ebbing and flowing as one soaks—sunset's a hallucination, silver-streaked scarlet sky with patches of indigo and purple, suggestive of artist renditions of fancied alien Eden-worlds. The camp staff spoke Spanish exclusively—learning Spanish was sink or swim, part of the reason my parents chose that camp, and I most certainly swam, in every sense."

"And you never breathed a word."

"Some things are for you to discover, Alex darling," she smiles, tapping his forehead. "I'm not going to just fling my entire history out there—you need to conjure it forth. The Game serves us well."

"Wouldn't have it any other way—you're a bottomless well of surprises, it's crazy how Puerto Rico's never come up, and makes me wonder what other wonderful surprises are in store. You're my brassy no-nonsense yoga instructor who's also quintessential Upper East Side elegance and sophistication, delicate and flouncy and fussy—ha ha!—when she wants to be." He licks her lips.

"And you're my choirboy," she smiles, scooting her hands up and down his arms. "To all appearances a devotee of the status quo, unquestioningly compliant, but nonstop thumbing your nose at it behind the curtain—a playacting master. Overcoming the mundane's your primary directive, you can't help but be secretly subversive, a dedicated devotee of playtime, and I'm lucky to be a part of it—you swirl me free of the falsely imposed priorities that'd like to hijack my life."

"And you're my guardian angel, watching over me during the too-long intervals when we're apart—joy's a flood in me as long as you're in my thoughts."

"Thinking of you soothes me as thoroughly as a Puerto Rican beach—sea breeze dancing on me as sun-glistened waves swoosh, frigate birds gliding on updrafts above, palm fronds rustling. And we both know and adore Puerto Rico, how wonderfully fateful—we really could make Puerto Rico happen."

"Absolutely—it's realistic aspiration, not far-fetched fantasy. I could raid the 401K, have been very dedicated in that department, employer matching funds are free money—tax penalties, yes, but matching funds offset them. A dozen acres, all ours in an unspoiled mountainous forest minus steep inclines, chances of mudslides. We lay a concrete foundation a foot high, respectful of torrential rainfall, build a modest hurricane-proof home—steel frame, brick walls, metal shutters, low ceiling—plant our garden, leave most of the forest untouched—add solar panels semi-financed by government incentives, a catchment for rainwater—live partially off-grid. I want to be realistic—we wouldn't want to be wholly off-grid, right? We'd want garbage collection, sewer access—reliable Internet's essential. I'd easily get freelance remote work via LinkedIn. Why not?"

"It's like Puerto Rico's been calling to me and I needed a loved one to awaken me to Puerto Rico's voice, share Puerto Rico with—inner floodgates flung open, sweeping me in Puerto Rico's direction, barriers in my feelings—predatory habits, false devotion—smashed! I raid my yoga and dancer savings (Thanks to an ex-student, well-informed finance guy, I've made sensible investments that husband's never troubled to pay any mind to and bring under the marriage-umbrella, even though they were disclosed, as faith in a fulfilling marriage-to-be would necessitate. Perhaps husband hasn't bothered because, in the end, I'm really just un-limited-credit-line hired help entitled to share his bed.) and we pool our money. Forget about going for a monster divorce settlement, launching an emotional neglect case for suitcases of cash—I loathe self-pity, want minimal ickiness. But I'm definitely entitled to a settlement due to lost teaching income. I didn't marry to avoid teaching, husband said no surgeons' wives work and he'd rather I didn't and I'd lack for nothing and he'd like me to be the 'fulltime face of our home.'"

"But if he's that controlling won't he make trouble?"

"He's not intentionally controlling—more like naive, as I found out too late. It could occur to him to make trouble because he'd be caught by surprise, has no clue the business of me lacking for nothing's something of a sick joke, since it's turned out to solely refer to materialism, a slick veneer veiling emotional deadness, but... OK, it's a sure thing avoidance of scandal would carry the day, shove wounded pride aside, and he'd agree to the smaller settlement, a drop in the bucket for him, without a battle. I could threaten negative publicity, a nasty ordeal, to get more but would never lower myself to do so and he'll realize that and appreciate it. I didn't marry a monster, I married a man who has no idea what a woman needs to stay sane, and that lap-of-luxury's not a stand-in for heartfelt attention."

"Sure hope that's it. I've seen people get insanely nasty soon as divorce proceedings step between them—they sometimes seem to be astonished by their reactions, accumulated resentment dredged up. Like it's a painful purge."

"Husband might sleep with his head under a pillow on the far side of the bed, a yard and a half between us, like I'm not there, but there's never been malice in the picture, only a baffling amount of obliviousness. I don't hate husband—he and I have turned out to be parallel lines that never meet and that's it."

"OK, Hilaria, end of subject."; then, after twisting from under her, spilling her alongside him, smiling into her eyes, "So what I'm *really* wondering is are we still playing The Game or are we using The Game as a go-between, means of making life-altering plans without admitting it? Like, if we were *openly* making serious plans wouldn't it be a lot tougher, scary? But if it's only The Game..."

"Scary question, Alex, although it's *wonderful* scary!" she interrupts giggling, falling onto her back, glancing for him to climb onto her; then, once he does, "I'm not sure I want to know how to answer that question yet, it's too soon too fast! But let's keep going, pretend we're plotting a pretend escape while aware it might not be pretend. If it's pretend then, yes, it's easier to spell out what's needed, because if it isn't pretend we'll need to spring to action and our world's suddenly on overdrive, demanding swift adjustment. The crazy thing's that casting off an unwanted life's stressful, since it involves a slew of tedious tasks and preparation, and also because familiarity, assuming it isn't outright threatening, doesn't require much effort to maintain and clings to us—inertia's a beguiling curse."

"Inertia's as deceitful as nefarious! Inertia's why some end up supposing they're content when they've the ability to upgrade to happier lives—it's too easy to put off tedious tasks, it can drag on for years, never end. We need to dig deep inside ourselves, identify what's best for us, summon the will to be free!"

"Exactly, sweetie! So I ask myself: what's keeping me in town, if I consider the question honestly? I love New York—oh, yes! Manhattan's energy's a surefire shot in the nerves, elevating drug—of course I adore it to death, every other American city I've been in, including LA, is a lethargic country village by comparison. But what about loving each other in a Puerto Rican rainforest during a downpour?—tropical winds whipping rain over us, tickling tingling, as the coqui sing? Or simply walking around naked in our forest, shaking papaya loose from their trees, leaping aside in time to avoid being struck?—tearing the bright red-orange fruit open with our fingers, getting messy? I want to acquire nature-illuminated senses, read the weather in the air's charge—want my reflexes aligned with the flight of birds, dapples of sunlight on the forest floor."

"Darling, we'd slip into wilderness-heightened senses, minimize civilization's stultifying influence, in no time—nature's happy to heal and guide us. As a child I attended summer camp in the Rockies, got very good very fast at photographing wildlife in the forest, especially the playful martens. Suddenly there was surefire anticipation of their movements in the trees, lightning fast coordination of sight and aim, framing of the photos—I could literally feel the martens through the air, sense their impulses—swear their footfalls in the branches, silent to my ears, reached me in the form of electrical pulses. I became attuned to the sounds and scents and motion—and freedom, grandeur—of the forest, hated returning to the camp-routine—a small band of us routinely skipped scheduled activities. In the wilds one acquires alertness so vivid it seems like a waking dream at first, but then one adjusts and realizes it's liberation from civilization bombarded and dulled senses, clarity restored. We'll recover our birthright, pre-civilization sharpness of sensation, in our new home. Humans evolved in the wilds, not in cities—the oldest cities are around ten thousand years, an eye-blink in the span of human evolution—an aberration. I want to cease to be domesticated, go feral with you—I think we'll take to living in a rainforest as readily as dry kindling combusts."

"Go feral together? Love it! Puts me in mind of feral cats! Cats are very much in touch with the wilds, able to go feral, return to their rightful heritage, with ease, survive and breed. There's a reason for the expression, 'Look what the cat dragged in.' Dogs are lousy at dragging stuff in—all but a handful of breeds have lost their hunting skills—but the laziest cat gets alert and focused if there's a mouse in the house and that mouse seldom lasts an hour. Yes, by all means let's go feral, escape demeaning societal restriction—race around like wildcats in our forest, yeowl at the stars! But to be realistic, my dear, we'd want a car, right?

So we could *very* frequently go on excursions, explore more of Puerto Rico's magnificence, visit *every* beach. I'd want to go shopping, have nice clothes, a PO Box."

"Absolutely go on excursions, visit every beach and *sleep* on every beach, assuming the no-see-ums (they once bit me so bad it looked like measles!) aren't in season. We live in the northeastern wilds and hit San Juan, zoom off to other regions, as we please—a wilderness base with the benefits of civilization. I know when and where I've been born, I'm a child of civilization—I've spent my life in civilization and it's in my blood, for better or worse—I'd never imagine being able to wholly cast civilization aside, such would be laughably delusional. I'll be a busy online bee in the tropics at first, putting the word out on LinkedIn and lining up work, securing a steady stream of cash. I want to see you in hot summer dresses, seamed stockings, wild makeup and accessories, almost as much as I want to see you naked in the forest! We'll hit the salsa spots—La Placita's the one I know, we'll find more. Turning entranced on the dance floor, then hightailing it home, barbecuing an iguana for a pre-dawn breakfast, lifting each other to greater euphoria under the stars... God! That would be as much heaven as I could hope to experience on earth, a kaleidoscope of wonder and bliss!"

"Barbecue an iguana?" Hilaria winces. "Yuck! Not eating a reptile—revolting! Exit me, Sir, if you please! We need to discuss!" She's shoving at his chest, twisting her face further into a frown.

"A succulent culinary experience, or so I've heard—haven't had the pleasure but am eager for it," Alex responds, glancing at her quizzically, taking his sweet time rising off her, lying alongside her. "A Honduran guy at my building assures me iguana's delicious and I believe him, same as I *don't* believe you're revolted. Iguana's unsullied wild meat, optimum nutrition unchanged for millions of years—I look forward to tearing into fresh-off-the-fire iguana. Many of the animals that sustained humans thousands of generations ago are extinct, or altered via domestication, selective breeding, antibiotics—not so iguanas, we need to take advantage. And iguanas are invasive in Puerto Rico, undermining biodiversity—I've seen them digging up endangered sea turtle eggs, devouring native lizards—no guilt in making meals of them, they don't pity their prey and I won't pity them."

"You *always* know when I'm fooling, Alex—I *love* our transparency—and only wanted you off me so I can get on you, which I know you also know!" Hilaria giggles, tapping his belly then climbing onto him again, he having rolled onto his back. "So happens I've had iguana! An amazing beyond-the-call-of-duty camp counselor, as devoted to teaching as she was to showing us the time of our lives, treated us to iguana on the beach, the bonfire's leaping flames blurring into sunset's blaze. Your Honduran friend's right, iguana's succulent, and I want more. Yeah, unsullied wild meat, unchanged since dinosaurs were alive—it's travel-far-back-in-time nutrition! I'll be an untamed wood nymph for you, rolling in the underbrush, wailing for love—my skilled hunter! I'm your primal girl—*feel* me now!" Grinding her belly into his, she licks him chin to forehead.

"I think I'm going to be hunting lots of iguana, feeding my family the time-honored way!" Alex exclaims, raising his fists and bouncing up and down. "I want my primal girl, fired up by an iguana dinner, pouncing on me in our forest during a thunderstorm! God, we'd be drowning in joy! It's as easy to relocate to Puerto Rico as to another state, no border issues—wild how the tropics are so close."

"We'd be nonstop out-of-our-skins jubilant, surrounded by verdancy instead of grating concrete and steel!" Hilaria cries; then, upon springing off him, rising to her knees. "Woo-eee! You asked if we're still playing The Game? Ha! Maybe The Game's playing games with us, prodding us towards the courage to shed our shackles, live as we ought to live. Nothing's naive about Puerto Rico—proximity and economics favor us, and knowing it through and through's additional advantage. We really could gather our money, purchase rainforest acreage, have the wildest of times going forward."

"Puerto Rico's not a bit naive—God bless The Game! I've said it before, maybe partially in speculation but now I'm inclined to wholeheartedly believe it: The Game's a means of dragging our subconscious into consciousness—uniting fantasy with desire and determination, guiding ourselves to a better future."

"I've never doubted that for a second. The Game guides us towards our shared truth via free-flow of emotion and thought, facilitates receptivity and enlightenment because our defenses are down—frivolity's transformative. So-called seriousness is anti-intuition, unbending and limiting—only shoves us into corners."

"Here's an anecdote about so-called seriousness: it's winter in Sun Valley a few years back, my brother and I are tearing a huge rotting fallen tree apart, tossing the chunks in a stream, building a logjam dam—running around yelling and laughing, howling like wolves. We become aware a dolt's paused on the trail ten or so yards away and is glaring at us, muttering what's clearly unkind commentary to his companion, arms angrily folded across his chest. In response we shriek louder, leap to grab the higher branches, swing from them like monkeys—ignore the judgmental killjoy. He's soon stomping away, loudly announcing people ought to learn to act their age, not directly addressing us but intending to be overheard. We discover by perusal of the local paper the next week he's dropped dead of a stroke in a supermarket, recognize his dour face in the photo. Moral of the tale's that disliking people for having fun's detrimental to wellbeing; or, more broadly speaking, that overmuch seriousness is hazardous to one's health."

"A valuable lesson, indeed," she says, scampering from the bed, facing him from across the room. "The unfortunate serious people inhabit self-manufactured prisons, but we're childish and play The Game and expand boundaries instead of narrowing them!" Gathering a blanket from the floor and two-handedly grasping one of its edges, she slings it at him with sidearm motion—it unfurls in flight, lands squarely atop and encloses him, its four sides flopping down.

"Amazing throw—the blanket unfurled and spread out like a parachute, flew like a Frisbee!" Alex shouts from under the blanket; then, upon lifting the side of the blanket that's facing Hilaria. "Get under here!"

"Yay!" she cries, dashing back to the bed.

Chapter Ten

We rejoin our couple approximately twenty minutes later, following playful tussling, including a pillow fight—most of the pillows are on the floor near the front door, they having concluded with 'target practice.' They're facing one another while lying side by side on the bed, raised on their elbows, palms supporting their heads.

"Don't think we're playing The Game anymore, Alex," Hilaria smiles, running a foot up and down his legs. "From seeming too good to be true, way outside of reach, Puerto Rico's starting to *demand* to come true, not only in our emotional readiness but in the practical implementation. Wildest dreaming's turning into urges tough to ignore—I'd say we're on a mission now, no turning back. All glory to The Game for sweeping us towards the life we're entitled to."

"Couldn't have said it better, Hilaria. I'll be eternally grateful to The Game for revealing us to ourselves, enabling us to swap flights of fantasy for necessary action, and now fondly bid The Game farewell. *(He blows a kiss into the air.)* We're on a mission, all right—fulfilling our shared destiny. I've felt we have a shared destiny for months, love that it's at last out in the wide open, and we're thinking that way." He swirls her hair aside, kisses her forehead.

"Bless The Game and our amazing chemistry and shared destiny!" she gushes, kissing him neck to shoulder—she's about to reverse direction, kiss him shoulder to neck, but pauses, saying, "And as to whether we're ready to bid Manhattan farewell, we've, even if jocularly, alluded to that before, wondered if there's more to be had here, if leaving would be healthy—whether we need to come to terms with undisclosed inner resolution and psychic alignment things, scratch itches we can't feel yet, delve deeper into what brought us here, in order to be authentically free to leave, without regret haunting us later. We don't want our subconscious kicking up a fuss because we left prematurely, all very tricky—something like trying to figure out if one's solved a puzzle without being sure if one's been given all the pieces. But of course there are also gut feelings, urges to pursue new avenues of fulfillment, to consider—I'm electric with the urge to play in Puerto Rico, call it a leap of faith in the interest of lasting joy."

"Right, I owe Manhattan beyond estimation for its personality-altering atmosphere, energy, intensity—nonstop opportunities to lose myself in unanticipated adventures. Dead of night doesn't exist in Manhattan and I've overcome my sheltered upbringing, shed my suburban skin, here—done things I couldn't conceive of doing when in school, reached the priceless 'I don't believe I'm doing this!' plateau too many times to count, turned inside out with amazement at how much I've changed for the better, so much so my old self might not recognize the new. And who can say what work remains to be done in the recesses of one's psyche, what new states of mind and feeling one needs to be swept into, before one's able to believe one's achieved lasting inner balance? But I *do* know having the opportunity to strive for such balance is what brought me to Manhattan. And now I realize I'm hungry for another change, as apart from civilization as I can go—one extreme begets another, Manhattan traded for the wilds. The next step's a Puerto Rican rainforest, mainly because I'll be in it with you. Without you in the picture, Hilaria, I wouldn't have a hope of..."

"So you'd *really* be willing to hightail it to the tropics with an older woman?" she breaks in; then, perceiving his dismay, "Sorry, honey, just checking—older people sometimes do that."

"Are you kidding me?" he responds incredulously. "I couldn't do a handstand or standing split if my life depended on it, so you're clearly the youngster—you know the gauge of age is health instead of years, you said so in your class. Sorry, but that question's the stupidest I've been asked in my life! How could...?"

"But I *am* older in years and a woman," she breaks in again, running her toes up and down his legs again, "so have to wonder sometimes, especially since I grew up in a world where the man was *always* older in relationships. Sometimes I wonder if people are wondering if I'm your mother, you being so fresh-faced choirboy and all, looking highschooler—well, unless we're doing things a mother and son wouldn't do, which is pretty often, glory be!" She swats his shoulder.

"Yeah, right! No one could possibly be loony or drunk or drugged up enough, or all three at once, to think you're my mommy—maybe they're thinking you're my daughter instead. Ever consider that?"

"OK, so maybe the business about me being your mommy's something of an exaggeration, although..."

"More like impossibly preposterous hyperbole," he interrupts, "equivalent to a drunk mistaking a streetlamp for a UFO! Your tummy alone's one of creation's finest achievements, a super fit dancer and yoga hottie of a tummy, that trillions of women would kill for." He's circling his fingertips about her stomach, lightly poking her midriff.

"Ooooo! Those are tickle-spots, you know!"

"Believe I'm aware of that," he grins, ceasing to support his head with his other hand, commencing to attack with all ten fingers. "A for effort, you're valiantly willing yourself to withstand the tickling, act like it isn't overly affecting, but your wobbling eyes, quivering skin, quicker breathing indicate otherwise, and it's unlikely you'll last much longer!"

"Nefarious brat!" she yells laughing, falling onto her back, frenetically rubbing her stomach, midriff, upper thighs, everywhere he's tickling her—swatting his hands away, kicking at the air, bicycling her legs, writhing. "Yeah, I didn't last long but who cares? The tickling's been erased, as if it never existed! So now it's your turn, I'm going to get you good, make you pay—no mercy!" She flips onto her stomach and rises to her knees, poised to push him over.

"Hope that's a promise—here you go, make hay! *(He falls onto his back.)* Pounce on me and tickle me to your heart's content, turn-about's fair play and I'll only pray for more!"

"Careful what you wish for, sweetie," she mischief-grins, straddling him. "Forget ticklish fluff stuff, letting you off easy—my kitty claws might be professionally manicured, done up to look pretty, but they're not averse to getting down and dirty and tarnishing their polish, are aching to be used!" Arching her fingers, she taps his chest, shoulders, neck, cheeks, forehead with the tips of her nails—hints at scratching—while gripping his torso tight with her thighs.

"And you think you're older than me? Ha! I'll be hightailing it to the tropics with a bratty schoolgirl captain of the cheerleader squad!"

"Good idea, sweetheart! I want to be a cheerleader for you—shake pom-poms, yell motivational slogans, support our team!" she cries, bouncing up and down, sliding back and forth. "Going to order cheerleader stuff, have it sent to Gloria—we'll play cheerleader games once we're settled in Puerto Rice, more motivation to kick our move into high gear! I'll be whatever you fancy, Alex, and hope you fancy many things! Cheerleader, wildcat, librarian, Egyptian priestess, Eleusinian Mysteries initiate, pole-dancing nun, Catholic schoolgirl—I'll doll myself up in any religion or fetish you wish, so fluid and fun! Want me in an Easter Bunny or Lady Claus costume? It's done! You don't try to train and restrain me, feeling swirls sky-high, no limits—behavioral barriers are figments of bad dreams."

"Hilaria, you turn me loose in my feelings like I've never been turned loose before and cheerleader and wildcat and librarian and all else sound good, and, yes indeed, I'll fancy many things—priceless that we're game for all games, hungering for constant invention! It's been killing me that we can't even meet a measly once a week, and that when we do meet we have to part before hardly getting started—there's much catching up to do, and I'll be unending heaven catching up."

"Right, much unfinished business—finally we'll be able to finish whatever we start, and start much more to finish!"; then, upon seizing his wrists, spreading his arms into a T, placing her knees on his biceps, "I'm *so* weary of playing a part for my keep! Because that's what it comes down to, right? I'm playing the part of surgeon's devoted wife for a living while withering inside! That husband's unaware I'm withering's no excuse, it's his duty to know what a wife needs, especially that no wife ought to be relegated to celibacy, and the farce needs to end. I'm done with being an ornament on demand, it's no better than being a paid companion, booked at some escort agency, no use prettifying it—I'm not blameless and need to own up. Puerto Rico with you will enable me to be the whole woman I want to be with all my heart, no more dispiriting kowtowing to appearances, faking of affection—forthright living's everyone's right."

"Puerto Rico with you will be life as it's meant to be lived, no more arbitrary external restrictions holding us back," he says, rubbing her back with his knees. "I'm getting *so* weary of having to set foot in an office! Employment in bleak surroundings, bland beige the corporate color of choice, is a crime against existence and I loathe being conned. Insane amounts of well-paid slacking or not, the office is a venomous jellyfish wrapping vitality-sapping tentacles about me—there's every reason to bail, telecommute from a tropical forest. I can be on our doorstep with a laptop, surrounded by breeze-rustled lushness, shimmering waterfalls of light, instead of slammed back on myself by a claustrophobic office—screw aping the part of corporate herd-creature for a living! In my humble opinion, we need to do whatever's necessary to relocate to the forest ASAP—it'll be otherworldly to arrange flamboyants in your hair."

"I'm up for the challenge with all my heart, Alex—it's as if I've been subconsciously preparing for months," she responds, bending to lick his lips while bunching her hair in one hand, holding it away. "No worries finding yoga work and I can work remotely too, have done so before, and our forest will be the perfect background. But mostly I'll want to teach in the studios because I love being present with my students, our shared energy elevating us—group euphoria soars through the roof but translates poorly to online. Plus there's yoga on the beach, paddleboard yoga in lagoons, yoga-grounded aerobics with weights, aerial's hammocks—it's wide open. I'm thirsting to be at the forefront of innovation while stressing the importance of tradition—it's insane how long I've been away from teaching, returning's long overdue! My goodness, sweetie, Puerto Rico was fun fantasy around an hour ago and now it's ASAP! We're flying miraculously fast!"

"Hilaria, I'm as amazed as grateful at how fast our escape plan's evolved from fantasy into actuality, spun into resolve," he smiles, caressing her thighs where he's able to reach, her knees still pinning his biceps. "But how could it be otherwise? Our chemistry's carried us."

"It sure has, from day one," she coos, releasing her hair, swishing him chest to face, before falling alongside him, wriggling close as he wraps his arms about her back, having slid one under her. "Our first rendezvous, eleven days after we met in my class, was priceless—no second-guessing, loss for gestures or words. We'd settled in with each other with calling and texting, knew it was safe sailing—I wanted to sink to the ground the second you hugged me hello but couldn't, since we were on the sidewalk. I *love* how we had no set plan and wound up heading to our hotel for the first time, I was dying of laughter when you told me your desk was across the way—no hesitation, it simply happened. Magnetism equals trust equals surrender equals—oooooweee!—a supremely wild time!"

"Love at the speed of light, or, rather, the speed of emotion, which might be faster," he smiles, grazing her lips with his. "Puerto Rico's firmly on our radar, we're committed—there's no escape and I'm in awe. I want to be your hunter and gatherer—spear and net fish, corner spiny lobsters in crevices, capture the crabs that scamper over rocks and up mangrove roots—gather conch, sea urchins, sea cucumbers, land snails, grasshoppers—as if we'll starve if I don't! We'll feast as if there's no tomorrow, then frolic in our forest all night."

"Sweetie, our tropical free-for-all-to-be's tingling in my tummy *(She rubs her stomach against his.)* and in my heart *(She presses her chest to his.)* and... My goodness, stirring in me all over, I know you feel it! *(She rolls with him until he's on his back and she's on top, emphatically squirms.)* Can't wait to feast on the fruits of your hunts, fish and other sea creatures, and thereafter see constellations glitter through the treetops while on my back on our rainforest floor, coqui singing loud as you do me proud! Many details to be worked out, we're still stuck in our Manhattan lives, but I have faith—this isn't whimsy, we've been sweeping each other towards heaven from the second we started eye-raping each other in my class."

"Honeybunch, today's the extra surge of yearning that's burst the dam for us—we're each other's ticket to a life unmoored from misguided obligation. It won't happen in a week, but... God, we'll be tearing into fresh-speared fish in our forest, naked in the tropical heat, the air charged with coqui and bird songs as from time immemorial! I'd like to think we'll now and then manage to drift far enough outside civilization in our blood and nerves to feel a hint of what people felt fifty thousand years ago. Is suspension of awareness of civilization on the *physiological* level, for even an instant, possible at present or are we too infiltrated?"

"Alex, I love that you're asking the question, have that aspiration, even if it's likely impossible to completely kick civilization out of our nerves for any amount of time. Civilization runs through all our memories, experiences—its pulsations surround us, never stop influencing us—there's nowhere to run from radio waves, microwaves, God only knows how many other waves, and that's only a small bit of civilization's constant bombardment of our environment, everything we do. But it'll be a thrill to go all out to taste of the Paleolithic—the pursuit's an end in itself."; then, upon rising from him, "So sorry to be a downer, Alex—I hate cutting us off—but what's the time? Unfortunately I need to return to pseudo home and maintain the farce, the better to plot escape without husband suspecting."

"Elephants will stampede Times Square before you'll ever be a downer, Hilaria, and in any case we're drenched in positivity, since nothing will stop us from relocating to Puerto Rico, making a vivid new life for ourselves."; then, upon grabbing his watch from the nightstand, "Bloody hell! 5:27 already!"

"Time accelerates insanely soon as we're together and then we're obliged to part ways while yearning for far more, never a break from *that*," she frowns, scooting off the bed. "Puerto Rico's absolutely going to happen, our future life in the rainforest's a done deal, but for now I need to act as usual—nuts how my schedule's stricter than yours, when I'm not bound to a corporation."

"The advantage of corporate bondage is it's impersonal," Alex says, likewise exiting the bed. "No faking of affection, need to turn up for dinner or social events, spend the night with anyone I don't want to. Time outside my shift is mine."

"You've pinpointed it, sweetie—can't wait to be done with dining in husband's dismal beige dining room, pictures of gloomy New England towns on the walls—yuck!" She's smiling over her shoulder at the bathroom door, he at her heels.

Suffice to say our couple are soon in the shower, lathering and rinsing one another. Less than half an hour later they've toweled each other off and Hilaria's combing and ponytailing her hair in the bathroom, applying a minor amount of makeup, while Alex, fully dressed, is on the bed. He's checked his email, ascertained odds are he won't be needed for anything else today—is demonstrating he's conscientiously on duty by sending inquires to the brand teams concerning upcoming assignments, even though he's already done so thrice. He fires off such inquires far more often than necessary, because, as he's explained to Hilaria, "If people consider me something of a pest they'll be less apt to suspect what I'm getting away with—they'll feel I need to lighten up. Being thought of as a humorless drone when I'm goofing off galore never gets old."

Chapter Eleven

By 6:10 our couple are at the door, preparing to exit. "Are we really on our way out?" Hilaria asks, turning to Alex, she being in front. "Don't want to go back to fake home yet—I'm done with worrying, being hyper-cautious. I'm already pushing it schedule-wise as far as husband's priorities go and don't care, it's insane I ever did—no more being on standby for image-upkeep duty! The only thing I do at hospital functions is act like a hooker hired to hover near husband, convince people our marriage is bliss—in other words, lie insanely, and I'm sick of it."; then, upon backing up to the door. "To put it another way, sweetie, I'm—pardon me—barring our way to the hallway! Apologies for getting assertive, but I think we ought to make actionable plans, set our escape in motion, right here right now. We've thrown Puerto Rico out there, know it's what we want, so..."

"One hundred percent agree," he breaks in, setting his laptop bag on the carpet. "Here I was worried you might not get back in time to avoid the awkwardness you describe so vividly and which pains me, and now you've popped a solution into my head. Like, only minutes ago I was wondering if I should dump my job, loot the 401K, gather my finances, head to Puerto Rico in advance, search for our home while consulting with you—sending pictures, calling every day. But that's stupid. Why abandon a path before reaching the next path? I think you should move in with me and I keep my job and you find yoga work. Meanwhile you start divorce proceedings and we fly to Puerto Rico at every opportunity, find our home together. We earn steady money, avoid dipping into our savings, while having ample time to do the move right—economic urgency won't be breathing down our necks, forcing decisions we might not be ready to make."

"My goodness, Alex!" she exclaims, her voice tremulous with joy—dropping her tote, seizing his hands and squeezing. "Only minutes ago I was unsure about simultaneously dealing with divorce and relocation to Puerto Rico, giving either the attention it needs, and you provide a solution. If we're together it'll be infinitely easier to handle the ickiness of divorce, plus husband will be more eager to sweep it under the rug. He won't be making trouble for me, only relieved I'm not making trouble for him—he has the money, not me. In the worst-case scenario (which won't come to pass) I'd instruct my attorney to announce emotional neglect could be added as a complaint and husband would cave, especially as the only compensation I'm seeking is what's my due because I was actively discouraged from teaching, deprived of financial independence. There's no reason for the divorce to drag on and get nasty if I'm not digging for gold, only want freedom without drama—husband's insanely image-conscious and that'll help it along."

"So clear out while he's at work, avoid unnecessary face-to-face confrontation," he suggests, kissing her forehead. "The faster you move in with me the faster we'll be moving our future along."

"Sweetness on top of sweetness!" she gushes, flinging her arms around his neck. "I was dreading having to hear husband's reproaches, be under his roof for a second after dropping the bomb—sneaking out will spare me mega stress! I'll be safely away, divorce handled professionally—communication solely via attorney."

"I can unfortunately imagine your husband trying to take the high road and blame you, make you feel terrible—it would tear my heart if you had to go through that and we'll make sure you don't."

"High road would be a given if I was around to hear it, and it's sweet that I won't! Don't want to hear husband's voice, see his eyes or body language, anything—face-to-face wouldn't make anything better, only far worse. Being forced to justify myself's poison—there's nothing to say. They say possession's nine-tenths of the law—well, maybe dispossession's nine-tenths of the law as well. Just let him try to make trouble when all I want is out with minimal mess."

"And out you shall be," he says, leading her to the bed, where they're soon seated side by side, she slinging a leg across his lap. "Why not move in with me tomorrow? I'll call in sick so I can help you get out of there. I have a friend with a van, have sent him lots of business, we once did mushrooms at a basement trans club, surreal party night—give the word and I'll book the move, he'll squeeze us in. And if he's unable to squeeze us in he'll find someone who can."

"Yay! Please book, sweetie! It'll be wild beyond belief to move from gloom-central to bliss-central, swap opposite worlds, in under a day—what an otherworldly dream! I'm shivering with... Well, *feel* me!" She presses his palm to her breast, inhales deeply.

"Impossible to focus on booking the move now!" he laughs. "Here, up on our feet, before I *need* to spill you on the mattress! *(He rises from the bed and brings her along, an arm wrapped around her waist.)* Now stand apart—discipline! *(He releases her, steps back.)* We need to drop out of free-dive so I can call Luis."

"Sure, Alex, as if I believe you'll ever drop out of free-dive—you're too bent on fun!" she giggles, stepping to him and pressing her belly to his—bringing his hand to her breast again while licking his neck, running her other hand up his back and massaging. "Oh, am I crowding you? So sorry—excuse me!"

"In my carefully considered opinion crowding will never be possible between us, and the closer we are the more expansive we get!" He seizes her behind with his free hand and yanks her tighter against him, licks her neck in turn.

"Ooooo, baby! Free-diving into energy together, and I'm flung out of my nerves! Weeeee! Catch me if you can!" She's tugs Alex back to the bed—soon as they tumble onto it twists and slides away from him.

"Flight's futile, my free-diving darling!" Alex yells, seizing Hilaria by her ankles, yanking her about a third of the way under him between his knees, he upright on them—she's on her back, all smiles.

"Not dreaming of flying from you, my love!" Hilaria yells in turn, gripping the backs of his thighs, pulling herself further under him. "But, then again," she switches tone, releasing his thighs and kicking at the mattress with the balls of her feet, backpedaling from under him, "please *do* book the move immediately! It'll be sweet to know, for a fact instead of a hope, that I won't be spending another night after tonight on husband's property." She rises to hands and knees.

"You'll be out of there tomorrow, if I have to rent a van and move you myself," Alex says, extracting his personal phone from his pocket. Within five minutes he's arranged the move, saying, "So, as you heard, Luis will pick me up at 10:45 and we'll come over. He'll have the supplies, boxes and tape and wrapping paper, you need. You'll like Luis—he's an ex-finance guy, kissed off corporate life a couple years ago even though he was raking in crazy amounts of cash—now a freelance photographer, mover, handyman. But will your building allow the move? Co-ops tend to require advance notice for moves. I can handle my building, am an entrenched shareholder—the staff will let it slide and I'll tip those concerned. How much will we be moving?"

"Mostly clothes and shoes, and also two suitcase sets crammed full and my laptop, scanner, second monitor. There won't be issues with the move because there's not enough for it classified as a move, no army of movers arriving and we won't be required to use the service elevator, since there's no furniture or appliances—I've seen people head to summer homes with more than I'll be hauling out. And I'm also cozy with the building staff—not one of those people, incredible to me, who haughtily come and go without so much as a nod to the doormen. Is it an indication of a doomed marriage that my pre-marriage furniture and appliances are in storage? Husband said he had everything I'd need and if I wanted something he'd get it and I didn't argue, thank God, and anything he's given me, aside from necessities, as in my clothes for God's sake, that I would've gladly bought with my own money had I been allowed to make money, will be left behind, especially this ring that's worth a mint." She taps her wedding ring.

"Whoosh!" Alex smiles, sweeping an arm through the air. "Just like that we're launched, on our way to soaring free of marriage and office—building a new future, uniting with our dreams."

"You bet—there's no obstruction we can't overcome," Hilaria responds, seizing his shoulders and bouncing, they face to face on their knees on the bed. "This time tomorrow I'll be safe at your place and how miraculous, yet simple, that is—it's been in front of us all along, just needed a nudge—needed Puerto Rico!"

"Isla del Encanto!" he yells, likewise gripping her shoulders and bouncing. "Puerto Rico pops into our heads in The Game and is compelling fantasy and then, before we know it—abracadabra!—turns into the life we've been longing for. Yes, there's serious work ahead—organizing finances, locating and purchasing our home, settling in—but it'll be incandescent doing that work. That we'll be together from tomorrow on, no more premature goodbyes, is already a trip to Paradise."

"Wildest Paradise, Alex—demeaning playacting's gone, pictures of rainforest abandon are in my head," she half-whispers, releasing his shoulders, framing his face with her fingers. "Already it's unreal, part of a dead and gone mindset, that ordinarily I'd stop at Gracious Home on my way home at this hour, buy baubles for the mantelpiece and coffee tables, or dinner party trinkets, napkin rings and placemats and candle holders—use shopping as a reason for lateness, bother with an excuse. Oh, because husband adores it when I turn up with prettify-the-home gewgaws, like a well-trained domestic pet! He announces to guests that I've purchased whatnot, as if wielding a credit card's an accomplishment, never suspecting how small it makes me feel. Come to think of it, trinket-accumulation's one of my duties—or, rather, *former* duties. Good riddance to being yoked to hollow appearances, pathetic show-and-tell! Well, almost good riddance! A final night in gloom-central, right? God! Tonight will drag on for centuries! I'll be too electric with anticipation, awaiting husband's exit in the AM, to sleep for a second! Soon as he's gone I'll gather my things near the front door, ready to toss into moving boxes. I'm aiming for military precision—hup two!" She salutes him.

"I'll be there by 11:15 with the boxes—military precision's right, we'll get you out fast," he says, returning her salute. "Luis will be idling nearby, ready to pull up front when I text. Glad you'll have everything at the door because I don't want to step too far inside your husband's place, nor see much of it, will shoegaze while helping you pack." He's gripping her waist, she bending backwards—gently swaying, tapping the mattress behind her with her fingertips, hair swishing.

"Sweetness, I want to fly out of husband's property as if trading hell for heaven, because I *will* be!" she exclaims, springing bolt upright again. "But please note there'll be at least two trips from husband's property to the van, even with the building's cart piled high, because I'm a girl who collects clothes."

"Which is off the charts delightful, and as if I didn't already know!" he laughs, spilling her onto her back, hovering above her on hands and knees. "I've never seen you in the same dress twice, and love the ways you changeup your makeup—now channeling ancient Egypt with black and gold, henna swirls on your ankles and shins—now club-hopping with purple, scarlet, pink—now a hooker, now a schoolgirl—now a beauty-mark, now none. You're a magician, darling dollface, altering your image lickety-split during your cab rides from uptown to here—I'll never get enough of the difference between your before and after selfies."

"Adore getting pretty for you once safe in a yellow cab hailed from the street, paid for in cash, so there's no record of the transaction—delicious surreptitious, and anticipation of a fresh rendezvous," she giggles, raising herself off the mattress for a kiss. "Later sadly having to wipe off the makeup before setting foot in fake home again, so as to look as plain and domestic and non-fun as possible. But no more wipe-offs after tomorrow afternoon, Fates be praised!"

"Mars will trade places with Jupiter before you're plain, domestic, or non-fun!" he smiles, reaching up her dress and seizing her thighs, softly squeezing. "If your husband's seeing you that way it's because he's seeing what he wants to see—willfully blind, robbing himself of the gift and joy of you. No one's more fun-loving and adventurous and stunning than you, athirst for anything-goes, and I can't wait for us to whisk each other further towards anything-goes."

"My goodness! I'll be leaping out of my skin with joy while escaping tomorrow and... Well, let's just say the building staff will figure out what's happening and, truth be told, I don't want to hide it from them. So I'll be telling them I'm leaving—I've known them a long time, had many unforgettable conversations. They've been refreshing support and grounding—made me smile many times when I didn't expect to smile. And they've discerned things, kept quiet, since I met you, treated me to 'Happy for you!' glances—interesting how they're aware of major beneficial changes and husband isn't. I can't imagine moving without making the rounds, hugging them goodbye, leaving notes of thanks for those not present, handing out bonuses. They've actually been something of therapists, helped me stay sane."

"Of course say your goodbyes. My building's staff also keeps me in high spirits—you'll love them as much as they'll love you. First, we load the van then you say your goodbyes. In fact, while you're saying goodbye Luis and I will get your things safe in my place, then I'll return in a cab to fetch you from fake home forever. We'll have an all day and all night and beyond house-warming! I'll prolong my sham illness for the rest of the week, keep our festivities going."

"It'll be The Rescue Damsel from Demoralizing Desolation Game, first and last time we play it!" she shouts, seizing his shoulders and yanking him onto her, wrapping her legs about his waist. "I'll be escaping fake marriage, free of the farce forever, and had no idea I'd be doing so when I woke up today, or even two hours ago—contrast so extreme it's borderline hallucinogenic."

"So time for more extreme contrast," he responds, tapping her thighs; then, after she's heeded the signal and unwrapped her legs from about him and he's slid sideways off her, risen to his knees and pulled her to hers, "Darling, in my humble opinion today's expansiveness, rebellion against ties that suffocatingly bind, won't be complete until I take you to my office—let's keep bashing our walls down, doing things we never thought we'd be doing. I know you're running out of time, bound to a last night under husband's roof—we'll be fast, a quick tour—I want to free myself from the farce in *my* life, announce by way of action, 'Hey, coworkers, I'm not the allergic to fun corporate drone you think I am!' Will you...?"

"Just try and stop me!" she gleefully cuts in, walking on her knees to the edge of the bed and exiting, Alex following. "As for running out of time, that's yesterday's me—I'm done with home-by-seven, as smother-ing as demeaning, and husband's place isn't even pseudo home anymore, it's ceased to exist. And now I'm going to, pardon me, *drag* you to your office!" Seizing Alex's wrist, she pulls him to the door, where she picks up her tote and he his laptop satchel from the floor; then, blowing the room a kiss while turning the doorknob, "Bye-bye, sweet room! You've not only been our Elysium but enabled us to hit upon plans to move to our permanent Elysium, kindest regards forever and I won't forget you!"

"So I won't be dealing with the smashed lamp at the front desk after all, putting on another contrition act—it seems so silly to do that now, there's a more important mission," Alex laughs. "They can auto-bill me."

"Correct—no detours allowed!" she grins, gripping his wrist anew. "But just thought of this: we shouldn't say goodbye to our wonderful hotel after all. I vote for coming back here for a freedom celebration, making a real reservation—imagine spending the night here for the first time, having breakfast in bed, after all the frustratingly premature good-byes! So simple, and what every couple has a right to expect from a stay at a hotel, yet denied us for ridiculously long."

"Absolutely, and I'd say a two-night stay's in order. After the first night I'll report to work from here and then pop back over throughout my shift, plus look over from my desk and see you part the curtains and know we'll be playing here all night! And we ought to do it at least once a month, until we're in Puerto Rico! Wildest dreams coming true, I'll be nonstop laughing when in the office!"

"And now to your office we go—time to smack down another wall, blast open new boundaries, alter your image! More freedom for you's more freedom for me, our freedom's joined at the hip." She hip-bumps him as they step into the hallway.

"Your freedom's the measure of mine and inspiration to acquire more," he says, hip-bumping her in turn. "Race you to the elevator!"

Chapter Twelve

Our couple have arrived at the back entrance of Alex's office building arm in arm. The entrance is on 39th Street's south side, directly across the street from their hotel, and almost directly below Alex's desk three floors up.

"And it's a deep double doorway—couldn't tell how deep from up there," Hilaria smiles, gesturing towards their hotel room. It should be mentioned that when Hilaria refers to a doorway as a "double," she means there's a second door a distance inside of the first, instead of two doors side by side.

"It's not only an optimum jump and clench vestibule, as if the architect had doorway frolic in mind, we have exclusive access," he says, hovering his company ID over the adjacent keypad—opening the door at the sound of the bleep, guiding Hilaria within. "No whiny killjoy out-of-town tourists interfering like earlier."

"Too good!" she giggles, wrapping her legs about his waist as he lifts her, presses her to the wall between the outer and inner doors. "Polished glassy marble, zilch surface peril situation—the architect really *was* thinking of us! *(Surface peril situation refers to rough-textured and/or unclean walls.)* And glass doors, perfect warning system—we'll see if anyone's down there *(She cocks her head towards the long hallway, visible via the inner door.)*, have time to decide if we should tone things down before they're close, and also see those about to enter *(She cocks her head towards the sidewalk.)*, when they pause to use keycards. Although please realize *(She emphatically undulates against him, licks his forehead.)* I have no reason to care on my account if there's a warning system—I'll go as far as you want to go in front of coworkers, won't flinch a bit."

"Hilaria, the more we take my coworkers by surprise the freer I'll be. Others bring loved ones to work without so much as holding hands, which utterly baffles me, and we'll behave otherwise. I'm likely thought of as one who's terrified of exhibiting affection in public, a situation begging to be exploited. It's almost as if I've created my false personality for the express purpose of burning it down—it'll be immeasurably fulfilling and amusing to do a one-eighty. Fear's a joke and freedom's boundless when we're together."

"Boundless indeed," she gushes, briefly nibbling his left ear while tightening the grip of her thighs. "Taking your coworkers by surprise is a worthy family project, I'm delighted to be on board. Positivity's off the charts now that we're a family, working as a couple, and... Ooooo! Tush smush and shoulder push will always be as incandescent as the first time, our sweet acrobatic feat!" She's referring to the fact that Alex, upon alerting her via three rapid squeezes of her behind, has lifted her high enough, she shoving herself higher from his shoulders, for her to wind her legs about his neck and sit on his shoulders, her stomach soft against his forehead. They routinely practice the move at their hotel, seek to set endurance records, their best times exceeding nine minutes, but never maintain it for long in public, for safety's sake, as abrupt intrusion's possible and it's a vulnerable situation for Hilaria to be in. Seconds later Alex lowers Hilaria until her elbows are on his shoulders, her chest level with his eyes and legs tight about his waist again, he continuing to grip her behind. "Will never get enough tush appreciation in a thousand lifetimes, Alex—your hungering grip's like... Well, just always wild!" she declares, nipping his ear again.

"As luscious a tush as will ever exist—union of shapeliness, texture, responsiveness! Remember our night of dancing—insane there's only been one—when I was grabbing you, we back to back? You were chatting with a yoga colleague, randomly encountered, on the dancefloor and my palm was smacked against your tush, savoring your softness—you were wiggling, encouraging me to grasp harder—and those two guys were staring gape-eyed, utterly mesmerized, wishing they were me. *That's* the look I want to see on the faces of coworkers."

"Admirable aim, and I'll do all I can to help you realize it—my tush is your property, your fulfillment's mine. But are many coworkers still around? You said no more assignments today."

"Right, it's past regular hours and nothing's hectic for any account, so there's probably hardly anyone left upstairs, plus this isn't the main exit."

"So why not relocate to the main...?"

"No chance to do the doorway thing at the main entrance on Broadway," he interrupts, anticipating her suggestion. "It's three revolving glass doors in an all-glass entrance—we'd be crystal clear to the building's security people, plus seriously obstructing traffic. This doorway's the only possible place for games—the out-of-the-way back entrance, used routinely enough during primetime. Gossip will fly off the charts if we're spied playing here."

"Got it, and can't wait to be on primetime duty," she smiles, thrusting her chest forward, lightly brushing his cheeks. "What about Friday? I'll be moved in, no more oppressive schedules and obligations, totally free to help you alter your image. But, whoops! Forgot you were going to fake illness all week so we can celebrate all week—seems I'm torn between two fabulous options."

"Actually, your idea's better—fewer vacation days burned up, which will come in handy when we're flying off to find our new home, and, anyway, soon as we're together it'll be an endless celebration in all circumstances."

"A constant flood of joy," she beams as he lowers her to her feet. "Negativity will be as vanquished as morning fog hit by blazing sun."

"So Friday it is, revamping my image at work's insanely overdue; but what's *really* insane is we haven't done the doorway thing here before, my fault! Me bamboozled by misplaced notions as to what's dangerous, preyed upon by unfounded fears, no excuse for waffling, and I hate the word 'waffling,' it's for..."

"Listen to me, you who've unshackled me from tedium, reunited me with the ability to hope and wonder, be a happy brat," she cuts in; then, upon taking a deep breath, gripping his waist, "Berating yourself's insane and not allowed, *period*—I'm not bothering to explain. We're having a ball so roll with it."

"Oh, you're rolling me, honeydoll, and doing the doorway thing here during lunch hour, when enough coworkers will see, will be incandescent. I'm gung ho to flip the script, create an opposite-of-expected workplace persona. I'll be reaching up your dress while some of them are passing through, that's a promise—we know they'll never know. How proud I'll be to give you a tour of the agency afterwards—we'll act oblivious of the double takes, whispers."

"Too cute! And I think we also ought to be soft-spoken and shy, insanely polite and well-mannered."

"But of course! Any more suggestions?"

"Well, since you're asking," she giggles, stroking his temples with her thumbs, forefingers quivering at his third eye, "why don't I dress non-conservative for a change? When you take me upstairs, after we're spied fooling around, I'll be picture perfect Upper East Side politesse—Miss Manners to the nines—while decked out like a hooker. My noticeable things are stashed at Gloria's and husband has no clue

I've ever gone in that direction, been a club kitty in the past. How do you feel about me in a fluffy pink plunging-V-neck angora sweater, to show off a hint of black lace bra, and a mid-thigh high black leather skirt, seamed black silk stockings, snakeskin booties—hair done B-52's style, face drenched in slut makeup—while I behave like a sheltered girl in Bible study?"

(We pause to mention that Gloria is Hilaria's older sister, a partner at the Fried, Frank, Harris, Shriver & Jacobson law firm. She resides at 400 West End, where she's recently been elected to the board.)

"Ha! Ultimate kid-in-a-candy-store experience, game-playing soaring to stratospheric heights in the most improbable place—I'll be losing my mind touring pink angora and black leather you through the office while acting the same as I would if you were a nun in her habit. Life's brief, fun's restorative, daring fosters health and wellbeing: you drive these truths home like no one else."

"Alex, the way the stars glitter, diamonds stabbing the dark, mirrors how you glitter me to my bones, unite with my heart-flow—life's pure candy store now, new treats every day!"; then, adding rather causally, "Head's up, three women just popped into the hall down there, are coming this way—maybe they're coworkers."

"Sure hope so and that they're huge blabbermouths," he laughs, trading places with Hilaria, his back to the wall now. "Let's put a picture in their heads."

"So now I'm one of your Tijuana pole dancers—have a heaping helping," she giggles, grasping the back of his head, lowering his face towards her breasts. "I appreciate that you told me about your Hong Kong Club fun, normal for a healthy man—that was a forceful statement of trust."; then, lowering her voice as the three women, chatting animatedly, come within a couple yards of the inner door, "Game for wherever you want to go—always your anything-goes girl."

"You're every pole dancer rolled into one multidimensional woman, darling—I felt safe telling you about Tijuana because you've completely eclipsed it, made it obsolete." Alex falls silent on account of the inner door opening: the three women enter the space, about five feet wide by three yards in length, between the inner and outer doors—rearrange themselves into single file, swiftly pass through.

"Didn't detect tension—no abrupt gestures, eyes stabbing me from behind," Hilaria observes. "Just nice people who have better things to do than pry, I think."

"Right, you don't need to see with eyes to obtain readings—you pick up on electrical pulsations in the air. They weren't coworkers—didn't bat an eye, politely swept on by." He taps her thighs in front up high, briefly squeezes her waist.

"Sure thing," she smiles at the signal, reaching inside her tote's topmost pocket for her rain cape, pitch black and of featherweight nylon, fist-sized in its compact state. Soon she's wrapped the cape about her shoulders, tied it in front at its top, and Alex is reaching up her dress, the cape veiling their fun. Our couple refer to this maneuver, also perfected before mirrors, as Rain Cape Misdirection Recreation. Alex is able to reach up Hilaria's dress on crowded sidewalks without anyone being the wiser, they merely appearing to be a happy couple standing close.

"Hardly matters, though, that those women weren't from the office," Alex observes, rhythmically stroking as Hilaria two-handedly grasps the back of his neck. "When we play here during primetime we'll be seen by coworkers in different departments and cliques, likely spreading the news within their circles, and it'll snowball, be well-advertised by the time we're upstairs. Stunning you decked out like a hooker—and immaculately mannered, sweet and shy and respectful as can be—while I matter-of-factly tour you through my office is outside dreaming! Contrast games accentuate the distance between surface appearances and our inner lives, enable us to toy with what's commonly classified as 'reality,' alter perspective and perception, and that's where liberation from restriction lies. In my humble opinion contrast games are a form of mysticism. What's mysticism if not shimmering with delight as realities clash, one exposing the other as a sham?"

"Love that you're mentioning mysticism while molesting me—interesting how the more you molest me the more mystical I feel!" she announces, mirthfully tossing her hair side to side. "Miraculous that by tomorrow afternoon we'll finally be free to get mystical all we please, play contrast games galore—thank God we're not yoked to pseudo-reality, imprisoned in mundane versions of experience. That I haven't been able to dress anything but conservative for you, per the stipulations of soon-to-be-ex-husband's world, is a shame. Once everything's moved from husband's place I'd like to—just thought of this—hightail it to Gloria's and get my secret things. I'm dying to deck myself out in what's stashed at Gloria's for you, appear in guises you've never seen—granted, it's only superficial alteration of costumery but I think our game playing's going to get extra kaleidoscopic."

"That's as sure as the sun will rise tomorrow, darling of my dreams, and I'd love to meet Gloria, although she'll doubtless be at work. How many secret things are we talking about? Will we need Luis?"

"An SUV cab will suffice and we can take our sweet time, dawdle all day, plus—ha ha!—raid big sister's fridge, something baby sisters are supposed to do—she'll be disappointed if we don't. And she's *very* curious about you—eager to meet baby sister's savior, see if you're worthy of my adulation."

"Well, that's *extra* daunting!"

"Absolutely nothing for you to feel daunted about, sweetie—my mention of worthiness is bad joking! *(She plants a row of kisses across his forehead, squeezes his waist.)* Gloria's already a huge fan, the proof's in how happy you've made me, revitalized me! She's given you good PR because she's seen selfies of us together, and heard some voicemails I've played—she's thankful for you."

"Very relieved!"

"Relief's unnecessary—you can do no wrong in Gloria's eyes. Maybe we can hook up with her family this weekend, have dinner somewhere. Finally, we get to have dinner together, do *anything* together! Insane how simple delights, that other madly in love people rightfully take for granted, have been denied us for so long."

"Insanely insane, and I'd love to meet Gloria's family. As for the secret things you have stashed at her place, of course I'd like to see you decked out in them, but please note I'll always relish seeing you dressed stylish conservative, just about the most vivid contrast experience I'll ever have—the way you flip into conservative's primal opposite after peeling everything off's a trip to my favorite place. Whether you're Miss Modest in church-appropriate attire or looking like the kinkiest streetwalker on the street, I'll be moved to the depths of my soul."

"Just eat up your honey talk and touching, honey! More grasp and un-grasp, please—well, a bit to the left—perfect! So whooshy, my spine's on..." Abruptly breaking off, she winks twice, intones, "Shsssss." It's a cease and desist signal.

"Over," Alex reacts, withdrawing his hands from under her dress.

"A security guard's left the desk down there, headed this way," Hilaria explains, stepping back. "We know he'll never specifically know anything, but maybe he's wondering why we've been here so long."

"That's my buddy Gerald," he laughs, upon perceiving the guard. "Nothing to worry about but we'll stop out of respect."; then, after he's held the inner door open for Hilaria and they've advanced a couple yards, "Hey, Gerald!"

"Everything good, Alex?" Gerald inquires smiling. He couldn't be more indifferent to our couple's doorway doings.

"Everything's awesome. How are you?"

"Shift's almost over—do the math," Gerald laughs. "Just need to make sure the loading dock's locked down, then I'm out of here."

"Lucky you—can't wait for my shift to be over. And this is Hilaria, my girlfriend. Hilaria, this is Gerald."

"Nice to meet you, Hilaria," Gerald responds, extending his hand.

"Nice to meet you as well, Gerald, and thank you," Hilaria smiles, taking his hand. "I teach yoga and have never been in a real corporate office—this visit's exotic for me."

"Wish I could say I've never been in an office, there's a long list of rules and they send emails warning us about horseplay, say we better not go there—no messing around with the loading dock carts. You might be in for a downer."

"That's what I told her, and you've said it better," Alex says; then, turning away with a wave, he and Hilaria continuing down the hallway, "Have a great night, Gerald!"

"You two do the same!" Gerald responds, also waving.

A few yards further down the hall Alex swipes his keycard beside a polished brass door, opens it onto a flight of stairs. "Do you realize that's the first time you've introduced me as your girlfriend, another simple everyday delight ridiculously overdue?" Hilaria asks as they ascend. "I look forward to *openly* being your girlfriend and introducing you as my boyfriend, and hope you realize hordes of women will be envying me! Speaking of which, and I've been thinking about this, I can't imagine anyone with half a brain believing you're a no-fun-toeing-the-line corporate stooge—you hardly project a killjoy disposition. Gerald wasn't surprised you were having at me in the doorway—discretely, and admiringly, smiling that knowing smile. Why would your coworkers be different?"

"Gerald isn't a coworker. The stooge act's office-only, devised to dupe potential informants. Most coworkers are bright decent people but also tend to be on serious career tracks and I've never felt safe in assuming resentment wouldn't rear its ugly head should any get an inkling of how much fun I've had while they're working. Better safe than sorry—I don't trust them because I'm convinced none of them are manipulating company time the way I am, treating it as a game. Many of my workdays aren't workdays, I routinely enjoy unofficial paid time off."

"Not buying it, Alex—look and act like a choirboy all you wish, and you're *very* good at it, but I still don't see how you could come off as being a bloodless droid. You say you're out to be thought of as killjoy central and, excuse me, but that's flat-out delusional."

"Sure, I get quizzical looks—I relish the challenge, it's another game. I act oblivious, acknowledge nothing, double down on stifling emotion, being a zombie robot with zilch capacity for fun—sometimes mutter aloud to myself in a spaced loopy tone, things like, 'Database is great, love the database—tagging and linking's what I wake up for and live for, studied in school for, need to improve my skills—it's a Zen thing, my religion and wellness, hope to do it well always, no one annoyed at me ever, want to stay in agency's good graces forever.'"

"Yeah, right!" she laughs, poking his ribs. "Ocelots will turn into ostriches before I'll believe you toss off that looniness."

"Darling, the looniness is opposite this door *(He lightly kicks the brass door in front of them, they having climbed three flights of stairs.),* where I mimic conscientiousness for a living."

Chapter Thirteen

"Grand tour, starting with a glimpse of the pranked creep's office," Alex announces after they've entered his agency, strolled a short hall-way—its white marble tiling gleaming between glass-walled conference rooms—and stepped into the open area. "It's in the corner at two o'clock—I'm not pointing or even looking there, giving myself away in any way, because of the spy-eyes in the ceiling."

"The spy-eyes are welcome to record my every move, I'm behaving as if in Sunday School," she says, briefly passing her glance across the indicated office in ascertaining-unfamiliar-surroundings fashion. "I'm your girlfriend, curious about where you work—an innocent situation." She clutches his arm as they turn to the right, advance towards the agency's front.

Within ten minutes our couple have visited the front, or west side, of the agency and then strolled to the back, or north side (As a reminder, the layout's an L-shape.), and are at Alex's desk. "Looks like there's only three other people here, all in the front where I hardly go and none of whom I recognize—glued to their laptops, oblivious of us," he observes. "Advertising you today's a bust but Friday's mission will set matters straight—looking forward to the new challenge of continuing to slack galore on the agency's dime after revealing I'm not exactly a humorless stoic. It'll be a higher degree of difficulty in the same game."

"Looking forward to Friday's mission, like none I could've imagined I'd be on, flying in the face of what I've thought corporate offices are—a reversal of perspective for me," Hilaria giggles, seating herself on the divider to Alex's left that's perpendicular to the front of his desk, he settling into his chair, extracting his laptop from its bag. "And how do you feel about me tossing in a yoga move or two, which may or may not cause my skirt to ride up a tad? I'll guard against the chance of inappropriate display *(She points between her legs.)* by wearing sports shorts in place of panties. Not about to flash, only hint at flashing."

"Hilaria, I'm blessed beyond imagining that I have a fearless and imaginative girlfriend, and get to play these games. One day I'm a killjoy drone at work, the next I'm shooting that down, daring more than anyone else. I'll have a high ol' time adapting to the new perception of me—needing to be extra resourceful in the flimflam department will help keep boredom at bay."; then, placing a hand on her knee while logging onto the laptop with the other. "Not too overt, right? It's acceptable for a boyfriend to touch his girlfriend's knee, even if there's a camera in the ceiling a few yards away at eleven o'clock—I was aware of it every second while mixing up the prank-medicine in the cereal box in the bottom drawer. *(He points at the third drawer down, where her heels are resting.)* Spreading a newspaper where you're sitting and pretending to read the top portion, most of it draping down and covering these drawers, was an effective shield."

"Very honored to be at the spot where you concocted your revenge," she declares, banging her heels against the bottom drawer, "just as I'll be honored to dance here—discreetly—during my primetime visit." Untying her ponytail, she swishes her hair while shimmying her shoulders, alive with motion from waist up. "Not too overstated, right? Just a happy girl moving a bit."

"Well, it's impossible you'll ever be understated, fail to attract glances as readily as blossoms attract bees. And that routine's perfect, just a woman who lives and breathes yoga innocently flexing, no intent of astonishing my coworkers detectable. I'd *so* love to spill you out on my desk, do here what we do over there *(He jerks a thumb towards the hotel behind him.)*, but the spy-eyes never sleep."

"How's this for an appetizer? Certainly no one perusing the camera feeds will object to an accidental hair-bath, if you'll be so kind as to gesture for me to examine something on the screen, as if it's important."

"No one's watching feeds at this hour, footage will be archived," Alex smiles, turning the laptop towards her, fluttering his fingers in its direction. "And unless something like theft or—ha ha!—the splashing of a creep's office occurs, there's zilch reason for anyone to examine archival footage. Waste of bandwidth."

"The only thing we're stealing's titillation in plain sight," she coos, slipping off the counter and bending forwards, her hair spilling alongside his head, leg brushing his; then, once he clicks on a thumbnail, "Wow! What a pretty ocelot—amazing!"

"Extra wild pattern on this one's fur," he says, inhaling deeply and savoring her hair's scent, she leaning closer. "And I'd say it's acceptable for my girlfriend to sit here *(He taps his lap, scoots his chair another foot from the desk to make room.)*, since we won't be going all out and making out." Seconds after Hilaria's on his lap, back to his chest, Alex swivels his chair to face their hotel.

"Why, hello sweet room!" she giggles. "Always the fourth floor and today it's the pair of windows third from the left—easy to spot by the pillow we left on the sill, swirly rumples in the drapes. And, sure, I've seen our rooms from here on FaceTime, and a kick it is, but it's a pale reflection of being here in person. I'm pinching myself *(She pinches her neck.)* to prove I'm not dreaming.

"Hilaria, I couldn't begin to count how many times I've placed myself back in your embrace between our meetings, sustained my-self with recollections of our fun, by looking across the way at our romp-rooms. Good riddance to relying on that and other compensatory measures—can't wait to embrace you every day."

"All the embracing you want, sweetie, and for me too!" she says, wrapping her shins behind his calves and interlocking ankles under the chair—seizing his wrists, stroking the backs of his hands. "Again, wild to be here in person, experience with living color senses instead through a phone screen—firsthand experience kicks secondhand technology-en-abled experience to the curb. Not that I want to go negative on technol-ogy, since it'll be priceless to FaceTime from cheerful places instead of husband's suffocating place."

"Suffocating places don't exist," he says, pulling her shoulders to his while thrusting his belly at her back, bouncing his legs up and down. "Bless our love for enabling us to shake off our shackles, sure as waves rushing ashore—tomorrow changes everything."

"Tomorrow flips us from stealth mode to proudly parading our love, unmolested by suffocating social circumstances!" She's reaching behind her shoulders, massaging his shoulders.

"No more looking across the way at our hotel room, as if it's millions of miles away, while stung by hunger unrelenting as mosquitos at dusk, after kissing you goodbye prematurely, you needing to rush uptown, and knowing it could be over a fortnight before I'm kissing you again! A special gift's that your scent, honeysuckle sugar, clings to me and lingers—I run my nose up and down my arms, revisit your embrace via your scent—am gazing into your wellspring eyes again, thrilling to your hair's feather-swish again, euphoria-dispensing strokes of your fingers, sinking into your soft electric skin—the whisper of your breath ignites my spine. You've enabled me to taste of bliss in this tedious claustrophobic place *(He sweeps an arm behind him.)*, where I never would've thought such possible, and I'm talking about the times when you weren't physically here."

"Honey, I know you know I'm thinking about us constantly, calmed and consoled—before we met I was frustration-flogged, high-strung and hyper, as good as bashed against a wall. I'd fantasize about setting off Roman candles during dinner parties, grabbing the tablecloth and yanking the dinner to the floor, whacking the chandelier with a bat. I'd hang out with the caterers in the kitchen, as much as I could get away with, and envied them something fierce, since they were free to go elsewhere in a few hours. What a Godsend when you appeared in my class, the Fates finally showing me mercy. I touch myself after fleeing the fake marriage bed in the dead of night and you're there instead of my hands, eliminating unease—serenity trickles through me like mist-rain. I can't imagine life without you and will do whatever's needed to make us happen in Puerto Rico."

"And now you're on my lap at my desk, something outside of imagining when I ditched the office to meet you today—all the useless trepidation, unhealthy hedging of feeling, done away with simply by bringing you here. Walls knocked down, indeed, and I can't wait for you to call my home yours. I'll put in for tomorrow as a PTO day around midnight, stating 'flulike symptoms' as the reason. Doing it later on will better convey it's unexpected, the real deal—not that I'm worried I won't be believed, since it'll be my first sick day."

"What's PTO? Corporate terminology's OtherSpeak to me. And being in a corporate office, by the way, isn't nearly as dismal as you've described—far as I can tell, it's highly enjoyable." She's opening and closing her legs, lightly bouncing, while undulating against his chest, still massaging his shoulders. "Whoa! Sorry, sweetie!" she exclaims, coming to a dead stop. "Getting carried…"

"Can't imagine why you're apologizing, when the reason the office isn't dismal is because you're in it," he breaks in, swiveling his chair to face his desk again. "As for getting carried away, I'm all for doing something here it's unlikely others have done—we need to play outside of camera range, the only possible area being under here. *(He jerks a knee towards his desk.)* Thanks to you, it's *essential* to dare more here than I've dreamed of and I won't rest until we do! Meanwhile, please sit here again *(He taps the portion of his desk, perpendicular to its front and above the three drawers, that separates him from his neighbor to the left.)*, so we can launch ourselves under the desks in a way that hides the real reason—don't want to invite suspicion by recklessly flinging ourselves under."

"Positioning on the launch pad!" she smiles, rising from his lap, swiftly seated with knees pressed together; then, after smoothing her dress and pulling her hemline further down, folding her hands in her lap. "Presto, I'm a demure exemplarily behaved girl, absolutely *not* planning on fooling around here! And sorry to pester but what *is* PTO? I don't even know why I care."

"Paid time off—*official* paid time off, as opposed to my untold hours of undeclared recreation and vacation during shifts. Like, could I have imagined in school, when the thought of gainful employment filled me with dread and school was very eager to reenforce such dread, that someday I'd be paid to fool around with the most wonderful woman alive? School did its best to pound work-yourself-to-the-bone-or-suffer-miserably propaganda into my head, brainwash me into being the stooge I pretend to be, and failed! Duping administration's a sport."

"Yeah! The trick to beating the system's telling administration what it wants to hear, parroting corporate positivity platitudes, holding the line of deception steady at all times, while goofing off galore (to paraphrase you!) and I couldn't admire you for it more, since it's the real deal with you, no empty posturing. I'm itching something fierce to fool around here, safely of course, and feel a good excuse to get under the desks would be to fake searching for a lost valuable. First we act upset at its loss, look for it out here, then reluctantly crawl under to look more."

"Beautiful! I dash to the end of the table (He's alluding to the fact his desk is technically an eighth of a table shared with seven others, four facing each other from each side.), urgently look around and under it for the phantom lost valuable, then fling my hands up in frustration, crawl under. You're doing likewise from a different area, say here at my desk, and crawl under at least a minute afterwards."

"That'll work," she smiles, tapping his leg with the toe of her shoe. "As for setting the lost valuable act in motion, things could very well tumble out of my tote and roll under the desk. We won't be searching for phantom things—they'll be as real as our fun."

"And that's brilliance on top of brilliance—can't wait to ravish you where I never dreamed I'd be doing so! Total free-for-all in the formerly oppressive office—reality's rapidly altering outside of wildest dreaming for the better."

"And not only altering outside of wildest dreaming here! Pseudo home's fading so fast it's like it never existed, was a predatory figment of my imagination—the notion of needing to head back there's just plain loony. It's like we're on an incomparably beautiful beach, free to unrestrictedly do as we please."

"So many walls smashed today—hail the domino effect, and the unexpected! Although... And this is atrocious timing, embarrassing, but I need to pause us to sign off on some training nonsense, fill out a stupid form—a client's requiring it. I've blown it off for a couple weeks and a convention's coming up, I need to be added to a certificate. If I don't do it now, while it's on my radar, I might not get around to it until people are getting restive about it, the last thing I want."

"Like I said, sweetie, I no longer care about flying back uptown—do what you need to do and the more you delay me according to obsolete scheduling the more delighted I'll be. It's a sure thing we'll be playing here and postponement, accumulating tingly anticipation, is something of foreplay."

"Christ! Worthless glitch-infested database crashed again!" he exclaims. "Client's rolling in billions and I have to log off, clear the cache, retry, and all for going-through-the-motions-bureaucratic trash that has zilch to do with real work! Even though I've worked on their projects for two years, made many people happy, they're requiring me to sit through modules explaining what I already know, attest I've done so. Then there's the request for feedback that's stated to be optional and confidential, when neither's true: it's tracked and I'll be pestered if I ignore it. Wish this client would go elsewhere and take their doddering database with them, the fewer clients the better. Hopefully we'll be playing soon."

"Cute when you yell at computers, Alex, especially since you remain even-keeled during actual stressful situations, like when drunks scold us."

"Yeah, I only yell at inanimate things—call it recreational yelling."

Chapter Fourteen

"OK, Hilaria," Alex says upon completing the training confirmation material about twenty minutes later, the database having crashed again, "we've flown past the hour when you're expected uptown and it's your call—say the word and I'll get a car. It's essential to play under the desks but we can play another day."

"I'm not leaving until we play today, that's a promise," Hilaria smiles, rising from her seat and standing close, nudging his thigh with a knee. "Finally, after years, I'm on a timeline that suits me, choosing my schedule instead of being shoved around! My reason for tardiness to fake home's bulletproof, as in..."

"Tardiness!" he interrupts laughing. "Terminology straight out of grade school—tardiness was a most heinous offence, subject of countless assembly hall lectures, punishable by detention and writing 'I will not be tardy.' fifty times!"

"Funny how my soon-to-be-a-memory marriage shares lots of grade school's bad things and none of the good! My tardiness excuse is I've been at Gloria's, too busy helping her redecorate to remember to call—husband will readily swallow it, since, to his mind, interior design's a nice inoffensive homebody female activity, precisely what a wife's suited for. But what about our mission?" She's pointing under his desk with an extended leg, wiggling her foot.

"Right, the cameras can't police us nearly as efficiently as the powers that be believe: a huge loophole, begging to be exploited, is the absence of floor-level cameras. Our unmonitored playground awaits."

"So here I'm fumbling in my tote clumsily," she giggles, "and—uh, oh!—the floppy butter-soft leather droops aside at the top and I'm not paying much mind and many things tumble out, at least half rolling under the desks! Think we need to crawl under to find them—I'm a frivolous spoiled damsel in distress who can't live without the runaway items, may faint if they aren't found!" She plops her tote on his desk, gesticulates alarmedly, drops to hands and knees.

"Your distress is mine—panic's singeing my bones!" he says, dropping to the carpet and shoving his chair behind him, such that it clangs against the heat register below the windows. They're gathering the escaped items side by side, reaching up to return them to her tote. About a minute later Alex rises to his feet, scans the floor near his desk and those adjoining, strolls a couple yards to the right, crouches down, emphatically points, announces, "A tube of lipstick's under there, and other things scattered around—an insane amount of stuff fell out of your bag." Suffice to say he crawls under the desks and she does likewise a couple minutes later at a location twenty or so feet away, after which they meet in the middle, are quickly lying face to face on the carpet. As a reminder the desks, two facing rows of them, are technically a table. The table's approximately eight feet wide by forty feet long and two and a half feet high, giving our couple ample room to maneuver. "Never thought I'd taste of our sanctuary across the street in the office," Alex smiles once their lips part. "Thanks for relocating our fun to here, turning reality inside out."

"Wild how my first trip to a corporate office is a ticklish kick of a time, polar opposite of assumption—further proof assumption's self-limiting, a prison! You're a doll for playing with me here—reconfiguring my mindset, obliterating stereotypes."

"I wouldn't have a pulse if I could resist playing with you! And the spy-eyes in the ceiling are recording every second, ramping up the pressure factor—anyone examining archives could find it unusual if we stay under too long. Not that I want to exit, mind you, but we might cross the threshold of suspicion soon."

"Killjoy cameras!" she laughs, chin pressed to his shoulder. "But I think they're also working in our favor, like that it's the infinity-reflected-in-a-raindrop thing, a world's worth of love-feelings, tingles and elevation, happening in instants, since we dare not stay here too long and must make the most of these moments. One of the most vivid of our intervals for me was last month when the text said the cab would arrive in seven minutes, and the driver wait for five more, and I needed to get uptown for that fundraiser, and we were half dressed at best and I was under you on the floor and you yanked me to your chest with one arm while on hands and knees, and I was pulsing against you, we kissing as if it would be years until the next time—maybe a minute at most passed between then and when we were springing for the rest of our clothes—each second's indelibly imprinted on my memory. It's all about quality, not quantity—time-compression intensifies stimulation. Sweetie, the intentness in your eyes is a thrilling me dizzy world unto itself, where I'd love to live forever, flowing through your regard." She rolls onto her back—is reaching for his biceps, conveying a wish with her gaze.

"Recall that interval so vividly it's as if it's happening now, fancy that," he grins, rising to hands and knees, positioning himself above her—wrapping an arm under her ached back, lifting her. "You took me to the priceless place where thought blurs like high fast waves in bright sun, words vanish in excitation-engulfment, but if I were to attempt to translate what I was feeling then into thought it would run something like, 'Savor Hilaria for all I'm worth while I can, inhale every scent and seize every curve of her, do my best to live under her skin and within her breath, because, given her marital status, another week or more—dismal deprivation—will follow and drag on forever before I see her again.'"

"We're so vividly in alignment—total telepathy, sweetie," she coos, chest pressed to his, legs wrapped about his waist. "You mirror me in a way I would've, before meeting you, thought only happened in romance novels. I was thinking, 'Let's see if I can hug Alex tight enough, pulse against him hard enough, to pull his essence under my skin—kiss him so intently I'll be able to hold onto the rhythm of his breath. I need to sustain myself until we meet again, not wilt away while waiting—there's nothing I dread more than the emptiness between our meetings.' Well, not that I *consciously* phrased it that way—it's what you said, translation of emotion into words once excitement's subsided."

"From day one you've redefined the word 'pulse,' turned it into a magical incantation! Near the end of your class you shouted *Pulse!* when we were in bridge, and then we're all pulsing up and down, thrusting high as we're able, after your example—my spine was afire. Wild that pulsing skin-on-skin with the gorgeous instructor seemed about as likely as the moon falling into the sea, and now here we are, and in my office no less, reality eclipsing imagination! Your pulsing lingers in my blood, hums strong, and..."

"Sweetest meshing of nerve-fields!" she cuts in, clasping tighter. "How could I know I'd be frolicking with the bright-eyed student, second row center, in a corporate office, exploiting security camera loopholes? Never thought I was a defiance-addict until you flung me into the situations, unleashed the joy—I fall under my skin, get electric and squiggly, land in undiscovered places, anytime you walk down my red carpet!" She unwinds from him, eases herself onto the carpet, happily turns her head side to side while tapping his shoulders.

"Honeydoll," he begins upon lowering himself onto her, albeit slightly to the side, they being on an ungiving floor instead of a bouncy bed, "surfing's all the more transcendent for the brevity of the ride, union with the ocean swooshing ashore, and that could be about as much time as we have before we cross the threshold of suspicion. Like, why have we been under here so long? *(He consults his watch.)* Whoa! Seven minutes flown by, maybe we ought to... But screw it! I want to catch more of your waves—energy sparkling through the silk of your dress." He's running a hand up and down her midriff.

"Well, it's cinchy to collect everything quick *(She waves a hand towards some of the scattered items.)*, exit when you make the call. But just because we can do it quick doesn't mean it couldn't take longer. Who's to say a treasured keepsake hasn't skittered to an obscure place and we're still looking, because it absolutely *must* be found?" She seizes his shoulders and squeezes, licks his neck.

"Maybe it skittered into that nest of wires *(He gestures at one of the table's support pillars, where landline wires, threaded across the table's underside, descend and congregate at its partially hollow base.)* and we haven't figured it out yet."

"So clearly we need to stay under here until we *do* figure it out, which might take a while!" She's released his shoulders, is raking at the carpet with her nails.

"Who knows how long it'll take?" he laughs, heeding her request and lying alongside her lengthwise. "But a more plausible reason to spend more time under here's to divide the time—we make an appearance outside, then dart back under. Like, that we've found some things but not all, including the extra valuable one."

"Meet you back here, sweetie!" Hilaria clasps Alex tight for a few moments, then is on hands and knees, collecting two of the scattered items—thereafter crawls to his desk and emerges from under the table, places the items in her tote. "Still no pearl earring?" she calls out, worry in her tone. "Valuable heirloom, I can't lose it. And sorry for getting intense about it, yanking you into my dramatics."

"Don't feel you're doing that, darling—there's nothing for you to apologize for—just hope we find it, I'm not going anywhere," he responds, emerging from the table's other side about twenty feet to her right. "In the meantime here's a couple consolation prizes. *(He's soon leaning over the table across from her, handing her a tube of lipstick and mini flashlight.)* Maybe the earring landed on my desk instead of rolling under it, skidded behind the big monitor."

"Doesn't look like anything landed on the desk," she says, sliding a hand about its surface, crouching to survey. "If the heirloom's lost I'll kick myself forever!"

"I'm going back under, not coming out until it's found," he announces, darting under the table.

"Thank you, Alex! I'll check to the left again, might have missed it." She ducks under the table and crawls to its left end, briefly emerges on hands and knees to fretfully gaze about—soon crawls back underneath, meets him in the middle—presses her chest to his, he on his right side. "Sea-drifting, please," she requests, resting her head on his lower arm, slipping a leg between his.

"Lolling on a sailboat's sun-drenched deck out of sight of land on a serene day, waves soothingly lapping—sea blurs with sky, erases horizons, limitation's illusion," he whispers, they shutting their eyes and going limp in their embrace, listening to their breathing.

"Tempting to drift asleep on our sailboat outside of time, serenity inundating my veins, muscles massaged, but I don't want you in trouble," Hilaria whispers after a spell, grasping his left wrist, turning his watch towards him.

"Well, no surprise," he grins. "Nine minutes flown by in seemingly one, looks like we need to do more acting to sell the reason why, come off as innocent."

"Innocent we shall be, despite how long under here," she giggles before kissing him for nearly a minute; then, upon righting herself to hands and knees, "I'll crawl out down there *(She indicates the table's left end.)*, look extra distressed because my earring's still missing. God forbid we've been rolling in sugar under here."

"It's unrelieved stress under here because we've failed to find your treasure!"

"Fun's a mirage until my heirloom's found!" Hilaria's crawled over a dozen feet away, is mirthfully glancing at Alex over her shoulder—seconds later is out from under the table, pacing back and forth, frowning—intermittingly halting, tapping the tabletop with worried fingers. "Any luck?" she calls out.

"Still looking, and lovingly so," he replies, admiring the shapeliness of her legs, swift grace, as she paces. "I leave it to you to figure out what I'm looking at."

"Well, I have a feeling!" she says, crouching to face him, legs spread as far as her dress allows, hemline stretched taut between her knees. "The feel of your eyes on me's unmistakable—crisp beamed energy, sweetest of stabs."

"Darling, there's not a more soul-stirring woman alive! *(He crawls close, taps the inner side of one of her knees.)* Always bringing on buoyancy, and—Jesus!—I wish we were back in our hotel room, free to play all night."

"Dearest," she beams, falling forward onto hands and knees, crawling under the table again, "since I'm losing my mind over my lost heirloom, dreading it'll never be found, I believe more consolation's called for—I need to be calmed."

"You flow golden in my blood," he smiles, they moving further under the table, rolling onto the carpet, hugging and kissing.

"Corporate office keeps delivering!" Hilaria observes once their lips part. "Priceless that I can go back out there, pace around and look worried some more, then fly back under for more fun, keep the merry-go-round going! Weeeee!" She swishes her hair up his left arm to his face, he on his back alongside her.

"A hair-bath's acceleration of my five senses into something like fifty-nine! It might take at least another hour to locate your heirloom."

"Oh, no! Bad me for suggesting we keep the merry-go-round going in the corporate world that I know nothing about, it's not for me to push playtime too far here—am going out, not coming under anymore." Instants later she's emerged from under the table, looking anxious, saying, "We've looked all over for my great grandmother's gift, it's gone and I'm in hell! How could I have lost it?"

"Fret no more—it's found!" he shouts, emerging from under the table's opposite side and holding the phantom earring aloft, his fingers bunched such that it's impossible to discern nothing's in his hand. "It rolled into a gap between sloppily installed sections of carpet—the light struck the pearl, caused it to sparkle and flare—it called out to me."

"Saved my life!" Hilaria cries, crossing her wrists over her heart. Then she's circling around to him with her tote, extending a cupped hand.

"Safe and sound," he says, placing the phantom earring on her palm.

"Glorious," she smiles, closing her hand; then, upon extracting a jewel box from her tote, placing the phantom earring therein, "Runaway heirloom's safe instead of loose in a side pocket, where it should've never been, shame on me!"; then, tapping his shin with a toe, lowering her voice, "Have we playacted enough to sell that we were looking for an extremely precious item under the desks or is more needed, mainly because it's fun to slip into the part, be fluid?"

"Discussing a fictional situation when no one's around to overhear it, acting for a nonexistent audience—just more of The Game, always enlightening," Alex laughs, wrapping an arm about Hilaria's waist, making a movement to dip her.

"But, sweetie, the spy eyes are *always* there and are bloodless robots, never our friend, and we're no longer out of sight," she reacts, avoiding the motion of the dip, taking a step back. "Soon as you handle me like that I melt to my bones and that's why I don't trust us to avoid winding up entangled on the floor! That our magnetism's constantly tugging at us is manna from heaven, but why carry it too far here, especially as we'll finally be a full-fledged couple tomorrow, free to frolic in private all we wish, me no longer shackled by social-ornament duty? What if one of the people up front comes over here? We've played under the desks so why risk giving the game away? Your job's straight out of a movie—slacker getting away with insane amounts of on-the-clock kicks, administration perpetually clueless! Sorry, but jeopardizing such a set-up isn't smart."

"Right, as always," he smiles, also stepping back. "Considering that the majority of jobs here are what I'd classify as utter hell, nonstop tedious meetings and hours spent on calls, having to placate clients at all hours, weekends and holidays never off-limits, it's incredible how much I'm unsupervised. And when I sign off for the day I'm out of reach, period, and not many others can say the same, so obviously I need to continue raking in cash without overmuch effort."

"And now that we're in agreement about *that*," she winks, briefly squeezing one of his shoulders and kissing his forehead, "I'd like to point out that you *love* boasting about your job as much as any top earning stockbroker!"

"Yeah, I'm a top earner, all right," he responds, they circling around the table to his desk, "and the currency's reimbursed kicks! Instead of boasting about the accomplishments I'm expected to be proud of, and list on LinkedIn, I boast about what's fulfilling and the gap between the two's Grand-Canyon-wide."

"Routinely indulging in well-paid recreation with full benefits will always be *my* definition of success, Alex, especially as you're the shining example," she smiles. "Your act's perfection, subversion's undetectable—I was intimidated by the corporate world before you came along—you've demystified it and I get to laugh. And here's a softball question, straight down the middle of the plate: what's a way you hoodwink the agency that you haven't told me about yet?"

"Sweet! An annual review question is, 'What are you most proud of?' and I respond with stuff like, 'Having remained at the forefront of my field by expeditiously becoming proficient in the utilization of new submission platforms, as well as updates to presently existing ones as they became available, always mindful of ancillary digital developments and mastering them as well, the better to continue executing my assignments in a timely manner without compromising accuracy, constantly endeavoring to inspire the unwavering confidence of our clients.' Ha! What does that *really* mean? It means I'm tossing off credible flimflam in the interest of faking that I'm taking the review seriously. The annual review's a golden opportunity to hoodwink the audience that matters most—administration—and I always obtain the maximum raise."

"I think your agency ought to steal your answer to that question and post it on its website, use it to stroke current clients and rope in more. I'll always wish your agency maximum success, since its laxity towards you not only enabled us to meet but has sponsored our assignations. Your agency's a beneficent agent of Fate."

"The funny thing's that shortly after arriving here I created a library of lists on the agency's server. The response was so affirmative that creating and maintaining such a library became part of the description for my profession across all agencies in the parent company's network.

My profession's new and I inadvertently contributed to requirements for obtaining employment in it. I've not only made it onto my agency's website, I've made it onto those of every agency in the network—again, purely by accident. After all, I created the library to eliminate unnecessary busywork, award myself additional playtime—I'm known for streamlining process and it's solely self-serving. Come to think of it, if I hadn't created the library I wouldn't have been free to ditch the office and attend your class, since the library greatly reduced prep time for a monster job."

"Yeah, a one-off substitution for a friend, opportunity impulsively seized that morning, and salvational life alteration, answer to my secret prayers, is the outcome," she smiles, grasping his shoulders. "I'll be everlastingly in awe of how we met—such a miraculous convergence of a crazy amount of contingencies."

"Wild how it's my determination to game the system, avoid being corporation-raped, that lead me into your arms," he says, hugging her as she wraps a leg about him; and he's on the point of reaching up her dress, but stops himself. "It's tough for me to act like where we are, Hilaria! Discipline, discipline!"

"Well, yes, yanked in our favorite direction, and it's sparkling up my spine, and regretfully *(Here she backs away, shrugs her shoulders.)*, and so sorry, Alex, but I probably should bite the bullet and get it over with and go, I unfortunately have to sometime. Gloria's an infallible reason for late arrival, I'll be on the phone with her when I arrive at pseudo home, still providing—ha ha!—valuable decorating advice, but... Hey, the new challenge will be to quench elation—anticipation of liberation will surely be glittering in my eyes, radiating from every gesture, adding buoyancy to my step. After all the playacting I've done for seemingly forever one would think it would be a breeze, but I was concealing discontent, not joy. And surely it's overcaution but I don't want husband suspecting anything's different for a second, the situation's getting intense."

"Yeah, the so-close-yet-so-far feeling, blazing under my skin—it's going to be an excruciatingly long night of waiting, anticipating," Alex says; then, upon reaching for his phone and opening a ridesharing app, "Getting a cab."

Chapter Fifteen

"Can you tell I'm nervous?" Hilaria asks, thrusting against Alex, they arm in arm on 39th Street, strolling east to 6th Avenue where her cab's due to arrive. "Skittish butterflies in my stomach, prickly heat scampering up and down my inner walls—I'm as knife-edged as exhilarated! By tomorrow afternoon my bad dream of a misguided marriage will be done, but the wait until then will be the longest of my life. I'll be mentally rehearsing the move all night—I want to pack but can't lift a finger until husband's out the door, and that'll be driving me insane."

"It shreds me that I won't be with you, Hilaria—I'll be awake all night, flying on sleep-deprivation adrenaline tomorrow. It'll be safe to text, right?" They're at the southwest corner of 6th Avenue and 39th, facing one another, hands joined.

"Silly, you *know* your number name on my phone is 'Sis Phone #2' and it's always been safe for you to text and call—the delight that hits me at the sound of your voice or sight of your words is easily passed off as love for Gloria, husband's never suspected. Can't wait to change your number name to 'Beloved'—it's loony that I've waited so long to do so, and miraculous the wait ends tomorrow."

"Just confirming, sweetheart, since it's the final night of faking I'm Gloria. I'm too accustomed to being called 'Gloria' when I call—our cue you'll need to act as if I'm Gloria, converse in code, and we won't be saying the half of what we're dying to say. Being free to say whatever we please whenever we call will be as rejuvenating as leaping into a wave! Meanwhile, since I'm still 'Sis Phone #2,' I'll be texting like mad—we'll buoy each other through the night."

"Please text millions! Easy to be buoyed and balanced when your texts are flying in. I'll be doing all I can to avoid husband's eyes tonight—eye-contact, likely inescapable, will be as ghastly as being with you's glorious. Don't want to speak to him again, hear his voice—his footfall on the parquet floor alone will make me cringe." She commences tying her hair into a ponytail, adding, "Husband's never liked my locks in freefall, probably another indication of a doomed marriage—guess we never had a chance."

"I'd sooner die than rob your locks of the right to freefall! And just thought of this: the doorway thing may have been born of having limited time together, needing to intensify every moment, but I vote for continuation. Reaching up your dress at instant's notice, toying with so-called acceptable public behavior, exploring and pushing boundaries, seeing what we can get away with, will always be refreshing and healing—precariousness multiplies sensation."

"Sweetie, I'll always yearn to be your doorway dolly, our lovingly rehearsed routines ensuring concealment while you—ha ha!—molest me in plain sight. Simply reaching high over my head, stretching taut, to claw a wall while you smush me electrifies me, and I'm looking forward to adding all seventy-eight of Puerto Rico's municipalities to our doorway thing collection."

"There's a weather-beaten lemon yellow shack with the door ripped off, visible from Torrecilla Baja's main road, and I'd love..."

"Love to ravish me in a doorless doorway?" she interrupts beaming. "It's the first place we go when we arrive in Puerto Rico together for the first time!"

"Beautiful, and I'm picturing the rustling pines and palms of Piñones, hearing waves slosh ashore, feeling sea breeze swoosh over me, smelling pinchos and empanadas, tasting Medalla, gold can glinting in blazing sun."

"Alex, it's as if I'm barefoot on a Piñones beach, sand pushing up between my toes as bracing salt air, wind-driven sea mist, tingles me—blurs the boundary between skin and sky, my sight lost in sun-silvered waves rolling in, and being there with you will lift bedazzlement to dizzy heights, turn living into a dream."; then, as she undoes the ponytail she's just tied, "And my hair will be flying free!"

"And I'll swish your hair over me, like so *(He steps closer, follows through.)*, and the swish of the waves and sea breeze and trees will mesh with the swish of your hair as... Ha! Are we in a doorway only we can see?" He's referring to how Hilaria's seized his shoulders and leapt onto him, legs wrapped about his waist.

"You do me proud with your reflexes, Alex," she announces, lips at his ear. "I grab and jump and, presto, you seize my rump and lift me sky high, swift as ocean breeze! Am I in Piñones or Midtown? Can't wait for you to grab me like this on the beach, and then we'll fall together—gently—onto surf-washed sand."

"Hilaria, you're the onrush of surf in shimmering light, and I'd love to bring you back to my office building's doorway—the more we play the more those who'd like to police us are illusory, a joke."

"Ooooo! Tummy's aflutter with honey feelings and I'd love to howl loud to high heaven for joy but it's advisable to purr instead, since our doorway's only visible to us. *Purrrrr!*" Then she's unwrapping her legs from his waist and returning to the sidewalk, taking a step back. "Presto!" she giggles. "It's like we haven't played a bit."

"Seconds of fun in an imaginary Midtown doorway in the wide open as the streets heat up, onset-of-night approaching, and hopefully we're as ghostly to others as they are to us. And speaking of ghostly, is there an urgent reason why you...?"

"Upon reflection," she breaks in smiling, "it appears it's silly to bother with hastily returning to husband's home, care when I arrive. After all, Gloria's expecting her second daughter and I've been helping convert the guestroom, am thrilled I'll have another niece to spoil—preparing for a newborn shoves all else aside, he won't quibble. And love where your eyes are leading us—I'm all in."

"First time I've cancelled a car," Alex says, tapping his phone. "Invisible doorway makes it *essential* to play in the real one, sparks fan a flame!"

Chapter Sixteen

"Tingling in every nerve!" Hilaria smiles, shaking her hair and kissing Alex's cheek as they emerge from the doorway of his office building, head towards the southwest corner of 39th Street and 6th Avenue again. "Returning to the marriage prison's so antiquated it hardly seems real—I'll be going through motions that already have little to do with me, as if they belong to a stranger. Beautiful that I'll be earning my way again doing what I love and coming home to *you*! Can't wait for you to be in my class, and if it's my last class of the day we'll race home afterwards riding our energy—all-night bacchanalias here we come."

"Riding our energy to bacchanalia after your class will lift incandescence to wildest heights—thanks for putting pictures of Dionysian rites in my head," Alex responds, halting a couple yards from the corner, facing and embracing her.

"No more unexpended energy stabbing me awake at night, making me feel naked and taut on a hot sheet of steel, and not knowing how soon I'll see you again," she says, licking his lips. "Who cares what husband's prim proper world thinks? Will Mommy Nature judge me for bailing on my marriage? Nay! Societal judgment's a shoddy brainwashing tool, as negative as Puerto Rico's beaches are dizzy bliss! Ha! I Love that Puerto Rico, our future, keeps returning to me."

"Can't wait to boogie board the Puerto Rican blue with you, catch the sweet spots of waves side by side, ride the swoosh, taste sea spray and tingle to our bones while howling—roll off our boards at shoreline, clasping tight *(He hugs her closer.)* as fresh waves tug on our wrist cords and toss our boards while splashing over us, the ocean's undying rhythm—electric elementalism—charging our veins."

"Yummy! An uplifting sequence to help sustain me through the night—so many luscious activities to absorb and transform us in Puerto Rico!"; then, upon hearing his phone ping and gazing towards 6th Avenue, where the SUV he's booked has arrived, "So sorry, Alex, but I can't lose this car. Now my reason to leave's that before long I might not be able to make myself do it—it's increasingly tempting to spend tonight with you instead and say I'm at Gloria's, helping her prepare for second daughter's arrival, then go move my things in the morning—tempting but, in the end, counterproductive. Better to be on location, poised to pounce on the packing, not forget anything, and... God! I'll be silently screaming inside all night, so impatient for husband to exit it'll be knives in my nerves! Well..." Trailing off, she steps from his embrace, slashes at the air with an arm.

"And if you don't leave immediately I might not be able to allow you to!" he teases, grasping one of her hands and pulling her towards the SUV, guiding her alongside it. "My night will be child's play compared to what you'll be going through, I want to keep you with me. But the move's arranged, Luis will be on time, all will transpire as planned—by tomorrow afternoon we'll be home free."

"Sweetie!" she exclaims, flinging herself back into his arms. "It's torture to say goodbye and how wonderful that is—you're a thrill-pill I'll never get enough of."; then, upon releasing him, sighing deeply, taking a step back, running her hands up and down his arms. "Unfortunately I really *do* need to go, plus call Gloria, set my (thankfully!) last mar-riage-necessitated lie in motion. Nor must I forget to re-ponytail my hair, and *that's* loony beyond belief—I can't wait to be done with lies, manufacturing excuses, tying ponytails when I don't want to. Love you *insanely*!" Kissing him goodbye, she hops into the cab—upon shutting the door rolls down the window and leans out blowing kisses, the cab pulling away.

"Until tomorrow, Hilaria—love you insanely too!" Alex calls out, they exchanging blown kisses until a delivery truck obstructs their view. When he turns to return to the office, needing to fill out his timesheet, officially sign off, he's too elated to be more than fleetingly aware of Manhattan's scenery and sounds.

Excitation and Oblivion, or Kaleidoscopic San Juan

"There's every reason to toy with civilization's boundaries, scorn predictability, challenge and scare oneself—the unexpected's rich with revitalization. Call it modern mysticism."
—Bergendahl

OPENING EMAILS

Steven to Angie & Ella
Sent: Saturday, September 1, 2018 4:47 AM

Hello Parisian Pussycats!

Quick note from SJU.

Delay out of JFK but a strong tailwind accelerated flight time—was too excited to sleep, as always (So what if I came off a noon to eight shift after awake since 10:00 AM?)—elevation via anticipation, adrenaline cresting, is pure joy, slumber be damned. Although for flight-duration I'm in something of an electric torpor, eyes shut, awareness of time's passage blurry—captain's announcing approach to SJU in seemingly minutes—sight of San Juan's shimmering lights appearing out of the pitch black, delineating the shoreline where I'll soon be! It's magically as if I've slept for half a day, energy to burn. Puerto Rico's my favorite waking dream.

Unseasonably cold NYC and the job, dealing with goof-ass reviewers on the client end, gone poof!! Now outside SJU's terminal in tropical temperature, coqui hitting high notes—shuttle to rental car in Isla Verde on its way—WOW!

Are you having as much fun as me? Sure you are! Stupid question…
Love,
Steve

Ella to Steven
cc: Angie
Sent: Saturday, September 1, 2018 5:29 AM

Hey Wild Waterman!
Was dizzy fun making fools of ourselves at the Place de la Concorde whirl-around! Ditzy American tourist girls—hahaha! Taking turns driving so we could each poke ourselves through the skylight, wave to strangers like teens in limos at prom—making loony faces, savoring tackiness—sporting oversized camo T-shirts—I wrapped a fanny pack around my arm! For lunch casting tourist shenanigans aside, svelte in Parisian haute couture at La Coupole. We'll revisit tourist misbehavior, change back to atrocious visuals, in a couple hours—tonight we'll be unapproachable ultra-sophisticates at the Opera. Rapid-fire flipping the ways in which we're perceived is a highly addictive kick and aphrodisiac—we'll hardly be sleeping, surfing adrenaline too—Paris is effortless buoyancy.

Happy you've landed in a waking dream, Stevie! Have FUN!
Love,
Ella

Angie to Steven
cc: Ella
Sent: Saturday, September 1, 2018 5:37 AM

Stevie!

Everything Ella said, and stay safe—I don't mind admitting huge noisy waves scare me! We're lusciously in alert-frazzled mode, adrenaline-pumped—sleep's surprisingly optional in Paris! Landlocked here but purplish sea urchins were encountered in a Montparnasse farmer's market—spines catching the light, sparkling—we bought one for its ocean-scent. Pre-dawn tomorrow we're heading for Parc Montsouris to limber up on the lawn—won't be open yet so we'll boost and pull each other over the fence, just like when we were teenagers.

Smooch the sea for us, Sweetheart!

Love,

Angie

Steven to Angie & Ella
Sent: Saturday, September 1, 2018 6:41 AM

Quick note: am at Parque del Indio, surf highest and swiftest I've seen in PR, as intimidating as inviting—what I live for, just unreal! Yeah, sleep's optional, energy inundating and elevating me—happy you're playing fun games—Paris—Montparnasse—Montsouris—oh, yeah! Will text and call of course, but next email's not until am at the office Tuesday. Heading back to the car to get my stuff, stash the phone—had to see the wave-action first! Love you! Yee-haw!

Steven to Angie & Ella
Sent: Tuesday, September 4, 2018 12:25 PM

All's sweet, Sweethearts! Am at my desk in a delicious post-PR daze that's unlikely to be disturbed—the monster launch was in August, so the agency's in a lull—windfalls of downtime, opportunities to do my best to do Labor Day weekend justice—writing's extra enjoyable on the company's dime, especially since I'll be signed in from home in a couple hours. It's fun to check in at the office—it wasn't required—wanted to taste the contrast, I'm as emotionally distant from the lucrative account communications as if on Mars. Hell, the agency's so slow now—and seemingly only half-real, nothing to be taken seriously—it'll be something of a continuation of vacation while recounting my vacation. And can't wait for your Paris escapades—haven't been to Paris for centuries.

Still not much sleep and surfing the adrenaline wave, so the Italian place tonight for sure. But will turn in early—can't cheat sleep forever.

Love,

Steve

Steven to Angie & Ella
Sent: Thursday, September 13, 2018 1:50 PM

Hello 16th Arrondissement Party Crasher KittyBrats!

Your Paris escapades prodded me to knuckle down Monday, finish faster, so please find my Labor Day weekend doings below, done with chapter divisions—didn't plan on throwing in chapter divisions, turning it into something of a full-fledged tale, it simply happened and I enjoyed myself—was commenced and completed, and mostly written, on company time, of which I'm *very* proud.

Chapter One

Have obtained a rental car in Isla Verde, hightailed it to Guaynabo, picked up my boogie board and flippers at a friend's—north again to Condado post-sunrise, gold's chased scarlet from the sky—straightest line to the beach. Shimmering to my bones, every sinew eager, once I'm facing the waves at Parque del Indio—high and fast and hissing loud, their backwash geysering skywards, rumbling gray radiating—very brief intervals between breaks. Oh, don't worry—the surf's drawn fellow fans, up early and at 'em—safe to drop board and flippers and race at the sea, dive in—golden rule is *never* play in waves alone and few ignore it.

First swoosh of surf on my ocean-motion-starved skin, taste of salt! I'm assessing seafloor conditions with my feet—sometimes the sand's peeled away and it's rocky, a shoreline's ceaseless change. Beautiful! I'm digging my toes into dense layers of sand—rocks are safely buried—carte blanche to be bolder.

No easy rides in rip currents to offshore breaks today—surf's hammering too high too swiftly for me to discern rips—would imagine they're constantly shifting, snaking about, although—granted—I'm not the expert I'd like to be. But there's no awaiting sets—there's a steady supply of primo surf—and I'm frenziedly kicking against roiling foam following runs, oncoming crests shoving me towards the shallows. The water turns choppy near shore in places, motion-architecture falls apart—splinters, whips in contrary directions, batters me about, seeks to tear me from my board—I can't stop laughing—the sky's flipping upside down.

"Never seen it like this!" I yell to a fellow boogie boarder. "Very special!" he yells back grinning. Seconds later I'm spun under an advancing crest, my timing slightly off—flailing in blurred silver-aquamarine, seeking to escape a slam into the sand, regain the surface—sand's not soft at speed, when a wave's weight's grinding one down. When I break surface, seize a breath, I'm squarely facing a succeeding crest—diving under, rising once it shoots over me—regaining my board, yanking its front at the horizon, kicking hard. Spinning under and righting myself happens in a swirl! Frolicking in waves rejuvenatingly drives home how fragile we are in the face of the elemental—intensifies appreciation of life.

"Are you OK?" another boogie boarder calls out, poised to kick towards me. "Totally OK, thanks!" I respond. "Waves are off the charts, love it!" I continue. "Where are you from?" "New York City!" "Welcome and have fun and be careful! We'll be looking out for you!" "Thank you! I'm losing my mind!" Pumping a fist, he positions himself to catch a crest, soon sails off. There's a good chance I'm the oldest in the waves—most appear to be less than half my age—youngsters looking out for the older guy. Territorial nonsense is what gets media coverage—reality is most surfers are happy for others to experience their heaven—a source of pride. Immediate camaraderie in the waves is the *beautiful* normal—surfers know the sea's as euphoria-inducing as unforgiving. Urgency accelerates in the waves.

Later on I've joyously surrendered, willfully gone limp, allowed myself to be washed ashore—am laughing about the amount of exertion that'll be required to reach water deeper than my height again—when a teenager dashes up to me. "You don't stop!" he grins, gesturing at the waves. "A crazy man!" He salutes me and I return the salute—before I can thank him for one of the best compliments I've received in my life he's retrieving a volleyball upshore. Following an interval on my back just outside of surf's reach, relishing the blazing sun and spinning sky, I'm heading horizonward again—ducking under advancing crests, kicking hard.

A blur of runs later I'm preparing to beach myself a couple yards left of El Presby's rocks, a flipper-strap needing readjustment—call it giddiness-clouded judgement, or sleep-deprivation surreptitiously catching up with me despite feeling energy-inundated, hyper alert, I read the surf as pulling leftwards, away from the rocks, when it's thrusting me straight at them—surf-direction's shifted east to west and vice versa too many times to count. Suddenly I know I'm in danger—it's impossible to turn out of the wave, kick seawards, in time—I'll hit shore splayed sideways instead of head-on if I attempt it—am shifting my weight to board's right and leaning hard, aiming for the spot of sand between jumbles of boulders—just plain luck the opening's there. I hit the target—scamper on hands and knees, board bouncing behind me, before the next wave arrives and seizes me, churns me against the jagged wave-sculpted lava on either side. (I know the rocks well, often wade among them admiring the tidepools, rich with marine life, on calmer days.) In my experience seconds seem to transpire in slow-motion when danger's looming, risk of severe injury very real, and the astonishment's vividly imprinted on memory—I'll likely recall that lapse of judgment for the rest of my life.

So I got away with blatantly misreading surf-direction—seconds separated me from slamming into rocks and safe passage between them—and am torn between glee and fear once on my back on dry sand upshore. Gratifying to be spared unpleasant consequences of having placed myself in a situation I've no intention of placing myself in again, and a stern reminder to guard against sleep-deprivation-distortion en-meshing me in perilous situations. Yeah, I'm congratulating myself on my escape, combination of skill and luck, tingled and laughing, while also lecturing myself about vulnerability, presence of danger—must guard against hubris—overconfidence kills—time to avoid the waves, reorient myself.

Then at Condado's SuperMax, board and flippers and beach bag in hand—stepping into a supermarket after in the waves for hours, and on no sleep for over a day, is flat-out strange, aisles wobbling, vision mildly blurred in overbright artificial light. I exit with the grouper entree and two sides, yucca and plantains, and two twelve-packs of Medalla, shiny gold—keep six cans for the beach, leave the others at the rental car. Then on the beach again, near del Indio in a coconut palm's shade, careful not to be under the cluster—a coastguardsman told me falling coconuts kill more people in a year than sharks do in decades. I devour the meal and down a couple Medalla's, doze—ocean breeze rustling the palms.

Sunset's minus an hour away when I awaken, dozens of boarders bobbing up and down in the breaks, catching swift foam-framed rides. Fortunately I awakened! I'm in the water in a flash—slipping on the flip-pers, diving under onrushing crests, kicking towards the horizon. Over and over I catch waves and turn out before halfway ashore—darkness will soon overspread the sea, *no one* stays in the waves after dark—each ride's all the more precious because time's running out—it's a privilege to experience the speed and power of these waves.

How communicate the contrast between absorption in boogie boarding high surf and exiting an office, kissing off the job, twenty-one hours ago? Being eye-level with the sea's shifting sunset-tinged surface, whoosh of water and wind, saltwater taste upon one's lips, shooting up one's nostrils? And careful! Miscalculation may slam one face-first into sand, bloody chin and lips, contort one's body into dangerously unaccustomed postures at high speed! Swifter the waves the more elusive their sweet spot, when one's effortlessly cutting across their onrushing face, and the more likely it is one winds up sore and scraped—about seventeen hours ago I was at JFK and it seems like minutes ago.

So when one's, say, the last one in the waves because maybe one's annoyed one hasn't caught an optimum onrush for a spell, or is willfully refusing to acknowledge the hour—ignoring the flaring vermillion and purple sky, darkness steadily concealing surf-movement—or because one doesn't want one's first day in the waves to end, is determined to execute a 360-turn on a wave-face before heading ashore, managing 240s at best... Thank God for those freezing in place on shore, worriedly watching—beaming alarm that cuts across the waves, awakens me. Right—I'm an idiot! I catch a crest and ride it in—two of my saviors waving. It's not the first time people on shore have jolted me from stupidity—once a family stood up, waved towels. When oncoming darkness renders it tougher for anyone to make me out as I bob up and down people have hopped to—alarmed faces and body language warns me—they're my lifeguards and I couldn't be more grateful.

Chapter Two

Salsa's bone-shaking cheer saturates the air, gold light's rippling over the pavement, onset of night hours ago—La Placita's in full swing. Angie and Ella, good thing we're good buddies first and foremost and you won't get jealous if I celebrate other women, because I'm doing so! Stunning Puerto Rican women—pitch black tresses, shapeliness showcased in tight multicolored dresses, their energy charging the air—are awaiting invitations to dance. Am I shy or not-shy? I'm not sure I know! I can seldom bring myself to approach women directly, ask for a dance outright, but when their faces brighten, eyes leap at me and ask to be asked, I'm swept into the flow—I live for when overthinking's defeated.

I'm aware hesitation to approach women straightforwardly translates to fear of rejection, but also aware hours spent in the waves attracts favorable notice—elevated mood, aura of excitement lingering as if the sea's still swooshing about me. (I'd never presume to state such if not repeatedly informed, including by the two of you.) Besides, it's *only* dancing, not a date—people treating one another to fleeting excitation, no commitment apart from a turn on the dancefloor remotely implied. Each woman I dance with enlightens me, increases my dance-move repertoire—it's my *responsibility* to ensure they're happy they've chosen me.

My glance meets that of a woman leaning against the wall to the side of a club's entrance (one of the double-garage-door-wide entrances opening onto a dancefloor), amber light illuminating her beauty—her eyes brightening, smiling, inviting me to step forward—in a way, asking me to dance. Her name's Marisol and we're shortly dancing in the street—love how La Placita's also a street party—I'll be dancing with a darling in front of one club and wind up in front of another further down the block, waves of music sweeping us along—a band's between songs while the band next door's mid-song, it's instinctive to follow—dance floors mirror the sea, currents ceaselessly in flux. Marisol's in green, scarlet, and black, her skirt's pleats fly high during twirls—we're becoming bolder—intermittingly caressing, rubbing—hand-holding's evolving, our fingers massaging while clasping—touch increasingly affectionate instead of solely practical. We're high-fiving, hugging, exchanging cheek-pecks between songs, she lifting her curls high and letting them fall, proudly swishing them. At one point, beat quickening and the singer fairly howling, I see a man circle his partner with his back to her, rub against her, bump rumps, their hands joined over their heads, followed by a deep dip once he's facing her again, and promptly mimic, Marisol adoring the move. We execute the move many times—add hand-claps, forehead-kisses, crouches. Dancing with Marisol's exploration and challenge—delirium, freedom, delight.

Mojitos are the only form of hard liquor I'll imbibe but it's too easy to imbibe too many, the mint-mixture's beguiling, and I've had many on Puerto Rico's beaches and with Puerto Rican women so there's visual and sensual association, encouragement. Marisol and I have several, dancing slow with them so as not to spill, dancing wildly once our glasses are drained. Wandering in and out of clubs, circling the block—we find ourselves near a stage, the singer asking where people are from. Gesturing at me, Marisol yells, "New York City!" "Welcome to Puerto Rico, New York City!" the man responds, a spotlight directed onto me, whereupon the audience is shouting and clapping, Marisol kissing my forehead.

Not long thereafter Marisol's pressing me to a wall, tossing her hair behind her shoulders, thrusting against me—a leg wrapped about mine, dress riding up her thighs—we're caressing each other's cheeks softly, gazing into one another's eyes. Each woman possesses a unique tone of presence—vividness of energy, reverberation, manner of seizing one. "All cats are grey in the dark." is flagrantly and insultingly inaccurate, doubtless dreamed up by bloodless frustrated killjoys who'll never comprehend intimacy's impact. What's the advantage of being ashamed to be leaping-out-of-one's-skin moved? I'd sooner drain my veins.

A blur of clubs and it's anyone's guess how many mojitos later I'm leading Marisol from a thronged dancefloor to the street—when I turn to her, intending to inform her how fortunate I am to have met her, I'm facing a different woman. *Where's Marisol? How has the substitution happened? How intoxicated am I?*

Strange! The new woman's behaving as if I've been entrusted to watch over her—she knows my name and that I live on the Upper East Side—I don't recall informing her of either, nor do I know her name. She's attractive, vibrant, charming, svelte, adept at dancing, but she's not Marisol—she squeezes my hand, signals to dance—I twirl her as if on autopilot in a dream. My attention's wandering to a fruit vendor's table, heaped with multicolors, across the street—groups of frenetically dancing dolls, two feet to a yard high and absently porcelain-eyed, are to the table's left and right, garish in fitfully flitting scarlet light.

Chapter Three

Slight pause from the narrative per se, Sweethearts, for idle reflections. In Puerto Rico I attain heightened awareness of how miraculous and beautiful and precarious life is—how *essential* it is to be grateful, relish every second, fear less and dare more. Being turned loose from customary obligations via travel facilitates said awareness, but no other place I've been invites me to surrender to impulse as does Puerto Rico—losing an interval of time, acquiring inability to explain a consequential sequence of events to oneself, while wide awake's a *gift*. Excitation leads to oblivion, if one's lucky—interpretation of perception's subjective.

It's tough to do Puerto Rico justice and I *love* the challenge. One morning at sunrise after arrival, a friend picking me up at SJU, we're at Isla Verde's eastern boundary, a 24/7 place with to-die-for caldo gallego and octopus salad—the glistening swirl-pattern of a landsnail's trail, reflecting sunrise's colors, is on a bright white wall in the parking lot as birdsongs and coqui-calls charge the air—rustling palm fronds are silhouetted against multicolored clouds—ocean's breeze caressing, salt-scent tingling. Three women, having fortified themselves following all-night fun, exit the restaurant—one blithely calls out, "Hola!" "Hola! Have a great day," I respond. "Great day for sleeping!" another responds, all three tilting their heads onto prayer-hands, their giggles pinging up my spine. As they pass by the three are smiling over their shoulders, yanking their skirts, bright as the sunrise sky, tight against their immaculate rear ends, giggling louder—sweetly playful. Said interval's indelibly blazed upon my memory, one of a dazzling amount.

And how do air-travel justice? At this point in civilization's evolution air-travel's taken for granted, but it's absolutely off the charts amazing that one can complete a project in NYC at around 10 PM then be riding waves in Puerto Rico by 6 AM, and shame on me if I ever become blasé about it.

Enough—will resume endeavoring to do my Labor Day weekend justice.

Chapter Four

I find myself seated with my back to a pale orange wall, a tree's blossom-heavy branches dipping low, occasionally brushing me, in a dead-end alley, gazing towards the alley's entrance beyond which mist-obscured shadows tremble like ghosts in uneasy anticipation of cockcrow—my hands and chin are gooey with quenepa and mango juice, both fruits in a bag between my legs—I'm cramming quenepas in my mouth, their tartness vaguely countering dazed disquietude.

Attempts to ascertain how, or why, I've arrived here yield no explanations and I'm contrarily pleased—moods shift like shadows in streetlamp light in ocean's fog—emotions unassociated with identifiable causes, even if dread-tinged, are liberation from restrictive clarity of reason. On the one hand I'm feeling as if I'm being pursued by a mysterious malevolent something; on the other hand I'm feeling as if I'm pursuing a mysterious beneficial something—either way, I'm catching my breath before once more compelled to flee or give chase. I'm relishing my stupefaction without understanding why—simultaneously afraid of being unable to seize ahold of a nameless something and afraid of a nameless something that's hellbent on seizing ahold of me. And my fitness-tracker, means of ascertaining the hour, is gone—did a wave rip it from my wrist and I'm only noticing now, or was I aware when it happened and forgot? Maybe over a day ago I was at JFK but it's as if I've briefly napped and awakened in this alley.

How explain apprehension amidst breathtaking surroundings?—a flowering tree's scent, suggestive of women's hair and perfume and skin, permeating the air?—breeze-rippled palm-fronds whispering, coqui lustily singing?—tropical warmth making Manhattan's winter seem ridiculously unreal? Yet I'm devouring quenepas and mango as if I've no idea when I'll obtain another meal! It's not like infrastructure-demolishing Maria swept through last week and I need to think about gathering mollusks and capturing insects for protein, foraging for wild coconuts and other fruit and seeds, obtaining water from rainforest streams.

I swear I'm sane! And aware anyone who swears they're sane is immediately suspect, since sanity's rightly assumed to be the default frame of mind. Why apprehensive regarding my frame of mind after deliriously boogie boarding, dancing? Marisol's more stunning than a field of shimmering dew-drenched flowers at dawn—her eyes, radiant with affection and energy, are dizzy ascension. We were relishing one another—couldn't stop caressing, kissing—yet became separated, lost one another—I'm utterly mystified as to why, recollect nothing. And there's no telling how much alcohol I've imbibed, nor do I have a clue how much sleep I've obtained since around 10:00 AM in NYC day before yesterday. Sleep-deprivation's hallucinogenic, I'm as amped up as disoriented, in thrall to paranoia and expectation alike—grinding my back against the wall.

Can't stress it enough: arrival in Puerto Rico's a Fountain of Youth, kicks the "I don't care how a person my age is expected to behave, I'm spitting on that!" frame of mind into gear. So, again, what's with the trepidation, foreboding? But isn't foreboding merely a product of an overactive imagination?—reflection of one's present mood, form of projection? Certainly it's impossible to foresee the future. Then again, if foreboding's unsettling enough it could unbalance one to the extent a disturbing incident's more likely to occur, as in fear manufacturing the outcome, fulfilling its own prophecy. Can paranoia be a manifestation of desire? OK! Such is a sampling of the speculations preoccupying me as I stare blankly ahead, continue devouring quenepas and mango as if I won't eat again for days.

The breeze is speeding up—foliage hissing instead of gently rustling, leaves and litter clattering across pavement, scraping building fronts—clouds blotting out the moon, rumbling and flashes approaching. Impressions of disorientation, terror, awe, panic, confusion, a general feeling of being absolutely vulnerable, alone, in a chaotic unpredictable world are absorbing my attention; and pronounced, as it were rebellious, joy accompanies these impressions. It's dawning on me this situation's my heart's desire, even if I'm baffled as to why: I'm in a dead-end alley located I've no idea where, taut as a drawn bow, thunderstorm bearing down.

Chapter Five

Shimmerbang, flickerboom! Gust-torn sheets of rain, silvered in a streetlamp's glare, are slashing diagonally amidst lightning's zigzags, thunder's crashes—obscuring all but objects near enough to touch. The building opposite's a pulsating blur.

"Here kitty kitty kitty!" a voice calls, piercing the gale. I discern a silhouette near the alley's entrance—the silhouette sways, stumbles, rights itself, passes on. I've elected to ride out the storm in place, as the flowering tree's abundant foliage is deflecting a direct drenching, but the storm has other ideas. The overhanging roof's gutter, rapidly glutted, spills over—shsssssh! thoroughly soaks me, nearly knocks me over, as thunder crashes louder, lightning flashes brighter. Soon as I exit the alley gusts—whsssssh! grab me. I'm knocked this way—that! by wind-currents scattering pell-mell like schools of frightened fish. Storm-whipped rain's semi-stinging, I'm shielding my eyes from airborne debris; a trash-can blows over, clangs while rolling—I but vaguely see it, dash from the sound; a window splinters, hit by a projectile. One moment bursts of chilly air are shoving me against a wall, the next I'm running haphazardly, nearly flung to the ground! Did I miss a tropical storm warning? Wouldn't be the first time—oblivion's seductive.

Where's shelter? La Placita's clubs, assuming they're still active, are who knows how far from wherever I am, and same goes for my rental car—it might as well be in Ponce. The curbs are roiling, overflowing—a good inch of water sliding over the sidewalk already. Coqui are piercing the storm-din—tropical heat periodically penetrates the storm-chill, swishes on me. Do I care if shelter's found? It's *beautiful* that all of outdoors is a pie with the storm's fingers digging in it.

Where to turn? I'm walking, dashing, backtracking, pausing to ascertain direction, spinning about—surrounded by blinding haze, as directionless as the storm's contrary winds. I turn a corner—an illuminated entryway's not four yards away. I yank at the door, it gives, I enter—a bedraggled individual stirs at the second door's base. "Kitty!" the individual calls, intonation husky but feminine.

She's quickly on her feet in the dark amber light, gnarled mouse-brown hair hanging limp, heels clacking on the marble floor, fastening her eyes on me—their splintered half-mad look flying in all directions from the rims of their pupils. I'm about to bolt—she seizes my hand, agitatedly pats, strokes—raises it to her lips, kisses and licks, heats with her breath. Witchery! Her touch, nefariously vivid, whips up my forearm, shimmers my spine, induces the flipped-inside-out-buoyancy sensation—I'm spellbound while revolted, fascinated while repulsed. She's undeniably drug-ravaged, high-risk disease-wise, but there's magnetic vitality in her touch. Part of me's inclined to grab and hug, thrill to her energy, while another part of me's advising to flee fast. But I'm unable to flee.

"Can you hear me?" she rasps. "Can you do me a favor—a little favor? I'm a working girl—oh, ten dollars, that's all—I'll make you feel *real* special." She's rubbing her crotch against me, squeezing one of my thighs in front, her hand trembling—pushing me to the wall, sucking my neck, teeth soft-scraping.

It's surprisingly tough to distance myself, be detached, impose boundaries. The woman's deft crisp touch, slipping under and sparkling my skin, is conjuring hunger and imagery—the fact I arrestingly surged when she seized my hand is as scary as captivating. If I was blindfolded I might have the time of my life, hit stratospheric heights of stimulation, but I'm not blindfolded. A scavenging look's in her eyes—an illness-consumed frame's obvious in her drenched clinging dress. Who knows what's afflicting her? Surrender may yield a medical nightmare.

Yet I'm still riveted—marveling at her elemental sway, the absorbing discombobulation and inner fireworks she's birthing. I'm cautioning myself against uniting my lips with hers but only cerebrally, risk of disease-transmission dissuading me as emotion tempts. She's adept at jumpstarting desire—coaxing desire—and I'm (might as well own up) enjoying the situation—enjoying myself—despite myself. "We'll have a blast, I'm a professional and it's my treat!" she declares, hands sliding up my midriff under my shirt, teeth gently tantalizingly worrying my neck again—winding a leg about mine, pressing me to the wall with re-doubled insistence, her chest heaving, breathing audible, eyes widening, brightening—strength above what her rail-thin frame would indicate. Engaging encounter or not, caution finally gets the upper hand: if I remain much longer I may lose the ability to police myself, resist peril. How extricate myself tactfully?

The woman frowns. "Kitty, I'm a working girl and want to please you, a measly ten dollars is all because I like you! I'm a professional, don't worry, it's one and done—you need soothing, I can tell! I'm your mommy, baby, so suckle—it's my pleasure to offer, I'm lonely too! *(She lowers her top, exposes her breasts. Detecting hesitation on my part, she seizes my shoulders, switches tone)* You should be pleased and flattered when a woman wants to be *special* for you! I'm usually *very* expensive—men form lines to pay! When I danced on Honolulu bars, shot tequila from my hip, guys *begged* for my attention, all wanted a piece! My thigh-highs bulged with tips! You should thank your lucky stars—I've never been this cheap! What's wrong with you? Why can't you accept a gift?"

I don't doubt the woman's dancer-history—her witchery's undeniable, it's the rare woman who possesses such skills. I'm half-wishing I could allow myself to thumb my nose at rationality, laugh at caution, and surrender, consequences be damned. "Nothing's wrong with you and nothing's wrong with me," I counter, grasping her wrists, stepping from the wall. "We don't know each other and, sorry, but this isn't happening."; then, keeping her at arm's length, a hand at her breastbone, the other reaching for my wallet, "Here's something for you."

"You insult me?" she cries, flailing a hand, stepping back. "I don't throw myself out there for just anyone, curse your charity! It's not about money, I want to get calm! Why are you mean to me when I'm nice? You can do *anything*, I'm your pizza dough girl, shape me and mold me and eat me up—be a *man*! Unleash on me, exhaust me, try to make me pass out on this floor! I'm strong and want a firm grip—grab me and kiss me!" She thrusts herself at me, a knee on my belly.

"Goodbye, and sorry, but I need to go—call me whatever you want, I'm sure I deserve the worst," I say, gently but firmly seizing her shoulders and turning her away. "This is for you," I continue, tossing a bill at her feet—maybe it's a single, maybe it's a twenty. I kick the door open.

"Kitty, come back—I don't bite!" I hear as I reenter the storm dashing, unsure if the woman's following. Tropics or not, the wind's semi-chilling me—lightning's periodically illuminating immediate surroundings—the coqui are seemingly louder than thunder-cracks—amazing, and comforting, that such tiny creatures can saturate the air with song. Soon I'm leaning against a wall, steadying myself, gazing skywards—a flamboyant's wind-thrashed branches are overhead, shedding soaked petals—scarlet's clinging to my skin and clothes. I've boogie boarded, danced with darling Marisol, met by chance, with no recollection of how or why we separated, and now solicited by a professional with beguiling skills belying an alarming appearance. I usually welcome the unexpected—Puerto Rico's usually delight bordering on delirium—so why am I uneasy, arms held tight to my chest?

I bolt from the wall as if it's red-hot, turn the nearest corner, a blast of gust-whipped rain hitting me face-on. Ha! Suspicious figures are on my side of the street, approaching fast—I'm alone against three! Why am I supposing them malevolent? There's no rationale for paranoia's onslaught—I'm in incandescent Puerto Rico, for Christ's sake! Am I capriciously undermining ease of mind?—willfully, albeit subconsciously, flinging myself in stress-inducing directions for exploratory purposes? I'm discerning cruelty in the eyes of the three—feigning dreamy oblivion, seeking to appear too preoccupied with inner matters to be aware of them. Perhaps they'll feel I'm inoffensively abstracted and leave me be? I hope I'm overthinking! Why would they, chatting among themselves and in their own world, trouble to notice me, challenge me? But then one of them intently looks at me, announces, "Good for you, man—wish I had gobs of lipstick on me, looks like she wanted to rape your face!" Is he mocking me? Initially I believe so and likely appear taken aback, confused, alarmed—he's smilingly gesturing for me to examine my reflection in an awning-shielded window, illuminated by fluorescent light. Glory be! Crimson's smeared on my face, there are lip-prints on my cheeks and forehead, as if I've been making out for hours—tension disappears.

The three bid me good night, laughing that they're thoroughly soaked, one stomping a foot in the gutter, splashing—jollily stroll on. To think I'd supposed them hellbent on harming me, was reaching for ridiculous strategy, wondering if acting the part of one bedeviled, haunted and hounded—staring blank-eyed at the air, hinting at mental imbalance—would persuade them to bless me as a brother night denizen, leave me alone. Silly imagined drama, particularly as they were the opposite of enemies. But imaginary enemies? Does a portion of my personality thrive on inventing opposition, afflicting itself? Sure, experience intensifies and bedazzles, but I'm endangering myself and others—falsely believing someone to be malice-motivated could lead to real violence—not a bit funny. But did I come to Puerto Rico to devil myself?—split hairs, race in futile cerebral circles? Has such happened to me in Puerto Rico, on *any* vacation anywhere, before? *No!*

Chapter Six

Finally a location I recognize, the Maria-shattered seawall and little park (its name escapes me) at El Presby—was beginning to wonder if I was halfway to Isla Verde or somewhere south of Santurce, the storm not only obscuring landmarks but drowning out the Atlantic's sounds and scents and wind-direction and open sky, robbing me of ability to find a beach. I'd like to think I've arrived here via subconscious awareness of clues—reflexive locational memory, innate directional sense—but perhaps it's merely by chance. Stone benches are toppled, one's flipped upside down, partially buried in sand smothering half the lawn—chunks of jumbled concrete at seawall's center, many walkway tiles smashed. "Careful!" I inform myself, obtaining my bearings at the surviving table in the park's center, where I enjoyed succulent meals—fish tacos, crab and octopus empanadas, chicken pinchos—pre-Maria, when there was enough lawn for soccer. I'm strolling towards the blurred lights of Condado's westward hotels, able to avoid scattered concrete-chunks due to two miraculously surviving lamps—stepping down to the beach at the park's boundary. Rain's continuing to obscure details but I know ankle-high slabs of rock, precariously slick with algae, displace the sand about fifteen yards ahead, in front of Paseo Don Juan's intact seawall, three yards high.

My feet are in flipflops instead of shoes—a bag containing hard objects whacks my shin, smarts. I've been wearing flipflops, carried the bag, since...? Ha, since stopping at the rental car on Calle Maribel several blocks away! Seems I located the car on something of autopilot—I've no recollection of intention to find the car, somehow bested tonight's sensory and emotional distortions. Am too distant from the lamps to see what's in the bag so I stick a hand in, discover cans of Medalla.

Because I often go weeks without drinking, *thoroughly* surrendering to alcohol's a treat. Chasing oblivion with little concern for consequences, aftereffects—granting impulsiveness greater sway over my behavior—is just plain fun, enlightening even, and *especially* in Puerto Rico. "Yeah!" I yell, cracking open a can, my clothes so soaked rain's pouring off me quick as it lands. I'm at the cluster of sea grapes in front of Paseo Don Juan's seawall, their 8-inch leaves flailing, whistling—lift a fist towards lightning flashes, drain the can, fall onto my back, dig my shoulders and hips into the sand, scream louder and writhe. No chance of yelling loud as I can in NYC so I'm milking the opportunity.

Surf's higher than yesterday, audible amidst the storm, crests intermittingly catching lightning-light and San Juan's illumination. Before long I'm knee-deep in water racing over three-quarters up the beach—bracing myself against push and tug, fighting to remain standing as retreating water yanks sand from underfoot—while howling and yelping, mimicking coyotes (having heard them in the Sierras, Sun Valley, Rockies). Ocean's warmer than the rain and it's tempting to dive in, frolic in the churn, and overindulgence in alcohol's liberating, but... OK, it's *enlightening* to stoke intoxication, alcohol-fueled or excitement-fueled or otherwise—come close to casting sound judgment aside, rashly embracing ill-advised activities—while *yet* maintaining the ability to watch out for oneself, stay safe. Treading the boundary between safety and danger, as in storm-tossed surf tugging at me, seeking to beguile me, and choosing to remain upshore is therapeutic. I could lose visibility while seized by the churn, yanked seawards, if I stepped four or five yards forward—it's a privilege to catch a glimpse of primal vulnerability—civilization endeavors to blind us to how fragile we are.

This location's special: it's where I first waded into Puerto Rico's waves, when I didn't know one street's name and all was mystery. Now I'm bounced about by water foaming bellybutton-high while seated further upshore—opening another Medalla as rain tickle-stings my face—lightning's no longer in evidence, or I wouldn't be anywhere near ocean's edge. How many Medallas have I drained?

A bilingual sign's facing away from me on Paseo Don Juan a few yards away, its silver back vaguely shining—I know it states: "Peligro: Oleaje Fuerte/Warning: Dangerous Shorebreak" and that within an orange diamond is the silhouette of a person spun upside down. But I've never felt unsafe here, because I respect the sea; and respect that the western boundary of a semi-circle of razor-sharp wave-sculpted lava's to my right—beware if waves are pulling east at speed.

Whoa! Lightning flashes so close I hear electricity sizzle, a deafening bang—shock-waves vibrating my bones, very sand I'm seated on—silver-white briefly blinds. I'm on hands and knees, scampering clear of waves' reach as if swarmed by wasps—nearly tripping upon regaining my feet. Then arms wrapped about my knees at seawall's base, wind-thrashed sea grape foliage swatting me—I've been insanely heedless! I was respecting the sea? What about respecting the storm? How many times have I been in the waves when dark clouds, heralding electrical activity, swept in and I hastily exited? All the electrical activity earlier and I *really* brushed such aside, ignored an obvious threat? I thought I knew better!

Why scrunched in a ball? Will minimizing exposed surface area of my body reduce chance of electrocution, when all's drenched in conductivity? If lightning strikes wet sand I'm no better off than if in the waves! Why's the storm so long-lasting, unabatedly strong? Again I'm wondering if I missed a storm warning; but the instant I'm wondering such realize La Placita would've been shut down, alcohol unavailable—am standing, lifting my arms skywards, laughing—not defiantly, but because it makes no difference—danger's already a done deal and, besides, I'm exiting the beach posthaste, seeking shelter. So why not open another Medalla, celebrate the churning storm and sea, worlds removed from NYC? Am I imagining the danger, as when I supposed three randomly encountered strangers might be inclined to harm me? No! The storm's very willing to harm me.

Chapter Seven

Angie and Ella! Thanks, as always, for being my audience and inspiration, best motivation to continue recollecting—am gaining added appreciation of how life-altering my Puerto Rico trips are, and having fun. In my humble opinion one's closer to attaining enlightenment when one's senses are spun outside of ability to unite cause with effect—logic's limiting—blurred experiences are more enthralling, vividly persistent in memory, than readily comprehensible ones.

Was I dead center on the lawn in Plaza Antonia Quinones, another first-day-in-Puerto-Rico-seemingly-eons-ago (given all the psychic transformation, personality revision, I've undergone) location, lifting my arms to storm-thrashed clouds, alternately balancing on either leg—shrieking uninhibitedly, confident my noise would be drowned out by the storm and hyperactive coqui—hoisting more Medallas, toasting the unleashed elements? Were two girls making out under the pavilion's bright white curve, profiles undulating, features alternately blurred and sharp, in the rain-sheen? Is one in indigo, other in emerald—skin-tight storm-soaked one-pieces, mid-thigh-high—hair matted to their heads? Do they notice me, smile and wave, shout greetings? I can't make out their words, bring a hand to my ear, approach halfway—they shout louder—I hear, "We admire you!" I'm saluting, wishing them a happy night—resume balancing. Did such occur, or was it part of the dream-whirl when I passed out later on? But I'm getting ahead of myself.

To resume in real-time, or at least my perception of such at the time: rain's glutting the gutters, overspreading sidewalks—every step's a splash and ripples—inch-plus-diameter landsnails congregate on the sidewalk in places, where I tiptoe to avoid tromping on their spiral-patterned shells, light brown contrasting with smoky yellow with black. People are approaching: I'm aware of animation, electric fluidity, nebulous silhouettes—blind to physical attributes, alive to inner essence, vitality—I believe greetings are exchanged via gestures, their voices lost in the wind—they considerately become single-file and stop, allow me ease of passage, because an ancient tree, its gnarled trunk, is partially obstructing the sidewalk.

I have no idea where I am—*again*! Sheets of mist-saturated light are shivering, shifting—dipping, soaring! in the gusts—reflected orbs of streetlamps dancing on—igniting! puddles at my feet, windows to my left—headlights here and there slashing, taillights trailing crimson—a group of chickens scatters a couple yards ahead, vanishes within shrubs, and a cock's crowing—feral chickens are everywhere. INTRUSION: a sudden gasp, sigh—insistence of presence, projected tension, surprise—sparkles in my nerves; the bright—leaping! silver of a pair of eyes seizes my eye, yanks my glance down: a girl—alert, anxious! is seated on a doorstep, intently regarding me—I'm noting her toned thighs, silky as firm—the fullness of her chest, radiance of her face—slender arms, trembling hands, mussed hair, parted lips—dark eyes aglow with ineffable sweetness, body language softening—her litheness snug in a soaked pale lavender dress. I've paused and the girl's pleased—we're flowing towards one another, meeting in the charged space of air between us. She's illuminated by lights on each side of the building's door—her eyes widening, visage framed in pitch black hair. "Loving the storm," she smiles, lifting her hands and twirling them, thrusting out her chest. "Same here—the storm's beautiful—pure energy," I respond, sweeping an arm towards the sky; then, upon extracting a Medalla from the bag, "Would you like one?" "So nice, thank you," she says, standing and clasping one of my shoulders. "My pleasure," I say, handing her a can, "and I don't know what time it is and don't want to know—tonight's a gift, hopefully dawn's still hours away." "So I won't tell what time!" she giggles, kissing me on the cheek, presenting her cheek for a kiss. After returning her kiss I'm strolling away, we waving farewell—two strangers sharing happiness in probably not much over a minute during a storm-tossed night.

My flipflops have vanished and I'm barefoot—I've no idea how long I've been so. It's reassuring that, intoxicated and dazed though I be, I've been reliably, seemingly subconsciously, alert for hazards. San Juan's sidewalks can be precarious—some slabs are over an inch higher than those adjacent, poised to trip people—many oval 10x6 inch waterline access panels, of brittle metal, are smashed or missing, with gaping holes, risk of sprained ankles or worse, in their place—the rain's slashing as furiously as if the cloudburst's seconds old. At least a dozen landsnails are on the sidewalk alongside dense shrubs—I pick one up and the animal's writhing in protest, seeking to tug itself onto my forefinger via suction, escape—I'm holding it close to my eyes, admiring the shell's symmetry, architecture—nothing humans have built will last a hundred million years in fossil records—mollusks have thrived hundreds of millions of years longer than humans have a prayer of existing. Humans are evolutionary infants—civilization's a flimsy facade. I toss the landsnail into the far side of the shrubs, clear of the sidewalk—crouch to toss the others to safety. Then strolling again—measuring my steps, hyper-cautious on account of awakening to the fact I'm barefoot. INTRUSION: reflect-ed imagery upon a window to my right quivers—shakes! like a pond's suddenly disturbed surface, and I turn towards it—ha! meet myself, eyes unflinchingly leaping at—challenging! the observer, unwilling to back down, be trodden upon. And here I'd supposed I might very well appear abstracted and vulnerable, ripe for victimhood! It's electrifying that I'm nothing of the sort! It's not only the reflection of an elated confident person, but of one who's respectful of being alone in nighttime streets, alert to steer clear of conflict—I'm raising a fist, yelling, "Thank you, eye-opening Puerto Rico! You've altered my life for the better outside wildest imagining! I love you infinitely, Puerto Rico!"

"What are you looking at with a face like that?" I hear a few blocks later, unsure if I'm the one spoken to—abrupt movement, clang of an oil drum lowered to a driveway, leads me to turn towards the voice. A man's glaring, cheeks twitching—he's illuminated by floodlights at the head of the driveway. I'm still strolling cautiously, slowly, due to being barefoot—glancing at the man as if appraising a piece of furniture—not overly alarmed, because the situation seems unreal—I can't imagine how I've given offense when oblivious of his presence. The man waddles clear of the truck, still glaring—is wearing lime green bib overalls stamped with a company logo, and nearly six feet tall, grossly overweight—he could knock me down with a punch but could never catch up with me, walking's laborious for him. He likely wishes he could puff himself up, flex muscles, but there's only blubber. I'm noting all in about two sec-onds. Curious: an anonymous someone's gripped with hostility—flus-tered, quivering! at sight of me—apparently the mere fact of my existence upsets him. Had to make his presence known, try shoddy intimidation tactics. Why? Because I would've otherwise been lost in my thoughts? Not my fault he hates his job, or life in general, is clearly miserable, wallowing in frustration. "What are you looking at?" he repeats even though I've strolled past the driveway and a large tree and dumpster are obstructing our view of each other. He's yelling blindly, seeking to force a reaction. My attention's primarily preoccupied with negotiating the sidewalk, watching for anything able to cut my feet or trip me.

Gusts are weaker and less frequent but the underlying wind's un-abated—rain's uniformly slightly slanted, no longer slung every which way—no sign of pre-dawn birdsongs or light—I still have no idea of the hour but know I'm in Condado. Not sure why I turn to gaze in the intrusive deliveryman's direction—perhaps so as to gauge to what degree visibility's improved, a straight line down the sidewalk.

The deliveryman's truck, lime green with an illuminated casino ad-vertisement on its roof, is backing out of the driveway—it's a one-way street, he'll be heading in my direction. Is he after me? If so, good luck to him—a private parking lot's boom gate is here, all I need do is duck under, walk to the other gate near the beach and duck under that, hit the shoreline—he's too overweight to give chase, get anywhere near me—probably takes him half a minute to climb from the truck.

Ha! Unexpectedly prodded to action by the enemy's limitations, I find myself rifling through a trashcan under the streetlamp—discover a magnificent prize: cheesecake! Putrefying, slimy—cradled in a half-fold-ed paper plate—as if expressly made to be flung at a despised target, smack a wannabe bully—treat him to some just desserts. I pivot, the truck's almost alongside me—dart forward, throw the cake hard as I can, see it hit the windshield on the driver's side—optimum splatter-pattern, mucky white. The slob panics, hits the brakes too hard—truck skids on wet pavement, hydroplanes, spins—its rear jumps the curb, strikes a tree. Oh, joy! The truck's shuddering as if recoiling from sledgeham-mer-blows.

I don't linger to gloat, duck under the boom gate, walk fast (but not too fast, lest I attract the notice of unseen people, potentially a security guard) without looking back, equally animated by apprehension and glee—am shortly on the beach, relishing sight and sound of surf, waves swishing at my ankles. I surprised myself by whipping the cheesecake at the truck (it was as if an outside force seized ahold of me—guided my aim), but I'm not thinking about that for long. At one point I'm snow-angeling above waterline, relishing the sensation of shoving my fingers and toes into wet sand—at another point on my knees in the rock sheltered pool at El Presby near the swath of eelgrass, opening another Medalla, slow moving water sloshing my belly. The storm's subsided, rain's a light mist—waves hitting the rocks are spraying me—still no discernable light at horizon's line.

Chapter Eight

It's not often I'm treated to oblivion, Angie and Ella—utterly lose the ability to disentangle how I managed to wind up somewhere from somewhere else. I say "treated," but only an imbecile would intentionally induce the situation. A kick if one gets away with it but blessings must be counted—gloating's ill advised.

I'm on my back on lawn under blazing sun, partially shaded by cycads—judging by the sun's location it's barely past noon and I don't recall dawn. I know this yard: a code's needed to open the wrought iron gate—seems I keyed in the code and entered, collapsed. A gorgeous cat's licking my face, gently kneading about my breastbone with her paws—she's Pastel, named for her calico coat—she has pale gold-green eyes, a white splotch about a pink nose, extra fluffy tail. I've been told she's highly temperamental, disposed to confront and scratch, but she's always been an angel with me. Two years ago she meowled in greeting as I passed her yard—slipped through the bars of the wrought iron fence, rubbed against me, playfully swatted with retracted claws. Soon I was crouching on the sidewalk, she purring on my lap as I pet her. The lady of the house, Luna, weeding a flower-island's opposite side and observing through the flowers, saw Pastel cross the yard to greet me and jump on my lap—rose and approached, announced I must be a special person, since Pastel's locally celebrated for disliking people, fiercely guarding her territory. Apparently I tamed a tigress without trying, and to this day I'm questioning whether Pastel's aggressive with anyone, it doesn't seem possible—she cheerfully swishes against me and purrs, adores play and cuddles, her golden gaze ineffably sweet. After a few minutes of socializing two years ago Luna, in off-handed-not-a-big-deal Puerto Rican hospitality fashion, surprised me by giving me the gate's code, saying please come visit Pastel anytime. Playing with Pastel's *essential* on Puerto Rico visits, usually I bring treats and toys.

I'm in awe of the fact Pastel's befriended me, would sooner die than take advantage of such—never dreamed I'd pass out in her yard—such is just plain inexcusably tacky, and I'm as ashamed as worried—all too visible from the street. My t-shirt's spread out and dry on the lawn, near my flipflops and a bag—four cans of Medalla, one empty and three unopened, are scattered to the left of my head—I thought I'd lost my flipflops. I won't blame Pastel's family if they revoke my visitation privileges—I've violated their trust. I'm immediately bolt upright, putting on the t-shirt, placing the cans of beer in the bag. Sun's heating the back of my neck—two anoles scamper up a white wall—one of the small brown birds with the metallic trill is vocalizing nearby. Pastel, bless her, is on my lap purring.

Unreal! The lady of the house appears with a sterling silver serving tray, plate of eggs, salsa, yucca, plantains, cup of tea—says she didn't want to wake me, kept Pastel indoors until she made a serious fuss, as she's accustomed to being let outdoors during daylight on demand—notes my surprise and smiles, declares that because Pastel's adopted me I'll always be welcome—asks no questions, betrays no surprise. All the same I'm saying something like, "Luna, I know it's weird but I don't remember coming here, would never plan on sleeping off a long night in your yard, abusing your kindness—there's no excuse, I'm sorry and embarrassed." Luna laughingly waves a hand in dismissal, says, "Pastel's chosen well—you two have fun!" and returns to her house. I'm infinitely blessed Pastel's befriended me. Who knows where I would've otherwise passed out? Oblivion's not a toy.

I'm certainly famished—aside from last night's quenepas and mangos, I haven't had a bite to eat since yesterday afternoon, around twenty-four hours ago. As I devour the meal and quaff tea, the caffeine as welcome as the nutrition, Pastel's getting friskier by the second—soon flipping onto her side alongside me, pawing my front right pocket, attacking my wallet, one of our games. She's biting through my linen pants and I extract my wallet so she can attack it directly. Lo! A sheet of water-logged triple-folded paper's matted to my wallet. Begging Pastel's pardon, I momentarily lift the wallet outside her reach, carefully peel off the paper, unfold it. At its top I read: "To Steve from Marisol with love!

Here's a place wh…" Oh, no! The remainder of the message is smeared, illegible! On the other side's a patch of scarlet—a partial lip-print's discernable. There's every reason to believe Marisol provided her contact information and kissed the paper.

The note's discovery only intensifies the loss of Marisol, stabs me harder. Yes, that we'd planned on staying in touch, possibly arranged to meet at the blotted-out location, dispels some of the mystery, but I've negligently allowed rain to destroy most of the message, keep us apart—Marisol's lost and it's my doing.

Cats readily perceive alteration of emotion and Pastel abandons interest in play—gazes upon me sweetly with widened eyes, rubs against me, purrs—every aspect of her body language is communicating concern. "You're the sweetest sweetheart," I say, reclining onto my back, she climbing onto my chest.

I'm recalling Marisol's laughing eyes and vitality and svelteness, melodious voice, cascading pitch-black tresses, scent and touch. And I've no means of seeing her! Chance meeting's virtually never happen—she's gone! She'll be wondering why I'm not following through, when there's nothing I want more—the thought that she'll be wondering why I've changed my mind twists knives in my nerves. I'm still baffled as to how or why we separated—try as I might, I can't recall a goodbye. And Marisol wrote "with love"? Sure, the expression's slung about in friendly fashion among friends, but it reinforces how we felt about each other, amount of easy familiarity we arrived at—when Marisol clasped my hands, affectionately finger-caressed, sparkles reverberated through my depths.

Chapter Nine

So, Angie and Ella, it's a sun-drenched day in Puerto Rico and the unthinkable's happening—gloom's gathering—shadowy veils envelop eyesight—good cheer's opposite an invisible wall. Marisol is extraordinary, our communication spontaneous—dance-floor synchronization leapt into life on its own, swept us sure as high surf into laughter and hugs and kisses and play. Allowing her contact info to become illegible's an inexcusable betrayal!

Insane to be hemmed in—gloom-smothered—in the wide open, under a bright tropical sky, while strolling to the sea! I'm in Parque La Ventana al Mar (Window to the Sea Park)—a spot-on name, as nothing obstructs view of the sea from Ashford Avenue and an expansive lawn invites one within—wind's rustling palm fronds to my right—fountain-jets are whooshing, creating clouds of mist, to my left. I'm headed for the breakwater's path—hopefully sight and sound and feel of surf slamming the boulders, vibrating the path, will elevate my spirits.

Someone's waving in front of the fountains, jumping up and down, semi-blurred by breeze-wisped mist—accidentally glimpsed in peripheral vision and there's vague recognition of physique and motion. I hear, "Hey Steve! Yoo hoo!"

The Fates be praised! Marisol's speaking and I'm jolted from my nightmare, gloom instantly a figment of my imagination. She's flinging her hair behind her shoulders—laughingly doing the twist, dipping low, her smile surging up my spine. We're hugging in seconds. "Thought I'd lost you!" I blurt out.

"What?" she responds, eyes widening, clasping one of my wrists. "I'm early, wasn't going to miss our meeting for anything—got here ten minutes ago."

"Marisol, I woke up in a friend's front yard a couple hours ago with no memory of winding up there then found the napkin with your info in my pocket, except most of it was smeared and illegible because I was in the storm all night—was afraid I'd never see you again, running into you's crazy lucky!"

"Steve, that's slightly crazy to me—it was your idea to meet here, go out on the breakwater before surfing. I've been texting like mad, embarrassing myself actually—going to a mommy place, wondering what on earth could've..."

"For which I'm *so* sorry, Marisol," I break in, gently squeezing her hands. "I was terrified you'd think I changed my mind—I stupidly allowed rain to destroy your info, thought I had no means of finding you—was in hell and this is a miracle. Although...wait... *(I slap my forehead.)* If you've been texting, then..."

"Yes, Steve, I texted my info last night and you watched me do it!" she interrupts laughing, lifting my hands over her head and turning to back up against me, whereupon I wrap my arms about her, she playfully squirming.

"Haven't seen my phone since stowing it in the rental car before we met, but *huge* relief your info was secure and I didn't lose you. Although had I not happened along here I would've shamefully stood you up—mortifies me to think of it. As to why it didn't occur to me to check my phone—an *extremely* obvious thing to do—I can't explain that either. There's no reason not to have my phone on me now and sorry for not seeing your texts, all misunderstanding's my fault."

"Explains everything," she smiles, turning to lick my cheek. "And that napkin and others was us clowning around—you did stick figures of us dancing, which I'm keeping—I smooched napkins while you nibbled my neck, and with your hand up my dress, showing me a divine time, and I did things you liked. You don't remember *any* of that? How many mojitos did you have? Are you with me now? *(She places a hand on my forehead.)* OK, no hangover heat there—maybe you're jetlagged? How many fingers do you see? *(She holds up three, then switches to four, then to two and back to three, squeezing my midriff.)* Are you drunk?"

"Drunk with delight at finding you again, Marisol, and the round-about way I've done so, as if we're destined," I answer, squeezing her midriff in turn. "I was in a dark dismal place because of losing touch with you and here you are."

"You only *thought* we lost touch, Steve," she declares, kissing my forehead. "I didn't lose faith, felt something must be up, rational reasons why no reply."

"Swarms of loony reasons," I smile, reaching up her leg under her dress at her invitation, she meaningfully glancing at my hand and stepping close, nudging with a knee. "Was blurred in my bearings, yanked into altered states—surf and little sleep and the storm and alcohol, losing my way in the streets even though I didn't really venture very far (such is becoming clear), and an amazing woman's bloodstream-reverbera-tions—fear of having lost touch with you pummeled me."

"No loss of touch now," she giggles, thrusting her belly at mine; then, after arrestingly hyperventilating, "We travelled so far together last night, were marveling about it aloud, no chance was I letting that go. Sweetie *(She softly circles her fingers at my temples.)*, I would've *stalked* you had you not shown up—you told me where your rental car was and gave me your Guaynabo contact info, and New York too! And, anyway, we didn't need our phones to find each other—don't underestimate ability of our subconscious to grab the reins and guide us. I love that your subconscious took charge and brought you to me."

"Right, I came to Ventana al Mar to lift my spirits, drive darkness away, and succeeded beyond wildest hope—all's blissful light." I'm running a hand up and down the back of her thigh as we press against one another in front.

"So it could be a coincidence you're here," she winks, slipping a hand up the back of my shirt. "You mentioned loving Ventana al Mar, which is why we chose to meet here, but you've arrived on the dot. Give yourself credit: we made a rendezvous and that sank in and brought you here outside of conscious thought."

"Thanks for the faith, Marisol *(I kiss her forehead.)*, but I'm not worthy."

"How silly, Steve—no one could be more..."

"Marisol," I break in, "I literally don't recall saying goodbye to you last night. I was guiding us through the crowd outside, holding your hand, and when I turned to face you was holding someone else's hand—tried all night to figure it out. A complete hallucination! Like, I thought I was holding your hand but it was someone else's hand and she knew things about me. Just nuts!"

"Oh, Steve!" She cries, hugging me tighter. "So sorry, I should have clarified better! That was cousin Maria—I left you with her because I had to show a house this morning, and she *did* mention you appeared confused at first, mumbled something about slapping yourself awake. But then you assured her all was well, said you needed to leave, and she took a picture of you and sent it to me. See? *(She shows me the photo. I'm smiling, balancing on one leg, giving her cousin a thumbs-up.)* If you hadn't been so cheerful and self-possessed she wouldn't have let you go. Maria's a conscientious and forceful fourteen-year-old."

"Whoa! No memory of getting my picture taken, even though it's pretty clear I was aware at the time! Was I in an alternate universe? Because also no memory that the new woman was your cousin or that she was a child! Shame on me for abandoning a fourteen-year-old! Or...? Well, her parents were there, right? OK, I'm assuming they were there because you're still speaking to me."

"Steve, Maria's mature beyond her years and was entrusted to look after *you*, because I'm still not sure how well you know San Juan, and she was with her posse, adults among them, don't worry about her," Marisol says, earnestly looking me in the eye. "She made you *prove* you knew the landscape (gave you an oral geography exam!), and had you touch your nose multiple times with eyes shut, before letting you go. Again, my fault for not clarifying Maria was in charge of you! Steve, we lingeringly kissed goodbye, affirmed our rendezvous, and..."

"Marisol, of course you *thoroughly* clarified what needed clarifying, and it's on me for losing track," I interrupt. "I wound up having an insanely sense-distorted night in storm-thrashed streets—enough said and I'm not going to wonder why recollection deserted me, only laugh. Mainly, you're more resplendent than dew-drenched flamboyants at dawn—svelte in emerald, and the golden-palm-frond patterns bending light. Last night's strange journey into oblivion's gone!" She's reaching up my shirt, lightly pinching-tweaking my nipples, nibbling an ear.

"Have never been this transparent with anyone so fast, boundaries flying out the window, immediate trust and safety," Marisol declares. We've pulled each other to the lawn, are entwining arms and legs, licking and kissing.

"Marisol, your kisses in blazing sun combine two of my favorite things," I say a few minutes later, gesturing skywards, we having rolled onto our backs.

"We spoke about loving the sun last night but I didn't *prove* it—here's my proof. *(She slides away a bit, sits upright and faces me—pulls her neckline and brassiere down, reveals a vivid tan line nearly midway down her breasts.)* Although maybe I showed you last night—don't recall if I did, seems my recollection of La Placita's also somewhat engagingly distorted—I *was* flooded with wonder. Although I *do* recall we promised to dance in the fountains, defy the bossy security goons, another reason to rendezvous here. Or maybe I'm only imagining we did, or maybe it just occurred to me it would be a kick."

"There's questionable recollection of a great deal of La Placita's doings, but I definitely recall we made a solemn vow to dance in the fountains," I laugh.

"Yay!" she cries, springing to her feet.

We haven't danced among the fountain-jets, shooting at least three yards skywards, for a split-minute before security's frantically blowing whistles from a building's veranda at the park's western boundary. "Sounds like grade school playground monitors trying to stop kids from having fun somewhere off in the distance. Don't think it applies to us. Do you?" I ask, turning eastwards.

"I only hear splashing water," Marisol smiles, likewise turning away from security. "It's our duty to ignore them—lazy slobs need to get off their duff and get some exercise and come over here if they expect us to stop—it's a public service fitness program, unhealthy for them to sit all day." We're whirling from one fountain to another, water shooting up under and ballooning her dress and my shirt, whereupon we're uproariously swatting the fabric into place.

"As if we're going to acknowledge whistles, look over there and obey gestures, instantly hop to—they insult us by assuming we're blindly obedient stooges, trained monkeys. Plus the more we ignore them the longer we play."

"Extended play's the ticket," she giggles, kissing me up my right cheek to across my forehead and down my left cheek to my neck.

"Too deliciously distracted to realize those goof-goons exist," I respond, kissing the nape of her neck, blocking the water shooting up her back with one of my palms. "We're minding our own business, not bothering anyone or harming property, so they should let it slide, go back to playing games on their phones, but they're not going to do that—one's stepping off the veranda, frantically waving."

"Peripheral vision's a beautiful thing, they have no clue we're keeping tabs. *(She's alternately licking my neck and speaking.)* It's fun and *essential* to mess with them—they're not nice people, yell at kids for bringing dogs here."

"He's given up trying to get our attention from there—waddling over."

"I'm *seriously* atremble! Aren't you?" Marisol laughs.

"So atremble I can barely manage to twirl and dip you," I say, we smoothly executing the move. The security guy's fairly red in the face with blowing his whistle—*Fweet! Fweet!*—by the time he's within a couple yards of us, we feigning ignorance of his presence until he's yelling loud. We act astonished, profess ignorance of the rules—are extraordinarily polite, addressing him as Sir, saying we thought the whistle was kids playing, apologize profusely. "Plenty of water to play in over there—sorry again, Sir," Marisol says, pointing towards the beach.

What is it about a drenched dress, clinging to a fit woman's curves and motion, that's able to attract more notice than a barely-there bikini? Heads are whipping in Marisol's direction on the beach—she's upstaging the likewise fit nearly naked women by miles. I sometimes wonder if I'd rather deduce a woman's deliciousness under cloak of fabric, thrill to anticipation's pull, or have her glories revealed straightaway, and my opinion of the matter pretty much depends on what mood I'm in at the time. Straight-up presentation's enthralling of course but accuracy in deduction's a valuable skill—I've gotten very good at ascertaining a woman's attributes in advance of seeing her naked. Every ripple of Marisol's musculature, graceful playful stride, is vividly displayed—sunlight's sliding about the soaked fabric's slickness, contrasting highlights and shadows of emerald and gold. Getting to know Marisol's the pinnacle of good fortune—I couldn't be more blessed.

Chapter Ten

Right, Angie and Ella, I've—ha ha!—gone there, and no apologies. I'm always asking if you'll get jealous if I happily describe another woman's effect on me. I outright declare Marisol's my Holy Grail—an off the charts head-turner, and as whip-smart and enamored of pranking as you. But we three are friends with benefits and we benefit by being free to frolic with others, because friendship's our priority and always will be—we're insanely blessed to have each other.

Resuming narration: am at Marisol's 8th floor beachfront place between El Presby and Parque del Indio—a passion flower vine, heavy with frilly purple blossoms, is entwined in the hurricane-defense grating enclosing the balcony. The vine survived Maria because the steel shutters allow four inches of space between them and the grating. Marisol's shown me a video she made during Maria with shutters shut—the wind sounds like shrieking children and buzz saws—gusts hitting demonically high notes—one *feels* the knifing speed—terrifying.

Marisol has three surfboards and we surfed until sunset with a rollicking crowd—joyous camaraderie and encouragement in the waves, some almost a dozen feet, as fast and powerful as any I've dealt with—testing resolve and ability, forcing us to take frequent breaks—viewed from shore the surf's thundering intimidation, myself amazed I've been playing there while knowing I'll be playing there again—evanescently grabbing ahold of a small part of the ocean's surge, momentary absorption in energy like no other, is something I'll never tire of. Sunset's faded, darkness swathing the sea save where crests briefly grab shoreline light. I missed being face-slammed into the sand by seconds—my board caught backwash, nosedived, dragged me—I frantically spun sideways and up, a knee striking the sand. I was asking for it—foolish to admire the view while on hands and knees on the board instead of reading the sea—surf shifts lightning fast and doesn't forgive, part of the thrill. I've no idea how much sleep I've obtained since arrival—engrossing adventures swiftly succeed one another, excitement whisking me towards more. Running into Marisol in the park, either accidently or via subconscious direction, has apparently rendered sleep requirements a joke. Not seeking to be hubristic—am merely plugged into inner energy, oblivious.

I've told Marisol of last night's adventures, near as I'm able to recall them—she's particularly impressed by the deliveryman prank. "I'd like to play a prank like that," she says, massaging my shoulders, we facing one another on the balcony, sea breeze wisping her hair. "Are you in?"

"Absolutely, but the delivery guy was unjustifiably aggressive, I didn't do anything to him, was minding my own business, mostly alert for sidewalk hazards, smashed tiles and punched-in utilities access panels—oblivious of him until he yelled nastiness and challenged me for no reason. No premeditation—I didn't know I'd prank him, opportunity materialized—I surprised myself."

"Understood, Steve, but you've inspired me to do what I didn't know I'd be doing," she smiles; then, her voice acquiring an edge, "The prank I have in mind is disciplining a creep for disgusting behavior—he lives by SuperMax, his house exposed to attack. He kicked a dog and smashed a kid's toy against a telephone pole when he thought no one was looking. I was looking and want him miserable."

"So his house fronts the street without protection—no wall? And how far is his house from the street? How many windows and how big?—any shrubs or trees between the windows and street? If he has a car, where does he park it?"

"Love what you're suggesting," she grins, miming a pitcher's wind-up, throwing an imaginary ball. "His house is maybe five yards from the street, no wall in front, and there's a wide picture window, hurricane shutters pulled aside. Car's in a carport—open to attack. Seems I noted this stuff beforehand, as if subconsciously plotting. But how could I know a professional would help?"

"Only off-handedly experienced when a youngster, certainly no professional—excepting last night, pranking's years ago—very fountain-of-youth, though, to know I can still go there. So a house-attack's the least of what a dog-kicking creep deserves and we'll deliver, but there could be video monitoring. We need to get disguises, conceal identity with oversized clothes, broad-brimmed hats, uncoordinated gaits and gestures, act our opposites. The tackier and loopier and clumsier the better—we wear stuff we never thought we'd be caught dead in."

"Yay! Shopping for video identification avoidance—prank preparation! I get to dress atrociously, become a caricature and clown, go in fashion directions I've never been—goody-goody! What's the attack-strategy?"

"Beer and eggs!"

"Drinking beer and throwing eggs? Steve, I was hoping for more..."

"For more devastation?" I cut in laughing.

"A sicko that kicks a dog, or wrecks a kid's toy... Absolute scum, as if he's an invented villain, and no sympathy—yes, I want *much* more devastation."

"No sympathy will be given—I throw unopened pints through creep's picture window, blast it open, and we follow with eggs, then we're gone. The beer will be cans of corporate garbage dog piss beer I couldn't be paid to drink, match our disguises. Or should our prank be nondramatic?—gobs of superglue on his car's windows, then dirt's thrown on?—sugar in the gas tank if it's accessible? We *are* adults, need to act quickly, clear out—don't want a souvenir mugshot."

"Definitely a high drama prank—forceful statement!" she responds, running her tongue about her lips, rubbing her hands together. "What I've never done, never thought I'd do—a prank-project at my age! Am crazy stirred, feeling *changed* already, and also afraid! Safe and sound minutes ago, now conscripted for retaliation! Been waiting to make him pay somehow so thank you, Steve!"

"Honored to be with a woman who's itching to prank a sicko, entrusting me to assist—thank *you*, Marisol, and I believe reconnaissance is called for."

"Keeps getting better!" Marisol cries, playfully bumping me, seizing my wrist, pulling me towards the door. "It's like we're being kicked out of here! Duty first!"

"We'll do a quick stroll past the target—won't break stride, lingeringly glance—want to get an idea of the layout, best angle from which to attack."

"From which to attack!" Marisol merrily repeats, opening the door.

Chapter Eleven

After strolling by the enemy's residence, determining which battle-approach is best, Marisol and I find ourselves at the San Juan Supercenter in Santurce, open until eleven. "Second floor's the costume shop," I laugh, "and the first floor's stocked with all else we'll need. One-stop shopping for pranking."

"Immensely convenient and considerate!" she giggles, we happily scampering up the moving walkway to the second floor; then, once we're among rows of clothing, "Plenty of things I'd be pleased to wear but tonight I'm ignoring them—priceless to shop for the tackiest stuff. Maybe I should suggest my company throw a tackiness theme-party for the holidays? Coworkers will go crazy for it!"

"I'm going for the couch potato slob tourist look. Check this out. *(I hold up a polyester Hawaiian shirt.)* Love the orange collar, apparently added to make it look even worse, and what's with the shark heads mixed with flowers and *Aloha* spelled out in piss-yellow 1960s-flower-power-style lettering? It exceeds the bad taste criteria but we don't want to be too bright in the dark—loud is bad."

"Noted—must be in blend-into-nighttime shades. And no need for changing rooms since we want oversized stuff, but prank-preparation's pure adrenaline, extra intensely because it's a prank I never thought I'd play—follow me, please."

Angie and Ella, modesty disallows me from detailing our dressing room doings—oh, and *very* drawn out, mind you, we reaching home plate for the first time, hungering to do so. Although when Marisol slipped her scarlet and gold and lavender triangle-patterned summer dress over her head in the bright overhead light, was resplendent in violet-frilled diaphanous lingerie, and her svelte soft-firm tummy was before me, myself on my knees—my gaze following the light up her lusciousness to her laughing expression, bright eyes, as she massaged my shoulders, my shirt tossed aside along with my pants; then my tongue's tickling her gateway—she's pulsing, drawing deeper breaths, warbling soothing words meshing with sweet musk and nectar, blurring my... OK! Breaking off!

I'm soaring on excitation when we exit the Supercenter with a carton of eggs, undrinkable beer, revolting clothes, and ancillary items. Once at Marisol's we're playing dress-up with our new wardrobe, doing send-ups of runway routines. "Extremely effective," she observes, twirling before a mirror. "I hardly recognize myself—identity's buried—it's like getting a new personality."

"Some people feel fashion's superficial—I strongly disagree," I say. "We've overhauled ourselves—style of dress manipulates outward appearances and therefore changes how we're perceived which, in turn, changes how we behave, and—ha ha!—will enable us to dare more and get away with more."

"Right, we respond to the changed reactions to us and travel to unexplored psychological places—presto! inner expansion, and laughs, tonight! Because we're doofuses, right?—embracing what we usually avoid—there's strength in that."

Chapter Twelve

It's after 3:00 AM, we're heading south on Calle Marbella towards the enemy's residence. Marisol's wearing a 2X extra-large long-sleeved shirt with an energy drink's logo along with men's size 42 camouflage pants, held in place by two windings of string about her waist, cuffs rolled up. I'm wearing a 2X extra-large long-sleeved shirt with a casino's logo along with dark olive pants, likewise overlarge and with string as a belt and rolled-up cuffs. We're both sporting a bargain-bin-two-for-five-dollars felt women's hat—mine's black, Marisol's is gray, our faces shaded from streetlamp illumination by wide drooping brims.

"Never imagined I'd advertise a toxic-sweetener-laced energy drink—goes to show what a good choice I made," Marisol smiles, playfully bumping me.

"Since I make fun of suckers who get roped into casinos and wind up royally hosed, hand over whole paychecks to the house while supposing they're rebels against straightlaced behavior, it's fitting to advertise a casino."

"I'm layered in so much bagginess you can't beam your presence into me as forcefully as usual when you kiss me—maybe if I..." She trails off, presses closer as I kiss her cheek; then, laughing, "Of course totally *kidding*, Steve! Your presence is wildest flow and energy, like I'm floating instead of walking."

"As is yours, Marisol," I respond, wrapping an arm around her. "Your presence is *otherworldly* when mingled with the euphoria of rushing towards a prank, or when mingled with... Well, when mingled with *anything*."

"Euphoric jitters! Knify bliss! I know we'll smash that window, mangle up the front room with glass-shards and eggs, so tension tightens and elation blazes. Plus our mission's a surprise—it's not like I had a clue I'd be personally punishing the creep in a very physical hands-on manner. We're adults on a *vandalism* mission, because—face it—calling it pranking softens the classification, almost makes it seem like innocent fun. I've never vandalized, it was guy territory."

"And I've never vandalized with a girl; and, yeah, hyper-stealthiness is stirring—caution whipping into overdrive, no such thing as too careful—beautiful idea you had of adding fake stick-on tattoos, identifying marks, to our cheeks and hands. Tattoos are used by law enforcement to track down offenders."

"And our dishwashing gloves, almost transparent, lest fingerprints be searched for—wiping down the beer cans, because you grabbed them—deliciously immersive. Getting closer and my heart's thumping—tingles and fear."

"We slow our pace at the target but don't stop—if anyone's around we keep walking, avoid eye-contact, come back later—time to ready weapons."

"On it," she says, reaching into a bag for eggs as I reach into a bag for beer.

"Green light," I say, we a couple steps north of the enemy's window.

"Check."

I rapid-fire throw two pints of beer through the picture window, glass crashing down, Marisol following with eggs, after which I throw more eggs. I've seized Marisol's hand—we're dashing to block's end seemingly before the last eggs land—turning right, tossing our hats in bushes—Marisol undoes her hair, pinned to her scalp, swishes it free. Easy to slip off our 2X extra-large pants without removing our $8.99 sneakers—our outer costume layers, pants and shirts, are swiftly in a trashcan. Now we're snug in fitted navy blue, black, gray—no longer running, lest such attract attention—silently walking fast. Seemingly in a flash we're over eight blocks away, having turned twice, avoided straight-line travel.

"Priceless," I smile, we slipping into the space between a taller-than-me honeysuckle shrub and fence, immediately kissing. Nothing that was visible during execution of the prank is in our possession, we having ditched the sneakers, replaced them with flipflops stuffed in the waists of our regular pants.

"Whew! Changed back into a happy couple innocently doing what happy couples do," Marisol smiles at first pause in our kissing, squeezing my midriff and rubbing cheeks. "Accelerated bloodbeat and warped time—happened so fast it's like someone else dressed in horrible taste and threw my eggs. "; then, stepping back a bit, framing her face with her hands, "I slipped into something like energetic blindness while throwing the eggs, willing myself to aim accurately, eyesight a silvery blur. Ha! Maybe I was even temporarily physiologically a teen, liberated from adult understanding of risk and obligation, or maybe I was even temporarily a boy—now I get why boys are gung-ho for vandalism."

"Oh, yeah! Vandalism's liberating because transgressional, and insanely so if one dares go there as an adult," I respond, cupping her breasts as she arches her back, deliciously breathing deeply. "A fountain of youth in the sense we experienced emotions befitting teens, since most grownups have been browbeaten to not dream of doing what we did, never mind—ha ha!—numerous notions of what constitutes maturity are a society-propagated hoax, manipulation for the purpose of exploitation. Hell, the mere notion of ascribing to opinions, believing stuff, is manipulation! Do I *really* believe that? Who cares? It's *fun!*"

"Safe and sound after braving danger and infamy, chance of career sabotage—I'm feeling lusciously defrosted—hordes of restrictions are suddenly a joke, and all revolves around *fun*! I'm not the Marisol I was before pranking the sicko, swept along by our righteous mission! And not completely a blur—I was testing hand- and finger-reflexes in the minutes leading up to action—was high-stepping for flexibility—readying myself to hit the target and run. Similar to pre-surfing stretches, elimination of muscle-kinks, in case I'm caught by surprise."

"Was wiggling my toes in the half-size-too-large sneakers, confirming I'd be able to sprint if necessary—pronounced caution intensifies the feel of oneself in one's skin—danger can be therapeutic—day to day routine's suffocating, suppresses enlightening emotions."; then, upon picking flowers from the bush and placing them in her hair, "Honeysuckles for a honey, very appropriate, and they'll add to the difference between now and what we looked like minutes ago."

"Have some also," she giggles, tearing off sprigs and placing them in my front right pants pocket. "Pocketful of posies, bright as rosies! People who adorn themselves with flowers—ha ha!—simply do *not* do what we did earlier."

"Right, a beer and egg attack will *never* match flower children personality profiles," I chime in, gathering freshly fallen petals, tossing them over our heads.

"Weeeee! Flower child confetti! We're innocent newborn babes!"

Chapter Thirteen

We've arrived at Marisol's place—are changing into beachwear, packing a tote with beer, quenepas, berries—flying out her building's code-accessed gate (the wall a story high) onto the beach. "Whoa! Ocean wind on skin, toes sinking into sand, palms fronds flailing, surf higher than earlier. And we did *what*?"

"Punished a dog-abuser and child's toy destroyer!" Marisol yells, waves sloshing our ankles. "So lucky I met a man who'd inspire me to do that, and jump in and plan it. I discovered new things I'm capable of—you make me bolder."

"Planning a prank's tougher than executing one unexpectedly—no burden of thought involved in spinning that deliveryman's truck off the road with cheesecake—but you changed planning into a whoosh of delight. Cans of beer and eggs through a window at my age? Thought I'd foresworn adolescent antics long ago, and I couldn't be more pleased. As an adult perhaps I ought to be berating myself for succumbing to foresworn impulses—engaging in vandalism, risking arrest—but being with you renders such ridiculous. You're beautiful."

"Sweetness!" she cries, seizing the tote from my hand and tossing it upshore, out of surf's reach, then pulling me to my knees—we're soon face to face, waves splashing over our thighs. "We *did* risk arrest, didn't we? Seems unreal—there was the showing in the morning, papers are being drawn up, and I'm top earner at the agency and was party to an illegal military campaign! Throwing eggs through a window my accomplice smashed? Watch me snap out of the spell after you're gone and be scared of myself! But I'm liking that—what seductive subversion. I became a vandal, something I couldn't have imagined, but a sample's enough."

"Happy you're happy with a sample—wouldn't want to kickstart a vandalism addiction," I laugh, kissing her forehead. "Vandalism's a highly risky drug, no free passes from the law, although sometimes otherworldly in its effects. Uh, oh! Strike that! I didn't say it—have no business promoting what needs to be discouraged."

"Otherworldly in its effects is right, sampling of a drug I didn't suspect existed—the fear-euphoria mix leading up to action—the white-light swiftness of sensation when the window splintered—I threw eggs in a dream—then turning the corner and changing, I was jittery jumpy in a daze! Trees loud in the wind, sky tilting—then snug behind the honeysuckle bush, feeling electric squishy. Danger became safety so fast it's like I momentarily straddled opposite realms."

"Welcome to the pranking-party, Marisol, and very well put, you're so right! Clash of realms is the real appeal, no substance assistance needed—conventional addiction's emotionally flat—predictability's a dead-end. Uh, oh! There I go again!"

"Well, this respectable real estate professional *(She widens her eyes, taps her breastbone.)* will never see the world the same way after getting away with our adventure."; then, sweeping an arm eastwards, "Dawn's first glimmer—our first night together's speeding—one of the most unforgettable in my life."

"Enthrallingly seared in my memory, my dear."

Chapter Fourteen

OK, Angie and Ella, time to speed this along—a special guest arrives Friday, and I want to be 100% free to chase new adventures; and, besides, Labor Day sped along in a quick-change blur; and, yes, of course I relish reliving Labor Day's exhilaration, but... OK, we three understand the happy tug of war between an absorbing recollection and anticipation of imminent escapades!

Marisol and I are in the sheltered pool at El Presby—a natural wall of wave-sculpted lava, three or so feet higher than the sea's average height and forming a semi-circle against the shore, makes the pool possible—oncoming surf's hitting the rocks, spraying us—a steady mist-shower seizes the sunlight, shimmers with mini-rainbows—the sky's cloudless. We've had a breakfast of scrambled eggs, sauteed vegetables, and fresh young coconuts—haven't slept, are absorbed in splash-wars.

"You're in *big* trouble now!" Marisol shouts, two-handedly skim-swatting the pool's undulating surface, hitting me with well-aimed jets.

"Mercy!" I yell, falling backwards and flailing, elbows on soft sand.

"Plumb out of mercy," she giggles, flinging herself onto me—we're tickling and swatting each other, shouting louder and longer, howling and thrashing and kicking—no one's noticing, although the beach is holiday-crowded—people are too absorbed in fun of their own, many yelling as loud as us, and salsa's blaring. "Ow! Stabbing things!" Marisol suddenly exclaims, sitting bolt upright, craning her neck to look behind her left shoulder. "Something got me but I can't see."

"Hang on," I respond, circling to examine her back as she turns it towards me. "Yeah, something got you—there's a scratch-streak, white against your tan but not deep enough to bleed."; then, my attention drawn to my right thumb, as sensation there's slightly off, "Jesus! Two sea urchin spines are rammed up under my thumbnail, one sticking out far enough to scratch you. Sorry about..."

"*What?*" she cuts in with a shriek—whipping about to examine my hand. "My God! We need to get those out, makes me sick to look at them!"

"But strangely painless," I hasten to say. "Looks much worse than it feels—a bit of pressure under the nail, as if someone's pressing on it—visually terrifying without discomfort and I've no idea how long they've been there, where I obtained them. Seawater can deaden pain, but I didn't think it was *this* effective."

"Sea urchin spines jammed under your nail is seriously terrifying, never happened to me and I'm in the water almost every day! We're getting tweezers, the drugstore's closer than my place—let's go!" She grasps my other hand.

Within ten minutes we're on Ashford Avenue's sidewalk, Marisol wielding tweezers as I steady my thumb with my other hand. "First, getting the one that's way up under there—got it! *(She drops the spine, half an inch long, onto the sidewalk, grinds it to dust under her heel.)* Now the easier one."; then, upon repeating the process, "Admire your stoicism, Steve—not a flicker of a wince while watching, I'd be looking away, imagining I was elsewhere."

"Not a bit stoic—it's numb, thanks to seawater anesthesia."

"Tea tree oil will trounce infection," she smiles, extracting a vial from her tote, dousing my thumb—following application she's waving an arm westward, suggesting we rent paddleboards at Condado Lagoon—we're seemingly strolling to the lagoon before she completes the sentence—opening Medallas also purchased at the drugstore and toasting each other, tilting gold cans towards the sun—pausing on a bench at Plaza Antonia Quinones along the way, under the vine-bedecked tree with the two-yards-wide trunk about midpoint on the plaza's southern side.

OK, *attempting* to whisk recollection along, avoid lingering on transition intervals, as for instance when we were cuddling on the bench in Plaza Antonia Quinones, watching the lizards and feral chickens, semi-dozing for a spell, stretched out lengthwise, Marisol half atop me, an arm wrapped around me, we murmuring sweetness. Children are playing a spirited game of soccer, a couple dogs bounding along—the yelling and barking's soothing. Then a gas station pitstop for restrooms, then to Condado Lagoon, where I resume with us on paddleboards at its eastern side, heading for where it flows to the sea:

Wind's at our back—rippling the glassy surface, whisking us forward—minimal paddle-exertion's required—we indulge in splash-wars with the paddles, and are often sharing a board, ankle leashes securing unoccupied boards—crystalline azure water—pelicans, frigate birds, gulls, and terns wheeling above—mangroves to our left, high rises to our right—we share a Medalla, obtained from Marisol's watertight tote tied to the front of her board, then share another.

We're snug in rashguards, waist to neckline to wrists, but sunblock reapplication's needed elsewhere—I'm applying sunblock to Marisol's neck and face, and from toes to thighs as her litheness tautens and relaxes by turns—sunlight's gleaming on the cream as I massage it into her silky skin, and her hands dancing up and down my legs and cupping my neck, soft circular motion alternating with forceful grasping, her breathing nearing hyperventilation... How communicate what's sparkling in the center of my chest, tingling up my spine, birthing something of inner weightlessness, leading me to relishingly gasp for breath seemingly on the *cellular* level? Marisol's beaming radiance, intoning "Ummmmm," blurring awareness of sun and sea—stretching on the board, arching her back, figure-eighting her head, hair spilling about... We're lying side by side, embracing and pulsing, warmth and urgency of Marisol's lips and tongue meshing with the breeze and salt-mist, lagoon's whisperingly lapping aquamarine... "Call me Baby Doll," she giggles at one point, rubbing against me with redoubled insistence, as if seeking to blur our bodies' boundaries. "Call me Miss Vandal! Call me Miss Rectifi-er-of-Misdeeds-Done-Kids-and-Dogs! Call me Sun Girl! Call me Playful Prankster! Call me whatever you fancy, I'll go in that direction! Call me Kaleidoscope Girl! Your eyes shot through me at La Placita, made me feel scrumptiously transparent, when I was hunting for a partner."

"Sun Girl, I was knocked into a locked-in-a-dungeon frame of mind, dogged by paranoia—doing desperate things in the streets—because I believed I'd lost you, no other reason for it possible! Temporarily ex-iled to a negativity-saturated alternate universe, as if I wasn't in Puerto Rico—jumpy and suspicious, wanting to black out. Feeling desperate in glorious Puerto Rico's *unthinkable*!"; then, checking myself, kissing her forehead, "Kaleidoscope Girl, telling you this again so you know how thankful I am we're together—gloom was instantly blasted away when you called out to me at the fountains, your wellspring eyes elevating me." I'm tightening the grip of my legs about hers, she responding in kind.

"It tears at me that there was confusion on your end, sweetie," Marisol says, deliciously quivering. "On my end it was a done deal, an-ticipation of our rendezvous keeping me joyfully awake all night—I was charged with reverberations of our fun and hungering for more *(She licks my neck.)*, had no reason to doubt we'd hook up as arranged. Wild to me how you thought we'd lost touch, I was sending pictures of our meeting spot with smiley emojis. I was adrenaline-buoyed in the morning, there was crystal clarity regarding what needed to be said to the client, could *feel* I was—ha ha!—charismatic! Yes, crazy easy to close the deal thanks to you, because our dancing was still carrying me."

"Could gaze into your wellspring eyes all day, Kaleidoscope Girl."

"Equanimity floods me when you look at me like that, Steve, and do anything to me you want to do—we've travelled light years already—just amazing."

"Sunlight reflected in your gaze is wildest equanimity," I whisper, raising myself on an elbow, licking the nape of her neck.

"Sucker-bite-smooch me please, Kind Sir," she smiles, pointing to her preferred location for a hickey. Soon as I'm repositioning to heed her request our shared board, the wind having flipped its lengthwise edge perpendicular to forward movement, we too immersed in playtime to notice, catches too much water on said edge, dumps us overboard. "Weeeee!" Marisol yells once our heads are above water. "Shipwrecked!"

"This debris is all that's left of our maritime disaster," I announce, indicating our boards. "Need to grab on before it's swept out of reach and we drown! Another storm's looming, hopefully we reach land before monster waves slam us."

"Nefarious clouds are gathering fast—we're goners if they swoop in before we make it to shore, seconds wasted are a death sentence!" she yells. We seize the tails of our boards (paddles are lying atop them), frenziedly kick.

"Be a healthy workout if we survive, imagine how relieved we'll be, laughing about our ordeal—a stirring lifetime memory—good things can be found in bad."

"Positivity in the face of peril's aphrodisiacal," Marisol giggles, abandoning her board for mine—licking my neck, nibbling an ear. "Feeling *extremely* dilated, scrumptious—think I need spa treatment," she continues, tapping my board. Soon we've climbed onto my board—Marisol's taut on her back, arms above her head, fluttering her toes and undulating as I massage. "Your turn!" she announces not long thereafter, lifting herself while remaining centered—careful to grasp both sides of the board, mindful of balance. Once I'm on my back she's saying, "Special massage and oil treatment. *(She pulls her board's leash, unzips her watertight tote, obtains a small bottle.)* Aromatic therapy mix courtesy of a yoga instructor." She's pouring oil with one hand, rubbing it in with the other, and tickling my ankles with her toes—bending low, her electric fragrant hair streaming over me—sun's scattered through the swishing veil of her hair—a few egrets, bright white on dark green, are clustered on mangroves at peripheral vision's edge. "Spoiling me silly," I murmur. "My mission!" she smiles, reaching under my shoulders, spreading oil at the nape of my neck—I adjust position to facilitate access, the board slightly tipping—Marisol intentionally leans into the tip—*Splash!* we're doused again. "Hazards!" she yells. "Hostile animals in the water! Quick!" "Right, we're adrift on the amazon, caimans and anacondas are hungry," I say, we swiftly on our boards. "And swimming jaguars! A huge starving kitty's eyeing us from shore, spots blurred in the sun—being on our boards won't help!" she says. "We need to act like with mountain lions, make eye contact, look as big as possible, yell and threaten, opposite of dealing with bears," I say, waving my paddle and smacking it on the water, howling—Marisol's following suit—soon we're too overcome with laughter to continue. Then, once we're sharing a board again, "How do you know how to deal with big kitties and bears?" she asks, we facing one another, she squeezing my hands. "Hiking out west, including within San Diego's city limits, where mountain lions have enough deer and rodents to thrive." "Thank God you're an expert—the jaguar's fled," she smiles, gesticulating towards shore.

(Angie and Ella, I've sought to convey a hint of the spontaneity with which Marisol and I were swept from one roleplay to another—we didn't plan on inventing situations—it simply happened, as automatic as breathing.)

"My goodness—missed the turnoff!" Marisol laughs, gesturing to our right, we having drifted a few yards past Ashford Avenue's Dos Hermanos Bridge; then, once she's regained her board and we've paddled against the wind and passed under the bridge, are in El Boquerón inlet facing the Atlantic's oncoming waves, "It's usually friendly humps of non-breaking waves, the inlet's configuration restraining them, occasionally dipping deep but with soft motion, like now." "Been here before but never as elevated as now because I'm with you." "Right, forgot you know Puerto Rico well enough to be a tour guide," she smiles, playfully bumping my board with hers. "As beautiful a panorama as I'll ever see and mainly because you're part of it," I say, sweeping an arm from the horizon to her.

For likely over an hour we're kneeling on our boards in El Boquerón inlet—paddling seawards and flipping about, riding the surge towards the bridge, never rising from our knees—frequently maintaining our boards in holding patterns, minimal stirring of paddles needed, while facing the Atlantic's advancing pulse, softly buoyantly bouncing without speaking a word—Marisol's presence is sparkling me to my bones—sunlight on surf meshes with surf's swoosh.

"Until next time, El Boquerón," Marisol calls out, blowing goodbye kisses, we about-facing and standing, returning to Condado Lagoon under Dos Hermanos Bridge assisted by the Atlantic's forward motion—playfully buzzing each other, the edges of our boards rasping and squealing when they touch. Suddenly there's wind and current obstruction, we unkindly shoved opposite our destination.

"Whoa!" I say, awakening to the reality of wind-blown ripples rushing at us, gusts scattering silvered patches over the lagoon's surface. "Will be an insane workout to reach the paddleboard rental place—straight ahead's a treadmill."

"Appears to be a naivete-encountering-unpitying-nature event," Marisol obverses, deliberately deadpan, lifting a palm to the wind in clinical fashion. "The first time I was rudely awakened on a paddleboard, taught a lesson near here, I was eleven. Mom and dad bailed me out, we beached over there. *(She points to the lagoon's southern side.)* Foolish to fight this wind head on—we'll lose."

"Already winded by the wind," I laugh. "It's like ten paddle strokes yield forward motion of one or two—seriously sore shoulders tomorrow if we don't beach over there." We steer south perpendicular to wind-direction.

"Done this lots—we'll land over there. *(She gestures diagonally to the right.)* It's an action-yields-an-opposite-reaction lesson, or a don't presume to evade-laws-of-physics lesson, or maybe even a hubris-gets-swatted lesson—of course skimming the lagoon with the wind at our back means the wind will bar our way afterwards—it can be fun to pretend to be an idiot, recklessly ignore the obvious and suffer consequences, although... Well, hope you don't think I pranked you!"

"Marisol, the paddleboarding's a kaleidoscope of frolic and fantasy gloriously heightened by the tough return journey hanging over us—opposite reactions to stupid actions are educational—we learn to avoid behaving like presumptuous dolts, taking easy outcomes for granted, and speaking of pranks—*yeeeee-haw*!" I jump from my board to the far side of hers in back, tumble us into the water.

"Love it!" she beams, we shortly facing one another in the water, our ankle-leashes mildly tugged by our westward drifting boards.

—◆○◆—

We've arrived at Condado Lagoon's south shore, are dragging our boards on the path between waterline and highway. As the boards are bulky and heavy (thereby stable on water, readily single-leg balanced on), our progress is stop and go—two men note our predicament and offer assistance, which is gratefully accepted—soon we've carried the boards a distance past Monumento Román Baldorioty de Castro's obelisk, reentered the lagoon—a shore-hugging route, where the wind's milder, takes us to start point. Instead of returning the boards we enter the mangrove thicket to the rental place's left—there's room to paddle between the mangroves in spots, our boards brushing elevated roots—an iguana rustles the emerald above us, scampers to the end of a limb, and leaps.

"Belly smackers!" Marisol announces as other iguanas follow, nearly simultaneously; then, tapping my shoulder—whispering, pointing, "Baby barracuda cruising at the surface, using shadow and light, shifting mangrove leaf silhouettes on water, to hide—look at those razor teeth." The barracuda jets forward with a flick of its tail, seizes a fish—churns the water, splashing half a yard high. "Wow!" I say. "Front row seat on a barracuda's kill—*bam*! fish is grabbed faster than I can snap my fingers. Wildlife's on overdrive in Puerto Rico—San Juan often sounds like a rainforest, thronged with creatures lost in mating frenzy, louder than traffic." "Our wild kingdom," Marisol smiles, gesturing for me to come onto her board—we're soon lying alongside one another, reaching over each other to hold fast to elevated mangrove roots, secure us. Her board's wedged between two mangrove trunks and we need to ensure we don't roll off, as a dense bed of oysters is less than a yard below us. "Edges of oyster shells are as sharp as barracuda teeth, it would be like falling onto a field of knives—one incautious move, too much tilt on the board, and we're sliced and diced," Marisol grins. "Oh, I have us—not letting go of the mangrove," I say, vibrating my extended arm. "Not letting go either," she says, rubbing against me.

We're alternating kissing with licking each other's lips, cheeks, neck, forehead, chest—nibbling ears, lightly nipping shoulders, tease-scraping with teeth—inching away from each other at our waists, facilitating access—Marisol's quivering fingers, delicate electric touch, and drawing deeper breaths—I'm stimulating her moisture, she lusciously tense, sighing nerve-caressing tones—losing my face in her curls, inhaling deeply—the sweet tremulous depths of her eyes, body seemingly smiling from the inside out—I'm gripping the mangrove root tighter, sensing Marisol's doing likewise, arm pressed to my midriff—knife-edged oyster bed's looming below in crystal clear water, infrequently noted oblique-ly—contrarily relishing danger while careful to remain safe—coqui cho-ruses lustily greeting sunset's approach—patches of water reflecting or-ange, red, maroon—softness of Marisol's skin meshing with glimpses of fluttering mangrove foliage against multicolored sky—her warm breath and tongue, soothing touch.

We're wearing water shoes (ignored the meddlesome dolt who told us they compromise balance on paddleboards—absolute rubbish). Rub-ber soles shield us from oystershell knives, and prevent slipping, as we walk our boards from the mangroves in waist high water—easier to negotiate the above-water root-systems and low branches on foot in the dim light, we tilting our boards as needed.

"Oh, no—terrible!" Marisol gasps, abruptly starting—seizing my wrist, her breath a hiss—as we emerge from the mangroves at shoreline. A desiccated pelican's dangling upside down from a mangrove branch, one of its feet entrapped in fishing line. "Careless fisherman couldn't be bothered to bend the branch to disentangle the line, get it out of harm's way, easily done without getting wet—magnificent pelican unnecessarily thoughtlessly killed—just tears my heart out."

"Too many people are callously oblivious of nature's fragility—evo-lution hasn't prepared other species for extremely recent human inven-tions and activities. How could a pelican know there's deadly unbreak-able fishing line on a branch, or how to escape? They've been on earth millions of years longer than us, no reason for them to be prepared for our inventions—our destructive tricks. Humans wantonly killing constantly—countless animals choking on plastic, and the insane pes-ticide-saturated monoculture lawns, poison that's not even sprayed for food."

"People who're either oblivious of nature's fragility or don't care!" she says, quivering with suppressed rage. "It's too easy to avert my eyes from the pelican, try to forget the awful sight—not doing that—am taking a picture *(She unzips her waterproof bag, obtains her phone.)* and posting it online—yeah, *forcing* it on people. Abandoned fishing line's deadly and people need to see it in a gut-wrenching way."; then, after snapping a couple photos, "Now we can get rid of this sickening trap—more birds may get caught—lizards may get caught."

"Yeah, abandoned fishing line lurks for years, kills again and again."; then grabbing the branch about a yard and a half distant from the dead pelican, "I'll snap it here." I break the branch, toss it ashore. After turning in the paddleboards we deposit the branch, fishing line and its victim, in a trashcan. "Atrocious end for a beautiful bird," Marisol says, shuddering. "Pelicans are very much loved, admired as they glide on the wind, dive for fish—iconic and hypnotic."

Not long thereafter we're strolling on Calle Luchetti's southern side—a foot-long bluish lizard rushes at smaller lizards scattering into beds of ferns, fronds rustling—fronds violently stir, outright thrash, in one location—coqui choruses are seemingly louder by the minute, darkness swiftly engulfing distant details. I pause at Pastel's yard to symbolically say goodbye (explaining to Marisol why), having little hope of seeing her, since she's generally indoors after dark. Well, Angie and Ella, cats unquestionably possess perceptual capabilities we'll never comprehend! I'm gazing at the illuminated living room window, above the ferns in front, when Pastel leaps onto the windowsill, gazes at me and meows repeatedly (I can read her mouth), paws the glass—the lady of the house, Luna, is soon at the window waving, motioning for me to key in the gate-code—lifts a glass of wine.

Luna's opening the front door before Marisol and I reach it—she and Marisol availing themselves of happy exclamations of surprise at having yours truly in common, hugging each other—Luna's brother is dating Marisol's cousin and they met at a family gathering, became friends, and both are in the real estate business. Pastel's immediately outside to greet me, meowing merrily—all over me rubbing, shortly on my lap—Marisol, keeping her distance, smiles, "Pastel doesn't like me much, par for the course—not surprised she likes you, though." Luna's saying, "You would *not* believe—Pastel was wiped out on the couch, suddenly springs up excited and yowls, scampers to the window—I knew something was up."

(So we humans have our society-infiltrated and -manipulated brains, which allow for vanity and hubris—most of whatever perceptual capacity we possessed in our primeval past has surely been extinguished by civilization—a case of staring at a spot on a tree's trunk, losing the ability to comprehend it's a miniscule fraction of a vast forest—we ate of the fruit of knowledge, invented self-consciousness, exploitation—hooray for duped humanity. What the notion of subconsciousness really means is that civilization has suppressed our former abilities—subconsciousness is symptomatic of disease and, as with other civilization-imposed diseases, hordes of parasites are taking advantage to harvest haystacks of cash—extrasensory perception is attempted-recovery-of-stolen-abilities. But cats—species besides humans—don't suffer from sensory strangulation.)

Upon returning to Marisol's place we set our phone-alarms and flop on her bed, take a much-needed nap—amazing how rejuvenating an hour can be. I've informed my friend in Guaynabo, who's been teaching online all weekend, that the trip ran away with me and I'll leave my boogie board and flippers with Marisol.

After returning my rental car in Isla Verde we're racing down a path between high-rises to the beach—flinging ourselves into each other's arms, kissing as surf rushes and hisses as wildly as on Saturday morning, incoming wave-crests dancing in peripheral vision. We're allowed about twenty minutes on the beach.

After Marisol drives me to SJU, under ten minutes away, we're in her car at the departure terminal—cuddling, caressing, kissing. "Last pictures," I say a few minutes later, we having exited the car, my luggage alongside me—selfies snapped as we're cheek to cheek, or kissing (having aligned the phone with our profiles). "We don't have La Placita photos, none of us dancing. I want a twirl and dip sequence—let's ask her," Marisol says, indicating a woman who's bid three teenagers goodbye. The woman happily obliges—at one point, detecting our hesitation to full-out grab each other, demonstrate overmuch affection, in front of her, assumes directional duties, saying, "Go for it—I'm still young, and my kids are crazy and I'm proud of them. Who cares what others think? If someone says something I'm in your court." Voila! We find ourselves doing things we didn't do at La Placita (when, after all, familiarity was in its infancy)—I'm reaching up Marisol's dress with my free hand while dipping her—we're licking each other's cheeks, grabbing each other as if we've hungered to do so for years—at one point we're holding hands at arm's length, delightedly looking each other up and down. "Maybe she should get ahold of your shoulders for support and you pull her up," the woman suggests. "Weeeee!" Marisol cries, immediately stepping close, seizing my shoulders as I lift her, my palms squarely on her behind's immaculate globes, squeezing with gusto—we're aware the woman's taking pictures from all angles, crouching low for some. "Love seeing a happy couple," she says.

"Thank you for your encouragement—you carried us to new levels with our dancing, we met Saturday night at La Placita," Marisol says, the woman returning her phone. "This is Steve and I'm Marisol." "Nice to meet you, Marisol—I'm Alina," the woman responds. "Safe journey, Steve." "Thank you, Alina," I say, "and thanks for the pictures, I already know they're off the charts, and thanks for the peptalk and coaching." "My pleasure, all the best to you two and I think you need privacy, I'm off," she winks, smiling as she strolls away. "Bye, Alina," Marisol calls out. "Bye, Marisol," Alina answers, waving without turning around. A traffic guy's at Marisol's car, gazes at us questioningly. "It's mine, sorry, I'll move it right away." Marisol says, we resigning ourselves to a premature farewell embrace. "It's OK, had to make sure the owner's here—take your time, it's not crowded, no one's waiting for your spot," he responds, advancing to other cars.

"Thank you, Sir—appreciate it," Marisol says; then, turning to me and crossing her wrists over her heart, "See you in two Fridays. Dreading the wait but looking forward to rushing into heaven in NYC—like so!" She embraces me.

"The wait will be an inner circle of hell," I say, "but anticipation's a dizzying drug, and hugging you exceptionally so—deprivation will burst into bliss."

"Want to stretch these moments out—don't want to say goodbye!"

"Want to say hello infinitely!"

A last goodbye kiss, and then another, then three more—a different traffic guy, of dour demeanor, is eyeing Marisol's car, reaching for what's presumably a ticket pad. "Oh, no—rudely forced apart! Bye, Steve!" "Bye, Marisol—will call from inside!" Her eyes are leaping at me, flashing sweet silver, as she advances to her car, gazing over her shoulder—she speaks with the man, who refrains from writing a ticket; but he's watching like a hawk, unmoving with hands on hips, as she hops into her car. We barely have time to blow goodbye kisses.

The interval between exiting Marisol's car with my luggage and when she's compelled to depart is barely over five minutes, confirmed via time-stamp on Alina's photos, but I couldn't begin to capture the range of emotion experienced in said interval. I'm dizzy-buoyant with the last touch and sight of Marisol upon entering the terminal—soon obtaining the "USDA—APHIS INSPECTED" stickers, color-coded turquoise this time, advancing to my gate through the (blatantly) strategically located duty free store, it being the sole means of doing so—captive audience marketing, indeed—the slightest pause, glancing in anything's direction, brings a—ha ha!—salesperson to my side.

Then my flight's over the Atlantic, events of the trip flickering in and out of focus, running together and blurring kaleidoscope-wise, in my mind's eye—I'm seemingly suspended somewhere between sleep and wakefulness, as when vivid nameless impressions swirl and dance during Yoga Nidra. What occurred and what didn't? Or am I still on Friday night's San-Juan-bound flight? A glance out the window yields the identical pitch-black. *Has Labor Day weekend happened?*

Signing off, Sweethearts—Marisol arrives tomorrow.

Love,

Steve

Bonus Story: Why Waste English Setters on Dog Shows?

Gratefully dedicated to undisciplined dogs
and the people who love them.

———◦———

Steven to Angie & Ella
Sent: Sunday, August 28, 2010 10:47 PM

Miffed, my darlings? You ought to be. What girls worth their frilly underthings—that every man with a pulse wants to peel off—put up with being stood up? All the same, I ask for understanding.

OK, I bailed on our Pierre brunch after making the reservation, but ask yourselves: how often do I fail to show up after setting a meeting up and talking it up? I can count the total for the year on one finger. Is it my fault Byron, one of my oldest friends who I—at most—see every other year, chose today to swing through town on a drive to Cape Cod from Cape Hatteras? I'd say that qualifies as extenuating circumstances.

As to why I didn't bring Byron along so you could meet him: he had his dog Zuke with him and Zuke couldn't be left unsupervised in my apartment. There's no telling what would've been chewed beyond recognition or ripped to shreds.

Zuke's an English Setter—one of the wildest, most spirited, bouncing-off-the-walls-with-energy breeds; and, at eleven months, is in the prime of exuberant disregardful-of-authority puppyhood. Full grown size-wise, still a puppy disposition-wise—perfect combination for maximum riot. Turn your back on him for a second in my apartment, and he's mauling a pillow or chomping on electrical cords or overturning the trash. So that's why you didn't meet Byron and we went to Central Park with Zuke instead.

Yes, an English Setter: slender, swift of movement, graceful of bearing, a breed not often seen in this country outside of dog shows. As for dog shows, the contract Byron signed with the breeder stipulates that he show Zuke. Will he do so? Here's his take on the subject:

"I shell out fourteen hundred for Zuke and the breeder has the gall to inform me I'm to hit the dog show circuit with him! Free advertising's what she's after, as when his pedigree's announced—not to mention I'd be *working* for her without reimbursement, like some sort of whipped sucker. But having botched it with breeders in the past and been turned down due to being honest and naive, declaring I had neither the time nor inclination to go anywhere near dog shows, I was prepared and trotted out a barrage of fake enthusiasm, assured her I was looking forward to showing Zuke, winning prizes; said I intended to hand him over to an obedience school—named the school, well-known in the industry. Still, she was suspicious—subjected me to a borderline interrogation. So I dropped more names and locations of trainers, demonstrated familiarity with American Kennel Club applications, policies, etiquette—was very well-informed, as I'd anticipated invasive questioning, studied the literature. Finally, she swallowed my act and agreed to the sale.

"Christ! Forcing an English Setter, bred for hunting, to endure dog show circuit transport cages is *abuse*! Handing an English Setter over to spirit-breaking parasites at obedience schools is something I couldn't be paid anything to do! All I want is a lively pet, who's loved and appreciated and treated like royalty! Anything wrong with that?

"All the training rigmarole, dog shows... Follow the money, it's an obscenely lucrative industry! The breeder thinks she's going to enlist me in publicizing her business, at the expense of Zuke's well-being! Screw her! And what's she, located in Vancouver, going to do about it when she discovers I duped her, attempt to confiscate Zuke? Hello publicity nightmare if she attempts it! Zuke's going to remain free-spirited and out of control and race like a maniac through fields and up and down the beach to his heart's content and she can drop dead!"

Enough preliminary, sweethearts. By way of seeking to make amends for missing our brunch-date (again, I nearly never do!), I'll entertain you with our Zuke-in-Central-Park adventure. Because, hey, you adore gloriously free-spirited dogs as much as I do.

Once we cross Madison at 85th Street, Central Park's trees are visible at block's end and Zuke's excitedly whiffing the air—inhaling nature's heady scents, tugging at the leash as if possessed, half-dragging me down the sidewalk. I alternate hanging on with my left and right hands and both arms are tired by the time I release Zuke behind the Met after crossing the Drive—it's a privilege to be entrusted with holding the leash, connected to a magnificent dog's strength and energy. Drunk with freedom after being cooped up in Byron's car and my apartment, Zuke bolts towards Cleopatra's Needle, darting every which way.

An English Setter racing free's an uplifting sight. Zuke's on permanent overdrive, easily swifter than any other dog in the park, able to sharply switch direction with minimal loss of speed. He buzzes other dogs, compels them to chase him, but none can come close to catching up. English Setters are pranksters, I admire them unreservedly.

Another trait of English Setters is they love people, are social butterflies, relish attention. Zuke greets people by rearing up on his hind legs, placing his front paws on their chests, often rather abruptly. He's simply saying "Hello!" and is as harmless as a baby but some people don't comprehend and become discomfited, apprehensive. It's amusing to watch Zuke jolt people from their thoughts, force interaction upon them: one moment they're in their private worlds, the next they're compelled to deal with an exuberant—leaping, sniffing, licking—creature that, even if domesticated, has a foot in the wild kingdom.

Byron and I play catch with a Frisbee under the ancient oaks near Cleo's Needle, sun dappling through their sky-obscuring canopies, innumerable songbirds vocalizing, as Zuke races between us leaping and snapping in ineffectual attempts to seize the disk gliding just above his reach—finally, half out of his mind, he barks in protest, squarely facing Byron. So Byron tosses the Frisbee to Zuke and, upon snatching it, he's delirious with delight—capers about in such zigzag angles of abrupt switches of direction it's amazing he remains upright. Then we're chasing Zuke to snatch the Frisbee and he's teasing us in turn—crouching on the lawn, permitting us to approach, only to dash yards away soon as our hands are inches from his mouth.

"Zuke's really charged up," Byron grins. "Let's go over there." He gestures towards the densely populated Great Lawn.

We're shortly entering the Great Lawn via its nearest gate. (Feigning ignorance of the no-dogs rule—if anyone calls us on it we won't argue, let's see if it happens.) And, hey, a populated expanse of lawn's Zuke's ideal playground, be a shame to deprive him of it. He forgets about playing keep-away, indifferently drops the Frisbee—madly dashes across picnic blankets, pausing here and there to say hello to people, be praised, petted—nuzzles and licks some of those who respond enthusiastically. Softball games are being played and Zuke interrupts two of them. In the first instance bounds into the batter's box and, in a demonstration of affection, places his paws on the catcher's knees. In the second instance fields a base hit and dashes in circles with the ball, the defensive players flinging their arms up in futility, batter laughingly trotting home, then going to first base because it's not a home run.

It's then, darlings, that I'm rewarded with transcendent moments—as when the truly unexpected suddenly reveals itself to be a plausible and existing reality of which one's the cause and beneficiary. I'm as if hovering outside my body, gazing upon the scene from a distance: Zuke, softball in his mouth, is racing like a maniac while both teams' players take turns halfheartedly chasing him; Byron and I, making a show of attempting to catch Zuke and leash him, are shrieking "Zuke! Zuke!" at the top of our lungs. We're causing a great deal of commotion on this previously peaceful afternoon and many of those nearby have whipped their heads in our direction, and guess what? No one's lecturing us, cursing us, even though we're blatantly violating Central Park's rules regarding where and when dogs are allowed to be unleashed.

It needs to be experienced to be believed: despite dashing around and shouting and clearly sharing responsibility for the commotion, I'm enveloped in sensations of security. How so? Because I understand that, as long as Byron and I pretend to try to catch Zuke while dispensing profuse apologies, announcing he got away from us and ran through the gate, no one will voice opposition. *How do two adult men get away with sowing chaos in a public place? All they need is a spirited dog.*

I'm thoroughly relishing the situation: many people are highly amused, laughing; others are watching with interest, or no readily discernable expression; a small percentage are exhibiting traces of annoyance. Am I worried concerning the latter? Not a bit. They dare not voice annoyance because then they'd be branded as dog-haters and incur the contempt of the majority. (Is it too far-fetched to suggest that dog-haters, especially in the eyes of people who frequent parks, are situated towards the bottom of the totem pole, somewhere in the vicinity of snitches, telemarketers, and neglectful nannies?) Nor does it hurt that Zuke's a poster child for canine cuteness: wide trusting vaguely sad eyes, long floppy ears, soft sleek tri-colored coat, a grown puppy romping without a care in the world. As I overhear one woman say: "Such a pretty puppy-wuppy! I could hug him all day!"

Deeming it time to return the softball, Byron tosses the Frisbee to Zuke: he drops the softball to seize the Frisbee and a player scoops up the softball. The players, jovial fellows, shout things such as, "Hey Zuke, we could use you on our team!," "Gold Glove fielding, Zuke!," and "Now we have a spitball!"

We've created a disturbance on the Great Lawn for over five minutes—good fun, but unwise to push it. Tolerance for a madly romping dog, no matter how cute and friendly, won't last forever, especially since the Great Lawn's officially a dog-free zone. So Byron and I exit and head towards Belvedere Castle, Zuke following close, we immediately leashing him.

And that, Angie and Ella, was our secret all along: as long as we chased Zuke, he was going to dash from our grasp, customary in a game of tag. I like to think of it as our covert canine and human agreement: Zuke disrupts gatherings of picnickers, sunbathers, ballplayers and we count on him to avoid us while pretending to try to catch him. We've the option of ending the game at any time, simply by turning about and heading for the exit, whereupon Zuke will dutifully follow.

Additional adventures are forthcoming, we alternately releasing and leashing Zuke—when we're near the Drives, or children's play areas, he's leashed. We always make a point of rather theatrically leashing him following his romps, to give credence to our apologies for his having "escaped." But I'm not taking it for granted I'll always get away with allowing dogs to romp in many of Central Park's forbidden spots—luck had a lot to do with it. Unleashing Zuke and racing around yelling the way we did happened spontaneously, we were simply drunk with it.

In Bethesda Tunnel Zuke demonstrates his hunting skills: suddenly freezes and stares, apparently mesmerized; then a swift dash, and—presto—he's grabbing a bag dangling from a man's hand, giving it a sharp tug: out tumbles a roasted chicken. Zuke wastes no time in seizing the chicken and racing towards The Mall. Quite breathtaking.

"Jesus Christ!" the man yells, glancing about to see who's responsible for the nefarious chicken-snatching beast.

"Zuke!" we're screaming at the top of our lungs—the tunnel very effectively amplifies and echoes our yelling.

The man glances at us for a couple instants, then towards the end of the tunnel, where Zuke's devouring his prize at the base of the stairs leading to The Mall—upon his face is a mix of being none too pleased and amused despite himself. Before the man can speak, we're approaching and apologizing profusely, offering forty dollars for the inconvenience, adding one of us will happily go buy him a new chicken at the store advertised on the bag, within a fifteen-minute walk.

"Aw hell, I can get another bird for a lot cheaper than that and do it myself—lots of places to get one on the way home, it's not like you guys stole it," the man answers, refusing the money and the errand. He makes it clear the offer of recompense is recompense enough. "What kind of dog is that, anyway?" he asks, gesturing in Zuke's direction.

"An English Setter."

"Hunting dog, right?"

"Too much of a hunting dog for the city I think," says Byron, apologizing with his eyes. "He's a country dog and doesn't know any better, shouldn't be snatching grocery bags."

"He sure as hell knows what he's doing!" the man declares, smiling broadly. "That bird was out of this bag and over there in seconds! It's worth a bird to see that and blessings on Zuke! I'm glad he's enjoying it! And he's still got his nuts! Good for you! Don't neuter him!"

"Dead horses will fly to Mars before my dog gets neutered," responds Byron heatedly, no longer ill at ease, Zuke's thievery having been dismissed. "Break his spirit? Steal his manhood? Where do people come off assuming they've a right to make those decisions?"

"Neutering's criminal!" the man fairly shouts. "Had a dog awhile back—Black Lab, feisty and smart, bundle of energy. I took off on business, convention in Atlanta. The first wife goes off and hauls him to the vet, gets his nuts cut off while I'm gone! Brando wasn't the same after. Spark missing from his eyes—he got lazy, wasn't as quick and bright. Sometimes I thought he was asking 'Why?' when he looked at me—it was like he was wondering how I could let him be savaged. And I sure asked the wife why! Guess why? Because some bought and paid for toady of a journalist on TV said it was beneficial! She was always glued to the tube, mistaking blather for gospel truth! No one easier to hoodwink than the first wife! Once a beauty pageant winner, but with low mileage! As scatterbrained as she was unable to keep her looks, and with her bedroom skills flagging as fast! She's been swapped for one who ruts like a rabbit *and* has a head on her shoulders."

"Yeah, just because I have a dog I'm expected to blindly buy into pro-neutering propaganda! Dogs haven't chosen to be born into our civilization, so the least we can do is be kind to them, refuse to mutilate them. Neutering dogs suggests they solely exist for our pleasure, are toys to be manipulated by us, which is disgusting. It's not like I'm going to irresponsibly allow Zuke to go around knocking up other dogs, add to overpopulation of unwanted dogs in the shelters, but the control-freak zombified loonies don't care. They say neutering's in a dog's best interest, as if being robbed of sex-drive will make a dog happier. What they *really* mean is it makes dogs more submissive—easier to train to do stupid tricks that reflect more on the vanity of humans than anything that's good for dogs. They get a dog because they want a creature to boss around. They want to show off in front of others of their ilk, say 'Watch Rover roll over! Watch Rover heel!' They're controlling despotic creeps who victimize animals because they need to feel superior, excusing it as concern for the animals' welfare."

"Damn right!" says the man, pumping a fist. "It's disgraceful what's commonly accepted to do to a dog, and I don't see the pro-neutering people rushing out to sterilize themselves, so where do they come off doing it to dogs? Responsible dog owners let a dog be a dog, accept them and love them as is. Not those scaredy-cat twits who want them to be stupid and lazy, like my stupid first wife! Dogs *ought* to steal chickens and raise a ruckus! To hell with those that disagree!"

As if on cue, chicken-thief Zuke trots up to us; not only is he inapprehensive of the man from whom he's filched the chicken, he greets him enthusiastically, placing his front paws on his chest.

"You're a good boy, aren't you, Zuke?" says the man, caressing Zuke behind his ears, petting him. "Such a *good* dog!"

We part from the man the best of friends and continue on our merry roving tour through The Mall (after cleaning up remnants of the chicken) and thence to The Pond via a winding route, leaving bustle and fluster and laughter in our wake, Zuke unleashed at least half the time. Towards journey's end I'm near delirious with the license to carry on that Zuke's antics are making possible. When he's loose I'm screaming his name like a maniac, dashing about like a ten-year-old. Zuke has transferred a portion of his freedom to make a spectacle of himself to me and I'm savoring every moment. Thanks to our frequent yelling of Zuke's name, it's possibly engraved upon the memories of dozens of people.

Alas, the waking dream's over too soon: we exit the park at 59th and 5th and Zuke's leashed going forward; no longer surrounded by open spaces, he immediately settles down. We stroll back to my place, chat for a couple more hours over a salmon dinner, of which Zuke gets a hefty portion, then say our goodbyes. Byron resumes his journey to his ex-girlfriend's Cape Cod place—meaning they've placed their "ex" status on hold, are revisiting steady-relationship experiences. Who knows? Maybe Byron and Lisa will eventually stop informing themselves these meetings are one-offs (these so-called one-offs keep adding up!) and full-out surrender, possibly marry? But I digress.

So, dearest ones, there's my excuse for bailing on our brunch-date and why I ask for special consideration, something you know I nearly never do. And although Zuke had a huge hand in keeping me away from you, I think you ought to think kindly of him and send sweet thoughts his way. I owe Zuke much gratitude for placing my NYC self in touch with the animal world—I'm still humming with it, have zilch wish to turn in as early as I ought to, be well-rested for tomorrow's new-client tour, and the slideshow presentation, and lunch at Smith & Wollensky's that'll likely last until evening. (Lunches are the worst sort of emotionally draining *work*, since we need to balance lightheartedness with professionalism, neither be too serious nor too carefree.)

Sowing a bit of chaos in Central Park in plain view of hundreds and getting away with it—three Central Park employees, that we know of, even looked the other way, bless them—lifts fun to wildest heights, and more: it's shown me the sorry degree to which constraint's infiltrated my life, accompanies me everywhere, subconsciously and otherwise—understanding the enemy better enables me to deal with the enemy, test and extend boundaries. Being in on the capers of a spirited dog's rejuvenating, therapeutic, instructional. And, hey, has romping with a dog ever motivated anyone to chuck their job, sell their co-op, relocate to an inexpensive foreign country, live free of obligation henceforth? But don't worry, it's just idle speculation—I'm not chucking everything, taking off anytime soon. NYC's too much fun.

Why do we love dogs, easily bond with them? It's not only that dogs are blind to our shortcomings, unselfishly offer affection and devotion, it's that we travel back to unrecorded history with them, when the first wild dogs approached us, inquisitively, and we tossed them scraps, and they wound up accompanying us on hunts, assisting us on hunts, providing companionship in the face of unpitying nature. It's miraculous how we bonded with dogs and that they trust us, and they turn us into better people. Dogs exist in our civilization without being fully of it and remind us of our authentic ancestry, when we lived unencumbered in emotional expression, non-splintered in our heads. Countless generations preceded us and our present state of civilization-engendered emasculation's an aberration, encompasses a minuscule amount of human history. How can we not want dogs among us, when they temporarily liberate us—gift us with glimpses of what we once were, when human freedom was boundless, vanity nonexistent?

I'm totally disinclined to sleep, only want to continue riding today's euphoria—can't stop seeing Zuke's tricolor coat flashing in the sun! Will have to brave tomorrow sleep-deprived, even if the stakes are high, new client introductions, urgency to put on a show. But we all know it's far from the first time I've gone there, since it's usually the two of you who irresponsibly—ha ha!—fire me up too much to sleep!

Good fun and goodnight, sweethearts!

Love,

Steve

About the author

Robert Scott Leyse was born in San Francisco, grew up in various locales about America, lived in Paris for over two years, and presently resides in Manhattan, Sun Valley, ID, and Puerto Rico. Upon arrival in Manhattan he lived in East Village dumps and worked as a New York cab driver on the night shift, with the aim of atoning for a sheltered upbringing and having adventures the likes of which he'd never had before and expectation was vastly surpassed. Subsequently he worked in the legal field, where he was pleasantly surprised to find adventures of the office shenanigans variety were to be had and sought them out at every turn. Thereafter he switched to the more tech-friendly advertising industry, where he favored working remotely (well before COVID), and amazed himself by getting away with an insane amount of escapades on company time. He eats insects and drinks blood, but can't be paid to eat potato chips or cake.